THE DIRTY DINER

GAY EROTICA ON THE MENU

**Edited by Jerry L. Wheeler
for Bold Strokes Books**

Riding the Rails: Locomotive Lust and Carnal Cabooses

The Dirty Diner: Gay Erotica on the Menu

Visit us at www.boldstrokesbooks.com

THE DIRTY DINER

GAY EROTICA ON THE MENU

edited by

Jerry L. Wheeler

A Division of Bold Strokes Books

2012

THE DIRTY DINER: GAY EROTICA ON THE MENU
© 2012 By Bold Strokes Books. All Rights Reserved.

ISBN 13: 978-1-60282-677-9

This Trade Paperback Original Is Published By
Bold Strokes Books, Inc.
P.O. Box 249
Valley Falls, NY 12185

First Edition: July 2012

Credits
Editors: Jerry L. Wheeler and Stacia Seaman
Production Design: Stacia Seaman
Cover Design by Sheri (graphicartist2020@hotmail.com)

THE BILL OF FARE

AN APERITIF: SQUARE PIZZA FANTASY

One of the clearest memories I have of junior high school is the square pizza and the way he ate it. The pizza was crusty and chewy, with just-right-spicy tomato sauce and caramelized onions at its base—sometimes laden with pepperoni and mushrooms and sometimes layered with sausage and green peppers, but always covered with yards of stringy cheese. Baked to bubbling and cut into irregular squares as only hairnetted cafeteria ladies can, it was the only meal they did well.

Him? He was the best-looking boy in the eighth grade, with deep blue eyes and black hair, set off by the palest of skin. His lips were full and pouty, and from seeing him in the showers in gym class, I knew he had a lithe yet muscular body, bushy, dark pubes, and a dick of death that bounced from thigh to thigh as he snapped towels at his friends in the locker room.

I was not one of those friends. I was a geeky, tubby kid with the appetite of a horse and the metabolism of a giant sea slug—not a good combination—and I had to settle for admiring him from afar. We had no classes together other than gym, but we did have the same lunch period.

Oddly enough, he usually ate alone. His jock friends all had different lunch periods, and none of the girls also ogling him from nearby tables would approach him either. In a perfect *ABC Afterschool Special* world, I would have broken those caste lines and tried to be his friend, but I had already learned that life was far different from programs designed to sell pudding cups to the parents of innocent youths. Such a breach of eighth-grade etiquette would only result in being called a fag yet again, with the additional threat of physical violence. How could I have been so confused by what others seemed to see so clearly? No. Safety cautioned me to stay where I was. And watch him eat.

He ate enthusiastically, in big, manly bites—sometimes not even chewing thoroughly before he swallowed and refilled his mouth. If he sounds like a slob, he wasn't. It was beautifully masculine mastication of corn casserole, mac and cheese, hamburgers, grilled cheese sandwiches, or whatever meal they were serving that day. And he always washed it down with those little cartons of Twin Pines milk—two white and two chocolate—that invariably dripped onto his shirt.

But the square pizza was the best.

He'd pick it up with his broad, spade-like fingers and bite off each corner first, creating eight corners where there had been four, then he would bite off those eight, leaving a center bit where he'd stack the extra strings of cheese or whatever topping happened to fall off on his plate. And he'd pop that into his mouth, a red dribble of tomato sauce trailing from the corner of his satisfied grin.

One of my most fulfilling nighttime fantasies was him with two broken arms, forced to ask me for assistance to eat his square pizza. I imagined his hot, moist breath on the back of my hand as I held the morsel to his lips and felt the pressure of his lips and teeth as he tore into it, my encouraging hand on his strong shoulder. When he swallowed that last bite, I'd lick the tomato sauce from the corner of his mouth. And we'd kiss…

That was my first connection with food and sex. Since then, I've acquired a taste for the frankly voyeuristic aspects of watching men eat. And I prefer men with a bit of meat on their bones. Skinny men munching on PowerBars seem effete and somewhat pretentious to me. Give me a fit-fat dude with his big hand wrapped around a juicy corned beef sandwich any day.

I used to think this fetish was mine alone until my second or third date with my late partner, Jim. We went to a Mexican restaurant, and during a lag in the conversation, a husky, football player–type guy at a nearby table got a stuffed sopaipilla. I watched him take a huge, unself-conscious bite, meat and shredded cheese and lettuce falling all over the place. He chewed, swallowed, and took another monstrous bite. Suddenly, I felt Jim watching me watch him. "You too?" he asked.

We occasionally went out to Hooters for dinner—not for the marvelous food and certainly not for the hooters. We went to watch straight guys cram their faces full of wings and cheese sticks, wiping their greasy mouths on the backs of their hands. Then we'd have crazy hot sex in the parking lot—or, on one memorable occasion, in the restroom with a couple of those "straight" guys.

Delicious.

And even more delicious are these savory, salacious tales from some amazing writers. Last year's Lambda Literary Award winner David Pratt takes us to the kitchen prep room for an arousing encounter in "Revealed," our favorite Western writer Dale Chase loads up the chuck wagon for a cattle drive in "Cookie," and the ever-inventive Karl Taggart serves a tale of a foodie and his potential boyfriend with extra-sensitive taste buds in "Supertaster."

Starting your meal with dessert? Okay. Jeffrey Ricker whips up some special bread pudding in "The Key Ingredient," Rob Rosen goes on a late-night donut run in "The Munchies," and J.D. Barton takes the cake with his "Sweetbread Hill." But no restaurant tour would be complete without some foreign fare, so Tristan Cole hooks us up in a Mexican dive in "Mistakes Were Made," Lewis DeSimone takes us to Venice for an alley encounter with *spaghetti alle vongole* and *osso bucco* in "Wish You Were Here," and Jay Neal goes back to World War II for a little *Schwarzwälder Kirschtorte* at "The Café Françoise."

We haven't forgotten the domestic comestibles, either. Todd Gregory picks up a New Orleans treat at the Clover Grill in "Someone to Lay Down Beside Me," Jeff Mann gets all Southern fried in "Christmas Comes to Otters' Gap," and Daniel M. Jaffe shows us his salami in "Herman's Kosher Deli." Love, lust, and lunch are also on the bill in Hank Edwards's tale of a grieving son finding romance at his late father's diner, "Rick's Greasy (S)poon," and 'Nathan Burgoine plates a bittersweet story of ice wine and an affair to remember in "The Finish."

But no banquet worth attending would be complete without a touch of the bizarre, so feel free to load your plates with William Holden's curiously cured meats in "Acquired Taste" or join Steve Berman for a very special birthday treat ordered from the "Bottom of the Menu." No matter what you have a taste for, we guarantee a trip to *The Dirty Diner* will leave you breathless, sated, and satisfied.

In more ways than one.

REVEALED
DAVID PRATT

Duty is thrilling. And as a man goes about his duty, what is *just* hidden is more exciting than what he may choose to reveal. When it is *barely* concealed by a piece of clothing, half-interposed or less, almost proven but partly secret, still possessed of that sweet, unique, vulnerable person, it's an offer hinted at by signs that drive you to distraction thinking, what if *I* removed the interposing thing? What if I trespassed, seized power, tasted it, took it? What if I undid him? And put him in his glory?

A loose, open shirt and dirty, checked pants *just* concealed him from me. That, and his not knowing. A young man not awake to his glory is more compelling than one who knows. Don't we pay to watch them sleep? The ones that know are appalling. That leaves me breathless, too. But no one touches me like one who does not know, or who suspects but hesitates to reveal. Who would not be so bold as to disrupt his duty?

Performing his responsibilities, he leaned forward. His shirt, top buttons undone to relieve heat and damp, hung away from his smooth, shiny chest, and I saw down to the pale, innocent dark blond hairs trailing down from his navel. His nipples were facts without guile. He did not mean for me to see as he leaned to scoop ice cream. He did not mean to make the sight available. I just took it. When he stood again, the shirt clung to his damp skin. He raised his arm to wipe grease from his cheekbone, and muscle bulged, some of it concealed up his short white sleeve. When he helpfully lifted a bus pan to me, the cords in his forearm played diligently, responsibly. His bottom, muscled and practical, perfectly filled the seat of the grimy checkered pants. If he climbed for a box of napkins, extending his arm, blond hair just naturally peeked from the short sleeves, damp and curled and darkish. (I love, in blonds, the way the light turns dark to show they have been working.) His muscles bulged, hoisting the box. And as he climbed down, the checkered cloth of his pants stretched across the perfect roundness of his bottom.

He was night manager at Hibbert's Diner, where I was a busboy. His name was Michael. Yet even his name hid something. His real name was Michel. His parents, first-generation Quebecois. He talked like an American kid, though, and everyone called him Michael or Mike or even Mikey, the last requiring a warmth and sweetness, tempered with a gently pulsing, unquestioned masculinity, to pull off. But when his shirt fell away from his smooth torso, when he raised his arms, then I saw and I wanted Michel.

He clocked in every evening at five minutes to six. Mike or Mikey, friendly and outgoing, but Michael didn't stand around bullshitting like the other managers. Michael prepped and cooked and fetched and carried, kept an eye on the waitresses and on me, offered his help (or, I thought when he stood close and I smelled his perspiration, Michel's help) when he could, said "Yes, sir," "Yes, ma'am," "No, sir," "No, ma'am" to customers, and at evening's end scrubbed the grill clean and shining, legs braced, forearms working, with a stiff metal brush. Then the shirt clung. His hair stuck in wet spears to his forehead and the back of his neck. He did not hesitate to fix plumbing (forearms rippling, shirt riding up to reveal a soft, taut belly), change fluorescent tubes in the ceiling (shirt riding up again to reveal hair leading down from his navel, hair showing damp and curling under his arms), or reach to jiggle the plug to revive our temperamental freezer (leg extended, shirt pulling up in back, triangle of downy hair where the depression began that, unseen but breathtakingly imagined by me, deepened to make perfect buttocks and the place his warm shit squeezed out). Always there was something sweaty to do. Something wanting strength and ability. Forbearance. Or politeness. A smile. A twinkle. Michael did it. Michel did not complain. He could cock his eyebrow in annoyance, but if I made a mistake, he kidded me, then grabbed a mop to help contain a spill, or he knelt with me to pick up broken pieces of a dish. I wanted to do well for him. I wanted to do well for Michel. If I did well enough, I would see him full and clear and gain total access to him.

I could not help but wonder, kneeling there, retrieving broken pieces of a plate, him now risen and standing over me, what the neat overlap of his fly concealed. I imagined a cock as forthright and capable as its master. When naked and hard he got the job done as surely and as deftly as he did striding, bending, reaching, turning, pulling inside the white shirt and checked pants.

Jeff, now, was the opposite of Michael.

Jeff was appalling.

Jeff was the other busboy; he had trained me. From the first day he made no bones about what he was or what he did. "How are you?" I'd said, shaking his huge, veined hand. His clothes seemed to quiver, barely able to stay on him. Each vein and muscle showed right through, along with a generous bulge below his low-slung belt buckle.

"Fuckin' worn out, man," he said, and he explained: "Popped four, no, five loads today. Cousin's stayin' at my house, sleepin' in my room, first thing this mornin' I look over at that virgin ass, nothin' but a sheet over it, and my dick's so hard it hurts, so I go over and relieve myself. The kid was squealin'! Whole room stank of come, I swear. So that's one." He stuck out a large, dirty thumb. "Then later"—with a flick he extended his long, thick index finger—"the lawn guy comes over, and basically the whole reason this guy does our lawn is to get my cock down his throat or up inside. So we strip down back of the barn and I do him twice." He flicked out his middle finger. "Then I come back in and the kid, my cousin, is all whiny 'cause he saw me doin' some other guy. And he's complainin' and complainin', I lost patience, took him upstairs, yanked down his pants, threw him over my knee, and spanked the little fucker till he squirted in my lap. Can't do 'em no favors, man; you land that first one so they yell out and then you spank long and you spank hard and you make it *hurt* a hundred percent or they don't learn what life is like. You can tell a guy who's been spanked right; he don't ever go around foolin' himself. Anyway, by the time the kid popped in my lap I got a steel rod in my pants and I'm just lookin' down at all that sperm on my jeans, I just scooped some up, ripped open my fly and stroked it on. Hold the kid's face right up to my tool, get it all in his hair, his ear…fuck, it was a mess! So that's four." He flicked out his fourth finger.

My heart pounded.

"So, five: The kid's all sobby and sayin' he's sorry. He's actually crying, so I'm like, I take mercy. I undress him, undress me, and just, like, hold him. And I started feelin' bad, too, plus you got this sweet little virginal type—I mean, not literally—I took care of that in the morning—but innocent, you know. Sweet. And cryin'. Gives me the biggest stiffy of all. So I'm kind of rockin' him and playin' with his little nipples, and we both pop again. Five. Plus, he's gonna beg me to do him again when I get home." He grinned. "So that'll make seven. Seven pops in one day."

"Wait," I said. "Five so far. Plus one when you get home is seven. What's six?"

He grinned. "You. Later. When we're done washin' all the dishes and shit. We're goin' out back, strippin' bareass, and I'm fuckin' you. I want you havin' my seed, kiddo. I mean, I really feel it down here." He cupped the bulge in the front of his pants. "I wanna give it to you."

And he kept his promise, taking me out back to the alley at the end of the evening and asking, "Ass or mouth?"

As much as I craved to be face-to-face with what I could already ascertain was a thick, straight, magnificent tool, as much as I craved sucking, gulping, devouring that staff and symbol of manhood, I chose instead the activity that would reveal him more deeply, that would let me see the real man—at work, rather than passively absorbing the pleasure of being blown.

I chose to have my ass plowed, and I chose well.

Jeff may have been appalling, but he was...What can I say? An artist. An elite delivery system. A man who truly knew what a dick was for. A man unafraid of giving and receiving the most intense pleasure— or pain. A few times, pressed against the wall out back, under the yellow light in the grease smell, I was ready to scream. A few times I did scream. But the way he worked his achingly hard organ, diligently, patiently, confidently, deep, deep inside me, triggered relentless waves of ecstasy sweeping up my body, exploding my fingertips, disintegrating my lungs and heart. Then he would pull back and work just his head gently back and forth over my sphincter till I could only whimper God's name and pray, terrified of but craving even further disintegration. Here was what two men could have that a man and a woman could never have. I pawed helplessly at the wall, wailed incomprehensibly till I let go all over the bricks, convulsing, clutching at his shaft with my sphincter. Afterward, trembling, barely able to stand, my hair and face and chest drenched with his sperm, I believed that I truly understood who I was and why I was put on the Earth and why Jeff and indeed all men were put on the Earth. Hesitant to put such explosive knowledge into words for him, I only stammered out, "Man! Where'd you learn to do that?"

"My brother," he said. "I mean, did some fooling around before and shit. Strip poker where the winner fucked the loser. But it was my brother who really taught me what these are for." He took his cock and balls loosely in his hand. "Taught me it was an honor and a privilege to have 'em, and how it's a man's duty to give as much pleasure as he can. Once he made me fuck him for practically, like, an hour, to show him what I'd learned. I was sobbing, man. Bawling, like a kid. I'd come maybe five times, and I felt it building up for a sixth. I was shaking all over. Kinda like you now! Afterward he held me. He's got this real hairy chest, and he just held me against it and stroked my hair. I felt the hair on my cheek. A man's hair. The sign of his strength and authority. He let me sleep with him that night so he could look out for me. I remember him whispering in the dark in my ear, 'How's your cock feel?' I told him I was hard again. He whispered, 'Give me your seed.' I just rolled on top of this big, hairy guy, my brother, this guy who had the same seed as me, and I just let go. Again and again."

Then Jeff held me, the two of us totally bareass in the night air. I had never imagined he could feel this way, or that fucking meant so much to him.

I could not help but think, what would happen if Jeff met Michael? I mean, of course, they had met, as employees. But what if Jeff *had* Michael? What if Jeff were offered Michel? What would it be like?

I would not have to wait long to find out.

One slow night the following week, I stood next to Jeff, feeling the heat coming off him through his skimpy, damp white shirt, barely containing that manly energy. Suddenly it registered that Jeff, leaning back, thick arms crossed, had been watching Michael as he went up and down, cooking, greeting folks, calling out to the waitresses, and scrubbing down a greasy surface here or there in the few seconds he could steal between assignments. Michel at work. Doing his duty.

Jeff had a hard-on and was making no move to conceal it.

I wanted to tell Jeff how I felt about Michael. I wonder if Jeff knew he was Michel. I longed to whisper to Jeff about unbuttoning Michael's shirt, taking down his baggy pants, exploring with my tongue between those strong, capable legs. Would Jeff be jealous? Would he dismiss me?

Strapping, hunky Jeff surely would look down on Michael—skinnier, boyish with his prominent front teeth, nerdily hardworking.

Just then, Jeff purred softly, "What do you think of him?"

Though I had been watching Michael right along with him, I said, "Who?"

"Michael." I don't think I had ever heard the name pronounced with such tenderness in the long "i," such an elegant little slide off the "k" sound into the "l."

Still not daring to believe that Jeff was really asking what I thought of Michael sexually, I said, "Michael? What about him?"

Jeff didn't bother drawing me out anymore. He just told me what he thought. "I think he is a very fine young man," he said.

I looked into his face. Surely he was being the littlest bit ironic. "Fine young man"? Well, Michael was.

"He works real hard," Jeff said. "That's a sign of a man's good character."

I hadn't thought about it. When I said nothing, Jeff went on:

"Works so damn hard, but he never gets rewarded. I think tonight after work, you and me should reward him for his good work. He should get to lie back and let someone else do the work. He should know he's appreciated." He looked at me. "It's gonna feel incredible. For us, too. Just wait. Once, when I decided I was not just gonna make my brother feel good, but I was gonna thank him for all he'd done for me…? Jesus, I thought he'd go nuts. I thought I'd go nuts. I couldn't stop. You'll see." He looked down. "Just hope I don't cream before then. I ain't creamed all day, and it's buildin' up!"

That evening, after the last customers left and Michael with his big bunch of keys locked the front door from the inside, we all circulated, mopping, scrubbing, washing the last dishes and implements from the grill and breaking down the dishwasher. Michael came through the back room. Jeff stopped him and engaged him with this idea of his not being rewarded enough for his work.

"Um, well, I guess I'm paid pretty fairly," Michael said.

"I'm not talking about pay," Jeff said, grinning.

"Oh. Uh, what are you talking about?"

Jeff looked at me. "Why don't you show Mikey here what we mean when we say he ain't rewarded enough."

Michael must have had some idea, because when I knelt and

unzipped his pants, he was already hard. Rather than start with his cock, I gently wrapped my mouth around his balls. Jeff was right. Thinking what a good guy Michael was and how hard he worked and what good care he took of us, I just couldn't take my mouth off those balls. I couldn't stop thinking of the little guys inside, the little Michaels working hard. Finally, though, I let them go and took his shaft in my mouth. Michael sighed out a single word: "Fuck!" It came up from his crotch, from the center of his soul. Jeff stood over me, unbuttoning Michael's shirt, massaging his chest, talking low:

"Dude, you are so fucking decent. You work so fucking hard, the kid here and me thought we should reward you for it. We think it's time you were treated right."

"Oh, yeah!" Michael moaned. He was feeling the front of Jeff's pants. Jeff obligingly took out his cock.

"Is this what you want?" Jeff asked. Michael nodded. "You got it, boy," Jeff said. "You think you can take all of it?" Michael nodded again. "Good," Jeff purred. "It's all yours. Tonight's for you, Mikey." Jeff stroked my hair and said, "Go easy, kiddo. We want to let Mikey build up. When Mikey shoots his little puppies, we want him to be achin'. We want him to go abso-fuckin'-lutely apeshit."

I took my mouth off Michael's cock. I stared at the wet slit, and I could just imagine it shooting puppies all over the kitchen. Michael seemed like he must be a fountain of white gold, more than all the Jeffs and all the other hunks of the world. I gazed up at Jeff, the strapping muscle-bound one entranced by Michael's decency. I stood, and we all finished stripping. Jeff saw my look when he kicked off his sneakers and went barefoot on the greasy kitchen floor. "Gotta be totally naked," he said. "Totally naked with the other guy." I remembered how we had stripped completely, even out back. "My brother said it. Gotta totally reveal everything." He caressed Michael's soft, round bottom and pinched his nipples. "Once this kid came over from next door, kinda outta shape, didn't want to take his shirt off. My bro made him. He said, 'I don't care what it looks like, just gimme it. Gimme all of yours, I'll give ya all of mine.' That kid was beautiful, turned out. Beautiful, beautiful little chub. Now you come on, Mikey. You gimme all of yours, I'll give you all of mine."

And he did.

He put Michael naked on the table in the center of the kitchen and sucked his cock, while I, in turn, sucked Jeff's cock. (Michael did have a pair of those little ankle socks, and he left them on.)

"Get me off now," Jeff said, "so when I fuck him I can go the distance."

I complied, sucking Jeff's shaft vigorously until with a guttural snarl he emptied in my mouth. After I swallowed I grinned up at him, wiping my lips. "You got some pretty sweet puppies yourself," I said, and he tousled my hair.

"Let's you pop some seed now," he said, "so you can spell me on Mikey here." He and Michael took turns sucking my cock, and their tongues fought hungrily for the goo that shot out. Neither one wiped his face. I wished I hadn't; I wished that I still had Jeff's stuff on me.

Now Jeff reached for a plate over on a shelf with a big chunk of butter. He yanked the plastic wrap off, grabbed a handful of the butter and smeared it first on Michael's cock and all between his legs and around his asshole, then on his own cock and balls and then on mine. Michael shuddered as the butter went on, but Jeff said, "Easy. Easy, boy. Not yet. You can't fuckin' imagine what we're gonna do to you." He worked the end of his long, greasy middle finger into Michael's hole. Michael writhed and shuddered. "You been fucked before, Mikey?" Michael shook his head. "Ooh!" Jeff said. "Virgin hole. Shit, I can just feel myself ready to, like, spew a gallon." He brought the glistening tip of his cock up to Michael's pucker and pressed gently. Michael whimpered and spread his cheeks even more. In his right hand he held my spent cock, still dripping after coating my coworkers' faces.

Once inside, instead of sinking his considerable shaft all the way into Michael, Jeff just moved the flare of the head back and forth in small but authoritative strokes over the very edge of Michael's sphincter. Michael squeaked, dumbfounded, and Jeff slowly grinned. "Good, right?" he said. Michael bit his lip, and his head flopped around in some kind of nod. Jeff turned to me. "You wanna try?" He pulled out, then held me from behind, his cock pressed to my ass crack as I played my head across Michael's sphincter for a while. Michael gripped the edge of the table and his belly heaved with each breath he gulped. "Now sink it in," Jeff said, and I did. I felt the warmth of Michael's insides embracing me and the grip of his sphincter at the base of my tool. I remained aware of Jeff's embrace from behind, engulfing me, his stubbly cheek laid against the bump at the back of my neck. Fleetingly I was aware that, for all his spectacular ranginess and appalling talk, Jeff held in his belly a roaring need to be with and to love men. And with that fleeting thought came another: I looked down at Michael. Where had my sweet Michel gone? He lay like a fish, just taking it, skin tender and creamy, the hair under his arms and trailing down from his navel adorably assertive, but where was his naked desire? He had not yet *met* Jeff. Briefly, before I returned to being turned on by the warmth and the grip and what I thought and what I was doing, I guessed he was not going to.

A few minutes later Jeff took over again and sank deep into Michael, rocking and pumping and thrusting while Michael twisted on the table and arched his back and whispered, "Fuck me, dude. Come on, plow me, plow my fuckin' hole. Fill me the fuck up."

And I have to say, Jeff was the perfect fuck machine, strong, passionate, tender, tireless, his tough, powerful, perfectly shaped body and equipment all bareass naked, its every thrust and undulation calculated to drive Michael over the edge into a sea of pleasure and release. As Jeff had once told me after a session we had out back, "I don't care so much about me. I just wanna know you fuckin' see God, man. If you see God, I had a good night. You in a state of grace, I sleep real good."

Nor did Jeff forget me. Working away on Michael's behind, he reached over and did my favorite thing of the whole night. He stroked my hair. Over and over. Stroked my hair and looked into my eyes and smiled. Then softly he said, "You hungry?" I nodded. Without stopping his rhythm, his huge hand pulled a can of chocolate sauce from the shelf. He swirled his finger in it and held it out to me. As I licked he whispered, "Pretend it's my tool, just gushing, and you gotta get every drop." Then he looked down at Michael and said, "You hungry, too, Mikey?" and soon Michael was devouring drips of chocolate off Jeff's long, strong, veined finger. Next he pulled down some jam and fed it first to me in gobs that dribbled off my chin and then to Michael, after which he smeared a whole handful on Michael's chest and belly, then another handful in my hair and over my face. He finished by smearing his own torso and face with it and declaring, as he continued the whole time to pump in and out of a squirming, gasping, mewing Michael, "We are the cannibal tribe! Argh! We devour men's meat! Argh! We are the brotherhood of the warm puppies!"

That's how I felt that night: part of a brotherhood. A brotherhood of pleasure, a group of men that would do anything to help one another reach ecstasy. While Jeff pumped, I sucked Michael's cock and brushed his nipples, then I got the idea to grab the butter again and grease Jeff's hole. Why should Michael have all the fun? I hesitated because Jeff always called the tune. He said what would happen. What if he disapproved? The night would no longer be perfect. I would spoil something if having me inside him wasn't part of the plan. But I longed to feel big, strong Jeff's tiny, warm entrance, so I kept on, took the butter and before I knew it, my greasy fingers were between his pounding, muscled cheeks, probing in the hair, finding the tender, closed pucker at the center of the man. To my surprise and relief, he adjusted his stance so his cheeks were spread wider, and as my fingers entered him he growled, "Fuck, yeah, get in there deep, kiddo." I was so excited I pulled out my fingers, greased my cock, and fitted it into him as fast as I could.

I had none of Jeff's art—though I remembered to nudge my head in and out over his sphincter real slow a few times—but I had his desire. I wanted to be as deep inside him as I could get, and plant seed in his fertile ground forever. Jeff, I thought, you throw your whole fucking soul into pleasing Michael and me, someone's got to take care of little Jeffy. Someone's got to make you quiver, someone's got to fill you up. Already with each of my thrusts, he was twisting and grunting and chewing his lip. He fell forward onto Michael, madly licking chocolate and jam from his belly while still plowing his hole double time. I kept myself pressed to Jeff's backside and nestled my cock as deep as I could in the warmth, feeling his sphincter grip me in rough spasms. I'll take care of you, Jeff, I thought. I'll make sure you have the greatest fucking Vesuvius-Old Faithful-moon-rocket orgasm of your life.

And so he did.

So did we all.

Jeff worked Michael's cock with his butter-smeared hand, and Michael began to build. "Jesus," he gasped, throwing his head left and right on the table, "I'm gonna fuckin' lose it. I'm gonna fuckin' come like a fuckin' freight train, man!"

"Yeah, you are," Jeff said. "Gonna blast your seed like the fuckin' 5:31 to New York fuckin' City." And as he said it Michael arched his back and bellowed like I had never heard a guy bellow. Jeff pulled out and began jacking himself. Suddenly he screamed, "Fuck!!" and the two of them shot long, thick spurts all over Michael's face and chest and belly. I had pulled out of Jeff, and I joined them, surprised myself with my triumphant cries and spilling my seed into Michael's chest hair. Jeff threw his thick, heavy arm around my shoulder, and I drained my last drops with my head nestled into his armpit. Without thinking I kissed his chest. Then again and again. Jeff squeezed the arm around my shoulder tighter. I nuzzled his chest hair. The air reeked of come. Michael was gasping for air and saying over and over, "Motherfucker. Motherfucking fuck. You big fucking motherfucking stud, look at all that cream. Look at all that fucking hot cream." Jeff reached down and trailed his fingers through the pool of sperm on Michael's torso. "All for you, Mikey," he whispered. "All for my man, all for the working man. You got your reward, Mikey." With his left arm he pulled me tighter to him, palming my head with his left hand, crushing it to his chest and nuzzling and pressing his lips to the top of it.

"Smell that fuckin' sperm," he said. "Smell it, boys. That's the stink of men. That's what it smells like to be a man." He took a deep breath. So did I. The air also smelled of shit and butter and chocolate and jelly. My legs trembled, and I didn't think I could stand without holding on to Jeff. I licked at the hair on his chest. He was quivering, too. Michael lay there limp, eyes closed, whispering, "Motherfucking stud, man, you are the most perfect fuck machine in the history of the fucking world, man. Shit. Other guys call themselves men. You are *the* man. You are the bull. You are the bull's fuckin' master. You fuckin' *taught* the bull, guy…"

Funny enough, Jeff wasn't really listening to him. Jeff was kissing the top of my head, hard, biting at my hair and licking it. I was examining each and every hair on his chest, nuzzling and licking them and reaching behind to finger his still slippery hole. He played with my hole and licked the top of my head all over. Before I knew it, he squeezed out a new load on my belly. I realized I had another one for him. I dribbled it on his cock and balls and in his plentiful dark hair. I felt his hot breath in my ear: "I could fuckin' do it with you all night, little brother. I could give you seed till I went fuckin' cross-eyed."

And we would. But first we had to finish with Michael. He finally got off the table and walked, and we decided to have a little fun before we all had to go. Jeff teased me about how I'd forgotten to wash some platters, and pretty soon we decided the only proper punishment was for me to go over Michael's knee bareass and take it with a wooden spoon. Only there were maybe twelve wooden spoons in that place, so we had to try out a few strokes with each one. Naturally Michael and I were both still naked and hard, and in the course of trying out those spoons we both came again. Then Jeff had to be punished for some infraction or other, and he really wanted to see how many strokes he could take with the biggest, heaviest spoon. It may not sound like much, but that thing was the size of a frat paddle, plus the force was all concentrated in the spoon part of it, so it made a wicked smack on Jeff's ass and left a big purple mark. Michael got the idea of soothing it with some ice cream, so we smeared ice cream on Jeff's ass, then on each other, especially each other's cocks, so I had the pleasure of taking a mouthful of cold chocolate with Michael's warm sperm as the sauce. By that time we were pretty exhausted, and Michael said he guessed he had to get going, if we didn't mind closing up. Jeff said no, we didn't, and Michael started wiping himself down—all the jelly and chocolate and butter and ice cream and come and shit and whatever else.

Jeff and I cleaned up slower. There was no point because we were going to engage in some action after Michael went. We had found one another in that three-way and were itching to commune just between ourselves, the ultimate nakedness.

As Michael locked the door behind him and waved, Jeff and I were still naked, dawdling with towels. I was ready to run and roll on my back on that table in the kitchen. Instead, Jeff stepped over to me and wrapped me in his thick arms. I gripped him with my skinnier body. I felt a stirring in the base of my cock but did not get hard. We just breathed for a while in the low light. Finally he murmured, "That was great…"

I was about to agree when he went on:

"The way you thought of doing me. I'm usually the guy in charge. As you can sorta tell. I plan everything. Everyone does what I say. But when you just went after my a-hole like that…No one ever told me what to do. Well, my brother. But that was our deal. He told me what to do. He taught me. No one ever just thought I'd like my hole opened up. It was great. What made you think of it, kiddo?"

"I…I dunno," I said. "I just, you know, I like you." I felt his arms grip tighter. "I wanted to touch you in the place you touched Michael."

"It was sweet," he said, and licked at my hair again.

"I wasn't sure you'd be interested," I added. There was something I still felt self-conscious about.

"What?" Jeff said. "Me, not interested in having you inside me? Why the fuck not?"

"Well," I said, "I guess I don't always think of myself as, I dunno, part of the brotherhood."

Jeff looked utterly confused.

"'Cause I'm, you know, not as big."

Still utterly confused. Jeez, how much more was I going to have to embarrass myself? "My dick," I said. "It's not as big as yours or Michael's."

"So?"

"Well…"

"Like, why would that have anything to do with anything?" He was truly, helplessly baffled, and somewhat annoyed by it.

"I dunno," I said. "I just always thought…"

"So how did you like Michael?" he asked suddenly.

"Hot," I said, without thinking. "I mean, cute. He sure seemed to enjoy himself…"

"I was kinda disappointed," Jeff said. "He just took. Maybe that's all I wanted him to do. I just wanted to be the big, powerful provider, give him more than any guy possibly could. Just to show I could do it. Kinda boring. How was it when he spanked you with them spoons?"

"Like…tentative? It hurt, but…"

Jeff grinned and cupped his hand around the back of my neck. Drawing me with him he sat on a stool and bent me over his knee. He reached for a spoon one of us had left on the counter. Hard and with no preparation he whacked my ass so I actually heard it. I was actually struck by the sound. While I was still absorbing this, he whacked again and again and again. I was squirming in pain, but soon enough I understood that this was going to go on exactly like this with no slow-down or let-up until Jeff decided it was over, so I had to just take it. I drew in a breath, and I felt big. Bigger than pain, but I liked the pain. When it ended, at first I didn't notice.

"Was that better?" Jeff asked.

"Much," I gasped. "What was it for?"

"For? For the bullshit about the size of your dick. That's what it was for."

"Funny," I said. "While I was taking it I felt…big."

Jeff just nodded and smiled.

Then he took me in his arms and caressed my back. Finally he said, "Yeah, you pokin' my hole was a lot better than anything that happened with our friend there. I sorta liked who I was with you inside me." His large hand squeezed my butt cheek. Our cocks stirred.

"Don't put your clothes on," he said. "I like you naked. All over. At the mercy of the world. And I'm naked, and I'm at the mercy of the world, but not when we hold each other. We're two naked guys, but we're fuckin' powerful naked, we're kings, and no one can get to us. Mikey needs that uniform. That white shirt and dorky pants and the paper chef's hat. Huh! They're what make him work hard. They make him know who he is. Did you notice how he wasn't the same once he got naked. He didn't know what to do. Me, I think I know best who I am when I'm naked. There should be a job for that, right? Yeah, I know, porn star, hardee-har-har. No, I just wanna work naked whatever I do. Like if I could wash dishes and bus tables and do shit here naked? No little white shirt, no dorky pants. Bareass, getting' the muck all over me, walkin' out back in the alley with the garbage and lettin' the glass cut my feet. No, seriously, I got cut up a little when I fucked you. Went home, washed it out. When Mikey was whipping my ass with them spoons, I thought of tellin' him to do it real hard, make me cry. Seriously. I ain't cried in a while. But I guess I figured he wouldn't do it. Not follow through for real. I thought of makin' him fetch his brush, for cleaning the grill, y'know? And givin' it to him with that. He woulda felt so betrayed, though. Work is everything to Mikey. He never took them little white socklet things off. Huh! Didn't they look ridiculous?"

We giggled. He squeezed my ass and then smacked it. His rough, large hand then came around front and gently held my balls.

"I kinda want the world to ask everything of me," he said. "And I wouldn't've got that idea if you hadn't fucked me. If you hadn't asked that of me. I could answer you with my body. Good thing. I don't know, when I stop talkin', what you're gonna want. I hope I can give it to you.

I hope if you just wanna walk away, I can open my arms and let you go, and be naked and alone here. Without anyone. Maybe I'd go out back and walk on glass." He laughed a little. "And maybe I'd have the guts just to stand here."

And then he stopped talking. He loosened his arms.

I didn't walk away. I just laid my face against his chest, my breathing slowly aligning with his, and he held me, not so tightly now, just gently, until gradually he began to cry.

It was then that I knew what kind of man I wanted to be.

And I knew with whom I wanted to be that kind of man.

SUPERTASTER
KARL TAGGART

I want to meet the man of my dreams at Whole Foods. I want love to spark where produce is so artfully displayed I hate to disturb it, where I often lose myself gazing upon broccoli stacked to resemble a luxurious green puffed quilt with carrots lined into orange trim or artichokes topped with white asparagus arranged into a crown. I sometimes visit the store when I have nothing to buy, like when my last boyfriend and I broke up and I consoled myself among eight kinds of apples arranged in a fragrant red and green collage. It is therefore appropriate for me to meet my dream man in this most hallowed of establishments.

I want to brush his elbow as we both reach for the Napa cabbage. We'll share an "oops," then an "after you," followed by that indulgent foodie look. He'll move off toward the trail mix while I head to fine cheeses. He has no cart, which means his kitchen is well stocked and he's come out for a specialty item or to replenish a spice in his cupboard. We'll meet up in raw foods where we'll laugh at discovering one another again. We'll discuss the Lemon Pie Coco Roons and from this point shop together. When he agrees to coffee next door, we will be on our way toward a relationship made in my kind of heaven.

Whole Foods is miles away, but I drive there every Saturday and sometimes, when I feel lonely, on a Friday night. Then one Sunday afternoon I'm cooking chipotle beef tenderloin for friends and find I'm out of cumin, which rattles me, as a gourmet cook out of such a basic is like a clown who can't find his big shoes. Safeway is in the next block, a big, chunky fluorescent box that thinks ambience is screaming specials and carts fit for buffalo. I'm in a hurry because my guests are due at five so I rush down there, race inside, hurry to spices, and grab a bottle of cumin. I am zooming toward checkout when I round a corner and crash into a shopping cart. And the man of my dreams.

For maybe the first time in my life I forget food. The collision has knocked the cumin from my hand, but I don't care because this incredible creature has his fingers touching my shoulder. "Are you hurt?" he inquires in a warm baritone. "I am so sorry. I'm just not good with these carts. You sure you're okay? You dropped something. What was it?"

I have yet to speak. He squats down to search for my cumin, which seems to have rolled under one of the bulging shelves, thank you fate.

Until this moment I didn't know what my dream man would look like. I'd played the setting more than the substance, so I'm stunned to discover food is not even on the list. He has a scruffy look but it's purposeful as opposed to idle. He wears jeans and a faded navy tee with a pocket that seems artfully torn. While he hunts on the floor I scour his body from top to toe, starting with a riot of blond curls that doesn't seem to have seen a brush all day. His features are fine, almost elegant, his body lean and lithe, and when he stands up and hands me my cumin, I note his eyes a vivid blue. "Here you go," he says. "What is that anyway?"

"Cumin. It's for chipotle beef tenderloin which I'm presently cooking for friends, so I'd best get back, only…"

"Only…" he says, smiling. His teeth are perfect, of course, the only orderly thing about him.

"This is crazy," I stammer, "but…"

"I know," he says.

"So…what's your name?"

"Clay."

"I'm Elliott. Would you like to come to my place later for coffee? I can get rid of my company by ten."

He doesn't hesitate, which confirms the heat radiating off me is well received. "You're on."

I get a pen from the cashier and write my address on the back of my receipt. "See you later, Clay," I call as we part.

I am so giddy over dinner that my friends remark. "Have you met someone?" Donna asks, and I decide to make this work for me.

"Yes, I have, and he's coming by later, so you all have to be out of here by ten."

"Elliott is gonna get his clock wound," says Noah.

"His donut dunked," chimes Kurt.

"His knitting purled," adds Mindy, giggling.

"All right, all right. How is the chipotle beef tenderloin?"

Accolades all around and a fine time, the meal consumed down to the last morsel. Over dessert—mint-topped chocolate mousse—Kurt asks how I met the new guy. When I explain, they are amused. "Appropriate you meet in the supermarket," Donna observes. "Food rush."

"What are you serving?" Noah asks and before I can answer, Kurt says, "Himself!"

At ten I push them out the door amid demands to call each and every one with details. I then clean up the kitchen, tidy everything else, myself included, and put on coffee. It's been a month since Lance and I broke up, Lance the chef who I'd thought was the ideal man until he left me for a waiter at La Maison. I am thus giddy with anticipation.

Clay arrives at ten after ten and hands me a package of Hostess powdered sugar donuts. "To go with the coffee," he says with a smile.

"How sweet. Thank you. Come in."

He looks around and we pass some inane conversation before he says "ah hell" and grabs me. What ensues is a veritable feast, the two of us devouring each other on the living room floor, the bed, and in the shower. Come is everywhere, as are sweat and the reek of sex. We wash it off only to start up again. I don't know who this guy really is, but he is the man for me, an absolutely perfect fit. And I tell him this when we crawl back into tangled bedding to play with spent bodies. We can't keep our hands off each other. "We never had that coffee," I note. It is two a.m.

"I have to go to work in five hours," Clay replies as he fingers my tit.

"I have to go in six," I reply as I squeeze his thigh.

"We should sleep," he says.

"You first."

He's still playful, and while part of me begs for rest, another part wants to eliminate sleep altogether and keep on with this wonderful man until I expire in the throes. He curls his arm around me. "Let's try to doze awhile."

I nestle against him and am overcome by sleep. It is light when he says "lie still" and I feel his hard cock at my backside. "Good morning," he says as he enters. I swoon.

As opposed to our frantic coupling the night before, this is gentle. An easy thrust awakens me butt first, awareness gradually working its way up to my mouth, which falls open, and then my mind, which starts to dance with excitement. Along the way, my heart is nudged most pleasurably and I begin to squirm on this impressive cock, urging it to do a little damage. Clay gets the message, begins to push with some force, then says that "ah hell" again, flips me onto my stomach and drives it home. Pounding my ass, he issues no more than grunts in time to his thrusts while I frantically work my dick in hopes of getting off with him. When he starts to growl, I know he's there. His fingers dig into my hips and I pump myself until I feel the rise. As he rides out his come I shoot a good morning load into the bedding, ecstatic with not only my climax but with his. When he's done he pulls out and falls over beside me. I roll onto my back and as we lie in recovery he takes my hand. It is this gesture that seals my fate. I am in love.

"I have to go," Clay says, squeezing my fingers. He hops out of bed and is into the bathroom before I can reply. "I'll start the coffee," I call as I scramble into my robe and head for the kitchen. It is then I spy the Hostess donuts. I finger the box but cannot bring myself to open it, no matter how endearing his effort. He had to have been in a powerful hurry to settle for such fare but I push this from mind, set out croissants and fresh blueberries, which are stunning on my Fiesta ware. I am pouring coffee when he comes in and slips his arms around me from behind. "You are fabulous," he coos, nuzzling my neck, "but I'm afraid I have to run. Breakfast meeting with the owners."

In with last night's sex we'd shared bits of life. He manages a downtown gallery, likes classical music, and lives alone in a studio apartment.

"Not even coffee?" I ask.

"'Fraid not. I'll call you later." A kiss on the neck and he is gone. I pour a solo coffee and eat a croissant before returning to the bedroom where I fall into the bedding and inhale our scent.

I'm office manager at a downtown insurance company not three blocks from Clay's gallery, but I try to keep from rushing over to see him. I call Donna and Mindy, leave a message—success! Then I catch Kurt, who will share the good news with Noah. But talk of Clay does me in, and by lunch my resolve is gone. I walk to the gallery where I see him standing with a customer before a large and splashy painting. They are deep in their assessment so I keep back, but Clay glances over as if he can feel my presence. He smiles and lifts his eyebrows, which melts me. Can I get any more in love? Apparently so.

"Let me cook you dinner tonight," I gush when he's free. He is impeccably dressed in light gray Italian suit, pale blue shirt, and gold patterned tie. His blond curls are still a riot but a quieter one.

"Wonderful," he says. "I'm off at six."

"Six thirty?"

"See you then." And he kisses my cheek.

I float back to the office where I set aside all work to plan my menu. Running through my mental recipe files, I settle on saucy Thai beef noodles, honey, pecan, and goat cheese salad, French bread, and wine. For dessert lemon berry parfaits. I stop at Whole Foods on the way home where I glide along in a serenity possible only in cooking for a man. Cooking for friends is fun and I do it often, but cooking for a date is the ultimate as it shows how strongly I feel. Food is as expressive a medium to me as art. In fact, it is my art and I am a master—at least in the kitchen.

This time I don't let him push me into bed first. Crazy, I'm sure many would say, including part of me, but I've gone to great lengths with this meal, set a fine table, and have the wine breathing. We can fuck later. Food has a timetable.

"I hope you're hungry," I say as Clay eyes the table and then me. "I mean for dinner," I add, smiling. "You are going to love what I've prepared. Why don't you pour the wine while I finish up in the kitchen. Make yourself comfortable."

He is adorable in chinos and a blue polo that sets off his coloring. His hair is halfway tamed and I can't wait to get my hands into it, but first things first. The Thai noodle dish is a stir fry and the beef is already done, as is the peanut sauce. I toss vegetables into the wok and after a bit, add the beef. Clay comes into the kitchen with two glasses of wine. I take one, we clink glasses and share a deliciously long look which I break only to stir the stir fry. "What is that?" he asks.

He listens attentively as I describe what he's about to taste. "Salad's in the fridge," I add. "Will you get it, please?"

He does as asked, takes it and the bread to the dining room. The stir fry has reached the optimum point. I add the peanut sauce, give it a toss, and slide it into a large bowl where I sprinkle it with cilantro and chopped peanuts. It is a work of beauty.

Clay is modest with his food. He takes small portions of noodles and salad but two slices of bread. When he begins to eat, he spears a piece of beef and pauses before he puts it into his mouth. If I didn't know better, I'd think he was sniffing it, but surely nobody would do such a thing. He downs the beef while I devour beef, noodles, and vegetables like I'm starving. Clay next twirls noodles onto his fork, appearing to take great pains to avoid the rest. Once he's consumed the noodles, he pokes around for a bit of carrot, spears and eats it. In this manner, he eats some of the Thai dish, and when he starts his salad, it is much the same. He eats the greens and maybe one pecan but avoids the goat cheese. He spends more time with his bread, eating both slices without butter. He also drinks two glasses of wine.

Of course, I dive into the entire meal, as it's a favorite not only of mine but of all my friends. Maybe Clay is simply cautious, although such a thing is difficult to imagine. I've heard of finicky eaters, usually parents moaning about children, but Clay doesn't seem the fussy type. He's just the opposite, quietly robust I would say.

We finally get to know each other over the meal. I share stories of insurance company life while he enlightens me with pursuits of the gallery and his own early artistic endeavors. "I still dabble," he confesses, "but I'll never make it as an artist. Once I saw myself more suited to appreciating art than making it, I became much happier. I seem to lack the artist's necessary angst."

By meal's end I am giddy, enamored, and ready. "Coffee?" I say. Clay has eaten maybe half of what was on his plate, and that wasn't much to start with, but who cares.

"No thanks," he says. "How about we get comfortable?"

We do not clear the dishes and we do not make it to the bed. Clay may not have eaten much but he is well fueled and we end up naked on the dining room floor, half under the table at one point. God, I love that! The only thing better would have been fucking on top of the table amid the food, peanut sauce and noodles smeared over us. As it is, Clay rams his dick home while his blond curls flail like some shaggy dog. I lie with legs reaching for the table's underside as that cock spears me toward bliss. My come is prodigious and Clay, as he lets go, declares he will fuck me to eternity. Fine with me.

"Dessert's in the fridge," I manage once we've settled. "I don't know if I can walk in there to get it."

He rolls over to me. "I don't need any dessert but this," he says as he starts to lick a nipple. I am totally spent, completely done, yet something in me stirs. I lie under that table floating on his languid attentions, giving my entire body up to his efforts while my hands trace whatever part of him is nearest. Finally he sucks my dick into his mouth, climbs over me, and drops his sausage onto my tongue and we make a long and satisfying meal of each other. Ages later, I suggest bed. "My butt is getting chafed on the rug," I tell him.

He laughs and we crawl out from under and hurry down the hall. In the bedroom he embraces me, kisses me, and most gently settles me onto the edge of the bed, where he parts my legs and resumes sucking my dick. This allows me to run my fingers through that blond hair, which thrills me almost as much as his tongue on my cock.

We are at it until I insist we break for dessert. It's around midnight and I retrieve the parfaits which are stunning with their layered lemon and blueberry combination in tall fluted glasses. Clay is impressed. "Such presentation," he enthuses.

Sitting in bed, tray between us, we take up our parfaits, and as I dig into mine I note Clay is picking at his. "Sorry," he says. "I don't like blueberries." He is pushing them aside to get at the lemon cream.

"Oh, I'm the one who is sorry," I tell him. "Had I known…well, just go around them. The lemon is the highlight anyway." I hear myself babbling, undone by some silly berries and not quite understanding why. Does my dream man have to like everything I do? No, of course not, but who on earth could dislike a berry?

Dessert somehow dampens things. Once Clay has eaten some of his parfait, he says he has to get going. "We're preparing for an opening on Saturday, Otto Lansdale, and there's a ton of work to do," he says. I want to tell him he need not make excuses, but don't. He dresses and I walk him to the door, kiss him.

"It was wonderful," he says. "You were wonderful. You are wonderful."

"How about we meet for coffee tomorrow?" I ask.

"Sure. I'll call you when I have a break." Another kiss and he is gone.

Tomorrow has already arrived and while I am happy with our incredible evening and enamored of this new man, there remains a finger of concern at those damned berries. If only I hadn't served them. I should have made lemon cream with ladyfingers and served them not in flutes but in dessert bowls. I could see the presentation, a dollop of whipped cream on top. When I last glance at the clock, it is two a.m. I force myself to let go of dessert and of Clay, which eventually gets me to sleep.

It is payroll day at work and the numbers make no sense. I've always breezed through this mundane task but everything now appears silly. I mean, a two is ridiculous if you look at it long enough, and there are far too many on the page. Then Clay calls and everything rights itself. "Yes," I tell him, "I can steal half an hour."

"How about we meet on the Freddy bench at that park down the street?" he says.

Freddy is a statue of city father Frederick J. Foster that stands beside a long orange bench, but I don't really feel like the park. "How about Starbucks instead? It's closer and I need a caffeine jolt."

Clay hesitates, then agrees. I find him outside Starbucks, smashing in a trim navy suit, pale pink shirt, and vivid black and white tie. I think I might cream at just the sight of him but then I see he has two bottles in hand. "Lemonade," he says. "I'm really not into the coffee thing."

This takes a second to sink in but I manage, taking the lemonade bottle because I crave Clay more than coffee. We walk the extra block to the park and settle onto the Freddy bench. I examine the bottle in my hand, which I find is not a blend that would attract notice but some common sort. Still, I open it and drink, finding it does indeed taste like lemonade but little more. No effort. Just lemon and sweetness.

I ask about his day and plans for the opening and he asks about what I am up to. Payroll sounds lame at this point. "Let me fix you dinner again," I say. "I think you didn't care much for my Thai beef noodles."

"No, they were great, but I have kind of plain tastes. Forget haute cuisine with me. I'm really a burger sort of guy."

"Fine. I'll do burgers. Burgers and fries and dessert with no blueberries."

"I wish you wouldn't go to such trouble," he protests with a smile.

"But I love doing it," I insist. "I love food and cooking it for someone special."

He takes my hand. "You are wonderful."

Holding hands is dangerous for us as the air begins to crackle with our heat and my dick starts to rise. When I look at my lemonade, I expect to see it boiling. "Feel that?" I ask.

"Oh, yes. If I didn't have to get back, I'd drag you into the bushes and have my way."

"I'm going to be ruined for work," I declare, squeezing his hand.

"What time is dinner?" he asks.

"Seven, but we have to eat first."

"Not easy."

"Burgers and fries," I remind him. "Fuel."

I manage to get payroll done by two and from then on troll the web for burger recipes, cringing at Stuffed Cheeseburgers and worse. I briefly consider Cajun Beef Burgers, then discover perfection: Fig Pork Burgers. I am entranced as I read the ingredients and think I may come as I see how to make them. I then look at French fry recipes until I cringe, giving way finally to a spectacular bean salad using basmati rice, kidney and black beans, corn, onions, red pepper and cilantro. The dressing is a delight of oil, vinegar, and spices, including cumin, which tells me this salad is meant to be. I make my list and leave work at four, pleading a dental appointment but, of course, I am off to Whole Foods.

Of the necessary ingredients, I have the walnuts, onion, bread crumbs, and red and white wines so I buy the dried figs, fresh sage leaves and arugula, ground pork, Gorgonzola cheese, and hard rolls. For the salad I need everything except spices and oils for the dressing. I hurry home and set to work making the burgers, trying to remember the last time I made one. When I can't, I decide this works in my favor. Clay is bringing something new to my life. I am elated.

He arrives in jeans and a loose orange shirt that causes me to remark on squeezing him until the juice flows. He has in hand a six-pack of beer and I haven't the heart to tell him I don't really drink the stuff. I hand him one and put the rest into the fridge. "I'll have one with dinner," I lie and when he is settled in the living room, looking at my DVD collection, I put away the wine.

"What are these?" he asks when I set the platter of burgers on the table.

"Burgers," I tell him.

"What do I smell?" he asks.

"Oh, it's pork. I hope that's okay. You do eat pork, don't you?"

"Yes, of course, but never in a burger. What's that on top?"

"Fig sauce and arugula. It is to die for."

He nods but does not help himself so I take the serving fork, slip it under one of my creations, and slide it onto his plate. I serve one to myself, then offer him the bean salad. "I know I promised fries but they are really so limited, while this salad will delight the palate." He takes the bowl and spoons a miniscule amount onto his plate, then hands it to me. I sit with the bowl in hand for a second before I dish myself a portion.

"I'm sorry," Clay says. "I thought you'd grill some beef, throw on a slab of cheese, some lettuce and tomato. You know, regular burgers."

I realize then my enthusiasm has trampled his plain taste, but like a trooper, he picks up the burger and takes a bite. He doesn't cringe but I do because I see he is making an effort to get a little bit down. I glance at the salad and wonder if he might choke on it.

"I'm sorry," he says again. He sets down the burger and eats a forkful of the bean salad, then attempts to suppress a recoil.

"You don't like beans?" I ask.

"Oh, no, I do, but what's on them?"

"Well, let's see. Cilantro, chili powder, ground cumin, garlic."

He looks down. "I am so sorry," he says once more. "I told you I have plain tastes, but I don't think you realize how plain. I think we would be better off if we ate out from now on. Nothing personal, but you go to such trouble only to have me disappoint you."

"No, you can never disappoint me. Difference of tastes, that's all. I should have taken you more to heart, but I guess I've been cooking this way for so long, I don't know what plain is."

He stands, drops his napkin onto the table, and comes around to pull me up into his arms. "Food is not what I'm here for," he says with a kiss.

He leads me down the hall to the bedroom, and I try not to think this is an effort to get away from the food. My fig pork burgers linger, never mind I took not a bite. But the effort, the love behind it, is going cold. As Clay undresses me and falls down to suck my dick, I attempt to hold on to disappointment, but it's futile with his tongue at work.

We pass another passionate night and he stays until six the next morning, fucking me awake again. We stink of sex yet I still want more and he takes me with my legs on his shoulders, going at me like he just arrived with a week's store of come. I work my prick as he does me and manage a few good spurts as I gaze up at him in his throes, his head back like a lion about to roar. He is absolute masculine perfection, and I am the luckiest man on the planet.

"I'm sorry about dinner last night," he says when we're quiet.

"That's about the fifth time you've said that."

"Well, I feel bad."

"It's okay."

"Shower with me?" he asks and we are off to the bathroom where we eventually get ourselves washed up for work. Finally dressed, he prepares to leave. At the door I suggest dinner at Chez Mignon. "They have a seared yellowtail with coriander that is to die for."

"I can't," he says. "The opening, remember? I'll be working late tonight, but why don't you come Saturday? I'd love you to be there."

I beam at the invitation. I don't think I've ever beamed at anyone, but I feel myself absolutely glowing. "I would love it. Count me in," I tell him. A kiss seals the date and I watch him depart, the scene playing out like some forties movie.

I sail into my workday, serene as I float upon the tide of paper. Problems occur but do not bother me, and when an employee known for whining sits down to tell all, I am most indulgent. After work I stop at Whole Foods to pick up radicchio and blue cheese because I feel like a salad, and this combination with a fig ginger vinaigrette is wonderfully simple. Checking out, it occurs to me that this impulse toward simplicity is Clay's doing. At home I devour the brilliantly red salad with gusto while I think of him at the gallery, working in shirtsleeves.

Saturday is a dreamy day of preparation for the date, and I savor every minute in a sort of excited calm. Clay stirs my most base desires but also brings a kind of serenity, and the combination is deadly. I call

Donna and Mindy, who take the call as a team, and I feel myself puff up as I relate details of the relationship thus far. It thrills me just to say Clay's name. "Someone is in love," Donna coos and I do not disagree. After this I call Kurt and then Noah, indulging myself fully with long talks about my man.

As it is fall, I choose a charcoal suit, white shirt, and magenta patterned tie. I fuss with my hair until the wave is perfect. My shoes are shined, my beard trimmed to a fashionable hint, and at last I set out. I have never heard of Otto Lansdale but am grateful for him having enough talent to merit the exhibit that will pair me with Clay. I enter the gallery and find a good crowd. As I look for Clay, a red-haired young woman comes up. "You're Elliott, aren't you," she says and before I can say yes, she continues. "Clay said to watch for you. 'Special attention,' he said. I'm Marcy Witherspoon, his assistant. He is going to be wrapped up a lot tonight but I am here to guide you if you wish or leave you alone to explore, your choice. I just want to say I have never seen Clay happier." Here she squeezes my arm. "He's a lucky man."

Just then a waiter comes up with a tray. I seize what appears to be stuffed snow peas and find crab at the center. "This is wonderful," I gush, seizing a second before the tray gets away.

"You like it?" Marcy says. "Oh, good, I wasn't sure."

"Delightful."

I see Clay in a corner with an older couple and as the last of the crab and snow pea combination melts away, I feel a surge of pride. "There he is," I tell Marcy.

"He is indeed," she chimes, then excuses herself to attend someone else.

Sipping champagne, I wander about, glancing at Lansdale's work, which seems rather morbid. Indistinct shapes blurred in dark blues and heavy grays seem to pull down the room, so I look for another waiter with another tasty morsel. This time I find an artichoke and goat cheese bruschetta and seize two. From then on I examine not the art but the food, making sure, in the course of the evening, to try it all. I have just polished off several smoked salmon and caviar toast rounds when Clay comes up and surprises me with a kiss on the cheek. "You have made my evening," he says. "Seeing you here. And I love the tie." He tries to say more but is suddenly waylaid by a tall woman in black who drags him off to meet others.

"Who is that?" I ask Marcy, who has come back to me.

"Elsa van der Poole, wicked rich, but I think of her as Elvira, wicked witch."

This cracks me up and we share a private laugh. I like Marcy. Outside of Clay, she and the food are the best of the evening. "Great food," I tell her. "Clay did a fabulous job."

"Clay?" she says with a sharp laugh. "You are kidding, right? Clay and food?"

"He didn't arrange it?"

"Honey, I won't let him near a menu, let alone a caterer. If food is needed, I take over. He is not allowed to participate in any tasting appointments with caterers, nor is he allowed to decide anything about what is served. If I turn him loose we'll end up with cheddar cheese and saltines."

"I had no idea," I say.

She studies me. "Aha, I see. You haven't gotten out of bed enough to find out."

"Find out what?"

She pauses. "He'll kill me for telling but, well, you're special. He's a supertaster."

"A what?"

"God, does anybody know about this? Okay, here's the scoop. It is a scientific fact that fifty percent of the population are normal tasters and twenty-five percent are non-tasters, meaning they have fewer taste buds, which makes them use lots of hot sauces and spices trying to make food taste good to them. The other twenty-five percent are supertasters who have extra taste buds, which makes them extremely sensitive to taste. They tend to eat few foods, no spices or hot things, and don't like trying new dishes. Tastes are vivid to them. Clay explained it to me once and I went online and it was a revelation."

I am stunned. "He said he has plain tastes," I manage to say as I cringe in recall of what I tried to feed him. "When I think of how polite he was over dinner and his attempts to eat what he couldn't handle, I feel terrible. I fixed him all my favorites, which he probably hated."

"Relax," Marcy says, stroking my arm. "He's used to it and he doesn't judge. If anything he's embarrassed, so he won't talk about what he calls the 'affliction.' Poor guy. Has to go through life hating cilantro."

I look over at him, so urbane, so grounded, and I want to rush over, apologize, and make him a grilled cheese sandwich. He catches my eye and winks and I want to cry. I grab another glass of champagne from a passing tray and gulp down half.

"You okay?" Marcy asks. I've forgotten she is beside me.

"I will be. Thank you for telling me, Marcy. It shows how much you care about Clay. I can't tell you how grateful I am. Will he be upset that you broke the confidence?"

"At first, but he's incapable of staying angry. He's too good a person to be that small. In the end, he'll thank me."

"You are a dear," I say and I kiss her cheek.

She smiles. "And just so you know, Elliott, I've never told anyone before."

"Really?"

"Never. But I've never seen him this happy."

After a while I sit on a little bench away from the crowd, avoiding the nearest painting, from which I fully expect Heathcliff or maybe even Dracula to emerge. Downing yet another glass of champagne, I try to imagine life with too many taste buds and cannot, as it seems to me a blessing rather than curse. Wouldn't it be better with more buds doing the savoring? I am deep in contemplation as the crowd thins. Clay finally comes over. "Another hour," he says as he sits beside me. "Can you manage?"

"Of course."

"You're an angel," he says before going over to a man with an inquiring look.

How can I do it? I ask myself as I take the last spinach cheese square from one waiter's tray and champagne from another's. How can I say to Clay that food doesn't matter when it is such a big part of my life? I think on my cookbook collection and my delight in fine dining. Seared yellowtail with coriander. Clay must have blanched, but he never showed a thing. Poor man. What must it be like? I cannot imagine not liking spices. A world without dill or basil or even garlic. No pork chops with plum sauce, no chicken meridian, no beef Wellington. Plain food. I don't even know what that is. Beef patty on a bun? Cheese on white bread? Does he eat chicken? How do you fix it plain?

I spend the final hour eating the last of the food and drinking champagne to excess while trying not to fall into a plain food maelstrom.

By the time Clay comes over, I'm somewhat a wreck and rather drunk. "Take me home," I beg.

"You don't want to go for a late supper?" he asks.

"You are all I want."

We leave my car and take his to the fourth-floor studio he has near the theater district. As this is my first visit I should be interested in his books but I cannot get my mind past his "affliction." When we get inside his apartment, there is but one recourse. "Fuck me," I demand.

"My pleasure."

It takes forever to undress, or maybe not. Everything is off-kilter, time bent to an angle. Then I'm naked on the bed and he is inside me, and the world returns to its axis, but boy, does it spin. My last recall is coming. I think.

"Elliott," I hear through the fog. Then a nudge. "Sweetheart, it's almost noon. Come on, open those baby blues."

A headache says not to obey but it is Clay's voice, so I attempt to wake, light stabbing me as I admit the day.

"Here," he says. "Sit up. Aspirin, then coffee, then food."

I ease up, take the pills, then the mug of coffee. It is not bad. Not great but not bad. I sip and begin to fully wake, noting the smell of bacon frying.

"You didn't eat last night," Clay soothes. "You need food."

"I ate everything in sight," I tell him.

"That stuff? No, I mean a real meal. Bacon and eggs. How do you like them?"

I almost say over easy but even a partially runny yolk is revolting. "Scrambled."

"Wheat toast okay?" he asks.

"Fine."

"Here's a robe if you want." He wears only plaid pajama bottoms, making him the cutest cook on the planet. His hair is tousled and I don't want him to tame it. Not ever. As I right myself, get to the bathroom for a long piss and some washing up, I recall the night. And then the revelation. Supertaster. The word leaves a bitter taste on my tongue even though I haven't said it aloud. And it doesn't even make sense, I decide. Why super? That makes it sound good. Should be hypertaster. I'll have to ask him about that once I broach the subject. Oh yeah, that. The broaching. Maybe after breakfast.

Clay's kitchen is miniscule, truly made for one. He works at one end while I perch on a stool at the other where a breakfast bar sits below a window looking out onto an air shaft. Fresh air feels heavenly and I suck in long breaths. Two places are set for us, melamine plates and colorful plastic glasses. At least the forks are metal. Clay pours orange juice and dishes up the meal which includes hash browns.

"These are great," I say as I dig into the potatoes.

"Ore Ida, Potatoes O'Brien."

Frozen fare. Okay. Admit it. You like it, you food snob. The eggs are just that, eggs. No scallions or cheese or peppers. Not even salt and pepper. I season and devour them, as I do the crisp bacon and thin slices of toast for which a tub of margarine is offered.

"I don't like butter," Clay says as I reluctantly run my knife into the imitation.

"Really? I've never met anyone who doesn't."

He pauses, then blurts out, "Marcy told me she told you but I don't care. I can't change, even for you, so if that's it, I'll understand."

"If what's it?"

He is almost in tears and I suffer a pang as he lays it out. "You're a gourmet, a total foodie, and I am the polar opposite. I don't like most of what you eat. I have things I like and stick to them and I know it sounds ridiculous but I can't help it. I hate spices. Ketchup is hot to me. Salsa is unbearable, as is coffee."

"But you made coffee."

"For you, yes. I make it for others but I hate it. Even the smell."

"You made a wonderful breakfast," I tell him as I bite a piece of bacon. "I love it all."

"Frozen potatoes, plain eggs. I know people add cream and onions and chives or whatever but here you get egg, pure and simple. No frills."

"But you like them and I like them," I say. "Yes, I haven't had plain eggs probably since childhood, but you know, it's good to get back to basics. And look." I take a forkful. "I like them, Clay. I really do. They're good. Please don't be so hard on yourself. I want to understand."

He throws an arm around me and leans in. I put down my fork and slide off my stool. We stand and embrace. "I can meet you halfway," I tell him. "Isn't that what opposites do?"

"You'd be willing?"

"Of course. Food isn't everything." We both laugh at this so I add, "Okay, it's something but we can work it in. Compromise is part of every relationship."

As I kiss him I realize my headache has gone, as has all upset and concern. I push him to the bed and throw off my robe. He slips off his pajama bottoms and slides onto me, his dick rising between us.

"Iceberg lettuce," he says between kisses.

"Dressing?" I ask.

"Mayo."

"Can we add a tomato?"

More kisses, some grinding on his cock. "Okay."

"Salt and pepper?"

"Okay."

"Garlic?"

He pulls back, stricken.

"I'm kidding," I assure him.

He is suspect for a moment, then breaks into a smile. The conversation is then lost to inquiring mouths and heavy breathing. Soon we are wet with readiness. I raise my legs and he enters, begins an easy thrust. How could I ever think food an obstacle to this man?

"Spaghetti," he says as he pumps in and out.

"Marinara?"

He shakes his head. "Fresh tomato."

"Parmesan?"

He nods.

"Garlic bread?"

He shakes his head. "Crusty sourdough and margarine."

I would quibble but he picks up the pace, seriously drilling me.

I think I could starve for this man.

COOKIE
DALE CHASE

I never expected peach cobbler on the Chisholm Trail. Drawn west by wanderlust and dime novels, I signed on to drive cattle from San Antonio to Abilene and was told to expect a diet of beef, beans, and biscuits. It was thus a surprise to lift the lid on one of the cook's Dutch ovens one evening and discover peaches swimming in hot juice under a crust so light and flaky it put Mother's to shame. Eating this delicacy with fourteen cowboys in the middle of a Texas plain made it seem all the more peculiar. The supper itself had also been first rate: baked short ribs, spuds with onions, and sourdough biscuits along with Arbuckle's coffee, which was "strong enough to float a horseshoe," as the saying went.

"I did not expect to eat this well," I said to Drew Pulliam, also a newcomer, who rode drag behind the herd, said to be the worst job in the outfit due to eating dust all day. I saw this played out as Drew and the other two drag men always carried a layer of dirt so thick it piled half an inch deep on their hat brims and dusted eyebrows and mustaches white.

"Best part of the drive," he remarked. "That and Abilene."

As he went on about what all cowpunchers do at the end of the trail, I considered instead the cook, Wade Kuller, who was already done eating and busy at his chuck wagon table, setting beans to soak for the next day's supper. Kuller did not look like a man to make biscuits or cobbler, as he was big and bearlike and thus more suited to pulling fish from a stream barehanded or maybe clawing someone to pieces. That such a man could create pastry to rival a woman set me to thinking on him. He was older than the others, even the trail boss, Galen Bishop, and his second, Skip Audley, who had driven cattle together for fifteen years. They were around thirty, which made Kuller maybe forty, his thick hair going gray, face bronzed from the sun yet still striking. His hands were rough, as was his manner. He said only the necessaries and these often came out gruff. Though I enjoyed all aspects of this new world, it was Kuller who stuck to me, and after a week on the trail, I had to ask myself if it was the food or the man.

"Wrangler," Bishop had said when I signed on.

"Horses?" I had replied.

"Well, they aren't sheep. You'll be in charge of the remuda, the herd of eighty horses, and assist the cook as he requires. And don't call him Cookie. That is the stuff of dime novels. He is Kuller to one and all and is third in command, behind my second. When you are not tending the horses, you'll take orders from Kuller."

I was disappointed as I'd come west to drive cattle. I wanted to belong to that team of men doing the real work and enjoy the camaraderie such an effort brings. I had not wanted to be set apart to care for their horses, six to a man, not to mention become a cook's helper. But within a week I had come to prefer my job to that of punching cattle, as Wade Kuller had a pull I could neither define nor resist.

He told me up front what was expected. "When we get to the night stop, you'll unhitch the mules and put them into the remuda, and next morning, you'll fetch them and hook them to the wagon. You'll dig my fire pit at each stop and set up my irons. You will fetch water, wood, tools, and anything I need. You got that, Hoofin?"

"Yes, sir, I surely do, but the name is Hooven. Haskell van der Hooven."

"Good Christ, what a mouthful," Kuller said with a laugh. "I'll stick to the last part. Hoofin."

I did not correct him further and from then on was known as Hoofin to one and all. When the drive began it saw Kuller waking me at three a.m. to set up the rope corral and herd the day's horses into it so the cowboys could easily catch them to saddle up for work. Once I had the corral full of horses, I added wood to the fire, ground coffee, and did other chores as told. Before long, breakfast was cooked and Kuller was rousting the men, swearing at them to get their hands off their cocks and onto their socks, as grub was ready. After the meal, he washed his dishes, stamped out the fire, put his Dutch ovens and other implements into the chuck box, and folded up the lid, which had served as his worktable. By this time I had his team hitched. Soon as the men were fed, they did up their bedrolls and threw them into the wagon, where I then packed them around our supplies. Should a man fail to see to his bedroll, it was tied behind the wagon and dragged to bits.

Our progress was about ten miles a day, but if problems arose or weather turned bad, it was less. Bishop always rode ahead to scout the next good water and grass, and once under way after breakfast, he would later ride back to tell Kuller where to stop for the noon meal. At this stop, we repeated our routine, though the mules were not unhitched, and once the men were fed, we dismantled and set out again. Bishop then scouted the night stop, which had to have good grass and water. The cattle could be treated roughly at noon, but at night they needed their comforts so as to remain calm. We usually pulled up well before dusk to allow time to get them gathered in and settled. Once stopped for the night, Kuller got to work on the evening meal, and once that was over, we knew our first free time of the day.

Now, the peach cobbler but a memory, men fortunate enough to not have night duty lazed in an after-supper stupor, smoking, talking, and sometimes singing. After I'd filled the water barrel, Kuller set me free, so I joined the men to lie about. When his dishes were done, he came over but even then kept somewhat apart. I wondered at this, then wondered why I was wondering.

As the first week had progressed, I had found myself wanting Kuller to ask me why I'd signed on for the drive, but he did not do this. Nor did he ask my age or where I hailed from. Eighteen, I would have said. Gettysburg. But I saw after a while that none of this mattered to him, or to me come to think about it. The trail drive was its own world, and once in it, little else mattered.

There had been time for Kuller to make the peach cobbler because we were laying over at Soda Springs for a day. When I asked why this was, Audley told me they pushed the cattle hard at first to tire them so after a week they were easier to manage and thus we and they could have a rest. This stop also allowed time to brand calves born on the trail.

Camp was in good grass near a fine spring, and the day following our cobbler treat, everyone sought a bath. The cattle were guarded in shifts so every man might have a chance to wash. Cottonwood trees grew around part of the spring, so those bathing had shade in which to recline and soon clothes were scattered, the spring full of naked men. Even the trail boss shucked it all and splashed in, as did his second. It was when the two of them began to frolic that I took note of the manly aspects of a trail drive.

Galen Bishop was a handsome fellow, dark haired and powerfully voiced, while Skip Audley was fair and slight. The two had worked together so long they often finished one another's sentences, but until they hit the water, I saw nothing more than cattle driving as their bond. I stood on shore, still dressed, while about eight men bathed, most occupied either in serious washing or soaking in the cool water. Then I noted Bishop grabbing Audley around the neck, pulling at him, which caused Audley to laugh. They wrestled some, splashed a great deal, and when Bishop pulled Audley onto his back, his front broke from the water and there stood a ramrod stiff prick. They tussled a bit more, Audley still on his back, and I was most excited at the display, my own cock stirring. Just when I thought I could not be further surprised, Bishop grabbled hold of Audley's rod and, holding the man against him, began to pump the thing. The other men scarcely noted what took place but I was fixed on the sight as Audley soon began to spurt his stuff. He bucked against his friend as he let go and Bishop worked the cock until it had nothing more to give.

"Comin' in?" Drew called.

This broke me from the sight but not the arousal, and I did not see how I could disrobe with my dick stiff. "In a second," I called back. I then sat on the shore and observed not the men but the trees and sky to calm my poor prick. Only when I had softened did I strip down and get into the water, but once there, with manhood all around me, I could not help but note several hard cocks. My own quickly rose and soon I had no choice but to work the thing, which I did while staying hidden in the water. Though I maintained composure when I came, evidence appeared in gobs of spunk floating to the surface.

Drew swam over. "Don't worry about letting go," he said. "Everybody is working their dicks one way or another." He nodded toward Bishop and Audley as he said this, the two now entwined in a little eddy, Audley lying back against Bishop. As I looked over, Drew added, "Bishop's got his dick up Audley's butthole. They fuck all the time, so I hear. Been at it for years."

My prick came up again at this news, so I was already agitated when Wade Kuller stepped into view. He'd managed to shed his clothes without my notice and was full naked at first sight. And what a sight. My thinking him bearlike was correct, as his body was covered in dark hair. His chest was impressive, with pectorals most defined, and his pelt descended over a flat stomach to thicken around a big pink cock. Hair continued onto thighs and arms, but I was lost to the prick being up and further, to his not jumping in like most. He remained knee deep, splashing water onto himself, bending and turning as he washed, then stroking his cock while not appearing to care who saw. In fact, he seemed proud of showing his arousal, unfazed as the men turned to look. He worked himself with care, raising his face to the sun as he pumped until his stroke became frantic. He then unleashed streams of come, his spunk shooting several feet from him and in quantity befitting bear rather than man. The sight was so stirring that I grabbed my throbbing prick and pulled just twice before I shot my stuff.

Once empty, Kuller sank into the deeper water and rolled about like a whale, the great cock surfacing at times, a formidable rope even at rest. Kuller kept to himself as usual but I found myself unable to resist going over his way.

"I am still thinking on last night's peach cobbler," I said as I came up to him.

"Wait till you taste my apple pie," he said.

"You spoil us. I never expected such food out here."

"A man eats dust all day, he deserves some reward."

"You are a fine cook," I said, unable to hold back.

"You are a fine wrangler."

As we spoke, the parts of him above the water glistened in the sun and I saw a reddish cast to his fur. I also, when he bobbed up, found his pink tits prominent in his pelt. As if to acknowledge my interest, he slid a hand onto one and began to pinch and rub, his eyes now fixed to mine. "You know, Hoofin, Arbuckle's coffee has attached to each bag a stick of peppermint candy. I save them for special occasions. How would you like some?"

I cared not a whit for peppermint candy, but even in my youth I could see he was offering far more. "I would like that fine," I said.

"You come by the wagon later on, before supper work begins, and you can have a treat." As he said this, he ran a hand down his front, and though I could not see in the muddy water, I knew him to have hold of his dick. A shudder of anticipation ran through me. "You are getting chilled, boy. You had best get out of the water."

"Yes, sir."

As I climbed out, I felt his eyes upon me and realized he wanted to see all of my unclothed body. On shore, I turned to look at him, my hard cock pointed his way. He stood in the shallows, his own big thing stiff again. It took every ounce for me not to grab hold of myself and gain release.

I could not settle after this. Into my clothes, I checked on the remuda, which was calm, the horses likely appreciating the stop as much as the men. Beyond them, the cattle stood munching grass, their lowing and mooing now a welcome sound. The sun told me afternoon was getting well along, so I ambled over near the chuck wagon where the pot of beans was cooking. Beans were practical when laying over, as they took time to cook. Kuller would only need to make his biscuits and rustle up whatever else he had planned. As for me, I knew myself to be a meal of sorts or possibly a snack, but devoured in any case. I knew what men could get up to with one another as I had, in fact, done such a thing two years before in taking a neighbor's cock up my bottom regularly until his wife found us at it one day in his barn. I had replayed our fucking many a night while stroking my cock but until now had seen little promise of more.

I was already stiff-dicked when I saw him coming up from the spring. Leaning against his wagon, I found his eyes upon me and, as if to tell me what we were about, he reached down and adjusted himself. I about came at the sight. "Get into the wagon," he said when he reached me.

Now, the chuck wagon had canvas over the top so it gave some privacy but it was a thing crowded with foodstuffs, fifty-pound bags of flour, coffee, and salt, cans of peaches and tomatoes, assorted tools and implements. Nothing was left but an aisle halfway down the middle, and this was narrow. I did not see what we could get up to in such a space but I left this to Kuller who, as the senior man, would know how to accommodate.

I climbed inside and he followed, pulling down the front flap, which shut out the camp. The wagon's back, where the chuck box was attached, had no opening. "Drop 'em," he said as he began to unbutton his pants. When I stood staring at his crotch, he said it again. "Drop 'em, boy. Come on."

I pushed down my pants and underdrawers, my cock springing up. He also pushed down his to reveal the big pink prick growing out of that thicket. "You ever take a dick?" he asked.

"Yes, sir. Back home, a neighbor."

"Then you know to turn around and bend over."

I bent at a barrel and spread my legs, then felt his hands upon me. He parted my buttocks and ran a thumb over my pucker. "You are a morsel," he said as he prodded. "And I mean to have a fine fuck." With this he pushed his cock into me and fairly set the wagon rocking.

"Been wanting to do you since first sight," he growled as he thrust in and out. "You get my dick hard whenever you come around, which makes work difficult. I am going to have you regular now, Hoofin."

I held on to the barrel but needed no hand upon myself to come. I cried out as juice spurted from my cock, and Kuller seemed most pleased at this. "Drove it outta you, boy. Gonna give you a load you'll remember and Christamighty…" His words became strangled as he pumped so hard my knees nearly buckled. Never mind he'd had a come at the spring, a man such as this had balls churning spunk by the barrel. He went at me for some time, gradually slowing but even then, still keeping inside me. Only when his girth lessened did he relent and when he slipped out, his hand came around to take hold of me. "Boy like you is hard half the time. Now get it hard for me as I want to suck your stuff."

He began to grind against my bottom as he pulled my dick, and of course I came up again because no man or boy could hold back with such a thing upon him. When he had me hard, he flipped me around, dropped to his knees, and sucked me into his mouth. The feel of his tongue upon me and his powerful pull called my juices up all too quickly. He sucked and swallowed as I spurted, and it pleased me to be feeding him for a change.

When he stood he wiped his mouth. "Now, that is dessert," he said and he began to do up his pants. "Tonight you don't bed down with the others. You come put your bedroll with mine and we'll do up a double like Bishop and Audley."

Though I had spent several times, I was still excited, my hand on my prick again. Kuller laughed. "You boys, you never get enough. I'll do you again tonight. Now let's get out of here and see to supper."

Supper was that pot of beans, to which he added salt pork. Alongside were biscuits and coffee, and I found myself with a hearty appetite. The men were loose and easy and once they'd eaten, some went back to the spring as it was a warm night. I saw to the remuda, which meant hobbling every horse, then came back to the chuck wagon where Kuller sat rolling a smoke. As usual, he was off from the others and I could not resist asking why this was.

He took time to light his cigarette and take a long draw. He was hatless and most handsome in the fading light. Not pretty handsome like Bishop but rough handsome, like there was something formidable behind his looks.

"I like to think on things," he said. "The men's tomfoolery often wears thin."

"What do you think on?"

"Next day's meals, stores we need, farms where we can trade for vegetables or fruit." Here he looked at me. "Sometimes I don't think on feeding, though. Sometimes I think on fucking."

I could not contain the gasp that rose up out of me, and this caused him to chuckle. "I am just saying what every man thinks most of the time," he said. "You too. I look over the men on every drive and consider which will take my cock. It is the best part, Hoofin, and don't you think otherwise. Man can fuck whoever will take it out here, and those on the trail are always ready."

I was now so happily agitated I thought I might fly away—or faint. Nobody had ever said such things to me, not even the neighbor who'd had his dick in me. He had said almost nothing, just gotten out his thing and put it to me, then finished and gone back to pitching his hay or whatever task he'd stopped. Here was a man who not only spoke of the worst of men, he made it the best of men.

"I saw Bishop doing Audley at the spring," I managed to say, for I wanted the talk to continue.

Kuller chuckled. "You'll likely see more than that. Those two are a pair to behold. You tell me you haven't heard them go at it in their double."

"I haven't been near them and, well, I hear enough from the other men."

"Dick-slapping outfit means a good bunch, full of piss and vinegar and a good store of spunk. Give me hard-dicked men any day."

I paused to gather my wits, as this was almost too much to take in. Then I ventured a comment. "You said we would double up tonight."

"Yep. We'll roll out my canvas, put on both our blankets, and have your canvas on top, though it is so warm we may not need it. Shed your bottom drawers once you're in bed and I'll put my dick to you."

The men were now unrolling their bedding. Some coming from the spring remained naked and slid into bed that way, Kuller and me taking in the sight. I took note of Bishop and Audley, who had been out seeing to the herd before settling in. Both stripped away all, laid out their double bedding, and got in together. Night was upon us and the campfire was nearly gone. A summer moon gave some light. Under this I could see movement between them, Bishop clearly riding Audley's back.

"First fuck of the night," Kuller said, leaning toward me, "but not the last. Come on, get your bedroll." He laid his out on the side of the chuck wagon, away from where the men were gathered, and once I'd added my blanket to his, he set aside my canvas. "Now strip off."

He stood at the wagon to watch me and when I kept on my undershirt, he motioned for it to go as well. He then drew me to him and reached down to cup my balls. "Hard little nuts," he said as he squeezed. "Full of juice." I squirmed as he dropped to his knees and pulled my cock into his mouth. He began to suck and ran a finger up my crack, which caused me to let go in his throat. As I attempted to fuck his mouth, he remained fixed on me, his power drawing every drop I had. I was grateful the wagon stood between us and the men, allowing at least some privacy.

Wiping his mouth on his sleeve, Kuller murmured his approval, then stood and undressed. Though I'd seen him naked, this revealing still excited me, especially the big hard prick. Once free of his clothes, he guided me into our bed. We lay a spell, listening to the camp go quiet. A grunt or groan was heard now and then, Kuller whispering in my ear that "the come is flowing." He then rolled me onto my side, got up against me, and put his dick into my hole. We lay fucking for a good long time before he bucked and came.

Kuller's windup alarm clock rang at three and before he shut it off, he reached down to tug my dick. I was stiff from night dreams and soon as he got hold, I became frantic, even half-asleep, unable to stop myself from attempting a come. He was patient as I thrust into his palm and let go what the night had stored up. "Now you're done, get moving," he said as he released me.

The night had turned cool and soon as I was out from under the covers, I sought my clothes and boots. I then found my jacket and got the rope corral pegs from the wagon, trudging off to start my day's work, as we would be breaking camp and getting the herd moving again. This meant the men would be coming to rope and saddle their horses and I had to have them ready. Kuller, now dressed, rolled up our bed, threw it into the wagon, lit his lantern, and started breakfast preparations.

As I drove the corral pegs and then strung rope along them, I glanced over now and then to see him at work, thinking on how I was now pretty much his and how this was to my liking. I considered that his fucking me was driving the arrangement, and yet I found more in him than just his dick. What exactly I could not define, and I kind of liked this as I could think on it when at work. Once when I looked his way I saw him looking back, as if he'd already had his eyes on me. This threw me a jolt running from dick to heart and back. A horse snorted just then and I wondered if he had picked up on the scent of things.

By the time I had the horses into the corral, Kuller had the coffee made and biscuits on the fire. Bacon was frying, the smell of which caused me to nearly drool, such was my hunger. As I came over to him, I saw he was making flapjacks, which were considered a treat as breakfast was usually a slab of bacon or beef along with biscuits and molasses and, of course, coffee. "Flapjacks," I said like some kiddie.

"I am in an agreeable frame of mind, which leads to better eats."

"You need me to do anything?" I asked.

"Possum is getting low on wood. You'd best come up with some today, else I'll have to throw your clothes into the fire and leave you go naked."

"You'd like that," I ventured, playing with him as I thought he wanted.

"Liable to burn the biscuits at such a sight."

This talk warmed me as much as the coffee I sipped. Arbuckle's was indeed strong, but I craved it now as it fueled a man for most anything. The outfit drank it by the gallon, the men never having enough. "Why did you become a cook?" I asked Kuller, thinking this a good question. When he gave no response, I was lost. He took up a pan and spoon, walked to the men, and began to strike an awful clatter, which got them moving. He then came back and tended his flapjacks and bacon. He did not answer my question until breakfast was over and I was hitching his mules.

"A man does not choose to become the cook," he said, drawing on a cigarette. "To a one, they come by it as the end of a road. I was a cowpuncher like everyone else but twelve years in, my horse stepped in a gopher hole, snapped his leg, and threw me. I landed wrong and something in my back gave. I could scarcely move for the first weeks but gradually became myself except I could no longer tolerate life in the saddle. I then had a choice. Find work elsewhere or become the cook. As I could think of no life but this, I signed on and have been sweating over a fire ever since."

I did not know what to say. He was such a good cook, it seemed wrong to offer sympathies at his loss of cow punching, and yet what he had endured sounded awful. He also seemed unencumbered by his injury, what with his driving that dick of his. As if to read my thoughts, he continued. "I came to terms with things long ago, Hoofin, so don't go thinking on it. If I can keep on cooking, I can stay out here until I am a hundred."

The men were now coming by the chuck box to pick up plates and eating irons. With these in hand, they filed by the row of pots and pans to serve themselves their flapjacks, bacon, and biscuits. They also took their first coffee of the day. Once they were settled with their food, me included, Kuller made another pot of coffee, then dished up a plate of his own. He sat beside me to eat and I felt most proud in his company, knowing the men had surely seen us sharing a double the night before.

When breakfast was over, the men placed their dishes in a tub for washing, then sought their horses. Once they'd gone I took down the rope corral, tossed it into the wagon, hitched up Kuller's mules, and set to tending the remuda, mindful I had to pick up either wood or cow chips for chuck wagon fuel. The possum, which was a canvas slung underneath, was indeed nearly empty.

My horse was a snappy little paint called Bob, and once astride him I guided the remuda behind the chuck wagon so as not to make

Kuller eat dust. Everything and everyone had to remain downwind of that wagon. I had been told hell would be paid by anyone breaking this rule.

Bishop rode ahead to scout our noon stop, and behind me the men got the cattle moving. It was a sight to behold, two thousand steers kept in line by little more than a dozen men. Though I was a good distance ahead, I could still look back and see the herd, which to me had a certain majesty. Spilling across the plain, here was food for the country, beef on the hoof. I liked the idea of being part of that, but more, I liked the feel of just moving in its company. Bob and I rode along most happily.

I could not see Kuller since I had to keep back with the horses. Being smarter than cattle and broken to man's authority, they fairly welcomed my efforts at keeping them together. From time to time I entertained myself thinking on Kuller with reins in hand, smoking as he guided his wagon. And I began to consider him not as cook but as man and how he'd wanted to keep to this life at any price. That he felt unsuited for other work gave him an appealing rough quality, a true outdoorsman preferring the hard life among men.

Just as I lulled myself into comfortable contemplation, a gunshot shattered the calm and my horses became agitated. Audley, riding up front, came back to check on the remuda, and once he saw it in control, he raced back toward the cattle as the ground had taken on a thunderous quality that rose up through Bob into me. "Stampede!" Audley shouted for all to hear.

I had no idea what to do. Looking back, I saw the herd running in all directions, most toward me but others branching left and right, cowboys in pursuit. Up ahead, Kuller set his mules to a gallop. Realizing the danger the cattle presented to him, I got the horses up directly behind him so the cattle, when they reached us, would split and go around the horses rather than trample the wagon. At least I hoped they would.

The thunder of eight thousand hooves was worse than the worst storm. An awful fright rose up in me, heart pounding, hands shaking, throat gone dry. My horses began to run as they heard the cattle closing behind, and all I could do was ride from one side to the other in an effort to keep them from breaking away. Then the cattle were upon us, for they were in a panic and crazy mad, galloping out of control. They came around us like a great brown flood, kicking up dirt so thick I could hardly see, and I knew then I had lost my horses. I held fast to Bob and hoped Kuller could keep the wagon upright.

He now pulled up to let the herd pass, as there was no point attempting to flee. I rode up directly behind him as my horses mixed with the cattle, every animal save Bob running away. Some of the cattle fell and were trampled by others, which created further chaos. Then came the men riding breakneck to get ahead of the stampede and turn the cattle while other cowboys attempted to contain the side branches.

It went on for what seemed forever, the ground shaking like it might collapse under the weight. Dirt and dust were thick. I had pulled my kerchief up over nose and mouth, but my eyes stung and watered, which made it worse as mud formed on the lids.

At last what was left of the main herd was turned and began to slow. Audley directed the cowboys with great skill, riding and cutting until the cattle stopped. The wagon and I were well back now and I rode up alongside. Kuller was covered in dirt, as was I. Only then did I think upon his anger at such circumstance.

Bishop rode up at this point and headed for Audley. Their exchange appeared most heated. The boss then rode from man to man shouting instructions, as cattle were now scattered far and wide while some lay dead. Once Bishop had spoken to the men, he rode over to me. "Round up your horses. Get them away from the cattle and keep them away."

"Yes, sir."

I rode off and set to work but looked back to see Bishop talking to Kuller. I doubted we'd move on to a noon stop.

Kuller drove his wagon some distance from the herd and set to work, dropping his worktable down. I continued regaining my remuda, which was mostly getting them unmingled from the cattle so I could from time to time glance over to Kuller. He had a fire going and coffee boiling. I then realized the chance of a noon meal was slim, as the men would work until the cattle were rounded up. When they brought in a bunch, they stopped to drink a quick cup of coffee before starting out again.

It was late afternoon when I finally had the horses gathered. Audley came by to tell me we were camping here for the night as we couldn't get to grass or water before nightfall, nor could the men get the scattered cattle rounded up. "Some are likely still running," he said before he rode off, and I did not know if he was joking.

I hobbled the horses, then went over to the chuck wagon where Kuller was brushing dirt from the chuck box. Didn't matter it had been closed. Trail dust gets into everything, and the quantity stirred had left a layer over all his pots, pans, spices, and such. He was wiping off the plates and implements when I rode up. "No water hole," he explained. "Water barrel is all we have, so you may eat some dust, as I can't waste it on washing dishes."

Most of the herd had been rounded up by supper, though, as Audley had said, some appeared to still be running. The men were dirty and beat and hungry. When they came to supper they found stew in Kuller's pot. An older fellow sniffed and said "Son-of-a-bitch stew" at which I had to ask what that might be. "Innards cut up and boiled with onions and chile powder."

"Innards?"

"Things usually left for the buzzards, only now you get to eat it because of the damned stampede. Brain, tongue, liver, heart, that kinda stuff. Cook's way of putting it to us."

"How is it?"

"Not bad if done right," the fellow said. "Took some getting used to, but I am hungry and will not quibble."

I spooned some of the stuff onto my plate, unable to tell one chunk from the other. A nudge from the next man in line got me moving and soon I was eating this remarkable dish that I found quite tasty. "Son of a bitch," I said, which got a laugh.

"That's how it got its name," someone remarked. "First fellow couldn't stomach the idea but found if he didn't think on it, it was right good." I too found it right good as I filled my gut. All the men were thankful for the meal and also to be returned to normal routine.

Horses and cattle could go without water two days if need be, but I had been told it made them cranky. To confirm this, Bishop announced over supper, "Double night hawks. No water or grass, so the stock will be restless."

"What caused the stampede?" someone asked.

"A new man fired his pistol at a rattler his horse stepped on."

Everyone looked at everyone else, me too, all except Drew Pulliam, who sat with head down.

"Hard lesson," Bishop added. "You don't fire a gun near the herd.

It is used only at a distance and even then with care. A pistol is to stop a stampede, not start one."

The men not guarding the cattle unrolled their beds and got into them as soon as they'd eaten. They were most contented after their son-of-a-bitch stew, having eaten the entire batch, but we were still a long way from peach cobbler.

Kuller and I slept double that night, but he came to bed late as he worked by lantern light still attempting to clean his kitchen. He refused my offer of help, thus I got into bed early like the rest. I did not know what to expect when he climbed in later on. I was half-asleep when he rolled me onto my stomach, got on top, and shoved in his cock. It was as angry a fuck as I'd ever had, a rough and quick go. He came in absolute silence, save for the slap of flesh. When he pulled out, he rolled onto his side away from me, acting like I'd caused the stampede. I had to allow he had been greatly inconvenienced by the day's events.

We could not lay over to rest or regain ourselves due to our inhospitable location, so we set out next morning as if nothing had happened. The cattle were now agreeable, as if they had never run crazy or at least had no recollection. The only thing Kuller said to me was, "Brazos River up ahead. Likely lay over once across, get a goddamned bath."

The noon meal this day was sparse as we were still low on water, the barrel attached to the chuck wagon but half-full. Salt pork, biscuits, and molasses was the fare and nobody complained. "We lost eighteen head," Bishop said as he walked among the men while we ate. "We'll reach the Brazos later today and will cross it, then lay over a couple days not because you earned it but because the herd is thirsty, as am I." He then stalked away and Audley followed.

"You are always going to lose a few," Kuller told me later when I was throwing cow chips into the possum. Wood was scarce on the plain, but cow shit was plentiful. "Eighteen ain't bad," Kuller went on, "but then we're not too far along. Best not have any more incidents."

The desire to offer condolence or apology or some such came over me, which made no sense beyond my feeling bad for the cook's wagon getting dirtied when he worked so hard at keeping it clean. "Rough day," was all I said, checking myself against offering more.

"I once saw a stampede run off a bluff," he replied. "Fifty, sixty steers went over and piled up below before we got the herd turned. Hell of a sight, some dead, some just broken to pieces and wailing."

I could not reply, as it was beyond imagination. Kuller looked up from washing his dishes with sand. "It is a hard life, Hoofin. Don't ever think it's not, I don't care you get peach cobbler."

When we reached the Brazos, the cattle were eager for water, as were my horses. The hard part was not getting them into the water but getting them out and onto the other side, as they wanted to stand around and drink and cool down. Finally Audley roped a calf and dragged it to the opposite shore, and the mother followed, which got the rest moving. At last they were across and turned out into good grass, as were the horses. The men who were free of night duty then set to bathing. I was grinding coffee when Kuller said, "Go on. Go have a wash. I am fine here."

I was filthy but wished him to join me. "Won't you come down?" I asked.

"Maybe after supper. You go on."

Drew Pulliam sat fully clothed beside the river. I don't think he'd spoken since the stampede. "C'mon, Drew," I called. "Have a swim."

He looked up, eyes red. "I ain't no cowboy," he said.

"Sure you are. If I kicked up a rattler, I'd probably shoot too."

"I feel like a marked man."

What else could I say? I stood and stripped. "Cool water don't care," I offered and I then waded into what felt like heaven, naked men all around. The water was a few feet deep and most welcome. I shed my dirt and kept on splashing, such was the joy of getting cool and clean. Looking up, I saw Drew idling and motioned to him. He finally got up, stripped, and came in. As he sank beside me, I patted his back. "Nobody holds a grudge here," I told him. "You have to move on."

The men, still recovering from the stampede and its attendant work, mostly lazed in the water. I saw only one stiff dick, and the fellow dropped to his knees to bring himself off. I was so relieved to be wet and clean that I was not inclined toward arousal. I enjoyed the sun on my body as I refreshed and cooled. I also thought on Kuller, hoping he'd bathe later on.

When he called us to supper, there was a scramble to dry and dress. Slumgullion stew was served, and I had come to like this mix of whatever the cook had left, bits of beef and pork, potatoes, tomatoes, and some stuff I could not identify. Kuller had once been accused of adding cactus to the stew and did not deny it. As always, his sourdough biscuits were served and they sopped the stew until they became heavy. I fairly stuffed myself.

As I sopped the last, Kuller called out "dessert" and heads snapped around. The men licked their plates clean, hopped up, and headed to his table where stood two pies, each with our L-bar-L brand cut into the top crust.

"What kind?" asked one man.

"Who cares," said another. "It is pie!"

"Apple," Kuller said. "Audley traded some farmer a calf for a bushel. You are going to get apples until you can't stand them."

"Never happen," someone replied.

The pies were sliced and carried back to the circle where the men sat. Quiet descended as the feast began. I glanced over at Kuller, who stood looking on, and though he did not smile, I knew he had forgiven these hardworking men. When he found me looking at him, he passed me a knowing look that I found most warming.

The moon was but a sliver late that night when he told me to get up. We were under the covers but had not gotten up to anything. I was content with my clean body and full stomach. "Why?" I asked.

"I want a bath and then I want a fuck," he said.

The camp was quiet, everyone snoring away, extra contented due to that pie. We crawled from our bed and crept down to the river. When I stumbled in the dark, Kuller took my hand and led me into the river. At best we had shadow. I could make out him lying in the shallow, splashing easy as I lazed nearby, savoring his company.

"Come here," he finally said. "Get onto me."

I found him mostly by touch and he guided me to straddle him. I felt the knob of his dick at my bottom and with some positioning, gave him entrance. As the cock went up me, I thought how I'd ridden so much on the drive, but this was to be the best. Then Kuller's hands were on me, raising me up and down until I got his motion. Soon I was bouncing on him, my own dick hard and flopping. "Ride me, cowboy," Kuller said. "Ride your man."

I set up a good canter and he slapped my leg to urge me on until he grew urgent and shoved up into me as he let go his load. His grunting was fierce and I took hold of my prick and pulled but a couple times before spurting onto the water. We thrashed until he'd emptied, then quieted and I slid off. He drew me to lie across him as his breathing settled. I could barely see him when he pulled my mouth to his. He had not done this before, not kissed me. No man had. His tongue sought mine and I responded, tasting him. He was most ardent and wrapped his arms around me as we remained upon one another in this most intimate manner. I decided then and there this was the life for me. I would do as Kuller had, stay with the drives year after year, as I knew myself now ruined for other work. And it was not a bad life. Hard work among men and beasts, but every now and then peach cobbler or apple pie. Or a good fuck.

THE KEY INGREDIENT
JEFFREY RICKER

Food was memory, which was why Jacob didn't want to go back to work. As soon as he started cooking, his thoughts were filled with Eric, and he didn't know how long he could stand that.

"But we need you," Carla said. "Luke called in sick and Rory hasn't shown up in two days, so I think she's gone and eloped. Ramon is about to have kittens, we've got two reservations for ten tonight, and I'm dying here. Please, honey."

Jacob was asleep on the couch when Carla called. He hadn't slept in the bedroom since the funeral. He stood in the doorway to the kitchen, a place that lately he went only to brew coffee and get another bottle of wine. He'd spent most of the past three months drunk or crying, or both.

"I don't know."

"Please," Carla said, then added, "We're all worried about you."

"I'm okay."

"Sometimes okay isn't good enough, you know?"

He pulled the bag of filters from the cabinet and filled one with coffee grounds. It was the last of the Sumatra roast, which Eric had loved. "The blacker the better" was his motto, which always made Jacob laugh, since Jacob himself was pale as a ghost. Even more so now.

"Jacob," Carla said when he let a long moment pass in silence, "I need you to come back, or I'm going to have to start thinking about hiring another dessert chef. A replacement, I mean."

"Oh."

"Damn it, you need to get out of that apartment," she said, then muttered under her breath, "God this makes me sound like such a bitch."

"Nonsense, that's part of your charm," he said, and she laughed louder than the joke warranted.

"Once the dinner shift's over," she said, "let's you and me sit at the bar. We'll split a bottle and talk about it, okay?"

He hesitated, empty coffee cup in hand, knowing she was right and that she could also never possibly understand.

"Okay."

After he hung up, Jacob poured himself a cup. Eric's mug was still in the cupboard, next to his. It was red with a white crown and the words "Keep Calm and Carry On." Whenever he opened the cupboard and the words were visible, Jacob turned it so he couldn't read it. Eric had a habit of reaching around Jacob as he stood at the counter to get to his mug, then wrapping his arms around Jacob's waist.

"Hey, sleepyhead," he'd whisper in Jacob's ear, his lips sometimes close enough to tickle. On more than one occasion they ended up naked on the kitchen floor. Eric liked to time it so they came right when the last burst of steam gurgled through the coffeemaker.

"Now *that's* the best part of waking up," Eric would say.

Jacob learned his way around the kitchen from his mother. She was a solid cook and could do the basics serviceably well. When she made dessert, though, the results were nothing less than magical. She showed Jacob how to bake a cake, but first she had him blow the eggs a kiss before she cracked them in a bowl. She taught him a song that he had to hum while he beat the sugar into the batter. And when he slid the pans into the oven, she had him make a wish. She taught him how to make cheesecake that didn't crack, soufflé that didn't sink, and cookies that were the right balance between chewy and crunchy.

She also taught him how to make bread pudding.

"I want you to make the bread pudding tonight," Ramon said.

"The bread pudding?" Jacob felt as if every pair of eyes in the kitchen were turned toward him.

"You can make it with your eyes closed, and you know what it does. The last time you made it, one of the customers said it was better than sex. I also have a shitload of day-old brioche. Make the pudding."

Jacob felt a little sorry for whoever that customer was. *Yes*, the bread pudding was good, but better than sex? That customer must not have been getting it on a regular basis.

The dessert had been Eric's favorite dish. It was the birthday request, the dish brought to parties, the pièce de résistance trotted out when they had company over. Sometimes, it was the thing he made when he just wanted to cheer himself or Eric. It could mean I love you, I'm sorry, or I want you to fuck me *right now*—sometimes all at once.

Mostly, at the moment, it meant remembering. He nodded at Ramon and felt like a condemned man as he went to the dessert station.

❖

Eric wasn't the first man Jacob had cooked for. There was a long history of impress-the-potential-boyfriend dinners, when he lit candles and pulled out the good plates his mother had passed on to him. There were soles and filets and roasts, chickens that nearly regained the power of flight as they sailed off the table. And there were desserts either rich and decadent or delicate and airy, depending on what Jacob guessed the man might want—or depending on what Jacob might have wanted from the man.

And then there was the bread pudding.

At the time, Jacob never realized his mother was teaching him about love when she showed him how to make bread pudding.

"The bread needs to have some life experience under its belt," his mother told him. He wasn't sure what she meant, so she explained. "Always make sure the bread is a little stale. Fresh bread turns to mush, and if it's too stale it just falls apart." She smiled and added, "Hearts are the same, really." He wouldn't understand that for a few more years, though.

She didn't like to use plain bread. Brioche had layers that made the texture complex (again, she said, like hearts). She used a few secret ingredients, as well. The first was Rainier cherries instead of currants.

They gave the pudding an edge that, she said, kept you from taking the sweetness for granted.

The other secret ingredient was bourbon in the caramel sauce. That just made everything easier, she said.

"Trust me, honey," she said. "You'll understand when you're older."

❖

The first time he made the recipe on his own was also the first time he had Eric over for dinner. They'd been dating for a couple weeks and things were going well, but they were taking it slowly: some movies, a couple dinners out, and a few tentative, searching good-night kisses. Eric was an accountant, and Jacob was starting to wonder if he wasn't a little bit of a prude.

It was Eric's first time over at Jacob's apartment, and he made the bread pudding because he had a bag of cherries that were about to go off, and at the bakery the sight of day-old brioche made him remember the recipe.

"This looks interesting," Eric said when Jacob brought out the pudding in sundae dishes. He picked up his fork, then set it down and picked up his spoon instead.

"My mom taught me to make it," Jacob said. "It's my favorite dessert."

"Pudding?" Eric lifted a spoonful and inspected it curiously. "I thought pudding was like that stuff that comes in the plastic cups in the grocery store."

Jacob laughed. "I don't know what that stuff is, but this is the real thing."

Jacob left his own spoon untouched and instead watched Eric's face as he took his first bite. It was something of a habit he'd developed over the years: watching the sometimes subtle, occasionally surprising ways people's faces changed as the food he'd prepared became a part of them. Eric chewed slowly at first, then stopped and closed his eyes. Did that mean he liked it? Jacob would have thought so, but then Eric made this noise—not one of disgust, or of pleasure, those little hums and moans Jacob had often heard when his dessert was a success. This was…like someone pushing a heavy weight.

And then Eric lifted his spoon again and took another bite. And another. He lifted the dish closer to his chin as he ate—no, as he *devoured* the rest of the pudding. When it was all gone, he stared at the dish for a moment; Jacob half expected him to lick what little caramel sauce remained.

"I don't suppose I could have some more?" Eric asked, almost timidly. Jacob smiled and took his empty dish into the kitchen. Asking for seconds was the best compliment he ever hoped for from his cooking.

There was a higher compliment, though, which he learned as he began to clear the table and asked if Eric wouldn't mind giving him a hand. Eric pushed his chair back and started to get up. He paused, a startled look on his face, and sat back down.

"I don't think I can."

Jacob set down the stack of dirty plates he'd gathered. "Are you okay?"

"I'm fine, but—"

"Did you eat too much?" Jacob started to walk around the table to where Eric sat. A sheen of sweat was forming on his forehead.

"This is kind of embarrassing," Eric began. "I'm—oh fuck it."

With that, he shoved his chair back and stood; for an instant Jacob glimpsed what Eric was so embarrassed about—a raging hard-on tenting his trousers—before Eric grabbed him and pulled him into a kiss more forceful than anything Jacob would have expected up to that point from the accountant.

Not that Jacob was complaining.

"So, you liked dessert?" Jacob asked, breathless, when Eric finally released him.

"It was great," Eric said. He pulled Jacob's shirt out of the waist of his jeans. "Really great." He fumbled with Jacob's belt and managed to pull it off. "Are there leftovers?"

"Lots."

Eric kissed him at the same time his hands went down Jacob's jeans and slid inside his underwear. Jacob gasped in surprise, the good kind.

"Think I can take some of it home with me?"

Jacob grinned. He was pretty sure Eric wouldn't be going home for at least another couple hours. "Sure."

"I wonder how it tastes for breakfast," he said, and drew Jacob's jeans and shorts downward as he knelt in front of him.

They left the dirty dishes until the morning.

❖

In spite of himself, Jacob felt his heart beat a little faster as the dinner rush began: the sear of heat from a burner firing up, the clank and rattle of pots and skillets and baking dishes. The caller shouted out orders—"Fire one salmon"; "Fire two specials"—it made him feel, sometimes, like food was combat.

"Sometimes you make things because you have to, not because you want to," Jacob's mother told him once. If there was one thing she hated making, it was angel food cake: sugary, spongy, virtually tasteless—what was the point? Nonetheless, she made the best angel food cake in the county, and it was always requested for the women's auxiliary bake sale.

"One of these days," his mother grumbled to him as she shoved a cake pan in the oven, "those women are getting a red velvet cake and they're going to like it."

Jacob knew she never would, so he figured there was no harm in egging her on. "How about you just give them devil's food instead?"

"Your mother has to draw the line somewhere," she said, but her smile told him she liked the idea.

Jacob made the bread pudding because he had to, and he took a little pleasure in the asterisk next to that item on the menu: *Please allow extra time when ordering the bread pudding.* Jacob made each serving individually, the caramel sauce in small batches, and he insisted on using Knob Creek, not the crappy well bourbon.

"How's it going?" Carla asked early on in the dinner rush. Jacob jumped, startled when she whispered near his ear.

"Be glad I didn't have anything hot in my hands," he said, "otherwise you'd be on your way to the burn unit."

"I'm more afraid of the big knife," she said. Jacob was cubing the brioche when she came up to him.

"Are things pretty slow up front?" he asked.

Carla shrugged. "Not too bad yet. I'm letting Sarah get some time in." Sarah was Carla and Ramon's sixteen-year-old daughter, but she looked old enough to be the cause of Ramon's ulcer. "So," she asked again, "how's it going?"

"Did you know your husband was going to have me making this?" He waved his knife at the cutting board.

"He had to go and buy all that goddamn brioche because he got a 'great deal'"—she made air quotes with her fingers—"and then I had to go and buy those fucking cherries out of season."

"You know it'll be worth it."

"I sure as hell hope so." She patted his shoulder. "Actually, it's worth it just to have you back."

Jacob purposely did not smile. "What are we drinking once the rush is over?"

"Something expensive," she said. "You'll love it."

"As long as it tastes free, what's not to love?" Jacob said, and went back to cutting up brioche.

❖

Jacob and Eric had, to the day, almost three years together. The December evening Eric stepped into an intersection at the wrong moment and met the cabbie who hit a patch of black ice, Jacob forgot his cell phone at home. He didn't find out about the accident until three hours after Eric had been declared dead.

"What do you mean 'gone'?" Jacob asked. Carla had come into the kitchen in the middle of his shift to break the news. When he finally looked up from his pan of gently bubbling caramel sauce, he noticed how white Carla's face was, a border of tears threatening to spill from her eyes.

"There was an accident," she said, her voice barely audible above the kitchen's relentless percussion. "A cab—"

The reality of her words gradually sank in. Jacob looked back down at the pan, turned off the burner, and watched the bubbles die away. He dragged his cap from his head.

"Next week's our anniversary," he said. "I was going to make the bread pudding."

"Oh, honey…" She sounded like she was already crying.

"What do I do now?"

The answer to that question, apparently, was drop out of sight. Carla and Ramon kept his job open and waiting for him longer than he could have expected—longer than he deserved, really—and now that he was back, standing in front of the same burner, making the dish he'd never gotten around to making one last time for Eric, the last three months dropped away and he felt like any moment Carla would walk through the door and tell him what he already knew.

It wasn't until the first tear hit the pan of custard that Jacob realized he was crying. Shaking his head, he watched as a few more drops fell, then gathered himself and wiped the back of his hand across his eyes. He took a quick glance around. No one had noticed, and the beat of the kitchen went on.

"People need to eat," his mother told him during his father's wake, when she kept her place in front of the stove, though her sister said she shouldn't be working at a time like that. "People need to eat, and I need to work. Besides," she added, looking down her nose at Aunt Joyce, "I'm not about to inflict your cooking on a house full of grieving people. I think they've suffered enough."

Jacob, who'd been eighteen at the time, had come home early from college for the funeral. Still, he remembered his aunt's fly-catching jaw drop, which vanished almost as soon as his mother started laughing and her sister joined in. At a time like that, everyone needed to remember to laugh as much as they needed to eat. Like always, his mother provided.

He would provide too.

As usual, the bread pudding flew out of the kitchen. More than one reviewer had called it out for extra attention when it appeared on the list of specials, and Carla had talked about making it a regular menu item.

About an hour into the dinner rush, Carla came back into the kitchen, her face darkened by a frown.

"Jacob," she said, "did you change the bread pudding recipe?"

"Change it?" He turned away briefly to check of pan of ramekins in the oven. "It's the same recipe my mother taught me."

"You're sure nothing's different?"

He matched her frown. "Why? Are people complaining?"

She shook her head. "No, but they're acting…weird."

At first, Jacob couldn't see what she was talking about. The two groups who'd made reservations for ten wound up being a party of six and a no-show. The dining room was reasonably full for a Wednesday night—mostly couples, a few groups of three or four. Everything looked normal.

After a moment, though, he noticed one of two things that were a little unusual. At one of the two-tops, a man and a woman shared a kiss that seemed like it would never end. Over in one of the circular booths against the wall, a woman was, literally, in the man's lap.

Until she slid beneath the table.

And over by the entrance were the Bugatchis, an elderly couple who came in for dinner at least once a week. When a Vikki Carr song came on over the piped-in music, Leo Bugatchi eased back his chair, took Loretta's hand, and they began to dance.

"What the hell?" Jacob whispered.

"Oh, it gets better. Carmine had to ask two guys to leave when he found one of them going down on the other in the men's room."

"Seriously?"

Carla nodded. "And then they asked him if he wanted to join them! The only thing all these people have in common is they ordered the bread pudding. I was going to ask if you slipped some Spanish fly into it or something."

Jacob shook his head. "There is nothing in that dish except what's in my mother's recipe."

Carla stared at the Bugatchis dancing a lazy circle near the foyer and shook her head. "This is completely wacko."

"Do you want me to stop making the pudding?"

"God, no." Carla lifted her glasses and massaged the bridge of her nose. "People have been asking when we'd have it back. They'll be so pissed off if I yank it. We'll just have to manage."

Jacob turned to go back to his station, but Carla put a hand on his forearm.

"Whatever you do, don't let any of the staff have it. Horny customers I can sort of deal with. Horny staff…"

"I don't know how to break this to you, but Ramon's had some."

"Great, just what I need: a horny head chef. Guess I'm not getting any sleep tonight."

Jacob managed a smile. "You say that like it's a bad thing."

"I'm glad one of us finds it amusing." She poked him in the ribs. "Keep that up and I'll send him home with you. See how you like it."

Jacob warmed to the banter, realizing how much he'd missed it. "A night riding your Italian stallion? Sign me up. Still want to have that bottle of wine after closing?"

"More than ever."

Somehow, they managed, though they did have to keep a closer eye on the bathrooms and make sure no one decided to sneak under the table and give their dining partners a happy ending. Ramon, contrary to the pattern, became laser-focused on his work, turning out entrées that were nothing short of outstanding.

Jacob wondered what he'd created. Though he'd told Carla the recipe was unadulterated, he knew that was a lie. He remembered the tears distinctly. But they were only a few drops. How could a little salt cause such a dramatic change?

Removing a pan of desserts from the oven, he drizzled bourbon sauce over one and took it back toward the walk-in, out of sight. When he tried it, he couldn't discern any difference, but would he have been able to detect the taste of his own longing, his own grief, after living with the flavor on his tongue for months already? He was so deep into it, not only did he fail to see its contours himself, but he couldn't see a way out of it either.

When Jacob walked back to the dessert station, Carmine was standing nearby, staring at the dishes of bread pudding. He looked as if he'd been caught doing something illicit, his almond eyes widening briefly when Jacob cleared his throat. Jacob started silently counting the dishes until Carmine spoke.

"Crazy night, huh? I'd swear there must be a full moon or something."

"No kidding. Things slowed down for the moment?"

"Sort of. I don't think most of them would notice if I never came back to their table, under the circumstances." Idly, he turned a pudding dish on the tray, and the clank and rattle of the kitchen seemed to subside as Jacob watched Carmine's hands, his olive skin dark against the white of the ceramic.

"So," Carmine asked, "how are you holding up?"

"Me?" Jacob picked up the pan of caramel sauce; he had two more orders up. "It's not been a bad pace tonight. I've been able to handle it."

"No, I meant how are you holding up being back here after, you know, Eric? It seems like no one wants to say his name, you know?"

Jacob set down the saucepan and looked at the tray of puddings, twelve little reminders of the man no one wanted to mention by name. "Yeah, it's tough," he said, and promptly burst into tears.

"Aw, hey," Carmine said. Jacob turned away. He could not bear to look at those sad little mounds of dessert anymore. He covered his face with his hands. He felt Carmine's hands at his shoulders, then they wrapped around him. All the while Carmine said, "Hey, buddy," and "Come on, buddy," and "It's gonna be okay, buddy," though Jacob wasn't convinced of that in the least.

Carmine turned him around and guided Jacob's head to his shoulder. Gently, he curled his fingers around Jacob's and made him uncover his face.

"Stop eating yourself alive from the inside out, buddy," Carmine said.

And then he kissed Jacob.

At first, Jacob was too stunned to do anything. He didn't even close his eyes, just looked down his nose at the soft blur of Carmine's face, whose eyes *were* closed. The faint scent of soap and olive oil clung to him. Carmine untangled his fingers from Jacob's and put his hands on either side of Jacob's face. He sighed contentedly, his mouth still locked on Jacob's, and that's when Jacob came to his senses. Instead of leaving his arms hanging uselessly at his sides, he put them around Carmine and pulled him close. With their bodies pressed together, it was easy to feel how much Carmine liked that. One hand slid up toward Carmine's hair—Jacob expected the tight, dark curls would be bristly, but they were soft, spring-like. His other hand drifted down Carmine's back and cupped the hard curve of his ass.

Which was when they both heard Carla clear her throat.

"Table six has come up for breath," she said to Carmine, "so you might want to get them their check while you have the chance." She glanced up and down at the waiter. "Though you might want to wait a couple minutes for things to die down."

Carmine followed her glance and immediately blushed. "Yeah, boss. Good idea."

As Carmine walked toward the doors to the dining room, Carla called after him, "So how'd you like the bread pudding?"

"I wouldn't know," he said, pausing just outside the door's swinging radius. Though he spoke to Carla, he looked at Jacob. "I haven't had dessert yet. Maybe later, though."

Carla turned back to Jacob, her expression somewhere between a smirk and a frown. Jacob wiped his eyes.

"Sorry about that," he said.

She shrugged. "Did he really not have any of the pudding?"

"So he says." Jacob took the two prepared servings and placed them on a tray, which one of the runners spirited away.

"Guess that means he must like you," Carla said.

"I don't know…"

"Hey." She put her hand on his arm. "I know it's only been three months, but the last thing Eric would have wanted is for you to spend the rest of your life alone."

Jacob smiled and covered her hand with his own. "Well, I meant more that I don't know if I want to get involved with someone at work."

"Please, I wasn't thinking relationship so much as a good lay. I mean, did you see what he's packing down there?"

"Carla!"

She waved away his modesty like it was a gnat. "Besides, he's a waiter. How long do any of them stay around? To be honest, I'm surprised you're still here sometimes. Happy about that, don't get me wrong, but surprised."

"I'm not planning on going anywhere any time soon, and I do not want to discuss the head waiter below the waist."

She pouted. "Killjoy."

"Well then, how's Ramon holding up?"

Carla rolled her eyes. "His hands are wandering. Normally, I wouldn't mind, but…"

"Still want that drink after we close?"

"Oh, hell yes."

❖

As it turned out, closing time came an hour earlier than usual. Ramon's hands wandered further, Carla had to slap him for doing it to her in a public area, and she sent him home and had Carmine flip the sign from "open" to "closed." Some of the waitstaff helped themselves to leftover bread pudding, and Carla worried there would end up being an orgy in the kitchen. She sent half of them home.

The restaurant bar was a small alcove off the main dining room. An oak counter and four bar stools divided the space, and Carla sat on one of the stools waiting for Jacob. When he walked in, she had two glasses of red wine waiting and an open bottle on the counter. He read the label; she wasn't lying about bringing out the good stuff.

He sat down and they clinked glasses. After they both took a long drink, Carla said, "So, after tonight, I'm thinking of retiring the bread pudding from the menu. You don't mind, do you?"

"I can't say I blame you, but even so, I think that's a fantastic idea." Jacob couldn't keep making dessert for the love of a dead man, no matter how much he was alive in Jacob's thoughts. And clearly, there were hazards beyond what it did to his heart. "How do you feel about crème brulée?"

"A little tingly," she admitted and took another sip. "Maybe you could change up the flavor each week."

"That would keep it interesting."

Carla set down her glass and nodded toward the entryway. "Speaking of interesting…"

Jacob turned. Carmine stood in the threshold between the bar and the dining room. He'd already put on his jacket and looped a fuzzy orange scarf around his neck. A plastic bag dangled from one finger.

"Are you heading home after this," he asked Jacob, "or would you like to get a drink or something?"

Jacob looked at his watch. It was already almost one o'clock. "Think there's any place still open at this time of night?"

He regretted saying it when he saw the hope dim a little in Carmine's expression. And the prospect of spending some time with him, Jacob had to admit, was not unappealing.

"Here." Carla wedged the cork back in the bottle and slid it across the bar toward Jacob. "It'd be a shame if it went to waste."

"You sure about that?" Carmine leaned forward to get a good look at the label, which brought him close enough for Jacob to smell him again. "This is in the top five most expensive on the wine list."

Carla patted Carmine's cheek. "Consider it a thank-you gift for being among the few people in the restaurant who managed to keep it in their pants until closing time. Now go someplace where that's not an issue. I've got to get home to Ramon."

Jacob threw on his coat. Carla locked the door behind them as they stepped into the chilly March morning. Carmine reached for Jacob's free hand and drew him into another kiss, a little more tentative than the one they'd shared in the kitchen.

When they parted again, Jacob held up the bottle. "Your place?" He wasn't ready yet to bring someone back to the home he'd shared with Eric, but at least he could imagine someone else drinking coffee from the "Keep Calm and Carry On" mug.

Carmine held up the bag. "My place. I live just across the square."

Still holding hands, they headed for the crosswalk.

"So what's in the bag?" Jacob asked.

Carmine managed to look innocent and wicked at the same time. "Bread pudding. I want to see how well you can cook."

His innocent façade lasted all of another second, and he grinned wickedly at Jacob, who threw the same grin right back at him.

"Um, you *are* talking about my kitchen skills, right?"

They waited for a car to pass, then Carmine said, "I guess we'll have to find out, won't we?"

BOTTOM OF THE MENU
STEVE BERMAN

Standing outside the restaurant, a young man leans against a parking meter and smokes a cigarette. I pause to watch him for a minute or so. His most prominent feature is a carefully maintained mane of loose brown curls. His face is turned away, toward the sun, but I see he has a mesomorphic build that complements the long-sleeved T-shirt and worn denim jeans he wears. He isn't texting or talking on a cell phone, which seems an anomaly. When was the last time you ever saw someone under the age of thirty, by himself, idle, without the ubiquitous handhelds clutched with devotion? No one daydreams any more. Perhaps the young man's battery died and now he finds himself suddenly so alone in the world.

Yes, I am a sarcastic bitch. But on my forty-fourth birthday, I have license.

As I walk by the front glass windows of Stylus and peer inside at the many small tables, nearly all filled at that hour, a puff of bitter smoke reaches me along with the words, "You must be Mr. Berman."

I turn to find the young man facing me. He has a natural tan, clean face with a small nose almost lost above his wide mouth, which grins at the moment. Nicotine has tinted his teeth a bit, but whenever an aging queen looks at any boy, he's forgiving of minor imperfections.

"I might be."

He transfers the lit cigarette to his left hand before holding out the right. "I'm Baker. The menu."

"The baker?"

He chuckles. "No, no. Baker's my name. But I am the menu."

I assume he's flirting. Could he be a hustler? An unprecedented hustler on this street that doesn't have much gay traffic, unlike Twelfth or Thirteenth. Or a foolish one. I thank him for whatever overture and step to the brass and wood door of Stylus. He moves faster and holds it open for me, then follows me inside.

Air-conditioning too meager to dispel the summer heat greets us. Old-fashioned ceiling fans, belt-driven, spin above. A cheerful hostess bounces our way. "Welcome to Stylus, Mr. Berman."

Now a bit of dread stirs in my empty stomach. Has my nephew orchestrated more than a free dinner—some sort of celebration? The last thing I want is the attention of strangers, an entire restaurant full of curious faces, all cruelly aware of the fact I am dining *alone* on my *birthday* due to friends who are out of town on summer vacations and my cherished nephew regretfully starting a new evening job.

"I see you have met your menu." She motions like a beauty queen toward the youth beside me, who must have abandoned his cigarette outside.

"He's never had the special before," Baker says and then leans in to kiss the hostess on the cheek.

She copies Baker's grin. "You *are* in for a treat then, Mr. Berman."

"My table?"

She leads us—Baker has seen fit to place a hand lightly on my back—to a table toward the rear of Stylus. Thankfully not too close to the kitchen. Baker pulls out my seat for me. Hustlers must go to school for etiquette now. I shall have to revise my view of the twenty-first century.

The hostess does not offer menus to either of us, though. She rushes to greet another patron before I can mention this oversight. I glance around, and other expectant diners are ordering off folded paper menus.

"I know what you are thinking," Baker says.

I raise an eyebrow and lean forward. The round table is a mite small, swallowed up by glasses, bread plates, cutlery and napkins, let alone my elbows. "All of what I am thinking? You're a magician, then."

"Of sorts." He rolls up the sleeve of his left arm. "What would you like to drink?" His entire forearm is covered in black ink. Tattooed script, fine calligraphy. I peer closer and read *Vieux Carré = Rye whiskey*

& *Cognac & Sweet Vermouth & Benedictine w/dashes of Angostura*
& *Peychaud's/Broken Halo = Plymouth Gin & Dry Sack & Williams*
& *Humbert & Oloroso w/Maraschino liqueur/Witch Doctor = Malibu*
coconut rum & Reposado tequila w/pineapple juice & orange juice &
Meyer's lemon juice.

"I…I'm at a loss for words." Unlike the menu. I dare to reach out to touch his inked forearm. The young skin is smooth and warm, like the burn of good Cognac. So I choose the Vieux Carré.

"Deux Vieux Carré," Baker calls out to a waitress passing by.

I cannot begrudge him a drink, but I doubt the gift certificate my nephew had sent me will cover the cost of feeding two. Actually, the certificate, which arrived in the old-fashioned mail, lacked an amount. The sliver of parchment featured only a massive $ beneath Stylus's information and a reservation for my birthday.

"Now your appetizer." He exposes his right forearm. "I recommend the green mussels gratiné." His fingertip underlines the rest of the dish: *Dijon butter, sweet sausage crumbs.*

"How often do you do this?"

He opens his mouth to speak, but the waitress interrupts him as she set down our drinks.

I raise my glass of liquid French Quarter. My alma mater, Tulane, would be so proud of me. "Don't tell me. If you answered 'All the time,' I'd be more perplexed than disappointed—how come I had never heard of walking, handsome menus."

"And if I said 'never'?" He sips.

"Then I would feel awkward that anyone would tattoo their body on my account. I'm not that special."

"But today makes you special—"

I clink my glass against his. "As well as the other umpteen number of men and women born today. Shania Twain. A Japanese composer. Jack Vance—he's a writer. Oh, and Jason Priestley. There once was a time when a guy might get inked to impress Jason Priestley. But the only thing you'd have on your skin in the nineties was baby powder, right?"

Baker laughs. "You're not a fossil. I think, if I told you I had 'dry-aged beef' tattooed across my chest, you would make some remark about—"

"About myself." I shrug. "I can't say what I want on my birthday, such a special day." I realize I have steadily sipped my drink down to the bottom and can feel the early euphoria of alcohol loosening my thoughts.

"You can say whatever you want. Until the entrée. After tasting that, you're allowed no questions."

The waitress returns. Or the hostess. Or maybe the hostess's twin. I order the mussels and two more drinks.

"So, the entrées..." Baker begins removing his T-shirt. I feel flushed, from the alcohol, from the sight of someone attractive committing a cardinal sin: No Shoes, No Shirts, No Service! I lean back in my chair, as if to distance myself from him, and nearly topple.

But no one in Stylus stops to stare. They continue with their forks and knives and spoons, their chatting and gossiping and flirtations or admissions of guilt. I wonder if Baker (now shirtless—and how his illuminated chest glistens with a bit of August sweat) and I have been seated in a section of the restaurant belonging to some pocket dimension. So I drop my knife. It clatters against the wood floor. A woman seated nearby glares. She could be the hostess's sister, they look so much alike, down to the same highlights in her hair.

"Steve, do you like chicken?"

I search his face for guile. But his fingers caressing the damp skin of his chest draws the eye, the black lettering askew as it flows over a pec, down the vale, then rises again. The black lettering hypnotizing me like the swirl of a cartoonish disk spun at a carnival.

"Here you can indulge..." He takes my hand and guides it to the ink, as if it were Braille.

Pygostyle in spicy ginger sauce w/sautéed kale & carrots
Green pasillas stuffed with criadillas w/black beans & rice
Welsh faggot & marrowfat peas

I want to lick from my fingers the drop of sweat caught underneath the word *marrowfat*. Would it taste salty? Sour? Have I drunk too much Cognac and rye to even discern a new taste?

"Your mussels," says the waitress and sets a plate between us.

"The portions here," Baker says (do his eyes drift to the plate or down to his crotch?), "are generous. So we'll share."

I bite a mussel—delicious—but not the muscle I want. Oh, I am tipsy. I may have even said this aloud because Baker is chuckling as if I said something whimsical but suggestive. My appetite extends beyond the seafood. I want to nibble on his unkempt hair, test the thickness of the cords at his neck, lick and see if the ink is nothing more than food coloring artfully applied.

Oh, what a generous nephew I have!

And that makes me suddenly worry. My twenty-two-year-old nephew's generosity extends to raiding Dumpsters outside of restaurants and grocery stores to bring freegan harvest back to feed his neighbors in the inner-city building where he squats with three other roommates. "You're not a friend of Zach's, are you?" If so, Baker would be one of the Untouchable caste.

"No. We've never met."

Would Zach find Baker attractive? He prefers his men dark, maybe with tiny dreadlocks, white tank tops, and sagging shorts, but still likely to Occupy Christopher Street.

When the pygostyle arrives, Baker cuts the meat and offers me the first bite, the fork held to my lips. It's the gesture of young love, of hearts worn on sleeves, a gesture that repulses cynics like a crucifix brandished before a vampire. He notes my hesitation. He cocks his head. "Relax, no one is watching."

"I find that hard to believe."

"Honest. Watch." He sets the fork down, balancing it at the edge of the hot dish. He pushes his chair back and stands up. "No menu is complete without listing desserts and digestifs." He unbuttons the top of his jeans and pushes his palms past the waistband, revealing a trail of unruly hair.

Why is no one staring? I am staring. Why no one else?

"It's your birthday. Don't question, don't worry. Have a good meal," he says, sitting back down.

"Asking if you are a daydream would be questioning."

"Yep." He holds up the fork.

I want the chicken to be like pomegranate seeds in Hades, keeping me with Baker for months out of every year. But the potent, savory taste does not linger past another sip of Cognac that I don't remember ordering anew.

"I'm drunk."

"Good," he says. "You'll be less skeptical."

"I want to know what happens when I get to the end of the meal."

"You do?" He offers me another forkful. I am so eager to take a bite that my teeth hit metal.

"So," Baker asks, "have you ever gotten laid on your birthday?"

The bold question chokes me. "N-No. Not my birthday." Why is there nothing but alcohol to clear my throat? "Halloween, many, many years ago, I blew a boy in my car. In a graveyard. Full moon, too. And one New Year's Eve in New Orleans I went down on a guy on a crowded dance floor." The memories rush back, filling spaces in my head like the vapors rising from the glass at my lips.

"You like to spend your holidays with your mouth full."

I chuckle. Because I am drunk and I have to think carefully what to say next, for it not to be a question, for it not to be something so raunchy that I fear it would clatter like the dropped knife.

He takes a finger and dips it into the sauce. Slow. Even slower, he lifts it to his lips and sucks the tip clean. I have begun to salivate anew.

"The cook here told me that melting a piece of chocolate in your mouth affects your brain." He fluffs his curls. "Lights up the gray matter like you were kissing someone."

"Then I better hope chocolate is on the dessert menu."

"Eager for dessert?"

I nod. Not that the food at Stylus isn't delicious…

He leans back in his chair and gestures for me to stand and come close. "You have to open it."

I stumble a bit rising. A passing waitress—always the same one, the same face, as if Stylus employs no other—winks at me. My napkin lands on the floor. I must not step on it. I must not trip as I walk around the table and kneel in front of Baker.

I take my time unbuttoning his jeans. I have to. I think my hands are trembling. I see the coarse hair of his slightly rounded stomach reach the band of a bleached white jock strap. He lifts his ass to let me slide the denim down to pool at his feet, I can see running up his left thigh the desserts:

Red banana confit w/Moscata d'Asti

"In Central America they think the sap of the red banana tree is an aphrodisiac." Baker adjusts the swollen front of his jock strap.

Fresh pound cake w/ confiture de lait

My mouth has grown dry as my mother's pound cake. And how much the faygele am I to be thinking about my mother while on my knees before a crotch?

Chocolate Scoville, assorted cacao squares dusted w/variety of dried pepper flakes

"A bite of that chocolate would be a very torrid kiss," I say.

"Singe your lips. Blister your tongue."

On his right thigh are the digestifs, which I just glance at. I don't need any more alcohol. But I do run a hand over that leg. I squeeze the flesh, the bony cap of knee. He smells a bit sweaty.

"I can't decide. Order for me."

He reaches down and strokes my hair. "That would be against the rules."

I almost ask, "There are rules? Still? To all this wonder?" but he prevents me by moving his fingers down my face to press shut my lips.

"There are always rules. And a price. Your nephew paid that so you could play with me here. Those are the rules."

Zach. Worry sobers me a bit. I cannot ask about him, though. Not directly. "I once wrote a story about an oven that came to life and ate German children. Never finished one about a were-oven. I don't know why I am obsessed with ovens. I don't even cook at home…maybe I've used the oven three times in all the years I've lived there. But I am afraid of being burned."

"The management is fair here."

"They say presentation matters." I sigh and rub again his legs. "I'll have the confit. Too much pepper and I'll worry about burning my throat."

I return to my seat. I do not step on my napkin.

"The confit is still very tasty," Baker says. He reaches out but I busy my hands in my pants pockets—no, not to adjust myself but to get my wallet. I pull out the gift certificate. Maybe the waitress heard my choice because a moment later she is there with the plate. It looks tempting. She plucks the certificate from my hand.

I could laugh at all this. Baker, though incredibly attractive, a feast for the eyes, does look a bit ridiculous with his pants down. I've drunk enough to laugh. I wonder if there is still one last bit of the menu that hasn't been revealed, inked and hidden underneath a layer of taut cotton.

He nods at me. "Finish the meal."

I scoop up a bit of the confit, which is blood-red and drips off the spoon to splatter my slacks. Baker watches me. His stare thickens the air so it seems forever before I taste the dessert. Its sweetness is cloying and warm.

"There," I say.

Baker smirks, stands and pulls up his jeans. "There's a spot, just behind the kitchen. The ovens, actually. The brick walls hold the heat well, much like a sauna, so you have to strip bare before going inside." He throws his T-shirt on the floor, where it lands next to my napkin. "A tour comes with the meal." He holds out a hand to me.

As I follow his lead, I glance once more around me. Out the window, another young man stands in the exact spot I met Baker. His head is turned away from the restaurant but I know who it is and the ink drawn on his skin paying for an infamous dinner.

SWEETBREAD HILL
J.D. BARTON

The four of them sat on the pier, their various ages and states of undress apparent only to them since no one else lived nearby. Chris gazed at the boys lying next to him, took in a large amount of sweet air, and smiled. There was a sun up there somewhere, he told himself, but it had bled across the sky and turned the whole world white. So he luxuriated in its warmth as it beat down on his skin and dried his underwear in its own time.

Someone took a swig of beer, then handed it to him, but he closed his eyes and passed it on to the boy next to him. The tangy aroma of the brew was enough for him and he didn't want to sour his stomach, since he knew that suppertime was nearing.

"Look," someone else said, and Chris opened his eyes just in time to see a large blue-green fish jump out of the water, then dive right back in. He was amazed that the flat, gray lake could be broken, then return to its pristine state. He examined it as if it existed only to reflect the diamonds of light that spangled it, as well as to provide refreshment for the four boys when their thermostats rose precipitously high. He was happy he'd stopped to swim with them.

The day was his and he knew it. Chris had nowhere to go and no one to report to, and the thought didn't make him happy or sad. It was his usual status and one he had long gotten used to before this beautiful day. The bicycle he'd propped against the ancient water oak gleamed in the daylight, and he squinted as he checked it out one more time to make sure it was safe. Yet, he knew it was.

He had ridden by the house he knew as Sweetbread Hill many times on his way to school or his part-time job but he'd never given it much mind. As stately and grand as it was, it had an air of genteel years on it, like an old man in aging suit. He'd found it benign yet interesting, and like most things in his life, Chris only noticed it when something enticed him. Today, it was the three boys who hollered at him from the pier behind the house. They had asked him to join them for a swim and the rising heat of the street and his own curiosity made him decide to stop. It was a decision he came to appreciate.

Their names were Sebastian, Luka, and Cam, and Chris noticed their manner was as languid as the humidity they all inhaled. He came to like them immediately and admired their various shades of light and dark and white as they dipped into the water, then climbed back onto the pier to sun themselves. Their obvious beauty was not lost on him.

He watched as they kissed each other deeply and then groped each other through their underwear. And before he could feel left out, one of them, Cam or Luka, he couldn't remember, reached over and grabbed his rising erection and pushed his underwear down. Chris took the cue and lay back onto the pier as a plush pair of lips sucked on each of his nipples, then kissed down his chest, licking the bitter water away and replacing it with warm saliva.

Slowly, the strange mouth and anxious tongue traveled down his hairless belly, then stopped at his cock, which throbbed into the warm mouth. Chris went flush from the heat of his phantom lover's tongue. Slowly, he arched his back up only to have it pushed down. His cock slid down the slick throat as the firm tongue tickled the base. The skin beneath the shaft seemed to be on fire as his lover slid the cock out of his mouth and then gently bit the taut skin up and down. After what seemed like an eternity of these same motions over and over again, Chris was sure that not only would he come but the rest of his body would explode as well.

Finally, as the unknown mouth arrived at the tip of his cock, the familiar pressure re-built. The soft mouth sucked with an inhuman desire until Chris came and came, a small cry erupting from his throat and his head slamming against the wet boards underneath him. The entire episode probably only took a few minutes, for Chris was perpetually horny, but the orgasm seemed to last all day.

It was the best blow job he'd ever received, and the accompanying exhaustion lulled him into a short nap. When he awoke, he had the hollow feeling that he was alone. Chris sat up on one elbow and looked around for the other guys, but all he could see and hear was the empty lake and the slow drip of water off the pier. Suddenly, the overpowering aroma of something sweet hit his nose, and he stood up to find out where it was coming from. What the hell was happening? he asked himself.

"Chris, pull your pants up and get over here," one of the guys hollered to him. The fact that one of them actually knew his name surprised him but not enough to keep him from pulling his now dry underwear up and heading off into the woods between the lake and the house.

His naked toes brushed against the soft grass as he regained his senses and followed the path through the woods. A finger of Spanish moss dusted his head and momentarily blinded him, but he could hear the voices at the house, so he continued on his way. Finally, he came to the end of the path and saw four bodies gleaming like gold statues, clustered around the back door of the house as they smoked cigarettes. The fourth body was one he had never seen before. It was taller than all of them, lightly muscled in a rangy sort of way and crowned with a cap of dark blond hair. His torso was naked and as amber as the beer the boys had been drinking, but his legs were encased in a tight pair of white jeans. Chris caught himself staring at the man, who appeared to be at least a decade older than all of them yet was clearly "one of them" in a strange sort of way.

As he approached the group, one of them turned around and said, "Chris, come here and meet the guy who owns this place."

He came forward, feeling a bit shy since he was clad only in his underwear, but he realized that most of the group was half-naked, so he smiled, extended his hand to the man and introduced himself.

"I'm Chris Lambert."

The man came forward, shook his hand firmly, and smiled back. "I'm Lucian Lorde. Welcome to Sweetbread Hill." Then he laughed and swept his hand over the vista of his back yard and said, "Actually, welcome to my *cucina*."

"Your *cucina*?"

Lucian laughed again and said, "Yes, I call my back yard my *cucina* because it's where I cook up all my goodies."

The other guys broke into laughter, as if they had all just shared a private joke, but Chris began to feel uneasy. Something about the whole scenario made him a little nervous and wary. All of a sudden, here he was, talking to a man he never knew existed behind a house he had been sure was always abandoned. In all the time he had driven by Sweetbread Hill, he had never once seen signs of life in the house. Now he was being welcomed by the true "lord of the manor." Where had he been all these years?

Before Chris got up the nerve to ask, Lucian ushered them all inside and told them to "light anywhere."

Within moments Chris's eyes beheld a beautiful home filled with buttery light and rustic antiques. The inside of the home was not at all like the outside, for every room seemed freshly painted and decorated with gentle care. They walked through a spacious hallway to a living room, which was even more perfect in its décor. Chris found himself flinching when he saw that the three other guys had flopped onto the delicate furniture. Their burnished arms and legs matched the gleaming wood of the floor, which quickly became a repository for their cigarette ashes. But Lucian didn't seem to mind; as a matter of fact, the smile he had greeted Chris with never left his face.

Chris looked around and told himself that he didn't belong in such a fine place. Even if the other guys didn't seem to appreciate their surroundings, he certainly did. He opened his mouth to excuse himself and quietly leave, but before he could speak, Lucian turned to him and said, "What would you like to eat?"

"Um, I'm sorry, but what?"

"We usually have a snack around this time of day."

"Yeah, and it's always the same thing," one of the guys called out from the living room.

Before Chris could answer him, Lucian had dipped into the kitchen and appeared beside him with a plate.

Tentatively, Chris took the plate from his host and looked at the beautiful slice of cake adorning the fragile china. It was a dark, creamy color, the consistency silky and smooth with a dark red frosting on top. Automatically his mouth started to water, so he took the accompanying fork and ate a small piece. The first bite confirmed his first impression. It was the most delicious thing he'd ever eaten.

"This…this is wonderful," he said between bites as the other guys nodded in agreement. "What is this?"

Lucian sat down on a crimson velvet chair, spread his legs out onto the Persian rug in front of him, then threw his head back and laughed.

For a second Chris was convinced he was being laughed at, but the gentle lilt of the big man's laughter told him that wasn't the case.

"Why, it's sweetbread, Chris. What did you expect?"

Then Chris laughed himself as the other guys joined him, and for the first time that afternoon, he relaxed and began to feel at home.

Every bite of cake made him feel calmer and even sort of drunk. A few more giggles escaped from his throat, and out of the corner of his eye he saw Lucian wave the others away. Then he felt his host take his hand, and he marveled at the iron strength hidden in the muscles beneath the smooth skin. He was guided deeper into the living room as he finished the last of the cake and his host gently took the plate and laid it on a table.

"Chris, I've watched you," Lucian said.

Trying to focus, he simply shook his head and said, "Lucian…"

"I've watched you and waited for you. And now you're here."

Just then Lucian laid him down on the floor, spread his arms and legs out, and then covered him in warm kisses as his hands swept down every inch of Chris's body.

Chris found himself coming alive under Lucian's touch. The slow, dreamy feeling the sweetbread had induced gave way to an alertness bordering on hysteria. He kissed his host deep and long and let his tongue linger on Lucian's masculine lips until a familiar taste arose. Sweetbread, Chris told himself. He tasted sweet and seductive like the dark cake he had just eaten.

He arched up to kiss him again but Lucian let him go and stood up slowly. Looking down at him, the tall man unzipped his zipper and peeled off the white jeans. Within seconds he was covering Chris's body with his own, his slender cock snaking its way across his belly. The two of them writhed up and down on each other as their hands locked and their legs interlaced. Lucian found Chris's tongue and ignited the warm flush he had felt from the cake. An explosion of want and need made Chris lose all control, and he grasped at Lucian's body as if he wanted to devour it entirely.

They humped each other until Chris was covered in Lucian's sticky sweat. Then, just as he thought he could stand no more, he felt two strong hands pick him up and turn him over onto the floor. He landed on all fours instinctively and his ass rose into the air. Suddenly, the warm triangle of his host's tongue kissed the down on each cheek and then traveled beneath his balls. Its warm silkiness enveloped one and then the other until Chris's arms and legs spasmed outward and he collapsed onto the wooden floor.

Lucian took advantage of his prostrate position and opened his ass as wide as he could, then buried his tongue in Chris's asshole. The newness of the sensation overpowered him, and every nerve he possessed seemed to end in the cosmos of his ass as Lucian licked him furiously.

Almost fainting from the sensation, Chris found his mind going blank and he wondered if it was the sweetbread or his host's sweet tongue that sent him to such a place of warmth and light. But he really didn't care.

Lucian's tongue began to stroke and flick the area between his ass and balls, and Chris could swear that it had punctured the skin and dug deep into the core of who and what he was. Tears began to fill his eyes and he almost cried out until Lucian did something that jerked him back to reality.

Without missing a beat, his host's tongue dove back into his asshole and flicked it open, then Chris could feel the silken warmth of his lips pressed up to it and he shuddered as a low, rumbling laugh vibrated into and through his body. The thrill of what had just happened made him shiver all over, but he was now aware enough to realize that the laugh was not one that evoked humor. No, just the opposite.

His balls gathered into a tighter sac and Lucian caught them again and traced every line and vein on them, then his mouth cupped them together and his tongue went back and forth over every inch. Chris felt as if the lower half of his body had become its own land of electrifying, vibrating sensation, sending him into another spasm of pleasure.

But Lucian continued on his journey, coursing his hot tongue along the slick, clear space between Chris's balls and asshole, licking faster and faster. Chris began thrusting his hips back and forth as his host found his asshole again and this time sucked on it and licked it with an almost inhuman speed.

Finally, Chris grabbed his own cock and jerked it until he came in long hot ropes, striping the floor and landing on the velvet chair. It was an orgasm from the very depths of his being, and he only stopped jerking and moaning when he felt his host move away.

He rested on the floor as Lucian stood above him and shrugged on his jeans. When he heard the zipper go back up, Chris turned over and saw that his host was smiling at him.

"Well, sweetness," he said. "*That* was my afternoon snack. And you were delicious."

Chris smiled back at him and said, "Thanks," then slowly rose up and slipped his underwear back on. "But you didn't come."

"Later," Lucian said. Then he took his hand and guided him into the kitchen. "We have plenty of time. Now tell me about yourself, Chris. I want to know *all* of you."

Lucian gestured for him to sit on a kitchen stool as he leaned his slender frame against the granite counter.

"I was in school…"

"Colonial University? The one down the road?"

"Yes. And I was studying…well, nothing really."

"Of course. And you were bored."

"Yes."

Lucian leaned toward Chris and he could see that his eyes weren't as light as he thought. Instead, they were as dark as the cake he had been served, with streaks of red like the delicious frosting. His aroma was a mix of musty and sweet and for a second, Chris lost track of what he was saying and began to stammer.

"Go on, Chris," his host said as he ambled over to the refrigerator and pulled out two bottles of water. He handed one to Chris, then resumed his place against the counter.

"Well, I…I'm staying down the road. Trying to figure out what I want to do with myself."

"And your family? Gone?"

"Most of them."

The conversation seemed to die off and Chris swigged a big gulp of water as he watched Lucian watching him. But now there was no wariness. Instead, he was just glad to be in the tall man's presence.

Finally, Lucian stared intensely at him and said, "Are you lost?"

Without hesitation, Chris nodded and then wondered what made him admit to his nebulous state so fast. Usually he kept his solitary status to himself.

"Well, now you're found," Lucian said, provoking a quick smile from Chris.

They stared and smiled at each other until Chris noticed the first announcements of night outside the kitchen window. The lines of gold on the lake became more liquid as the blue of the sky edged into a sensual indigo, surrounding Sweetbread Hill until it seemed like an island of something particularly sweet to drink. Chris had never felt so warm and wanted, and he became totally at home in the old mansion.

"It's getting dark. Do you have any other clothes?" Lucian said.

Chris suddenly felt awkward and shook his head. "I think my jeans are out on the dock somewhere."

His host found a T-shirt, gathered it up, and gave it to him. Chris slipped it on as Lucian disappeared down the stairs outside the kitchen then quickly reappeared with more sweetbread, which he fed to him with his fingers.

Laughing, Chris said, "I'm not a child." But Lucian fed him slowly and deliberately until the dreamy feeling ignited inside Chris's head once more.

That night they joined the three other boys in their bedroom. Still floating from the last slice of cake he had eaten, Chris untangled the arms and legs that they had draped over each other and thoroughly enjoyed himself. When the effects of the night and sweetbread wore off later, he noticed Lucian standing in the corner of the room, looking at all the beautiful bodies arranged haphazardly on the floor. His face was as intense as it had been earlier, and his skin glowed with strength and beauty. Chris could swear that he was slowly licking his lips.

It went on this way for weeks with Lucian directing them all—telling them when they would eat, sleep, and fuck. And, of course, he made sure that everyone had an ample supply of sweetbread, which Chris had to admit he was seriously addicted to now.

The days and nights melted into one another and Chris began to notice that his host acted differently with him than he did with the other guys in the house. Almost every conversation was directed to him, every glance was sent his way. He began to feel certain that his goal of experiencing every heightened sensation life offered would be achieved.

The house, the food, the bodies, and especially his host conspired to make this the happiest summer he had known. The dreamlike state he enjoyed almost every day was unbroken by anything, and a certain affection grew inside him for his new home. He told himself that

Sweetbread Hill had sated his appetite in every way and the perfection of this time would last forever.

However, one afternoon provided a wrinkle in his never-ending summer of contentment. It was another day of lounging and swimming in the lake behind the house with another blazing sun and air so sweet and moist Chris was happy just to drink it and nothing else. Luka and Cam and Sebastian were drying their perfect forms on the pier as Chris sat up and looked at them. There had been a noticeable drop in sexual play between them, but he attributed that to the quick boredom of youth. Yet the heat and the proximity of three beautiful bodies made him almost instantly hard, so he rolled over and slipped his hand into Sebastian's wet underwear.

He began stroking the stubby cock, enjoying the way it grew in his hand until it was blue with ripeness, then he filled his mouth and gently sucked the briny lake water off the young flesh. He found that as he licked up and down the shaft he could slide more of it down his warm throat and the fat head seemed to catch behind his teeth. He flicked his tongue at the precome flowing from its slit and swallowed it slowly, enjoying every drop. Then he got up on all fours and began to concentrate on sliding the cock in and out of his throat, pushing it farther until his lips brushed up against Sebastian's coarse pubic hair. He did this until his throat expanded and then he nibbled at the tight balls just to give his mouth a break.

There was something vaguely familiar about the taste of the cock as he sucked and licked the hard skin. Sweetness had replaced the brine, but Chris told himself that they were all so saturated with sweetbread that it was only normal for him to be aware of the taste. Yet he also noticed an underlying chemical flavor, bitter and distasteful. He continued to suck, telling himself that he was imagining things. Finally, he flicked his tongue down the large blue vein on the underside of the shaft, fascinated as it pulsed as fast as his heart. Then he slid the cock back into his mouth and into his waiting throat. Sebastian groaned as Chris intentionally sucked the entire cock harder and harder, then slowed down to a deliberate pace, sliding his tongue up each side, then washing the head again with a string of saliva and plunging the entire shaft down his throat.

He got ready as the predictable rhythmic thrust of Sebastian's hips told him it was time. So he grabbed the base and sucked up and down, going faster and faster until, with one gigantic push and a low "Yeah," Sebastian released an ocean of come in his mouth. It washed down his throat as Chris licked all remaining drops off the tip of the cock, kissed it tenderly, then lay down beside him again.

As he lay beside Sebastian, he thought about his time at Sweetbread Hill and began to realize that there were some odd things going on with the three other boys. When they were asleep, Chris noticed a constellation of pinpricks dotted their bodies. At first, the signs of drug usage didn't really concern him. After all, he was no angel. But the location of the marks was very strange, for most of the boys had them either behind their knees or between their fingers. Also, Chris had noticed an increased lethargy in the three, with their main activities now whittled down to swimming, sleeping, and, of course, eating sweetbread. He only saw them in their beds or on the pier anymore. And for some reason, Lucian seemed to have distanced himself from the group. Intentionally.

"Chris? Are you dry?"

Lucian's voice startled him out of his thoughts and he sat up to see his host towering over him.

"Yes," he said.

"Good," Lucian said, then turned to the trio that was sharing the pier with Chris. Calmly but firmly, he said, "Luka, Cam, Sebastian?"

All of them shaded their eyes at the same time. Lucian looked down on them, then said sharply, "Go inside. Now."

All of them got up and moved like wobbly marionettes as they followed the trail back to the house, quiet and unquestioning as always. Finally, after they were out of sight, Chris stood up and said, "Lucian, what's going on?"

Taking Chris's face in his ample hands, Lucian kissed him, then whispered, "They've been using drugs since they got here, Chris. And I don't allow that, so they have to disappear. But don't worry. You can stay as long as you want. You were always the main...one."

The wary feeling Chris experienced returned again, and although the rest of his time with his host was warm and sweet and sexy, he felt as if the ground had shifted beneath his feet.

He tried to stay aware of everything that happened around him at Sweetbread Hill, and he noticed that there were times when Lucian would disappear for hours, then reappear abruptly. And Chris could also swear that he caught glimpses of the boys from time to time, but when he would run to catch them, they would vanish.

When he admitted that he had seen them to Lucian, a sweet lilting laugh would be his answer. Then his host would simply tell him that he was hallucinating. A plate of sweetbread would lull Chris back into a state of acceptance, and he would forget his concerns for a while.

But one thing became apparent after the trio of boys had gone; one thing Chris wasn't overly upset about. His nights with Lucian had become more dramatic as the sex between them became more aggressive and passionate. He thoroughly enjoyed the difference, and it even made him feel somewhat safe with his host.

Yet one night in the dying days of a stale summer, Chris reached his limit. After dinner, he noticed a dark, blank look in Lucian's eyes, and before he could say anything, he was being lifted up and thrown onto the dining table.

"Look, I—" he began to say, but before he could continue, his clothes had been ripped off and a naked Lucian landed on top of him. Before Chris could catch his breath, his host bared his teeth and began biting down his right side, grabbing and ripping the flesh, almost chewing it to shreds. Chris screamed for him to stop, but Lucian continued his attack from the nipple to the groin.

Another scream ignited another round of bites and Chris saw the streams of his blood pouring onto the table beneath them. "Please, please stop!" he yelled, but Lucian ignored him and continued to bite every inch of Chris's bare flesh. This went on for only a few minutes, but Chris felt as if hours were spent ripping his skin open.

Just as the pain became too much and he began to lose consciousness, Lucian picked him up and turned him face-down. Crying from relief, Chris thought he was returning to the journey he had taken on his first day when Lucian's tongue almost found him, but he wasn't so lucky.

No, this time there would be no gentle probing; this time his host's slender cock was thrust all the way up his ass, eliciting another scream from Chris. The rock-hard head seemed to go all the way to the root of his hunger, first massaging then attacking what was once a pleasurable spot. And then every vein in Lucian's cock throbbed in his ass, increasing the fire that had erupted there.

Chris tried to relax into it, but his host's rugged fucking wouldn't allow him the luxury. The more it went on, a feeling of being halved, or butchered, overwhelmed Chris and he begged for it to stop.

Finally, he found the strength to try to push Lucian out of him, but his hand was swatted away and the pain exploded as he was fucked even harder. They were now one being, connected by their hunger and blurring into one thing, he told himself. But the thought didn't soothe him. Nothing would ever soothe him again, and he let himself cry and scream, oblivious to anything else except the table underneath them. It began to creak so hard and so loud that he thought it would collapse. Then he began to pray that it would.

But Lucian fucked him with abandon, sliding his hot cock in and out, then picking Chris up by the hips and pushing him toward the base of his shaft. He did this over and over again until the pain overwhelmed Chris and he fainted as he cried out one last time for his host to stop.

When he awoke, Chris realized that he was in bed with Lucian, whose bronzed arm and leg were draped over him. Their weight ignited a roiling anger mixed with a newly found fear. As roughly as he could, he threw the limbs off him and climbed out of bed. He didn't bother to dress and wasn't sure what he was doing; he just knew that he didn't want to be near the man who had effectively raped him just a few hours before. So he walked down the stairs, gently touching the pink bite marks on his chest. The fire inside him still burned, but he decided to ignore it, at least for the evening.

A slight midnight drizzle had begun, with a hint of lightning, but it didn't faze him as he walked into the dark *cucina* and headed for the refrigerator. As he opened the door, the inside light illuminated the stairs outside the kitchen and Chris noticed there was another light at the bottom of the stairs. He had never been to the basement before, had never even inquired about it, yet now he was curious to see what Lucian kept down there. His steps were shy at first, then more assured as he walked down the wooden stairs.

Stopping in front of a large door with a brass knob, he jumped as a crack of lightning announced the arrival of sheets of rain that pelted the house. Chris thought he heard the storm calling his name, but shook it out of his head as he opened the door and found the light switch on the wall. He saw a spacious but plain room with a large silver freezer against the opposite wall. The sight of such an ordinary basement appliance calmed him as he told himself that most people kept freezers in their basements. But what he saw next unseated his initial impression of a mundane storage room.

To one side of the room was a metal tray at least six feet long, above which hung a pole with two loops. Upon closer inspection, Chris saw a long tube with a thick needle protruding limply from one of the loops. His heart began to push against his chest as he followed the trail of the tube until it ended at a wide grate on the floor.

Pinpricks, he thought. That's where they came from. Pinpricks between their fingers and behind their knees. Fear kept him grounded to the spot for a second, but another flash of lightning startled him and he caught himself looking at the silver freezer. He made himself walk over to it and stood in front of it until he could slow his breathing down. Then, he took hold of the handle and jerked the door open. And there were the answers he never wanted.

Clasping one hand over his mouth to stifle a scream, he slammed the door closed and stood in the middle of the room shaking like a live wire. Fright and shock raced through his mind as the rain increased its angry assault on the house and lightning raged outside. He was sickened by and still couldn't believe what he had just seen.

Operating solely on instinct, he ran back up the stairs and out the back door into the night storm. Then he headed down the now-muddy path to the lake. When he got to the pier, he fell onto his stomach and got sick over the side, well aware that he would never be able to release everything. The storm coated him and Chris drew his knees up to his wounded chest and began to cry and howl with the wind.

He sat and rocked there on the pier as the lake boiled in the storm and the rain drenched him. But the coolness of the rain eventually cleared his head and he was able to stop crying and think about what he had seen. For there, in the vast freezer, he saw three metal containers with the names Luka, Cam, and Sebastian written on them. And behind them were identical containers with other boys' names. When he had looked inside one of the containers, a mélange of remains blasted his senses. Only vaguely did he remember seeing the recipe for sweetbread taped on the door as he slammed it shut.

The violence of the storm slackened and the rain slowed enough for him to hear the long drops of water plop down from the trees into the lake. He had to think quickly, so he asked himself what he should do. Should he call the police? Should he run away? Should he pretend he'd never seen anything? Finally, he slicked the rain off his head and looked up at the night clouds in the sky. It was as dark as what he was feeling and he contrasted it to the white day of just a few months before when he arrived at Sweetbread Hill. A few more tears fell, and he hiccupped the rest away as he told himself it was the only thing he *should* do. The only thing he *could* do.

He found his way back to the house, climbed the stairs to Lucian's bedroom, and stood and looked at the monster lying in the bed. Then he went into the bathroom, dried himself off, and got back into bed, turning his back to his host.

Lucian immediately scooted over to him, spooned him and whispered gently into his ear, "You okay?"

"Yes, just thinking."

"About what?"

"About how hungry I am."

Lucian laughed, pulled him closer and said, "I'll make you some more sweetbread tomorrow."

Chris swallowed hard, caught his breath, and then said, "Okay… but, Lucian?"

"Yes, sweetness?"

"Tomorrow?"

"Uh-huh?"

"*I'll* make the sweetbread."

SOMEONE TO LAY DOWN BESIDE ME
TODD GREGORY

"You *really* see some tragic drag in this place at four in the morning," Dennis said, shaking his head. He said it a little too loudly, and I glanced over at the counter nervously. He rolled his eyes and smiled at me. "Don't look so worried. She didn't hear me." He looked over at her with disgust on his face. "Besides, she's so fucking wasted she doesn't know what day it is."

He plucked a packet of Sweet'n Low out of the little caddy next to the ketchup and mustard bottles and shook it a few times before dumping it into his red plastic cup of iced tea. He took a big swig before using a paper napkin to wipe beads of sweat off his forehead.

It wasn't quite four in the morning, but I wasn't going to be sleeping anytime soon. The digital jukebox was blasting a remix of Rihanna—"Only Girl in the World," which weirdly enough seemed like the appropriate soundtrack for the episode of *The Real Housewives from Hell* playing on the flat-screen television mounted on the wall I was facing.

I wiped my own forehead with a napkin. It was hot in the Clover Grill and the air seemed thick and heavy with grease. Burgers were frying on the grill, and French fries were sizzling in the deep fryer. The smell was making me more than a little nauseous. I didn't know how Dennis could possibly eat anything. I felt a wave of nausea coming on, so I closed my eyes and took some deep breaths till it passed. My lower back was aching, so I turned in my chair and put my back up against the wall. We were sitting at the table in the absolute back, and Dennis had his back to the front door. I put my feet up on the extra chair at our table and leaned forward a bit, trying to stretch the ache out of my back.

I took another big drink out of my red plastic cup of water and couldn't help smiling to myself. I recognized the tragic-looking drag queen sitting at the counter. I'd seen Floretta Flynn perform any number of times at various clubs in the Quarter. She was one of the better drag performers in the city and was actually quite funny. She'd been hostess of the show we'd caught earlier in the evening at the Parade while we were waiting for our dealer to show up. She'd clearly had too much to drink since then—Dennis swore drag queens were always smashed when they went on stage, but I couldn't tell. It was obvious now, though. She was seated at the counter on one of the revolving stools, leaning against a hot muscle boy who didn't seem quite as wasted as she was. Her massive 1970s country-singer wig was askew and her lipstick was smeared around her mouth. Her mascara was also smudged around her eyes, and it looked like she might have tried to wipe off some of the foundation and rouge on her cheeks. Her bright red sequined dress looked dirty, and she'd spilled something down the front of it.

"The wreck of the *Hesperides*," I replied in a much lower voice, just in case she had some kind of bat-like hearing.

"Drag queens also should always avoid direct overhead lighting." Dennis shrugged. "Even when their makeup is fresh it isn't pretty. Don't they teach that in drag school?" He rolled his eyes and took another swig of his tea. "I'd think that would be Drag 101."

I gulped out of my water glass. My buzz was already wearing off. I hadn't drunk much—a couple of mixed drinks, a bottle of Bud Light, at most—and we'd smoked a joint on the balcony, but it had been enough to alter my mood. But the energy in the club had been off—it seemed like there had been far too many drunken straight girls at Oz, the ones who come to gay bars to show how cool they are and make complete fools out of themselves in the process. One had sloshed some of her drink on me on the dance floor, and if I'd had a dime for every time one of them almost burned me with the lit cigarette she carelessly waved around like it was an accessory, I'd never have to worry about where my next meal was coming from ever again. So when Dennis finally said "the hell with this" and suggested getting something to eat at the Clover, I was more than happy to put my shirt back on and follow him out the front door of Oz.

If I'd only known those stupid drunk bitches were going to be there, I thought as I looked around, *I wouldn't have wasted my time or my money there.*

The problem was I was still horny—and the likelihood of getting laid was getting smaller by the minute.

The Clover Grill was pretty empty. Floretta and her muscle boy were the only people at the counter. Besides a group of large and extremely hairy bears at the front table, we were the only people in the whole place.

I adjusted my shorts again and wondered if Dennis would be up for some meaningless sex. I narrowed my eyes and watched him worrying his straw. He was looking out the picture window across the street at Lafitte's, which was also pretty deserted. A drop of sweat had pooled in the hollow at the base of his throat.

He was so fucking hot. He was wearing a Saints baseball cap backward—he always claimed it wasn't to hide his receding hairline, but methinks he doth protest too much—and his features were strong enough to pull the look off. He had enormous, expressive brown eyes, a square jaw, and thick, eminently kissable lips. His years teaching aerobics and working as a personal trainer had given him a thickly muscled yet defined body. His tight white tank top showed off his dark tan. His arms were crisscrossed with bulging veins. He turned his head back toward me and smiled. He was one of the few people I'd ever known who smiled with his entire face.

My balls ached.

I opened my mouth to ask, but before I could form the words he yawned and said, "All I want to do is eat and go home and take a Xanax and sleep till Monday." He took the ball cap off and ran his hand through his sweaty hair, smiling at me again as he put the cap back on. "Probably just as well the night was so off," he went on, "who knows what trouble we might have gotten into?" He winked at me.

This was the kind of mixed signal he'd always given me, the kind that had always made me think there was a chance of something more between us than just being friends. I closed my eyes and decided to not bring it up. Even though I knew it wouldn't mean a damned thing other than two friends scratching an itch, I couldn't forget the one time it had happened.

Dennis would think I was still hung up on him if I suggested it, had backslid, or worse, had never ever gotten over him in the first place.

And to be honest, as hot as Dennis was, the sex wouldn't be worth dealing with all of that shit the next morning.

Fuck it, after I eat my fries I'll head down to the bathhouse and fuck someone there, I decided. Dennis didn't approve of anonymous sex in bathhouses, so I'd have to walk him back to his place and pretend like I was going home. I glanced at my watch. A little before four—I could be there by five, and hopefully pounding someone's ass by five fifteen. By then all the guys coming down from their drugs but not ready to go home yet would be there—and wanting it bad.

"Are you still high?" Dennis shrugged his shoulders. "Mine wore off a while ago." He made a face. "What a shitty night—we should have just stayed home and watched movies or something." He frowned as a couple of guys walked past the big window in the direction of Esplanade Avenue. They looked slightly familiar—but I didn't get a good look. The scowl on Dennis's face, though, let me know he knew and didn't like one or both of them. "Last weekend sucked too," he went on as our waiter put a plate of French fries in front of me and a grilled chicken sandwich down in front of him. "And tonight was a total waste of money."

"No shit," I replied. "It's not like I've got a lot of extra cash to throw away." I closed my eyes and tilted my head back against the tiled wall. I didn't get paid again until Wednesday—and I thought I had exactly forty bucks in the bank and no food in my apartment. *Should've just stayed home tonight, found someone online*, I lectured myself. *Ah, well, I still have credit on my card—I can use that for the bathhouse and some groceries. Yeah, should've stayed home and found a trick online…stupid stupid stupid.*

I opened my mouth to say something else when I realized the guy with Floretta was looking at me. Our eyes met, and he smiled at me.

I was dazzled as he stood up and stretched.

He was a blond, with his hair cut close to the scalp in a military style that emphasized his square jaw, strong nose, and wide mouth. He had blue eyes and was wearing a pair of khaki shorts that reached his knees. His red T-shirt had the sleeves cut off deeply, so that his entire side was exposed. He grinned at me with dimples cutting deep into his tanned cheeks. His arms were huge, as were his shoulder muscles.

Veins stood out on his arms, and his waist was narrow—he was widely built from the front, but from the side his waist looked tiny. His pecs were big, and his shirt clung to his big, hard nipples. He walked along the counter toward our table. He kept smiling at me as he walked. I knew Dennis was still talking between bites of his sandwich, but all I heard was mumbling. The loud music from the jukebox was nothing more than white noise in the background as he walked slowly toward where I was sitting, that big smile still on his face.

God, my cock ached.

He walked past us, and I turned to watch him go out the door to the courtyard, where the bathrooms were. His back was broad, and the muscles twitched beneath the tanned skin pulled tightly across them. His ass was round and full—not as big as maybe I would prefer, but it would definitely do. For a brief second I pictured him underneath me, smiling that big grin up at me while I slid my dick into his ass—

"Earth to Gary? Are you there, Gary?" Dennis waved his hand in front of my face and, to add insult to injury, snapped his fingers.

Irritated, I pushed his hand away from my face. "Don't do that," I said. "You know I hate it when you do that."

He smirked at me. "That's pretty, all right. Why don't you go say hello? Introduce yourself?" There was a taunting tone to his voice that made me want to smack him.

I started to snap back at him, but stopped myself. Instead, I smiled at him and said, "You know, I think I will." I got out of my chair and walked out the side door and through the courtyard to the bathroom. Once in the courtyard, I leaned against the side of the building and closed my eyes. *Idiot, idiot, idiot,* I moaned. I never had the nerve to actually approach anyone—especially not someone as hot as this guy. But my dick was still semi-hard, and my balls were still aching. I was about to turn and walk back inside the diner when I heard the bathroom door's bolt being slid back, and it opened.

I opened my eyes as he walked out of the bathroom.

Our eyes met, and he smiled. "Hey."

"Hey," I replied, stepping out of his way.

But instead of going back inside, he just stood there smiling at me. It seemed like we stood there in the moonlight staring at each for an eternity before he finally said, "My name's Trey." He stuck out his hand, which I stared at stupidly for a moment before taking.

His hand was warm, enormous and strong. "Gary." I said, feeling like a complete idiot.

"Nice to meet you." He didn't let go of my hand. "Don't you have to go to the bathroom?"

"Actually, no." I heard the words coming out before I could stop them. "I followed you out here." I was mortified—I certainly didn't want him to think I cruised bathrooms in public places.

Before I knew what was happening, he pulled me in closer and kissed me briefly on the mouth. His big thick arms went around me, and his hands cupped my ass.

Our crotches brushed against each other, and I could feel his hardness.

I pulled my head back and whispered, "Um, you want to come back to my place?"

He nuzzled my neck. "How far is it?"

"Not far. Just about a block."

He licked his lips. "Works for me—if you want to."

I let my hand brush against his crotch. "I don't want to make out here in the Clover Grill's courtyard," I replied, although I'd done much worse in more public places before. "Come on."

I took him by the hand and led him back into the grill, pausing at the table long enough to give Dennis a five for my fries. I didn't wait for him to say anything—but he had that judgmental look on his face that always pissed me off. Trey kissed Floretta on her makeup-smudged cheek, and she gave me a crooked, approving grin. Trey took my hand again and led me outside. Once outside on Dumaine Street, he walked alongside me as we headed up to Dauphine. "Your friend didn't look too happy," Trey said over the music blaring out of Lafitte's as we walked past.

"Dennis—Dennis thinks I'm a slut," I replied.

Trey laughed. "And he's not?"

I stopped walking. "You haven't slept with him, have you?"

He laughed again and shook his head. "No—would it matter if I had?" He pushed me up against the side of a house and kissed me long and hard again. When he pulled back, I gasped out, "No."

When we reached the side gate at my place, he kissed the back of my neck as I fit my key into the lock and turned it.

I barely had time to flip the light switch just inside my front door when he pushed me against the wall and hungrily kissed me, his tongue probing inside my mouth. I sucked his tongue, refusing to let it go and making him keep kissing me as I fumbled with the button of his jeans, finally getting them open. I pushed his jeans down while we still kissed, and grabbed hold of his bare ass with both hands as he put his hands into my armpits and lifted me easily. I let his tongue go and gasped while he kept me up in the air. I wrapped my legs around his waist, and he held me there as he pulled his jeans up so he could walk—and headed over to the couch, where he gently lowered me down onto my back. He pulled his T-shirt up over his head and I couldn't help but stare at his smooth torso, the big heavy pecs, the huge round erect nipples, the ripples in his flat stomach as he kicked his shoes off and slid the pants down and off, standing there over me, his long hard cock standing out away from the golden pubic hair. He straddled me, a knee on either side of my rib cage, and I leaned up and licked the end of his cock.

He moaned as I started sucking—no, worshiping—his cock. It was magnificent, the skin soft and smooth and hot, tasting of salty sweat and smelling of musky manhood as my mouth moved slowly up and down its shaft, my free hand cupping and gently squeezing his thick, heavy, shaved balls as I slurped away at this amazing rod. I ran my other hand up his torso, tweaking a nipple before sliding down the ridges of his abs, and I opened my eyes, looking straight up at him. His head was tilted back, so I could just see the straight line of his throat, and still I worked on his cock, teasing the slit with my tongue while he emitted guttural groans of delight from deep inside his diaphragm.

He pushed my head away, and I looked at him, puzzled.

He simply smiled and got off the couch.

He grabbed my shirt with both hands and yanked hard, lifting me up off the cushions. I heard the fabric tear as he kept pulling, and then the fabric gave way completely and tore free. He tossed my shredded shirt aside like it was nothing and undid my jeans, sliding them down and off me, tossing them over his shoulder. He tore my underwear off me.

The sound of it ripping in his hands and the feel of my hard cock springing free was so hot, so arousing, I would have let him fuck me right then and there.

Instead, he got down on all fours on the couch, facing away from me, and backed up until his balls and cock were in my face. He leaned down and took mine in his mouth, and I reached up and started licking the underside of his balls before moving on to his cock.

The feel of his tongue, of his warm wet mouth, on me was so intense I thought I might come—which I certainly didn't want. I didn't want this to ever stop. It was incredible.

I started trembling and let his cock slip away from my mouth as I took some deep breaths to keep the wave of pleasure from overwhelming me.

But *he* was still working away on my dick, and oh my God it felt—

Amazing.

So good I didn't know if I could handle it.

Like the top of my head was going to blow right off.

I turned my head to one side and bit my lip as tears filled my eyes, as joy swept through my body, and I tentatively stuck my tongue out and let the tip touch his thigh.

His skin tasted salty, and I licked his thigh again, tracing little circles while waves of pleasure crashed over me.

I was barely aware as he stopped what he was doing, but I noticed when he moved out of range of my tongue.

I opened my eyes and looked up into his eyes. He smiled at me, and I fell into the deep blue of his eyes, and it was like we were merging into one person as his lips touched my throat, his hands pinching my nipples, and it was so incredibly arousing, it felt so fucking good, no one had ever driven me so wild with desire before, and I wanted him, I wanted to be part of him, I wanted our skin to meld together so we would be one creature, one combined, and I felt the head of his cock teasing my asshole and I was so deep in his eyes I couldn't resist him, and he started to slide inside me and I couldn't draw breath, I couldn't breathe, all I could do was gasp as his tongue traced along my throat up to my earlobe and then the lobe was between his teeth and he was nibbling taking little bites all the while his fingers were pinching and tweaking and pulling my nipples and I wanted to scream it felt so good but I was so deep inside his eyes I was afraid if I made any sound, any sound at all it might deafen him cause him to pull back cause him to withdraw from me and we would separate and I didn't want that I didn't want that at all I wanted him to be a part of me I wanted to be a part of him and I could feel some pressure inside me as he pushed against me yet his tongue and lips never stopped moving and my nipples my god my nipples he was pulling and twisting and working them no one had ever worked them quite that way before oh my god what was he doing to me I never wanted him to stop—

"You're high, aren't you?" he whispered in my ear, and his breath tickled my skin, sending a tingle through my body that didn't stop until it reached my toes and went out into the universe from there, and his voice echoed inside my head.

"A little bit," I answered, and I looked into his blue eyes and was lost in them, into the beautiful deep azure, and then his lips were on my throat again, his teeth taking little bites out of my skin. As another wave of pleasure washed over my body I wanted him to take me into his mouth. I wanted him in my mouth again, and I reached down and wrapped my hand around his thick cock. "Fuck me, please," I heard myself saying, "I want you inside me," and before I knew what was happening he had pushed me down and was between my legs, pushing them up, and the head of his cock was pushing inside me.

It felt like I was being torn in half but it was good, it felt right, like it was how I was meant to be, like I'd been born for this one moment, and I closed my eyes, tilted my head back, and gave myself over to the pleasure.

Wave after wave coursed through my body as he slowly fucked me, sliding his dick in and out of me in a rhythm intended to push me to my limits. My body was trembling uncontrollably as he worked my ass, his big hands tweaking my nipples, and I could feel drops of precome working their way up my own cock, dripping out of the slit onto my abs as he kept pushing and pulling inside me, occasionally stopping to let me experience the feeling of being completely filled by him.

I tried to breathe but I was gasping as my body shook yet he still didn't move. I looked up at him and he was smiling at me. I watched a drop of sweat run down from his forehead down his nose. It hung there for just a moment on the tip before dropping onto me. I felt it splash on my chest, and I reached up with both hands to grab his thick pecs. His smile didn't waver, he didn't move, he was still shoved all the way inside me as he raised both of his arms and flexed his biceps muscles, veins thickening over them and in his forearms, his chest hardening under my hands as I kept squeezing them, and I wanted him to start fucking me again, harder and nastier, I wanted him to shove inside me so hard I'd move, so I start twisting under him as another drop of sweat flowed down his nose, beads of water forming in the deep canyon between his chest muscles, his tanned skin glistening in the light.

"Oh, you want me to fuck you some more?" he asked, his low, deep voice getting under my skin, the words echoing inside my head.

"Fuck me," I hissed, my eyes narrowing as I tried to move. "Pound me, make me your little slut pig bitch, come on, stud, give it to me!"

His smile faded, and his lips curled into a sneer as he slid slowly out of me.

I gasped.

When all that was left inside me was the head, he snarled, "Beg for it."

My body was trembling with need and desire.

He twisted both of my nipples. "Beg, you fucking bitch."

He kept twisting as I gasped, and the shock of the pain turned to pleasure.

It was like my nipples were wired directly to my balls.

He slammed all the way into me before I could say a word, before I could react to anything.

The intensity of the pleasure overwhelmed me and I screamed.

I bucked upward, my upper body rising, but he roughly planted his hands on my chest and slammed me back down on my back.

Now he was pounding, slamming into me so fast that I couldn't even gasp. It felt so good, but his thrusts were coming so quickly I didn't have time to moan or groan or make any noise other than the gasps as I tried to suck in air before he slammed into me again and drove it all back out of me.

Come shot out of my cock, splashing on my chest, my stomach, hitting me in the face.

And still, he kept pounding on me.

Sweat rolled down his face, his chest glistened wetly as he grunted from the exertion.

I grabbed his nipples and pulled.

His head went back and he screamed.

I could feel his cock jerking with each spurt inside me.

With each jerk of his cock he howled again, his body shaking.

His eyes were still closed.

Finally, he stopped.

He slowly slid out of me and smiled down at me.

He bent over me and licked my come off me.

"You have an awesome ass, man," he said, running his hand through his wet hair.

I made room for him beside me on the couch, and he dropped down, sliding an arm under my head. He was on his side, and I slid over until our wet skin was touching.

"I don't usually—I don't usually get fucked," I replied, resting my head against his chest and listening to his heartbeat.

"It felt so good I didn't want to come," he said. He pressed his lips against my forehead. "Sorry if I was rough."

"I liked it," I replied, a knowing smile coming onto my face. I turned and faced him. "You could have gotten rougher."

"Let me rest for a bit, and then I'll show you rough."

I reached down and grabbed his dick. "Let's go into the bedroom."

I got up off the couch and led him back to my bed. As he lay down on the bed I glanced out the window.

Dennis was sitting on a chair outside his apartment door, and I wondered if he'd heard us.

A smile crossed my face. I didn't care if he did, and why should I? He'd made it clear more than once that I wasn't his boyfriend, would never be. What right did he have to judge me?

I nestled inside Trey's big arm and rested my head on his sweaty chest. It felt good.

It felt right.

"Whenever you're ready," I whispered as I lay down next to him. "Sir."

Wish You Were Here
Lewis DeSimone

I ate my way through Italy. Italy was my revenge.

Naples was greasy slabs of pizza Margherita, plucking off clumps of mozzarella and dropping them into my mouth like stringy ambrosia. Rome was saltimbocca, crisp slivers of sage balancing the sweetness of tender (and, in the States, politically incorrect) veal. In Florence, I lingered over plates of creamy risotto dotted with juliennes of fresh asparagus. And in Bologna, the eponymous meat sauce sent a shudder through my limbs.

I wanted to be spoiled by Italian food. I wanted to indulge in as much decadent flavor as I could. If I could get my appetite back anywhere, I knew, it would be here, where the aromas of garlic and onions filled the air, where the plates were overflowing, where food was an expression of love. I was tired of halving recipes to fit a single plate. In Italy, I was determined to have my fill.

But I had been warned that the Italian flair for food didn't necessarily extend to every corner of the country. "Don't expect much of the cuisine in Venice," Clarice had told me. (You remember Clarice, don't you? No, of course you don't. My friends' names never quite made it into your vocabulary, did they? The faces may have looked familiar after a while, but that was about it. "I have nothing in common with So-and-So," was your constant refrain—and your excuse for not getting to know So-and-So, never finding out if indeed you might have something in common with her, something other than me—as if I weren't enough.)

I had my own trepidation about Venice, but it had nothing to do with the food. It was everything else I'd heard—the picture-postcard views of the canals, the winding streets and dollhouse bridges, the grand palaces reflected in murky water: Venice, they said, was the most romantic city on earth. Even Paris, with its fabled light, its sensual airs, its very Frenchness, couldn't compete. No, in the collective imagination, Venice was the city of love. Venice was where people went on their honeymoons, or to recharge their romantic batteries. It was not a place you visited alone—and certainly not right after a breakup.

But it was there. And I wasn't about to fly halfway around the world only to miss one of its most legendary spots. So Venice claimed its place on my itinerary—the last stop on my way up the boot, food and romance be damned.

My hotel was a short walk from Piazza San Marco. A short walk if you knew where you were going—but in Venice, only the natives know where they're going. After getting lost the first couple of times I dared venture outside, I was tempted to carry bread crumbs on subsequent trips. Each time I looked for markers, some way to memorize the route, but I was never able to completely retrace my steps. Venice was a labyrinth, a series of concentric circles with little bridges between them. If I wandered long enough, I would inevitably find my way, but by faith more than intent.

The sun was still well above the horizon on my first day when I realized I was starving. You have to understand that hunger and I were just getting reacquainted on this trip. After the breakup—to be honest, for a couple of weeks before that, once I realized the end was on its way—the thought of food disgusted me. I came to understand how anorexics must feel: The sensation of emptiness is seductive. At first, the only thing my stomach could hold was anxiety—a jittery hollowness that saw any incursion of food as an act of war. Before long, I began to confuse the emotional emptiness of my heart with the literal emptiness of hunger. Little by little, I was starving myself to death, yet always convinced that the next bite would kill me.

Italy cured all that—not just because delicious food was everywhere, but because *you* were nowhere to be found. There was nothing in that landscape of Renaissance palazzos and cobblestone streets, of tight alleys where Vespas wound their way quickly past unsuspecting tourists, of old women arguing on narrow sidewalks with hand gestures as loud as their voices—nothing in any of it that bore the slightest resemblance to the life we had shared. There was no remnant of you anywhere.

So I took it all in. I gorged on art and architecture and lasagna and Chianti. I devoured an ancient civilization that was still alive with passion and faith. I filled myself up with it, hoping with each sight and each bite to leave no more room for you.

I found a small restaurant on a side street near the piazza. At this point, I was so hungry I didn't care if Clarice's prediction came true. Along my way up the peninsula, I had already experienced the most amazing food of my life, so something pedestrian might actually be welcome. It would help me get used to the idea of going home to my steady diet of fried chicken and Prego.

Throughout the country, restaurants had also provided the least stressful opportunity to practice my Italian. It wasn't only that waiters were used to tourists, but that in a restaurant, I could pretty much get away with communicating only through nouns. At worst, I could simply point to something on the menu and smile.

But not tonight. Tonight's waiter wanted a whole conversation. And a three-course meal.

"Scusi, signore," he said, smiling enthusiastically, "you start with a pasta? *Spaghetti alle vongole*—with clams. Is very good." His English was only slightly less skilled than my Italian, and given his obvious eagerness to practice it, I decided that it was more polite to communicate in my native tongue than to butcher his.

"Okay," I said. "Great."

"Is good," the waiter repeated, his smile growing even broader. His look could best be described as swarthy—olive skin slightly pockmarked, furry eyebrows guarding deep-set eyes, the head a mass of almost black curls. "Is good for here." And he pointed toward my belly, finally reaching out to gently pat it. Yes, I thought, spaghetti would be good for the stomach.

He straightened up and began scribbling on his notepad—suddenly officious again, as if nothing had happened. I told myself it had just been an innocent gesture, no more meaningful than the casual behavior I'd already seen all over Italy—men walking arm in arm, kissing each other's cheeks on the street. In Italy, they weren't afraid of the body: They recognized its sensuality without investing every touch with sexual innuendo. Sometimes a feel was just a feel.

I asked for a half-carafe of the house white and some water. He nodded, pouting his lower lip to reveal the fleshy pink underside. "And the second?" he asked. *Il secondo*—the main course. I was still getting used to the fact that, in Italy, pasta was merely the *primo piatto*, rather than a meal in itself.

"What do you recommend?" I replied.

His eyes opened wide, almost glowing. "The osso bucco is *magnifico*," he said, one hand curled in so that all the fingers met around the thumb in the classic Italian gesture.

While I was waiting for the spaghetti, he brought a full carafe of wine to the table. He had already poured a glass before I was able to come up with a pidgin-Italian protest.

"Your eyes," he said, ignoring my concern about the wine, "they are very beautiful. Like the sea." He stood at his full height, gazing down matter-of-factly. "How are you called?" he asked, tilting his head to one side.

I fumbled with the words in my ears, the familiar idiom so strange in literal translation.

"Your...name," he said.

I debated with the truth. For good or ill, it won. "Paolo," I said. *"Mi chiamo Paolo."*

His eyes brightened, his mouth hanging open in a perfect *O*. "Ah, it is...how do you say, fate? *Mi chiamo Francesco*." He winked and delivered the rest in a whisper. "Like *Francesca,* no? Paolo *e* Francesca. *La Divina Commedia*."

Of course, I thought, smiling awkwardly: The adulterous lovers who spend an eternity in purgatory. How romantic.

More likely, he was just making it all up. If I had said Leonardo, would he have claimed to be named Mona Lisa? Would we have found ourselves lying to each other, both putting on false personas, playing a game that no one would win? I began to understand how women felt in Italy—the transparent flattery they had to put up with, the constant, shameless stares, the suggestive remarks from unremarkable strangers.

"If you like," he said, leaning in, "we get a drink later tonight. I tell you all about Venezia. Yes?"

I smiled. After two weeks in Italy, two weeks of wandering around alone, marveling at the sights with no one to share a comment with, I was craving company. Each night, when I finally tired of sightseeing and returned to my hotel room, the weight of loneliness settled upon me like a suffocating blanket. I would have loved to see the real Venice in the company of a real Venetian. But he didn't just want a drink. He wanted something I was unprepared to give. This trip wasn't about men. It was about getting away from men. This trip was about food.

"Maybe," I replied, relishing the ambiguity.

"Bene," he said, nodding. He was playing with a napkin, holding one end tight and pulling the rest through his free hand. And then he was gone again, back into the loud kitchen.

When he passed by a few minutes later, I reiterated my request for water.

"Maybe later," he said and bolted into the kitchen.

He busied himself with other customers for the next several minutes, as I anxiously nursed my wine. The spaghetti, when it finally arrived, was delicious—the pasta the epitome of al dente, fighting delicately against my teeth, while the clams melted creamily on my tongue. My first thought was to tell Clarice she had obviously gone to the wrong restaurants. The only problem was that the sauce was so spicy my eyes started to water after a few bites.

As I twirled the strands of spaghetti around my fork, Francesco kept gliding back and forth through the restaurant, winking at me each time he passed. I poured myself another glass of wine, but it only exacerbated the fire in my mouth.

Finally, when I wasn't looking, he placed a half-carafe of water on the table. He stood solemnly beside me as I poured out a glass and looked up. "The water," he said flatly, "is good only for cleaning the face in the morning."

I drained the first glass and smiled politely as I refilled it.

"You like the clams?" he asked.

I nodded, managing a mouthful of spaghetti.

"Is very good," he repeated. "Very good." And suddenly, so quickly that I had to wonder whether I'd imagined it, his hand moved to my belly again—and then, suddenly, slipped a little further down. So what exactly were the clams good for? I'd thought oysters were the only aphrodisiac shellfish, but apparently not in Italy.

"Enjoy," he said and dashed toward another table, where a large man was gesturing impatiently.

I was only halfway through the spaghetti, but suddenly the thought of another bite brought back a familiar anxiety.

It's not that he wasn't my type. Francesco was tall, with square shoulders and a rugged look, just this side of handsome. His arms were hairy and muscular—the white shirt hugged his biceps like a tightly stretched sausage skin—the type that could lift you into the air or effortlessly crush you. In America, no one would think he was gay, but here it was impossible to tell. So far, my gaydar had been pretty useless in Italy—like an electrical appliance that couldn't fit into a 220-volt plug. I could hardly believe he was flirting with me. He just didn't look or act gay. Except for the touching my penis part: That was pretty gay.

Maybe I was just out of practice. I didn't trust my own desire or my ability to assess anyone else's. You'd taken that away from me.

Throughout this trip, I had admired the men I saw, but only as objects—like the statues that presided over every piazza, cold and off-limits. That had been enough. None of the statues had ever tried to touch me. Until now.

It was still early, the restaurant only half-full. I had a whole evening to kill after this, another evening alone in a foreign city.

"Ten o'clock," Francesco said, stopping by a few minutes later. "I meet you at ten o'clock, on the corner."

"Okay," I said, just to shut him up. I looked at the half-empty plate. "But is it too late to cancel the osso bucco? I'm not as hungry as I thought."

"Ah," he said, "a handsome man must eat to keep up his strength. You need energy tonight, maybe."

I chuckled. "Really," I said, "could I cancel it?"

"Of course," he said. "I tell them now."

I forced myself to finish the pasta. The water was long gone, and the wine was already having its effect, but I poured just one more glass to get me through.

The plate was respectably picked over by the time Francesco came to retrieve it. Along with the bill, he brought a couple of amaretto cookies and a glass of port. Apparently, the wine wasn't enough. I felt like a hostage, forced to partake. The port was delicious, and I wondered how much more I would enjoy it if my stomach weren't turning cartwheels.

I paid the bill and got up slowly, conscious of the wine sloshing its way to my head. Francesco walked me to the door, unable to hold back his excitement. Outside, on the cobblestone, he took my arm and turned me to look down the street, toward the right. "I meet you there," he said, pointing to an alley a block away. "Ten o'clock. We have drink."

"Yes," I said, smiling. "Yes."

He went back inside, the same energy in his eyes. Perhaps he did like me, I thought, listening to the slow echo of my shoes on the sidewalk. But then the paranoia resumed. He was so aggressive, I could only imagine what he would be like if I actually were alone with him. *No* may have sounded the same in Italian as in English, but that was no guarantee that he would hear it. I had already observed that the Italian man seemed completely fixated on his penis—constantly scratching, repositioning, or simply holding it—as if to prove to the world that it was there, or to give some indication of its dimensions. He might rape me. That is, if he was gay at all. If he wasn't simply planning to mug me in that alley and stab me in the heart. Suddenly my life seemed like a Verdi opera.

It was still early, the street glowing in crepuscular light—always my favorite time of day, when the shadows vanish and every object stands in clean relief. I meandered from bridge to bridge, gazing down into the myriad canals. How many tourists, I wondered, fall into the canals every year—the Venetian equivalent of DUI.

Venice, I thought—the most romantic city in the world, and I didn't want to be touched. If we had only come here a year ago—together, you and I—it would all be different. The narrow alleyways, the bridges arching over the canals, would present an adventure rather than simply an opportunity to get lost. The reflections of colorful buildings swaying on the water would remind me of Monet, rather than simply making me seasick.

Italy had been your idea—the music of the language, whose syllables rolled off the tongue like profiteroles; the history that was still alive in every building. It was you who had wanted to come here: I was just going along for the ride. But when the time came, and you were gone—when I faced the inexorable urge to get away on my own—Italy was all I could come up with. I had planned it already. I could have gone somewhere else on this now solitary sojourn—London, Paris,

Barcelona—but any other destination would have taken too much effort. My heart had been set on Italy, and I was determined to make sure my heart got at least one thing it wanted. No reason an entire country should become collateral damage from you.

I hadn't come here to forget anything, to supplant one memory with another. I didn't want to replace you with another man; I simply wanted to be reminded that the world was bigger than us. Sex had never been part of the agenda. Since the plane landed in Rome, I had been more interested in the ancient ruins, the museums, the restaurants, the busy cafés, than the men. In every city, every teeming piazza and cathedral, I was a wanderer—invisible, untouched. And that was part of the excitement: Here, I could be a fly on the wall, observing life rather than partaking of it. I needed the cocooning effect of that. The beauty of Italy was enough of a distraction. At every turn, I tried to focus on that.

But Italy, I quickly discovered, was all about passion—the passion for food, art, love, for life itself. No matter how mundane the task, the people I saw approached it with gusto and commitment. A woman shaking out a broom made a little symphony by clanging it against a balcony railing, and a tornado of dust plummeted down from her perch. Children ran noisily through the streets, darting around pedestrians, who barely noticed because they were so deeply embroiled in conversation.

I didn't see as many couples at this hour, the intimidating honeymooners whose locked hands swayed between them like the pendulum in an old clock. They were gone for the night—huddled over tiny restaurant tables or ensconced in the far end of a gondola moving languidly through the canals. And yet the stones glowed in their absence, all the more so as lights went on in various windows throughout the town.

Still drunk on the wine that Francesco had continued to pour each time he passed my table, I floated through the city. I held tightly to the railing when climbing a bridge, refusing to gaze into the dark water below. As night fell, my footsteps echoed more loudly on the cobblestone, one sense giving way to another in the dark. I had no idea where I was going. There was no point in knowing where I was going, actually: In this town, all destinations were equally impossible to find. That was the main thing Venice had taught me: Somehow, without trying, you may not arrive where you want to be, but you will nevertheless arrive. Everything looked familiar after a while, everything circled back to itself.

I had no idea how long I'd been walking when suddenly an amber light shone through the encroaching darkness, an awning aglow over an open doorway. My restaurant, scene of the crime—the crime of running away. I stopped in a shadow across the street and gazed through the windows, aged latticework dividing the panes of glass.

There were only a couple of tables still occupied. In the background, busboys dashed around, carrying dishes into the kitchen, wiping down tables, pushing in chairs. I couldn't make out anyone specifically, not even the couple in the front leaning toward each other over a small bouquet of roses.

We went to restaurants all the time, you and I—sat at tables like that, shared a bottle, finally walked away into a different darkness. I'd never lingered before, watching the whole process. It was like studying an ant farm, the way the ants march from one spot to another, busying themselves with tasks too small for the human eye to grasp.

I watched the couple in front settle their bill, as the only other remaining guests—four loud Italians—appeared in the doorway, one singing drunkenly as his companions made a show of holding him upright. I smiled. This, too, was Italy.

Finally, the couple emerged as well—a woman with long blond hair that glowed eerily in the light shining from inside, a man who took her hand and gently led her down the street. They walked slowly. They'd learned that you can't rush anything in Italy.

And then, a few minutes later, he was there in the doorway— Francesco, lighting a cigarette behind a cupped hand. He looked even swarthier in this light, and a bit shorter than I remembered, a silhouette against the bright interior. He took a few puffs from the cigarette and glanced casually in either direction down the street—but not directly across to where I stood. He was waiting, but not anxiously. He would not be disappointed to simply be on his way.

I pulled myself out of the shadow, and as my feet scuffled on the cobblestone, Francesco's gaze moved toward me. His lips, beneath the brooding mustache, curled into a knowing smile. He stepped out of the restaurant's glow and met me in the middle of the street.

"You had a good evening?" he asked softly. And—not waiting for an answer—"We walk, then," he said. "This way."

I was tired of walking, tired of the circles that led nowhere.

"Come," he said. "Is not far."

I followed, my footsteps uncertain beside his firm gait. He turned toward me several times, eyes aglow, as bright as the orange flame at the end of his cigarette.

"This way," he said when we reached the next corner.

I lagged. He had walked a few paces ahead before noticing, then turned around, his eyes quizzical—as if my hesitation were completely foreign to him, absurd.

I found myself backing away, toward the corner. It was more an alley than a street, and I continued to hover beside the entrance, the familiar emptiness rising in my belly.

Francesco approached, and his fingers grazed mine—so gently that I suddenly let go and embraced the fear. That's all you can do after a while. Fear doesn't go away until you give in to it.

Somewhere in the distance a woman's voice bellowed indecipherable words. And as we moved deeper into the darkness, Francesco's hand rose up to my wrist, over the sleeve to my elbow, where his fingers lingered. Up close, he had a gruff face—hard edges, a Roman nose that looked as if it had been in one too many fights.

He stopped in the darkness, very close to a windowless wall. The main street was barely visible at one end of the alley, the other end completely shrouded in darkness. I let him take my shoulders and move me delicately toward the wall.

His arms curled around me, and suddenly his lips were against mine, his mustache brushing my skin softly as his mouth opened. He tasted of cigarettes and garlic. A faint scent of basil lingered on the fingers that stroked my face. As he pressed more firmly against me, my back arched into the smooth masonry of the wall. I wondered at the age of the stone behind me, how many other secret lovers had stood here over the centuries, hidden from public view.

I wish I could say I thought of you as Francesco's hand traced a line gently down my side, as his tongue darted in and out of my mouth. I wish I could say that I imagined your hands, your tongue, your hips holding me against the wall. But at that moment, there was no memory—no cognizance of past or future. As I closed my eyes and leaned back, letting the moment wash over me, there was only the moment—one moment at a time. Now fingers stroking my skin, now teeth nibbling at my lip, now breath warm in my ear. There was only now, an endless now.

Francesco turned his head down, and my lips fell to his neck, the surprising sting of tomato sauce on his skin. A drop must have splashed on him as he was carrying a plate through the restaurant—too small to notice by eye, but pungent on the tongue. I sucked at it, the sweetness of the tomato, the acidity underneath that revealed a touch of balsamic.

And all at once, the air was full of scents wafting from open windows throughout the neighborhood. Somewhere, meat was sautéing. Somewhere else, chopped herbs caught a draft of air and whispered through the alley. It was late, past dinnertime even for Italy, but the aromas lingered, like the echoes of Puccini that had stayed with me a couple of weeks earlier, as I skipped down the steps of the opera house in Rome on the way back to my hotel.

Francesco's hand found its way to my belt, loosened my pants, worked itself inside. I gasped and bit into his neck. The tomato was gone now, only salt playing on my tongue.

And as I reached down to return the favor, holding him in one hand, he cried out. *"Sì, sì,"* he murmured. The Italian reasserted itself, driving away the halting English words that had defined his seduction of me.

He became more verbal, but the words spilled forth too quickly for my comprehension. It was just music now, the unmistakable rhythm of Italian, backdrop to the scents in the air, the pressure of his hand, the insistent darkness.

When we were done, when the air thinned around us and breath came more easily, he leaned softly into me and tenderly pecked at my neck, my cheek, my lips. And the English returned, but only in a whisper. "You are beautiful man," he said, lips against my ear.

The old Italian flattery, even now. I could only smile. I feared opening my eyes, seeing the world again. I had felt so at home in the dark.

"When do you leave Venezia?" he asked as we reemerged into the blue light of the street.

"In a couple of days," I said. "Then home to New York."

"We meet again?" he asked. His eyebrows lifted, hairy caterpillars.

"Forse," I said. Now it was my turn to practice a new language.

"I am here," he said, nodding toward the restaurant.

"Sì." I knew where to find him.

"I live this way," he said, pointing to the left.

"My hotel is that way," I replied with a chuckle, gesturing toward the right. Not that it mattered. *"Buona notte,"* I said.

He smiled broadly, revealing large white teeth. *"Buona notte."*

I waved from a few yards down the street, and watched as he turned around and headed on his way.

Piazza San Marco, I soon realized, is best at night, when you're a little tipsy and the world is gorgeous. I found it, once again, led only by the sporadic signs and my own instinct. My feet tapped out a rhythm on the gray and ivory stones of the square, enclosed by the Basilica, the Palazzo Dogale, the majestic and phallic campanile, the open-air cafés all closed for the night.

The crowds had thinned, stragglers meandering through the streets to capture one last glimpse of beauty. Even the pigeons had resigned themselves to the coming quiet, no more tourists holding handfuls of bread, begging to be swarmed.

There was a sadness in the few faces that turned to me, those whose eyes were not inaccessible, gazing up at the palace or down at the stones. Their cheeks looked softer than in the day, their eyes more liquid. They walked past me now with the heaviness of endings, no longer denying—unable to deny—the fact that time is the only winner in life. Time takes everything away.

The wine was still swirling in my head, the memory of Francesco's lips still dancing on my neck. The campanile vibrated, as if it were really the Tower of Pisa trying desperately to right itself, and the sky was alive with stars that lit the space.

I walked toward the edge of the piazza, where brackish water lapped at the stones. Beneath my feet, ancient, now petrified trees had been driven deep into the muck, and a city—an absurdly beautiful city—had been built upon that perilous foundation. It was, of course, ridiculous—romantic less in the sentimental sense than in the grand style of poets. On my first day in Rome I had headed directly to Keats's house, beside the pink stone of the Spanish Steps. There, in a glass case, was the poet's death mask—alabaster white, surprisingly small, capturing a gentle expression of peace, a belief in something beyond the daily suffering of the world—Xanadu, or long-dead figures dancing on an ancient urn. Keats must have loved Venice, too, I thought now.

I turned around and ran back to the middle of the square. The buildings seemed to close in on me—all I could really see were vague shapes and twinkling lights. Any minute now, I thought, this whole exquisite place might sink back into the mud. Someday, like everything else on the planet, it would all be gone.

In the middle of Piazza San Marco, I stopped and looked up at the sky, the stars that, to my drunken eyes, seemed now to tumble down to earth. And I laughed. Boldly, loudly, my laughter echoed through the empty square.

It's a wonder you didn't hear it.

HERMAN'S KOSHER DELI
DANIEL M. JAFFE

I was skeptical when Dr. Rosa Handelmeyer first brought me to California for sex angel training. At age seventy-two, could this old dog really learn new tricks?

"You've been coping on your own long enough," she explained, referring to the sad fact that I hadn't known I was a sex angel until recently. Ever since my bar mitzvah when, without my awareness, I was anointed a sex angel, I'd been sustaining assaults from men of all ages. "You've got to get a better handle on the rights and responsibilities of those who spread sexual joy," said Dr. Handelmeyer. "First off, you've got to get a regular job because sex angeling doesn't pay—charitable work never does, and you can't rely on Social Security."

Given my love of pastrami, Dr. Handelmeyer arranged a job for me at Herman's Kosher Deli in West Hollywood. After all, she explained, "if you know how to chow down on meat, you automatically know how to dish it out. Besides, working with people and temptation all day will give you practice managing your skills." Whatever the good doctor advised, I'd do.

That first morning at Herman's Kosher Deli, I sat in Herman's office while he stood over me, breathing heavily on my neck as I filled out new-employee paperwork. Herman said he was in his eighties, but didn't look a day under a hundred.

With a skeletal arm around my shoulder (he kept tweaking my nipple, and I kept swatting his hand away), he took me out of his office and into the restaurant proper to introduce me around. We first encountered the deli's one-and-only waitress, Sadie. Pink uniform, black stockings, sensible white shoes, greasy gray hair bunned into a black hairnet. "Just don't steal my tips," she said while picking her teeth with a chipped fingernail, "and we'll get along fine, you shmuck." Irma, the cashier, Sadie's identical twin sister but with even more wrinkles under her cracked makeup, introduced herself with, "I catch your fingers in the till, you putz, I shove 'em into the meat slicer." Friendly. To tell the truth, I was used to such disdain from women. The sexual energy I radiated toward men had the side effect of irritating women like steel wool panties, except, of course, for Dr. Rosa Handelmeyer, my sex angel mentor.

Then Herman led me through creaky swinging doors to the kitchen, patting my butt as he did so, and introduced me to the mix of older Russian Jewish immigrant cooks and younger Mexican immigrant sous-chefs. A mix of khellos and holas. Lots of smiles. Lots of leers. Lots of crotch scratching. Lots of tongues sliding between lips. Herman apparently noticed—he put a hand over my crotch and growled, "Anyone bothers my deli counter man and you're fired." Hostile. I'd grown accustomed to this sort of reaction from men in charge, as if their authority entitled them to possession of all my services.

Out front behind the deli counter, Herman himself tied a white apron around my waist, his stubby fingers sliding down my butt and squeezing while he studied my eyes as if to check if I'd object. You might think a man like me in his seventies would be grateful for a grope, even from a snake in his eighties (or hundreds) like Herman. Maybe if I'd been an ordinary, sexually invisible seventy-two-year-old man. But after a lifetime fending off every man with dick and balls (and even a few eunuchs—don't ask), this sort of attention wearied me. As Dr. Handelmeyer knew, I needed to practice controlling my energies and charitable givings.

"Anything you need during the day," said Herman, "you let me know. Anything." He winked.

In the distance, a young man with thick red hair flexed muscles beneath his white shirt. As he lifted empty plates from tables into a gray plastic tub, he gave me the eye. "Our busboy, Charlie," said Herman. "Working his way through college. Clears tables. No reason for the two of you to interact. Not ever."

Old stags never like young bucks.

That first lunch hour—the customers' lunch hour, not mine—I was kept really busy behind the deli counter, what with the take-out customers ordering sandwiches and Sadie dropping off sandwich tickets for the sit-down customers. I could barely keep up. Sadie snapped at me for my slowness, women customers uniformly insisted I sliced the corned beef too thin, smeared on too much mustard, or looked so sweaty I made them lose their appetites. Irma kept yelling across the lobby from the cash register that I was marking wrong prices on the brown paper sandwich bags, which I don't think was true.

After one look at me, each of the men take-out customers could barely stammer out their orders and drooled so much onto the top of my deli counter that my cleaning sponges got soaked. They pressed their erections so hard against the front of my deli counter the glass nearly cracked. How much was I being paid an hour? I kept sighing and reminding myself that my real purpose here was to learn how to control my talents after a lifetime of disorganized, chaotic, constantly exhausting homo-sex.

At my 3 p.m. lunch break, I snuck into the kitchen storage room, huddled in a corner with a roasted chicken leg, and hunkered down onto a crate of cling peach jars for a moment of peace that lasted all of two minutes until one of the Russian cooks walked in looking for chicken fat from the freezer. His grin revealed a mouth of gold-capped teeth; I smiled back. He stepped in front of me with his crotch at my face level. No point in resisting because I knew he'd hound me until he got what he wanted, so I set my half-eaten chicken leg on a can of beans, unzipped him, and complied. *"Spasibo,"* he grunted in thanks, and returned to the kitchen.

No sooner had I popped open a can of ginger ale and done a quick gargle when the other Russian cook came in, apparently having been told by his buddy of today's storage room special. Another quickie, another *"Spasibo,"* another gargle.

I was glad to help out, but was this all there was to being a sex angel? Whoring for free, satisfying other men's lust whenever and however they wished with no regard to my gleaning any satisfaction from the experience? I thought my calling deeper than this. Two of Dr. Rosa Handelmeyer's related sex-angeling lessons came to mind: "We're angels in the nation's service. Suck it up and do what you have to." Rather cold. Then she added, "But never shut yourself down. If you do, you won't be able to relish the special times."

"Which kind of special times?" I asked in our most recent seminar. She gave that rueful smile of hers with the lift of the left eyebrow, and walked away.

I stood from my crate in the storage room, took another chomp on my chicken leg, and was about to step out when both Mexican sous-chefs stepped in. "You make Russians *muy* happy," said one, his wide face stretched in a smile, his dark eyes glistening with hope.

I winked and crouched down into position, but he lifted me to my feet. "No, *papi*, me." He dropped to his knees, unzipped me, and went to town while the other one grabbed my face in both hands, leaned forward for a kiss, slipped his tongue between my lips, and stroked the back of my neck. I was done in an instant. *"Chicos,"* I said, somewhat stunned by their generosity and tenderness. *"Mil gracias."*

"No, *papi*, *gracias a usted.*"

If only gringos understood such respect, my life would be way easier. The three of us hugged it out and the young men left.

So much for my lunch break. But what a great experience of multi-cultural LA.

Soon as I arrived back behind my deli counter, Herman showed up, a sad expression on his face. "I been looking for you. I thought we could share lunch in my office."

"Oh, I didn't realize. Well, maybe tomor—"

"I want company. Come with me now."

"But, Herman, I've left the deli counter for a good fifteen minutes already. We can't leave it unattended any longer."

"Irma!" barked Herman. "Get your fat butt off that cashier's stool and come work the deli counter."

"What? With my bursitis you think I'm gonna work that slicer?"

"Just keep track of orders, that's all. Our man here will be back at the counter in no time."

"And you want I should run back and forth to the cash register too, I bet."

"Blackjack, you win! Now go."

Grumbling and glaring at me, Irma waddled to the deli counter as Herman grabbed a bowl of chopped liver and led me through the restaurant to his office.

"Sit on my desk," he ordered. He was the boss, so I complied.

Holding the bowl of chopped liver in the crook of an arm, he continued, "Open."

"Thanks, but I already ate a chicken leg."

"I want to feed you chopped liver. Open!"

I sighed. It made sense that a restaurateur's fantasy was to feed. He shoved a fistful of chopped liver into my mouth and I chewed and swallowed. "That's the way," he said, breathing hard. "Take it just like that."

He set the bowl down on his paper-strewn desk, unzipped, took out quite the shlong, I must say, and jerked. With his free hand, he scooped another mound of chopped liver and held it in front of my mouth. "Eat my meat," he mumbled.

"Herman," I protested gently. "You think, maybe, I could get an onion roll with that?"

"Eat!"

I complied and his eyes began to glaze. Satisfying Herman was one of my greater challenges. He was a stringy pot roast of a man in desperate need of basting, one of those Southern California oldies who spent so much time in the sun, you could easily mistake him for a crocodile handbag.

"Rattle for me, you old bag of bones," he said.

What? This carcass nearly ready for soup was calling *me* an old bag of bones?

"Rattle for me!" he repeated.

This was a new one, but Dr. Handelmeyer taught that it was our sex angel duty "to remember that any and all fantasies are valid."

"Rattle rattle," I said.

"More."

"Rattle rattle rattle. Clang clang clang."

"More, more!"

"Jingle jangle go my marrow bones."

"Yes!" gasped Herman. "Yes!"

"Clickity clack clickity clack—all my bones banging together in an aluminum soup pot, jostling and clattering and soaking and boiling until their marrow gets tender so you can suck out every soft sweet bit of mush."

"Ahh!" he cried, spurting all over the papers on his desk. "Ahh!"

I sat there, silent and still, waiting to see how he wanted the fantasy to end.

"You're disgusting," Herman said, smearing the remaining chopped liver all over my face. "Disgusting." He leaned forward, licked the chopped liver off my eyes. "Never leave me," he whispered, "promise you'll stay, you decrepit skeleton."

"Dignity comes from knowing that one has rendered meaningful service," explained Dr. Rosa Handelmeyer, "not necessarily from others' expression of respect, although respect is nice when we can get it."

"Yes, Herman, I'll stay." Hearing that, he burst into tears, wrapped his arms around me, wept on my shoulder. "You're a dream come true. After you clean up this mess, you can go back to your deli counter and I'll even trust you with staying late and closing the restaurant by yourself this evening so I can pick up my wife from her karate class."

"You're so generous, Herman."

"That's just the kind of boss I am." He left his office.

After cleaning everything up with paper towels—the come-covered payroll records on his desk would simply have to air dry a little crusty—I went back to my deli case where Irma's face was red as beet borscht. "The boss's new favorite gets to eat lunch in the office while the rest of us have to make do with the storage room."

"Hey," I said, a little ticked off by now, "If you wanna trade places, you got a deal." I sneezed a wad of chopped liver smack onto her pink uniform.

She looked down, scraped off the chopped liver with her fingernail, and looked up at me with an expression of compassion I'd seen only in Rubens altarpieces. "He chopped livered you?"

I nodded.

"Oh, you poor man." She hugged me tight, pressing her breasts flat against my chest. "He used to do that to me until he decided I wasn't good-looking enough anymore. Sadie!" she cried out, waving over her identical twin sister. "Sadie, Herman just chopped livered the new deli man."

"No!" said Sadie. "Herman's gone queer?"

Such was the effect I had on all men, regardless of their labeled orientations prior to our meeting. "Sexuality," I said, "is a continuum, you know." Dr. Rosa Handelmeyer always said "we should never miss a chance to educate."

"Did he make you do the bone thing?" Sadie asked.

"What bone thing?" asked Irma.

Sadie blushed.

"Is there something you never told me?" Irma asked. And so began an argument over Herman having stopped chopped livering Irma once she turned sixty and turning to Sadie for boning. "Jealousy is the scourge of human experience," instructed Dr. Rosa Handelmeyer.

I was sorry the women were upset, but at least they no longer hated me. "Nothing builds camaraderie like shared oppression," said Dr. Rosa Handelmeyer, "sexual or otherwise."

It was now close to 5 p.m. and dinner business picked up. We all had to return to our stations. As with the lunch crowd, my dinner deli crowd was a mix of snarling women and goofily grinning men.

By the time we were just fifteen minutes shy of closing, I felt beat.

Then a shriveled prune of a blue-haired lady approached my deli case. (It must be the preservative in deli meats that keeps all these oldies going.) "So, tell me," she said with a Central European Jewish accent. "You're new here?"

"Yes, ma'am."

"New—shmoo. So I'll tell you vhat I vhant so you shouldn't forget. I come every day."

"So do I," I mumbled, trying to make a joke for myself.

"Vhat you say?" she said, cupping an ear. "This hearing aid I got is crap."

"Nothing, ma'am. How can I help you?"

"Roast beef sandvich, but thin and tender, you know? My dentures, they can't handle thick and tough. Lots of mayo."

I nodded and turned to my meat slicer while this crone watched from across the deli case, nodding in approval. But just as I was slathering on the mayo, I felt a hand on my zipper. I looked down and—wow, it was the hunky young redheaded busboy. Apparently, he'd snuck around the refrigerated glass deli case without my noticing, and was hidden from the old lady's view by piles of knishes. Before I could pull away, he had me in his mouth.

"Vhy you stop my sandvich making?" demanded my customer. "I'm very hungry. You vill finish, please, young man."

To this Bride of Methuselah, I was a young man. I had to get the kid off me or there was no way I'd be able to finish the old lady's order. So I dropped the mayo knife—"oops!"—and as the clatter startled the kid, I slipped out of his mouth, crouched down, kissed him on those lips that tasted like me, and whispered, "If you can control yourself until closing time, I promise to give you all you can handle."

His eyes widened bigger than prunes in fruit compote and he nodded and crawled away, whispering, "I'm Charlie and I'm yours."

Picking up the mayo knife, I stood and smiled at my customer, who said, "You gonna vash that filthy thing, right?"

I admit to being startled for a moment until I realized she was referring to the fallen mayo knife and not my dangling participle. Tucking myself back in my pants, I washed the knife in the sink, mayoed her roast beef, wrapped the sandwich up in brown paper, and handed it to her.

"You handled that very well," said the customer, suddenly without accent. She dug fingernails into the flesh just below her hairline, then proceeded to tear her face off like they do in horror movies. But instead of revealing some lizard face, she revealed…

"Dr. Rosa Handelmeyer!"

"I'm very proud of you," she said, smacking her lips and stretching her smile to get her face back into shape. "You took wonderful control of the sex situation with that busboy. You're on your way to becoming a model sex angel."

"This was a test?"

"Not really, more an observation. Charlie behaved on his own. I was just here to watch."

"You mean you could see what was going on behind the potato knishes?"

"I am a PhD, after all."

That explains a lot.

"After hours," she said, unwrapping the roast beef sandwich, "be sure not just to perform your sex angel duties for that young man, but to enjoy them. He's a sweetheart, I can tell, and you deserve him."

"Thank you, Doctor."

She winked, gave that rueful smile of hers with the lift of the left eyebrow, and took a bite. "Mmm, good sandwich. See you at the next seminar." And she left.

"Here are the keys," said Herman, waltzing up to my deli case and presenting them to me with a ceremonious flourish. "The busboy's still loading the dishwasher, but I gotta go pick up Mrs. Herman. Once the busboy's done, you can go, you sexy skeleton, you. Woof!"

I forced a wan smile.

Waiting for Charlie to come out front, I dusted the shelf containing pickle and sauerkraut jars, polished the meat slicer, scraped dried precome dribbles off the front of my glass deli case (which customer had been so bold as to unzip right then and there?). In the silence of the restaurant, I heard the kitchen's swinging doors creak, but pretended not to.

I wanted Charlie not just because he was so adorable and because he really knew how to use that tongue of his, but because he represented an achievement for me. Finally, I'd been able to take control of my sex powers, finally I'd been able to negotiate a time and place of my choosing. And it all came about so naturally. Charlie would be my reward.

The soft puppy pad sound of knees crawling around the deli case, the gentle lift of my apron, and there he was, nuzzling my crotch while reaching around and untying my apron in back. Off with my black slacks and tighty whities, white shirt and sweaty undershirt. Charlie gently sucked in my left ball, which hangs a good deal lower than my right, stroked its underside with his tongue, slapped my increasing hardness against his face. He muttered, "Your white pubes are a total turn-on, Daddy."

"Daddy's good boy," I said to this man who might well have been the quarterback of a college football team. I stroked his red hair, and he whimpered. "Daddy's good boy," I repeated, and he whimpered louder, pressed the side of his face against my lower belly, reached around and squeezed me tight. This is the part of sex angeling I like best but rarely get to experience, the affection part, the connection. As Dr. Rosa Handelmeyer taught: "Despite what proctologists say, the way to a man's soul is not through his anus, but through his heart."

I knelt onto the white-speckled linoleum floor, rested Charlie's curly-haired head onto my shoulder, and we held one another, daddy and boy sharing a moment of intimate bonding.

With the lightest of strokes, I ran my fingertips along the white shirt still covering his granite back. I squeezed him to me, he lifted his head, kissed me full on the lips, slid his tongue deep, and moaned as his hands roamed and groped me. I pulled back and ordered, in my lowest baritone of authority: "Take off your clothes, boy."

"Yes sir," Charlie said, scrambling to comply. Off with his shirt, off with his slacks, off with boxers and socks. He positioned himself before me on all fours, his haunches nearly in my face. "Please sir, if you would—mayo me."

And so I stood, grabbed the gallon jar of Hellmann's from the refrigerated deli case, opened it, scooped out a gob, and shoved as much of the cold goo as I could up his butt. He shivered, muttering, "Yes, Daddy, yes. Make me take it."

Another palmful of mayo, then another, and then he said, "Please Daddy, make me your kosher pig."

Ever a sucker for irony, I slapped those hindquarters, slapped them repeatedly with my mayo-greased hands, then positioned myself behind him, fumbled a condom from my apron pocket (I was nothing if not ever ready), and slid slowly in. The mayo had melted, of course, and was oozing out of him. He felt so slick and warm that I had to distract myself or—you know. Thinking about lamb chops, kasha varnishkas, and schav borscht slowed my rush toward the finish line, but then my sexed-up mind drifted to matzoh balls, stuffed cabbage, and thick juicy dill pickles so firm the way they glide between the lips—I pulled out.

"Don't stop, Daddy," begged Charlie. "Please!" He turned his head to me, revealed desperate eyes.

I slid back in.

"Yes, Daddy, yes. Pork me good. Go hog wild!"

I'm a tad embarrassed to admit that this blaspheming in a kosher deli made me thrust all the harder. Charlie snorted and oinked, I slapped his ham hocks, me an angel sent to earth to spread joy to mankind, an angel servicing a soul like a heathen Sodoming his Gomorrah, primitive and ancient, each of my thrusts banging Charlie's head against the glass deli case, each slap of my balls on his ass an affirmation of my masculinity and his, each man giving what the other man needed, all thanks to the teachings of Dr. Rosa Handelmeyer and the slick properties of mayo.

"Now!" I yelled as I shuddered inside him.

"Now!" he screamed while creaming the linoleum.

He collapsed, and I onto him. My Charlie. I whispered sweet words of ownership and he whimpered as he had before. He belonged to me now, to my psyche, to the notchings on my nonexistent, imaginary angel wings. My Charlie squeezed me gently out, rolled onto his back, pulled me to his broad hairless chest, and held me close, rocked. Who was the daddy now? How exquisite the interchangeability of men, the fluidity of soul roles regardless of the physical, the ability of two to soothe as one. "Be selfish," Dr. Rosa Handelmeyer taught, "in order to be selfless. Take what you need so as to give what is needed."

I knew, as I felt Charlie's fingertips lovingly trace the wrinkled furrows of my forehead, that I would continue in this job at Herman's Kosher Deli for as long as I could. Sure, I'd have to accommodate Herman's chopped liver and skeleton fetishes, but that was my duty as a sex angel. As was my task to satisfy the assorted male kitchen staff. But I had now gained a sense of how to impose comfortable limits on my services. And I'd found accommodation with Sadie and Irma, a sympathetic understanding that might lead to friendship. Most of all, I'd found my Charlie, every daddy's dream boy. A place to belong, a place to be myself, a place I could take on my own terms.

I was finally taking charge of my own life. It had taken only seventy-two years.

Rick's Greasy (S)poon
Hank Edwards

The smell of fried food hit him the minute he unlocked the door. It wasn't a bad smell, not really. It was actually comforting, like coming home. Which, Dave had to admit, was exactly what he was doing.

He stepped fully through the door of the diner and let it swing shut behind him. Seeing the place empty in the middle of the day like this left a cold ache in Dave's chest. He liked to remember it as it had been when he was growing up: busy, loud, and filled with the heady aroma of diner food.

With his father, Rick, right in the middle of it all.

But his father was gone now, and Dave had inherited the diner. His sister in Chicago was busy with her four children and her career as a marketing company vice president, and his two brothers were in Florida trying to launch their own Jet Ski rental business. So each of his siblings had signed the documents to turn the diner over to Dave and let him do with it what he wanted. They had all put their time into working at the place when growing up, just as Dave had himself, and wanted no further part of it.

He walked through the diner, running a fingertip over the dusty tabletops. Growing up, he had worked hard all day, most every day, at the diner, but Dave had been glad to have the chance to spend more time with his father. Each of the kids had put in time at the diner once they reached the age of thirteen, and his siblings, all at least six years older than Dave, liked to tease him that the only reason he had been conceived was so Rick would have more free labor when the other three had gone off to college.

But Dave didn't care. He had seen how happy and outgoing his father had been in the diner. He knew how good it had made Rick feel to see people on a regular basis, get to know them and their families, feed them all good food at a reasonable price, and still bring home a nice profit for his own family. Dave had been happy to be even a small part of that success.

The place had been locked up tight for months while his father's will had wound its way through probate, and then the legal documents to transfer full ownership of the diner to Dave had had to be drafted and reviewed and updated and reviewed and finally signed by all surviving heirs. Now Rick's Greasy Spoon was Dave's, all his, and he could clean it up and sell it, or clean it up and run it. Either way he knew one thing: He was going to have to clean it up.

Since he had come back home and moved into his father's house, Dave realized he'd missed Garrettville. Sure it was just a tiny dot on the bottom of the state of Wyoming, near the corners of Utah and Colorado, but it was where he had grown up, and those places a person grew up, no matter how dry, green, cold, or hot, stayed inside them all their lives.

There was no one back in Boston for him, not anymore. Not since Robert had decided he wanted someone younger and gainfully employed. Like it had been Dave's fault his company had released almost half of their in-house support staff a year ago. Dave had managed on unemployment and odd tech jobs to pay the rent and most of the utilities—who needed hundreds of cable channels anyway?—until he had received the call that his dad had had a heart attack and was in cardiac intensive care.

The flight home had been a blur and the three weeks his father had lingered seemed to drag on forever while simultaneously going by much too fast. At the end of it all, Rick had passed away without ever really regaining consciousness, and all four kids had been gathered by his bed. After the funeral, his siblings had returned to their homes and Dave had moved into his father's house, long since paid for, and hired Riley, a college-aged neighbor, to pack up his belongings back in Boston and drive his car out to him.

And now he stood in the middle of Rick's Greasy Spoon, the place that had provided meals and a decent standard of living for his family. His parents were both dead and he was really, truly, alone in the world.

A string of high-pitched barks took Dave to the window and he peered through the dusty glass to where he had parked his car at the angle-in spot just outside the diner. Dark, bright eyes inside a tan face peered through the windshield and into the diner, looking right at him. It was Zeus, his father's Yorkshire Terrier that Dave had inherited along with the diner. Well, maybe he wasn't entirely alone.

When Zeus saw Dave looking out at him, he threw back his head and let out a volley of yelping barks that finally drew Dave out to the car.

"Okay, okay, okay," Dave grumbled. He unlocked the door and picked up the wriggling Yorkie. "I know you love this place, too. Come on, let's go poke around."

Zeus wagged his tiny tail in response. Dave stepped back inside the diner and locked the door behind him before setting Zeus on the floor. The dog let out an excited yip and ran the length of the counter, slaloming around the stools bolted to the floor as his nails clicked against the linoleum. Zeus skidded around the end of the counter and disappeared, barking as he ran into the kitchen.

"Zeus!" Dave hurried after the dog, the cold ache within his chest expanding and pushing a ball of grief up his throat. He knew, without a doubt, that Zeus had been waiting to come back inside the diner to look for Rick. The dog had often come to the diner with Rick, probably more than the health department cared to know about, and Zeus knew Rick had spent most of his time in the kitchen.

Dave found the little dog sniffing around the bottom of the grill, tiny feet cushioned by the rubber mat Rick had laid there to take some pressure off his back. The imprints of Rick's large shoes remained, a spooky sight to Dave, as if the spirit of his father still slaved away in front of the grill.

"Hey, Zeus," Dave said, his voice soft as he leaned in the door to the kitchen.

Zeus turned twice and sat directly between the shoe imprints, then lifted dark, bright eyes to look at Dave and whined quietly.

"I know, buddy. I miss him, too."

Dave walked around the kitchen, noting the various items that needed to be fixed, cleaned, or replaced, until his mental list overwhelmed him. He let out a breath, scooped up Zeus, and smiled when the dog licked his chin. "Let's go out and get some bleach and gloves and stuff and come back here to clean this place up. What do you say to that?"

Zeus barked and wagged his tail and Dave took that as a yes, so he left the diner with the dog in his arms and locked it up tight. It was going to take a lot of work to get the diner ready to open, but Dave had time and, it appeared, a grieving Yorkie to help him out. And maybe Dave could convince Ava, the woman who had waitressed at the diner for more than twenty-five years, to come back and help him get the business running again.

Sliding in behind the wheel of his old Cavalier, Dave ducked his head to look up through the windshield at the neon letters that stood dark and sullen in the September sunshine. He smiled and said, "Rick's Greasy Spoon. Don't worry, Dad, I won't go renaming it on you."

❖

Dave stood in the early morning light across the street from the diner, scowling at the place with his arms crossed. He had switched on the sign, red neon letters that spelled out Rick's Greasy Spoon. But the "S" in Spoon flickered and went dark, leaving it Rick's Greasy poon, something Dave was sure would get a lot of comments, if not from the diner's regulars, most likely from the Garrettville high school kids.

The sound of a laboring truck engine caught his attention and Dave turned his head to look down the street. A mud-splattered pickup rattled to a stop at the curb in front of Polly's Place, the only other diner in town, and Dave sighed. Another customer he was losing to Polly Walker. He was about to turn back to his assessment of the front of the diner when the pickup truck's driver stepped out of the cab and snagged his full attention.

The man was tall, his broad shoulders filling the tan Carhartt jacket he wore like an easy second skin, and a faded ball cap perched atop his head. From his distance, all Dave could see of the man's features was a square jaw covered with stubble and a round ass beneath denim worn almost white by the number of washings. As Dave watched, the driver reached into the bed of the pickup and brought up two leafy green plants, then turned to step inside Polly's Place.

Dave wondered if the driver was going to order breakfast, a typical grease-laden meal at Polly's, and brought his own lettuce to give it a healthy side dish. He shrugged to himself, turned to glare at the accidentally inappropriate sign over his own diner, then crossed the street to step inside. Zeus trotted up to paw at his calf and Dave bent down to scoop up the dog, absentmindedly scratching the Yorkie's head as he looked around the place. There was still cleaning to be done, and no one to do it but himself, so he might as well get to it.

Sometime later, the sound of the bell above the diner's door and Zeus's excited yapping brought Dave out of the kitchen. He wore the only gloves he had been able to find at the local store: rubber dishwashing gloves, complete with tapered yellow fingers, pink painted nails, and a rubber diamond ring around the left ring finger. He was dirty, sweaty, starved, and about fifteen minutes away from becoming stark raving mad.

But the man who crouched just inside the diner door to scratch an obviously ecstatic Zeus behind the ears made Dave stop in his tracks. It was the pickup truck driver he had seen go into Polly's Place, and up close he was even more handsome than Dave had thought. At the sight of him, in his Carhartt jacket, ball cap, and scuffed-up work boots, not to mention the few days' worth of dark blond beard that covered his square jaw, Dave let out an involuntary moan. The visitor raised chocolate brown eyes that seemed to burn right into Dave's own blue ones, and flashed a smile full of even white teeth.

"Hi there," the man rumbled as Zeus licked his thick, strong fingers.

Dave cleared his throat and, trying not to envy Zeus too much, lifted a hand to wipe his forehead. He realized he still wore the feminine yellow gloves and quickly peeled them off, turning to toss them back into the kitchen. He smiled and shrugged, blowing out a breath as he said, "It was the only pair of gloves they had left at Earl's."

The man stood up to his full height of over six foot and grinned at Dave. "Yeah, Earl doesn't get much call for rubber gloves."

Dave rolled his eyes. "Yeah. Probably not."

Being careful not to step on Zeus, the visitor closed the distance between them and stuck out his hand. "Ben Ellerby."

"Dave Brighton."

Ben narrowed his eyes as he shook Dave's hand. "You're one of Rick's kids?"

Dave nodded as he released Ben's hand. "Yeah. I'm the youngest."

"I'm sorry for your loss," Ben rumbled. "Rick was a really good man."

A ball of grief seemed to be stuck high in his chest, and Dave cleared his throat as he looked around the diner, trying not to see the image of his father behind the counter, standing by the booths laughing with his regulars, or coming in the door with a smile on his face. When he found his voice, he said, "Thanks, I appreciate it."

"You from down in Florida?" Ben asked.

Dave shook his head. "Boston."

"Oh." Ben nodded and folded his arms over his broad chest. "Boston, huh?"

Dave let out a breath and glanced away, feeling that familiar pang of guilt at realizing his father did not talk about him much, most likely because he had been ashamed of his lifestyle. He pushed those feelings aside, nothing to be done with them now, and looked Ben in the eye again. "I know my dad didn't talk about me much. You don't have to pretend like you know all about me."

"Actually, your dad mentioned you more times than I can count," Ben said, his deep voice rumbling into Dave's chest and snuggling up against his heart. "I just never caught what city you lived in. You were on an in-house technical service team or something out there, right? For a bank?"

The heat of his blush caught Dave off guard and, to distract himself from it, he crouched down to pick up Zeus, who had started to paw at his leg. "Um, yeah. That's right. Sorry, it's been a long day and I didn't think—Well, it was out of line for me to say that to you, I'm sorry."

Ben was quiet as he looked him over. "The 'S' in your sign is out. You know that?"

Dave sighed and nodded. "So it reads Rick's Greasy poon? Yeah, I've seen it. It's on my list."

Ben looked around, then rested his eyes back on Dave. "Long list?"

"Longer than Santa's," Dave said with a sigh.

A smirk quirked up the corner of Ben's mouth. "The naughty or nice list?"

Dave smirked back. "Which one's longer?"

"Good point. So, you opening soon?"

A wave of exhaustion rolled over Dave and he felt his shoulders slump as his energy seemed to drain down his body and out through the soles of his shoes into the floor of the diner. "Well, I hope to. But I still need to figure some things out first."

"Yeah?" Ben shifted his weight and dropped his gaze. "Things like which food suppliers you're going with?"

Dave's exhaustion deepened. He hadn't considered anything that specific. "Well, no, hadn't gotten there yet. That list just keeps getting longer and longer." He gave Ben a tired smile.

"Sorry."

"No worries. It needs to be decided on." Dave set Zeus on the floor and turned to make a notation on the legal pad he kept on the counter. "I don't suppose you know someone reasonable?"

"Actually, I know a great person to use for produce."

"Oh yeah? Who's that?"

"Little place down the road here called Ellerby Farms."

Dave turned to look at Ben, noting the man's shy smile and hoping to see more of it. "Is that your farm?"

"Yeah, it is. I didn't know if you were a locavore or not, but thought I'd give it a shot."

Dave let out a surprised laugh. "Locavore? A werewolf?"

Ben's hearty laugh startled Dave and Zeus both. When he had regained his composure, Ben shook his head. "You're thinking lycanthrope. A locavore is someone who buys locally grown produce."

"Ah, got it." Dave chuckled to himself and shrugged. "Oops. Sorry."

"No problem, not many people know the term." Ben toed the floor, looking endearingly boyish. "So, what do you say?"

Dave narrowed his eyes. "You going to give me a good deal?"

Ben took a step closer and smiled. "I'll give you the best deal in town."

The tone of Ben's voice and the heat of the man's gaze made Dave's cock take notice. To hide his condition, Dave stepped behind the counter and busied himself doing nothing. "Well, I'll need to see how good a deal you're offering. How about a trial run?"

"I've got some stuff in the back of the truck," Ben offered. "I'll grab some things and you can sample their freshness yourself. Sound good?"

Dave leaned against the counter to press his hard-on against the edge and nodded. "Sounds good."

When Ben stepped out the door, Dave let out a breath and looked down at Zeus, who sat looking up at him. "Damn, Zeus. If I'd known the farmers around here looked like that, I'd have moved back home years ago."

❖

"This is pretty damn embarrassing, you know," Dave said.

Ben frowned at him across the table. "What is?"

Dave threw out his arms. "I own this diner, and here you made me lunch."

A shrug lifted Ben's broad shoulders. "Yeah? What about it?"

"It's just, I dunno, ironic, isn't it?"

"It's just a simple salad and some stir fry." Ben smirked at him. "It's not like I could afford to get you a diamond ring like the one on your pretty rubber glove."

A flush of embarrassment warmed Dave's cheeks, but he had to laugh. "Nice. Just had to bring that up again, didn't you?" He stabbed a few pieces of stir-fried zucchini and bit into them.

"Well, it is a pretty big ring."

Dave grinned in spite of his embarrassment. "Yes, yes it is."

Ben smirked. "Besides, I wanted you to see just how fresh my produce is, and the only way to do that is to eat it, right?"

"Well, ain't this cozy?"

The voice was low and ugly, almost a snarl, and the sound of it made them both jump. The day had turned gray and dark and Dave squinted into the shadows near the diner's door, wishing now he had turned on all the lights in the place. But he hadn't wanted people stopping to peer inside and maybe get the wrong idea about him and Ben, even though he very much wanted to act out that idea with the man.

A pulse of red light from the neon letters outside revealed a tall, heavy shape by the door. Dave squinted as a shiver ran up his spine; it was like a scene from a horror movie.

"Who is that?" Ben said, and something in the tone of his voice brought Zeus growling out from behind the counter.

With a heavy tread, the stranger stepped forward into the glow cast by the few lights Dave had left on. It was a woman, tall and heavy, with bright fuchsia hair pulled back into a ponytail, greasy red lipstick, and heavy blue eye shadow. Polly Walker, the owner of Polly's Place, the diner down the road, sneered at them.

"This what it takes to get a good price from you, Ellerby?" Polly asked. She looked at Dave and smirked again. "Your sign needs looking at. Or maybe not. Greasy poon seems to fit, for what I'm seeing."

"How'd you get in here?" Dave asked.

"Left the door unlocked." Polly glanced between them. "Seems you might have been a bit distracted."

"There's nothing going on here," Ben snapped, and Dave felt a cold knot of disappointment tighten in his gut. Nothing?

"Yeah, okay." Polly turned to the door, opened it, and looked back at them with a sneer. "I don't recall getting a free meal out of our agreement, Ben. Maybe I ain't got the right parts, though, huh?" She looked down at Zeus, who stood a foot away, barking and snarling up at her. "Keep your rat on a leash or it might get its neck snapped in a trap."

"Zeus, come here," Dave called, hoping his voice didn't sound as frightened and sad as he felt.

"Your father was a good man," Polly said. "He made a great pot roast. I respected the hell out of him, and I'm glad he didn't live to see you peddle your wares like this here in his diner."

She left and the door sighed shut behind her. Ben and Dave looked at one another as Zeus growled low in his throat.

"I bet she's not a very good tipper," Ben said, and Dave snorted a laugh.

They laughed quietly together a little and then Dave stopped as he had a thought. "Oh shit."

Ben's expression turned serious and he leaned in over the table. "What? You're not taking what she said seriously, are you?"

Dave shook his head. "No. I just realized that I have no idea how to make any of my father's dishes." A wave of nausea rolled through him and he put his head in his hands as he stared down at the plate of food he no longer wanted. "Oh my God. How am I going to do this? I'm not a cook. I can boil water and only sometimes make microwave popcorn without burning it."

"Your dad didn't leave you a book of recipes?" Ben asked, his voice gentle and soothing.

"No. I mean, nothing was mentioned in his will or anything. And he never came around after his heart attack to tell me anything." Dave took a shaky breath and sat back in the booth, lifting his wide-eyed gaze to Ben's face. "I'm fucked."

❖

Having lost his appetite, Dave carried his dishes into the kitchen. He leaned on the counter and stared down into the stainless steel sink. Without a recipe book, what was he going to do? He had no idea how to recreate his father's dishes.

Ben came up behind him, standing close enough for his body heat to warm Dave's back. "You okay?"

Dave sighed but didn't turn to look at him. "Yeah. I'm fine. I just don't know what I'm going to do. I was hoping to open the diner next week, but if there isn't any food I can prepare, well, then what's the point?"

"Look around the house again maybe?" Ben squeezed his shoulder and Dave's cock responded even as his spirit sagged.

Dave turned to face Ben, folded his arms over his chest, and shrugged. "I guess I could. I haven't really gone through the place with that in mind, you know?" He shook his head and dropped his gaze to the floor. "It still feels weird to be living there with all of his furniture and belongings, hell, I've even got his dog."

"Hey."

Dave raised his eyes to look the man in the face. Ben's expression was serious as he leaned in to rest his hands on the edge of the sink to either side of Dave.

"I can help you look for it," Ben said. "If you want me to."

Dave swallowed hard and tried to ignore his throbbing length of cock. Ben might not be coming on to him; he might just be a close talker. Besides, Ben was a hot, hunky farmer, there was no way, gay or straight, that he was single.

"That would be too much to ask," Dave managed to say. "I mean, you've got your farm to look after."

Ben grinned and leaned an inch closer. "I could spare an hour or two on occasion."

"Why would you do that?" Dave asked. "You barely know me."

Ben shrugged. "I like what I've seen so far. I think I'm a pretty good judge of character."

"You'd want to be seen consorting with the owner of Rick's greasy poon?"

The warm brush of Ben's breath was the only warning Dave received before he felt the soft press of Ben's lips against his. Ben's stubble grazed Dave's skin as his lips lingered, then the man pulled back. "I wouldn't mind being seen with the owner of Dave's greasy poon. Does that help?"

Dave smiled. "Yeah, I guess the other way is a little weird."

"A little."

They kissed again, longer, and when Ben's tongue traced the seam of Dave's lips, Dave opened to him. Ben's tongue twisted around Dave's, stroking, circling. Dave let all other thoughts fall away and focused on the kiss: the taste of olive oil on Ben's tongue, the scratch of whiskers against his skin, the heat of Ben's body as the man stepped up against him.

Dave felt the press of Ben's erection against his thigh and groaned low in his throat. The sound encouraged Ben to break their kiss and he pulled his head back, the bright kitchen lights illuminating the intensity of his gaze.

"It's been a while," Ben confessed, his voice deep, infused with lust.

"Me too," Dave replied.

"I really want to," Ben said. "With you." He raised his eyebrows. "If you're interested?"

"Definitely." Dave pulled him back for another kiss. He tugged the tail of Ben's henley out of his jeans and lifted the shirt to expose the broad expanse of Ben's chest, covered in dark blond hair.

"Oh fuck," Dave gasped as he ran his fingers through the fur and pinched Ben's hardened nipples. "You're gorgeous."

Ben kissed him before pulling the shirt over his head and then doing the same to Dave. Ben put his mouth on Dave's left nipple and rolled it between his teeth. Dave moaned, tipped his head back, and ran his hands up and down Ben's back.

"Look at you," Ben growled as he ran his hands over Dave's chest. "Dark hair over pale skin." He shook his head and looked Dave in the eyes. "It's like I ordered you out of a catalog."

They kissed, fumbling with belts, buttons, and zippers until each stood in his underwear, jeans piled around his shoes. Dave groped Ben's cock through the thin cotton of his white briefs, the material damp with precome and the prize underneath thick and long, making Dave's mouth water.

Ben's fingers slipped beneath the waistband of Dave's briefs, his skin rough from work on the farm. His touch sent sparks spinning through Dave's body, lighting up parts of him that had lain dormant for much too long. When Ben clutched Dave's cock in his rugged grip, Dave tipped his head back, breaking their kiss to let out a deep moan.

"You like that, huh?" Ben whispered.

"Yeah, I do."

Ben brought him close enough for a quick, tongue-filled kiss, then dropped to his knees. After a few licks that seemed to burn along the shaft of his cock, Ben opened wide and took Dave deep into his throat. The hot, wet tunnel of Ben's mouth closed around him, pushed a grunt up from the depths of his gut, and Dave leaned back against the counter, bracing himself with his hands as Ben worked him over.

After a few minutes, Dave put a hand against Ben's cheek, feeling the bristle of his stubble, and looked down into his brown eyes to say, "I want a turn."

They took some time to kick off their shoes and strip away the last of their clothes before swapping places. Dave knelt before Ben, using the pile of their clothes as a cushion for his knees. The broad, meaty head of Ben's cock hovered before him, slick and glistening, a runner of precome drooping toward the floor. Dave extended his tongue to catch the thick drop, followed it up to the fattened prize, and opened wide to swallow Ben to the root.

The taste of Ben exploded across his tongue, a unique blend of sweat, earth, and the bittersweet tang of precome, and Dave knew it would be a long time until he would be able to forget it. He sucked

Ben's long length, stopping now and then to purse his lips around the soft rounded tip. As he sucked, Dave stroked himself, feeling the approach of his orgasm but not wanting this to end just yet. He wanted, needed, for Ben to fuck him, to drive the big, powerful shaft deep inside him, possess him, take ownership of him. After the past weeks, hell, year, really, of Dave having to make so many life-changing decisions, he wanted someone else to run his body, even if it was only for a short time.

Letting Ben's cock slip from between his lips, Dave stroked the spit-slick length and lifted his gaze to look Ben in the eye. "I want you to fuck me."

Ben smirked, then looked disappointed. "I don't have a condom."

Dave looked up at him, into the man's eyes, and asked, "Are you safe?"

Ben nodded. "Tested last year and passed. Nobody since then."

"Same here," Dave said. "Question is, do we trust each other enough to believe that?"

Ben didn't say a word. He reached down to pull Dave to his feet and kissed him hard. As they kissed, Ben backed Dave up with slow steps, their cocks mashed between them, marking each other with sticky precome.

Dave's ass touched the edge of the prep table and Ben never stopped moving or kissing him. Ben lifted Dave up to sit on the counter, the stainless steel surface cold on his bare buttocks. With a final spin of his tongue through Dave's mouth, Ben leaned back to stare at him as he lifted Dave's legs. He held Dave's gaze as he lowered his mouth to the tightened sac of Dave's balls, painting them with the wide expanse of his tongue, then moved lower still to swipe his tongue across the trembling folds of Dave's hole.

"Oh, fuck yeah," Dave sighed and dropped his head back to the surface of the table.

Ben spread Dave's cheeks apart and drilled his tongue deep into his hole, flicking the tip and making Dave gasp. A finger followed Ben's tongue, pushing deep, then a second, and a third, as Dave groaned and writhed on the tabletop. Finally, Ben stood up and strode across the room, returning with a bottle of olive oil. He held it up and grinned at Dave. "Cook healthy."

Dave looked down between his raised legs and watched Ben tip the bottle so the olive oil dribbled along the crack of his ass. Ben dipped his fingers into Dave's hole, loosening and slicking him up. As Ben worked his hole with the fingers of one hand, Dave watched him stroke himself with his other, smearing olive oil along his cock, which stood hard as timber. A few times Ben's probing fingers grazed the sensitive knot of Dave's prostate, and Dave was worried he might come before the man even entered him.

But then Ben removed his fingers and stepped up between Dave's legs. He fixed him with a look of such intense want and need Dave lost his breath. The slick grip of Ben's fingers was hot around his ankles, branding Dave, and he felt the hot, rounded tip of Ben's cock poke at his eager hole.

"Ready?" Ben asked.

"Oh yeah," Dave replied.

Ben eased into him, the blunt head sinking slowly into the tight heat of his passage. Dave closed his eyes and heard a low moan slip from his parted lips as his muscles adjusted around the hot, bare shaft that burrowed into him. It felt so good to have a man inside him again, to be filled up, owned.

Just when Dave thought he would have to ask Ben to stop for a moment, he felt the brush of the man's pubic hair against the underside of his balls, and let out a breath. Ben stood gripping Dave's ankles, cock fully seated inside him, his dark eyes narrowed.

"God, you're fucking tight," Ben said.

"And you're fucking huge," Dave said. "I can't believe you fit."

"All in, baby." Ben turned his head to suck Dave's big toe a moment before saying, "Ready to ride?"

"Oh yeah."

Ben pulled back, paused for the space of a breath, then fucked him. The man's hips pumped hard and steady, dick pounding into him, opening him up. Dave tightened and released, imagining his muscles as a fist, gripping Ben and letting him go.

"Oh, fuck," Ben said. "You're grabbing on so tight. Fuck, that's good."

"Feels so good," Dave agreed. "I'm close."

"Me too." Ben leaned forward and Dave lifted his head to meet him for a kiss. Their tongues rolled together as Ben hammered Dave's prostate, and Dave reached down to take himself in hand.

"I'm coming," Ben gasped into Dave's mouth. "Coming inside you."

"Fill me up," Dave said. "All of it." He stroked himself to a breath-stopping climax, the come splattering up his sweat-covered torso as his muscles pulsed around Ben's cock, which jerked and spilled inside him.

Ben rested his head on Dave's chest, catching his breath, then eased out of him. He kissed Dave's nipples, ran his tongue through the puddles of come as he moved lower. Ben took Dave's softening cock in his mouth for a quick suck to clean him off, then pressed his lips to Dave's hole, still gaping open. Dave moaned as Ben ran his tongue around the oiled and come-slicked muscles.

"I love this hole," Ben whispered.

Dave chuckled. "It seems to feel the same about your cock."

Ben smirked before stepping away to grab some towels. He cleaned Dave up and helped him off the table, watching him stand on unsteady legs. Dave saw him watching and smiled. "I'm okay. Just got the balance fucked out of me, that's all."

"How you talk," Ben said and kissed him.

As they dressed, Dave kept looking for any sign of regret or discomfort from Ben, but the farmer had a soft smile and reached out now and then to touch him. Fully dressed, Ben stepped up to him for a kiss and pressed his palm against Dave's crotch.

"I need to get back to the farm," Ben said between kisses. "But I'm going to be hard the rest of the day knowing you've got my come in your ass."

Dave's stomach knotted at Ben's words and the tone of his voice. He tightened his sphincter, wanting to keep Ben's come inside him as long as possible.

"Now I'll be hard, too," Dave said.

Ben kissed him again, stroked his cheek, then turned to stride out of the kitchen. Dave listened as Ben stopped to pet and bid Zeus farewell, then moved to unlock the door and finally left the diner.

Dave took a breath and looked around the kitchen. He needed to clean, again, with bleach and water, but for now, he was going to savor the unsteady feeling in his legs and the well-fucked feeling in his ass.

❖

Dave sat at his father's kitchen table, a quilted barn coat keeping back the chill and a cup of coffee steaming before him as the rising sun warmed the eastern sky. Zeus was curled tight on the cushion that padded the chair to his left, napping after a breakfast of kibble.

It had been a week since he had been fucked by Ben, and Dave had not heard from the man. He knew Ben lived on a farm outside of town, most likely fifteen or twenty miles out on County Road 27, or Aspen Road as the locals called it, and working a farm took a lot of energy and time. But the silence gnawed at Dave each day as he worked to get the diner ready to open. He thought about Ben as he searched his father's house for a book of recipes, as he cleaned the diner, and as he interviewed for waitstaff, cooks, and busboys. Each night as he lay in bed, cock hard as steel and unrelenting, he thought about Ben. He felt again the push of Ben's cock in him, tasted the sweat and earth and salty-sweet precome. A few sure strokes each night was all it took for him to come, and he lay gasping afterward, wishing Ben would call, wondering what he had said wrong to make the man keep his distance.

With a sigh, Dave turned away from the sunrise to sip his coffee. When he glanced back out the window, he was surprised to see a tall, thin woman with bleached blond hair and a stern expression marching up to the front door.

Ava Hobbs. His father's hardest-working waitress, who had worked with Rick for over twenty-five years. She was smart, tough, and had made sure the dining area ran efficiently while Rick managed the kitchen. In some ways, Dave had always thought Ava and his father had a better, more understanding relationship than his mother and father ever had.

At the sound of Ava's sharp, firm raps, Zeus leaped off the chair to prance and bark at the door until Dave pulled it open. Before saying a word, Ava stepped inside and grabbed Dave in a tight hug that made his eyes sting with tears. He hadn't seen Ava since the funeral and realized how much he had missed human contact this past week. He had had no one to talk with, not since lunch and sex with Ben.

Finally taking a step back, Ava gripped Dave's arms up by his shoulders and looked him in the eyes, hers the brilliant blue of an autumn sky. "How are you, David?"

He had always been David to Ava, never Dave or Davey like he was to most people in town. It was one of the things he liked about her.

"I'm all right."

Ava narrowed her eyes and kept her grip on his arms. "No, you're not. But you're getting better."

"Yeah. That, too."

She released him and bent down to swoop Zeus up into the crook of one arm, scratching the dog behind an ear as she looked around the dark living room before turning her gaze back on Dave. "I'm worried about you."

"Come on in," Dave said to avoid a response. "I just made coffee."

"I'll get myself a cup," Ava said.

She placed Zeus on the chair where he had been napping before her arrival, moved to the correct cupboard to pull down a cup, grabbed sugar and creamer from another cupboard, a spoon from the silverware drawer, and poured herself a cup. Dave watched her move around his father's kitchen and wondered, based on her comfort in the space and knowledge of where all the items were kept, if her relationship with his father had become more personal after his mother's death ten years ago.

Ava sat across the table and stirred her coffee as she looked at him with those clear blue eyes. Zeus settled in on his chair once again and Dave turned away to look out the window.

"You've been working at the diner a lot," Ava finally said. "I've seen the lights on late at night."

Dave nodded and shrugged. "I've been cleaning it up and fixing what I can. I interviewed for staff this week."

Ava was quiet a moment, then said in a quiet voice, "Your father loved that diner."

"I know."

"The only thing he was more proud of was you four kids."

Dave took a breath and let it out before looking at her. "I had to do a lot of soul searching to decide to keep it, you know. I don't think I've got it in me to run it like Dad did."

"Then run it like you can," Ava said and reached across the table toward him, fingers outstretched on the shellacked wood of the table

Dave's family had eaten countless meals around. "That diner lives and breathes inside you, David. It is part of what made you the person you are today. Don't just sell that to some stranger. Your father, your family, played an important part in this community. That's nothing to give away lightly."

He sighed and looked out the window again. "I'm not a cook."

Ava snorted a laugh. "And you think your father was?"

Dave chuckled in spite of his dark mood. "Well, he was better at faking it than I am, how's that?"

"David, your father meant a lot to me. More than just as a boss, he was a good friend. And we talked a lot about you kids. He was sad all of you moved so far away, but he understood why you did it. Garrettville is a small town in the middle of three county roads and a lot of open space. He wanted you all to have a better life than he did growing up, and he was glad to see you get that. But he missed each of you, more than he admitted, I'm sure." She pulled her hand back and sat up straight to sip her coffee. "Out of all four of you kids, he always knew you would be the one to come home and carry on at the diner."

A tear surprised Dave and he quickly wiped it from his cheek. "Me?"

Ava nodded. "You were the youngest, and there was enough years between you and your brothers and sister to let him get to know you maybe a little better. He saw how hard you worked there when you were growing up, how quiet you were on the drive into the diner each weekend morning, not complaining like your siblings, but accepting, almost content to be going there." She smiled, and it softened the sharp planes of her face and made her look like a pretty young girl, though she had to be almost sixty. "He knew you better than you might have realized."

Dave looked away out the window. "I don't know how to cook, Ava. And Dad didn't leave a recipe book behind." He turned back, felt the sadness in his eyes as he looked at her. "I hate to think all his dishes, those favorites of the local people here, are lost."

Ava shook her head. "They're not lost, David. He mailed them to you a week before he…before the heart attack."

Dave blinked. "He did?"

Ava nodded. "He boxed it up and mailed it off. Told me he was trying to lure you back home since you were unemployed."

"I never received it," Dave said, his stomach a knotted mess. Had the book gotten lost in the mail somewhere? Was it gone forever?

"Well, he sent it book rate, maybe it didn't reach you until after you had left to come out here."

Dave glanced toward the door to the basement where he had stored all of his own belongings that Riley had packed up and driven out from Boston for him. "Oh my God. You mean I've had them in my stuff all this time?"

"He wanted you to come home, David. He needed to feel that connection with you again."

Ava finished her coffee, kissed Dave on the cheek, Zeus between the ears, and stepped out on the front porch. Turning back, Ava raised her eyebrows and said, "Call me when you're ready to open. I could use some extra income."

A wellspring of relief opened inside him and Dave smiled. Maybe things would work out all right after all, if Ava could help him get the diner running again. "I don't have your phone number."

A small smile, touched with sadness, raised one corner of Ava's lips. "Speed dial 5 on your father's cordless phone."

And with that, she turned to march down the walk.

An hour after Ava left, Dave climbed the steps from the basement with a heavy box cradled in his arms. His address back in Boston had been written on a mailing label in his father's familiar script, the sight of which sent a hot needle of grief stitching through Dave's gut. He tried not to feel as if his father were reaching out from beyond the grave to comfort him, reassure him he would be able to run the diner, especially with Ava around to train the new waitstaff.

Dave got another cup of coffee and sat at the table. The sun was full up and bright, flooding the kitchen with warm, yellow light the way it used to when he had been growing up. Everything seemed to slow down around him as he peeled the tape along the seam of the box, trying not to think about his father sealing the box a week before his heart attack, probably sitting in the kitchen, most likely in the very chair where Dave sat.

Wads of crumpled newspaper had been used for packing, the local rag his father loved even though it was nothing more than a glorified gossip column. Dave checked the date—a week to the day before his father's heart attack—and tossed a few of the smaller balls of paper for Zeus to chase into the living room. Then he found it. A three-ring binder, older than Dave himself by the looks of it, covered with stained and torn denim, lay nestled within the paper nest. Written across the front in blue ink in his father's writing: *Recipes*.

The tears surprised him, filling his eyes, rolling down his cheeks and dropping onto the binder, adding his grief to the stains until Dave pushed back from the table. He grabbed some tissues from the coffee table in the living room, kicked around a few of the paper balls for Zeus as he blew his nose and dabbed his eyes. When he was ready, Dave returned to the kitchen, refilled his coffee, and pulled the binder out of the box. He took a breath, opened the cover, and started to read.

❖

The day before the diner was to open, Dave worked with the waitstaff assembling the menus, washing dishes, wiping down tables, all the last-minute details. He had not heard from Ben at all and tried not to think about the man. Instead of counting on Ben's local produce, Dave had driven an hour to a warehouse store and stocked up on canned items. He would figure out something more permanent after they opened, but for now he had enough food for a few days at least.

At the end of the day, long after the sun had set and a steady rain had moved in, the red neon of the diner's sign glistened on the wet street outside the windows. Zeus lay snoring quietly on his cushion behind the counter as Dave bade the last of his staff good night. He locked the diner door and stepped around the counter to turn off the lights of the restaurant, leaving the sign on for now to act as a blood-red night-light as he finished up a few last details.

His back ached and his head felt fuzzy, filled with a million small details he had yet to check off his list, and another million things that could go wrong. Closing his eyes, Dave took a deep breath as he leaned against the counter. When he felt less anxious, he opened his eyes and looked out over the rows of tables and booths, every surface clean and gleaming red in the reflected light of the sign outside.

And then someone stepped up to the window and peered inside. It was a man, tall and broad-shouldered, his tan Carhartt jacket stained red by the neon buzzing above him, rain dripping off the brim of his cap.

Ben.

Dave stood still and watched Ben look around the diner. He wondered if the man had come looking for him or, seeing the diner dark, was merely curious how the place looked. Ben cupped his hands on the glass to see better and Dave could make out the man's shadowed face as he swept his gaze across the diner. Then their eyes met and Ben squinted as Dave felt a flutter of nerves in his belly.

Ben smiled, prompting Dave to smile back, and the farmer lifted a hand to wave. Dave waved back and nodded when Ben pointed to the door.

With his heart pounding, Dave walked out around the counter and unlocked the door to allow Ben inside. The man stood big and sure before him, rain splattered and smelling of damp earth and work sweat as he stared into Dave's face.

"Your sign needs looking at," Ben said.

Dave sighed and pulled his gaze from Ben's to lock the door. "Is it advertising my dad's greasy poon again?"

Ben grinned. "Yeah. But I like to think of it as your greasy poon."

"Well, that's a relief," Dave said, and they both chuckled a moment before an awkward silence draped over them.

"I haven't called," Ben stated.

Dave shrugged, then turned away, avoiding Ben's eyes as he moved back to the counter. "You were busy, I'm sure. You've got a farm to run and all."

"Actually, about seven times a day I started to call you," Ben admitted, "but each time I stopped myself."

Dave walked into the kitchen and busied himself straightening up items he had already straightened up six times that day. "I understand. We had just met and it was pretty intense. Don't worry about it. I'm a big boy, I know how things work."

"No, it's not like that," Ben said, and put a big hand on Dave's shoulder to turn him around to face him. "I felt something that day that was so amazing, so different from what I felt with anyone else before, I didn't know how to deal with it."

Dave blinked. "You did?"

Ben frowned. "Didn't you?"

"Well," Dave hedged. "It was intense, like I said, and I was, you know, really into it—" He stopped, looked Ben in the eyes, and took a breath. "I felt the same way."

The smile on Ben's face seemed to brighten the entire kitchen, and something that had been knotted tight inside Dave's chest for years loosened. A flicker of hope sparked to life in its place, burning through him, warming him as Ben put his arms around him and leaned in for a kiss.

"I've missed you," Ben said after the kiss.

"Me too."

Ben looked toward the thick steel back door that opened to the alley. "Think you could open that door?"

Dave furrowed his brow and frowned. "You want to go for a walk in the alley in the rain?"

"No," Ben said with another kiss. "Just open the door, wise ass."

"Hey, that's Mr. Greasy Poon Wise Ass to you, Farmer Ben."

Dave stepped around Ben, trailing his hand over the rounded bulge of the man's crotch before moving away toward the alley door. He twisted the two dead-bolt locks and pulled open the heavy door to find a large truck parked just outside. Two men jumped out of the cab, flashed tentative smiles, and began hauling baskets of fresh produce out of the back of the truck.

"What's all this?" Dave asked, stepping out of the way of the deliveries.

"I think you're going to be busier than you expected," Ben said and waved his hand at the canned vegetables and fruits stocked on the shelves. "You're going to need some fresh, locally grown stuff to keep up with demand."

"You think so?"

Ben nodded. "I know so." He stepped up and directed his employees to set the baskets in the walk-in refrigerator as Zeus ambled around the corner to bark at the men.

Dave picked the dog up and shushed him with pets as he watched the refrigerator fill up. When the last basket had been set inside, Ben closed the refrigerator door and waved to the men. The truck rumbled to life and Ben closed the back door and locked it tight, then turned to smile at Dave.

"Ellerby Farms delivers."

"In more ways than one," Dave said and set Zeus on the floor to walk over and kiss Ben hard.

In moments they were nude. Ben's kisses strong and passionate, his hairy chest pressed against Dave's, their hard-ons trapped between them. Dave dropped his mouth to Ben's nipple, licking and sucking at the hard brown nugget beneath the dark blond hair. He moved lower, tongue out and parting hair as he licked up the salt of Ben's sweat on his way down. On his knees before Ben, Dave leaned in to place a kiss in the tangle of wiry blond hair, breathing in Ben's damp, heady musk, wishing he could bottle it and use it for aromatherapy when he was alone. Running his tongue along the side of Ben's cock, root to tip, Dave swiped it across the slit and tasted the precome gathered there. Then he moved down the other side and once again into the fragrant bush.

"Not hungry?" Ben asked, voice heavy with lust.

Dave leaned back to look up at him and smiled. "Starved." Then he opened wide and took Ben into his mouth to the root.

Ben gasped and groaned, strong hands curled into fists as the muscles in his hairy legs tightened. As Dave sucked, he raised a hand to slide it over Ben's sweat-damp skin, parting the fine hairs until he reached the pointed nub of nipple. He pinched and tugged as he sucked and sighed through his nose when he felt the big, hot palm of Ben's hand on the back of his head.

Now things were going to get interesting.

Holding Dave's head still, Ben pumped between his swollen lips. The hot, sweaty length of cock filled Dave's mouth and retreated, faster, until Ben let out a deep grunt. A flood of thick, salty come filled Dave's mouth and he swallowed it down, drunk on the taste, smell, and feel of Ben. As Dave nursed the last of the come from Ben's cock, he stroked the length of his own, faster, until the snap and spark of his orgasm started deep inside and he came across Ben's bare feet.

Dave leaned back but kept his tongue extended, letting the top half of Ben's cock rest there as he looked up into the man's eyes.

"You were hungry," Ben said. "Think you've got another round in you still?"

Dave smiled, tongue still out, Ben's cock lengthening along it.

Ben picked Dave up from the floor for a kiss, then lifted him up to sit him on the prep table. Dave lay back, lifting his legs as he watched Ben grab the olive oil. A moment later, he felt the warm, slick oil coat his hole and shivered.

"I kept something out of the refrigerator," Ben said.

Dave raised his head to look between his legs at the man. "Oh yeah?"

Ben held up a long, firm cucumber and waggled his eyebrows. "Oh yeah."

Dave smiled. "I've never been fucked with a cuke before."

"Oh, baby, you haven't lived."

Ben made a show of greasing up the smooth, green cuke and held it to Dave's lips for him to kiss. He traced an oily line down Dave's torso, along the length of his hard cock, and then along the seam that ran from his balls to his asshole. Dave felt the blunt tip circle his hole and closed his eyes. At the first slow push, he groaned and Ben eased back. Pushing the cuke in again, deeper this time, Ben spun it and Dave gasped.

"Like that?"

"Is that your version of the Salad Spinner?"

Ben laughed. "You ain't seen nothin' yet."

He worked the cucumber in and out of Dave's hole, loosening him, greasing him up, taking him right to the edge before pulling the cuke free and using his fingers in its place.

"That looked so fucking hot I want a turn," Ben said, his voice deep with lust. "Slide down on the table."

Dave slid himself to the opposite end of the long table and watched Ben climb up as well. The man lay on his back and lifted his own legs, then pushed himself close to Dave. Ben poured oil on his fingers and reached down to slick up his own asshole. This action brought Dave up to a sitting position and he slid his fingers in alongside Ben's, feeling the hot, wet muscles clamp down around him.

"Oh, yeah," Ben groaned. "Get your fingers in there."

Dave's cock throbbed as he pushed his fingers in deep and eased them out, watching Ben's sphincter stretch around them.

"You've got a hot ass," Dave told him.

"It's hungry," Ben said. "Care to share a cucumber?"

Dave lay on his back and lifted his legs, twisting them around Ben's. He felt the smooth touch of the cucumber against his anus, then the slow invasion until it paused. Raising his head, he watched Ben adjust the cuke until the opposite end poked into the man's asshole. Ben pushed himself closer to Dave and his movement slid the cucumber deeper into Dave as it slid into Ben himself.

They groaned in unison. Dave reached out to grab Ben's oil-slicked hands, pushing and pulling to work the cucumber back and forth between them.

"I want you," Ben said. "I want you inside me."

Dave didn't need a second invitation. He disengaged himself from the cucumber, slipped it out of Ben's loosened hole, and tossed it into the sink. He stepped down onto the floor and pulled Ben to the edge of the table. His cock was harder than it had been in years, precome drooling from the tip to puddle on the floor between his feet.

When Ben was set, Dave pointed his cock at the rugged, glistening ring of his hole and pressed forward. He slid deep into him, the muscles slick and ready, embracing him. Ben tightened and released around him as Dave's hips found that old, familiar rhythm and he pounded into the man, staring in amazement at the hairy, masculine body sprawled before him. Was all this really his?

The second time took longer, but when Dave finally did come, it felt like gallons. His hips surged forward as if with a mind of their own, burying his cock deep inside Ben as he pumped out his load. Ben stroked himself, his fist a blur along the oiled shaft, and, still impaled on Dave's cock, shot a heavy load across his belly.

They kissed as they slipped apart, and Dave fetched towels for them to clean up, then helped Ben off the table. The farmer surprised Dave by grabbing him in a tight hug and kissing him hard. When Ben finally broke the embrace, he smiled at Dave and asked, "What time do you open for breakfast?"

❖

Dave stood behind the counter and watched the waitresses and busboys perform their ballet around the tables. Conversation and laughter filled the diner along with the clatter of silverware and the occasional crying baby. Zeus slept on his cushion in a corner beneath the counter, an accepted fixture of the place, even after the three surprise visits by the health department, spurred on, Dave assumed, by Polly

Walker. Polly's Place had lost a good chunk of business after Rick's Greasy Spoon reopened four weeks ago, and Dave was once surprised to see Polly's own sister, Molly, sitting in the back corner enjoying his pot roast.

"Good crowd," Ava said as she speed-walked past to grab the coffeepots off the warmers.

"Yeah, it is." He noticed her check the timer by the brewers and waved her off. "I'll make fresh pots, go pour."

She smiled and said, "Just like your father, David," as she breezed past him and out around the counter into the flow of the other waitresses.

As Dave poured fresh grounds into the filters, he heard a man behind him clear his throat and turned to find Ben sitting at the crowded counter. The smile on Ben's face ignited one of Dave's own and he nodded before placing a gleaming white cup before him.

"Coffee, Mr. Ellerby?" Dave said.

"That'd be good, Mr. Brighton." Ben jerked a thumb over his shoulder. "The 'S' in your sign is out. A bunch of high school kids are across the street singing a limerick based on it."

"Yeah? They any good?" Dave asked.

Ben shrugged. "Not much you can rhyme with 'poon,' really, but they're holding their own."

Dave nodded and wiped down the counter in front of Ben before smiling at him. "What brings you to Rick's Greasy Spoon—sorry, *poon*—today?"

"I'm hungry," Ben said with a smirk. "Why else would I be here? What's good?"

Dave grinned. "We make a mean cucumber salad."

Ben raised his eyebrows, fighting to keep from laughing. "Do you? Does it have a spicy dill sauce?"

"The spiciest."

The woman sitting next to Ben reached to open the menu. "You have cucumber salad?"

Dave kept his eyes on Ben's and prided himself on not laughing as he replied, "As a matter of fact, we do."

THE FINISH
'NATHAN BURGOINE

The last bottle I managed to track down is bleeding drips of condensation onto the white tablecloth in the private dining room. I feel sick, of course. Even the sight of the label—the Byrnes Vineyard dragonfly and frog design, done in gold pointillism on a red diamond—makes me feel queasy. It's a rare red ice wine, meant to be enjoyed after a meal and in small quantity. It's the tenth bottle—no, the eleventh—I've had in two days.

When I uncork the bottle, the scent of it is too much. I stumble to the men's bathroom barely in time and heave into the sink. I wash my face, not daring to look in the mirror, and then sit down again in the closed restaurant dining room, facing the bottle. I rub my chapped lips, still burning from the last glasses, then pick it up.

I pour, sniff, swallow. As always, I remember the words of a young woman who'd toured the vineyard the first time I'd been present to deliver a tasting of the label. I'd just finished explaining how the mild climate and the rich soil combined in the region, and a perfectly placed frost had garnered the ice wine. "It all tells," I'd said. "The rain, the grape, the soil—it all comes together."

"The aftertaste is like molten strawberries," she'd delighted. I'd explained that in the lexicon of wine, an aftertaste is called a finish. She'd laughed and said, "I'd like to finish the whole bottle."

It's still my favorite customer memory to this day.

To this wretched, wretched day.

I feel the wine—so sweet—in my throat, and the first hazy glimmers of change appear in the air around me.

"Please," I whisper, to God or Dennis, whichever might answer.

Dennis appears, hazy and indistinct, heading toward the kitchen.

It seems God isn't listening.

I take another sip, and feel Dennis become real.

❖

Giving summer tours of the vineyard, I often joked that if collecting the January grapes for ice wine sounded like fun, then anyone taking the tour should leave phone numbers. I promised to call if there was a January night frost cold enough to freeze the grapes, likely at around one in the morning.

Unsurprisingly, no one ever took me up on it.

Still, every January frost, if the conditions were right, I found people—usually vineyard workers, their families, or friends—to help.

That was how I met Dennis, who was just another helper of nearly two dozen, dressed in a scuffed black coat, with a thin scarf and knitted hat covering all but his eyes. I hadn't really done more than glance at him when he'd shown up to work—Terry said he was a friend of a friend of one of the waiters from the vineyard restaurant.

We'd worked all through the night and into the morning—fingers achingly cold, slowly filling baskets of frozen grapes and passing thermoses of coffee and hot chocolate back and forth that the kitchen refilled every hour or so. It was long work, uncomfortable and miserable. Every year I gathered everyone afterward in the restaurant and the chef made them all a good hot breakfast on the house. While they ate and warmed up, I stepped into my office and wrote out checks for each of the workers named on the list Terry had made for me. I considered it a point of pride that I worked with everyone else on these frigid nights. Terry had often told me I didn't have to, but I always believed it mattered to the staff that the boss also did the crappy jobs.

"You're rich, buddy," Terry said, shaking his head. "You can pay people to do that shit."

After cutting the checks for the workers, I'd handed them all out but one. Dennis Clarke hadn't come for his money when I'd called out his name. That surprised me. Cold bitter nights and thin gloves working to pick frozen grapes usually left people more than eager to get whatever compensation they could.

"Terry," I said. "I'm missing one. Dennis…" I glanced down at the list. "Clarke."

Terry nodded and went to where the group was rapidly moving off to climb wearily into their vehicles. The plates had been mostly cleared. Terry called out a few times. I went back to my paperwork, rubbing my eyes. It was a decent harvest, and it was going to make some fine ice wine.

"Got him," Terry said, a little while later. "He's deaf. Didn't hear you calling."

"Thanks, Terry," I said.

Terry nodded, and paused at the doorway to raise his eyebrows. "He's cute."

I shook my head. Terry and I had been friends for a long time, and had even dated for one disastrous year when we were much younger. Now we ran the vineyard together—though Terry handled more of the restaurant side, and I took care of the winery. We were better business partners than we'd ever been lovers. Built like a bulldog—and just as tenacious—Terry had a seemingly endless appetite for younger men who tired of him and moved on, generally with pockets full of presents before they left. He was terrible with money—he blew it on expensive toys and expensive boys. I was never sure where he was at, financially, and it had always been like that. It was one of the many reasons we hadn't made it as a couple. That, plus his temper and seemingly endless string of young things on the side.

Taller and—if I allowed myself some pride—in better shape for my age, I hadn't dated nearly as much, but still found I could get attention if I wanted to. I didn't hide the gray in my temples like Terry did, and still ran the half-marathon every year. If sometimes the younger men who did hit on me called me "Daddy"? Well. I could live with that.

A moment later, Dennis stepped into my office.

I looked up. Without his hat and scarf, he was indeed handsome, though a little rough around the edges. His dark hair needed a trim—it was just long enough to fall into his eyes, which were a soft green that didn't seem to fit with the rest of his angular features. He had the shadow of a day or two without shaving on his chin.

I handed him the check and thanked him, though if Terry was right, he didn't notice. He was looking down at the check when I spoke. Then he pulled a small well-worn notepad and a pencil from his pocket and flipped it open. He wrote something, then turned it to face me.

Can I get cash? I read.

He was watching my face—I hoped he could read lips. "I don't have cash at hand, but I can have it sent to you later on today once the bank opens. Where are you staying?"

He frowned, then wrote again.

The Y.

It bothered me, I'll admit it. He wasn't a kid—though it's hard for someone on the downward side of their forties not to think of anyone under twenty-five as a kid, I'd learned—but he seemed lean and hungry to me. This wasn't a young man who'd been having a good run of luck. He'd been a good worker, efficient and working hard without break or complaint.

I glanced out my window at the parking lot, then looked back at him.

"Do you have a ride?" I asked.

He shook his head. His lips curled in a slight smirk, and it suited him. That Terry and I were gay was well known in the region. I knew better than this, but I made the offer anyway.

"If you'll wait a few minutes, I can drive you."

He nodded, the smirk growing into what could have been a smile.

I really did take Dennis to the Y. He fell asleep on the drive over, and I stole glances at him. The neck of his shirt was a little frayed, and there was just the tip of an unseen tattoo below the smooth hollow of his throat. When we got to the Y, I tapped his shoulder, waking him, and he rubbed his eyes with one thumb.

I waited for him to look at me. "I have a spare bedroom," I said. "If you've got nowhere else to crash."

He regarded me for a long moment, then nodded once. He pulled out his notepad.

Gonna get my things. Be right back.

I nodded, and waited for him.

❖

He dropped his beaten canvas backpack—not much for anyone to carry their belongings in—at my front door and tugged off his boots without sitting. He shrugged out of his jacket and tossed it over the edge of the chair that sat in the entrance hall, and started to look around before I'd even finished untying my shoes. By the time I'd hung up our coats and followed him into the living room, he was standing at my bookcase, trailing his finger along the spines of the books and stopping every now and then to carelessly pick up a picture or an objet d'art from the alternating shelves where I displayed them.

"Big reader?" I asked before remembering he had his back to me. I felt myself blush when he didn't react. *Deaf*, I reminded myself.

He moved with the arrogant grace of youth—his shirt, faded and short-sleeved—was tight across his shoulders and chest, displaying his lean strength. His jeans rode a little low, exposing the small of his back when he reached for something. There was another tattoo there. When he did turn to look at me, it was with a picture frame in hand and a raised eyebrow.

It was an old shot of me and Terry.

"That's Terry, from the vineyard," I said. "And me. Back when we first bought the place."

He nodded and put the photo back on the shelf. He turned back to me, his amused smirk back in place.

"I'm going to go to bed," I said. "Let me show you to your room."

His lip curled, and he walked toward me. He came closer than was polite—until that moment, it hadn't occurred to me that what I was doing might not have been safe—and looked up at me, his eyelids low on his green eyes. I felt some small relief at being taller than him.

His hand cupped my crotch—and what had been a slight stiffness before began to harden under his fingers. He smiled at me again with that crooked smirk and then slowly sank to his knees. As he pulled at my belt and my zipper, I ran one hand through his messy hair.

That he was talented didn't surprise me—his fingers wrapped around my shaft, and his tongue teased my cockhead. He swallowed me, one hand slowly working my pants free, and I tilted my head back and felt the warm wet heat of his attention.

"Wait," I said. "Slow down..."

He'd brought me close to the edge quickly, and I had to take his shoulders and pull him away. He looked up at me, a small frown on his face. Again I remembered he couldn't hear me.

I pulled him back to his feet and tugged his shirt over his head.

The tattoo on the centre of his chest was a green man—a face of oak leaves—and I traced a finger over it before sliding my arms around him and pulling him against me for a long kiss. His lips parted easily for my tongue, and my hands shifted lower, gripping his strong ass and sliding between his warm skin and his jeans. He made nearly no noise—just gasps and soft breaths against my skin when we parted long enough for me to undo his jeans and for him to step out of them. Then we collided again, our cocks hard and hot against each other. One of my hands gripped his ass tightly, pulling him into me, while the other stroked us both.

His voiceless moans were more felt than heard. I wanted to devour him.

We went to my room, casting off clothes as we moved, kissing and touching with rougher and faster passion. At my bedroom door I finally got out of my shirt, and Dennis rubbed his hands across my chest, obviously surprised—and I hoped delighted—to see I was in good shape. I pushed him back onto the bed and crawled after him, licking his throat and neck and pinning his hands above his head while I lay over him. He shifted, making little breathy laughs and gasps while I teased his nipples with my tongue. When I let go of his hands he gripped my ass tightly and pulled me against him, wrapping his legs around my waist with a perfectly clear intention.

I paused long enough for lube and a condom, already so hard for him I could barely stand it. I braced his legs on my shoulders, and never once did his green eyes look away from my face as I pushed my way inside him. He pressed his hands against my chest and squeezed his legs around me, and I fucked him with a need I didn't know I had. He was no stranger to this, and I found myself thrusting into him harder than I'd dared with others. His legs urged me onward, and I tipped over the edge, driving into him deep while I came.

After, he shook his head when I tried to pull out of him, and his legs squeezed tighter. He jerked himself off like that, with me still inside him, and his quiet orgasm was little more than a ragged, throaty exhalation.

I kissed him again and then extricated myself to clean up. I brought a wet towel back and wiped him as well. He pressed against my side and pulled the blanket over us both. His eyes closed.

We slept.

❖

I follow the specter of Dennis into the kitchen, where I watch the sink fill with translucent foamy water. He's washing dishes, and false sunlight is falling in from the window that looks out onto the parking lot. I sip more wine, and his body firms around the edges. I watch him work, see wisps of other kitchen staff out of the corner of my eyes, but it is Dennis that is invoked by this vintage, not they.

"Why?" I croak.

He doesn't turn and doesn't answer, of course.

I see myself arrive in the kitchen, and suddenly I realize which day it is I'm seeing. I want to close my eyes, but I can't. None of these visions have ever had sound. I have watched us walk by the vines. I've seen us fuck by the pool. I've relived each vision as though it were Dennis himself spinning a tale for me—a silent tale from a deaf man. I can't close my eyes.

But I don't want to watch.

We interact, puppets of ourselves in the past. I remember the conversation, and flinch when the other me kisses his forehead and then holds up one hand, fingers curled a certain way. Moments later, this wine-conjured image of Dennis kisses me, and the other me leaves, more content than he has ever felt.

"Fool," I growl. "Fucking fool."

❖

At first, he tried to refuse the job I offered, scratching on his notepad that he was on his way out of Niagara. *Lost my job*, he wrote. *Laid off, not fired.*

"Where are you going?" I asked.

He shrugged. We lay in bed, still naked from the night before. When he'd reached out of the bed to get his notepad from his jeans, I'd enjoyed looking at the lines of his back, and his lovely ass. The tattoo at the small of his back was a series of moons—a full moon, with a waning and waxing crescent on either side.

He scribbled again. *I'm not a hustler.*

Reading it filled me with a kind of aching shame. I nodded.

"I know," I said, and his green eyes read the words on my lips. "And I'm not a sugar daddy." I thought about Terry and his penchant for boys—young men—just like Dennis. "But there's a spot open at the restaurant. It's just a dishwashing job, but it's a steady thing. I already know you're a hard worker. You can stay here while you get your feet back under you—in the spare bedroom, if you want." I added the last awkwardly, knowing I was blushing.

He looked around the room. I was suddenly aware of how fine my furnishings were.

You invite guys to stay with you all the time? he wrote.

Dennis flashed me that smirk of a smile while I read it.

"No," I said.

He reached over and ran his hand across my chest, down my stomach, and between my legs. He raised his eyebrows almost comically when he felt how hard I was.

"Yes, well," I said, feeling myself turn all the redder. "You're very handsome. But I'm serious. You can have the spare bedroom."

In answer, Dennis stroked me and shook his head.

"But…" I gasped as his hand worked my length. "You'll take the job?"

He nodded.

I rolled onto him and kissed him, taking his hands and once again pinning them over his head. I licked at his neck and heard the little gasping noises I'd eventually learn was his laughter. We ground against each other, licking, kissing, nibbling, and teasing in a more lackadaisical dance than the night before. We came in turns—I was pleased to tease his load out onto his smooth stomach by burying my face into his lovely ass, his legs on my shoulders, and he returned the favor by taking me into his mouth again, and I watched my own sperm spatter across the green man on his chest.

He looked at me lazily while we caught our breath.

"We need a shower," I said. "And breakfast."

He smiled.

❖

"Reports," Terry said, standing at my door. He had the weekly reports from the restaurant. Ever since he'd nearly run the restaurant into the ground with his fast-and-loose approach to finances, I'd had him keep me up to speed on how the restaurant was doing on a weekly basis. The man knew food and chefs, and was amazing at ambience and figuring out what the customers at the restaurant wanted.

He was an idiot with cash.

"Thanks," I said.

He hovered. I looked up at him.

"You always did have a thing for hard-luck cases," he said.

He'd seen me leave with Dennis. I'd been expecting some sort of comment. "Pardon?" I feigned innocence and took a glance at the reports.

Terry laughed. "Don't get me wrong—he's a cute little fucker. Wouldn't mind bending him over the sink myself."

I rolled my eyes. "He needed a job. He worked damn hard when we were picking," I said. "And we're down one dishwasher anyway."

Terry laughed, wide body shaking. "You are such a softie. Just like you to take him in."

I nodded. "He's a nice kid. And I think he'll take the job more seriously than yet another college kid just doing it for some spending cash."

"That's the truth," Terry said. Students were his nightmare, Terry often said. "I'll give him a shot. At least I know he won't talk back." He laughed at his own joke.

"Don't be an ass," I said. "And make sure none of the others give him any crap."

Terry shook his head. "Softie. And don't worry about that—he's a cool customer. I imagine he'll have 'em all eating out of his hand in no time. Just like you." He looked at me. "You seem awfully chipper this morning. Where'd you drop that kid off last night?"

"See you later, Terry," I said, voice firm.

He laughed as he left my office.

❖

We developed a routine that felt fragile and unsettling at first, but grew more firm as the days became weeks and the weeks turned into months. Some days I'd make four trips, leaving early to go to work while Dennis often slept in—I had to admit a slight guilt at enjoying having a lover I couldn't wake with my snoring or thumping around in the morning. On my lunch break, I'd come home and pick up Dennis, who'd start at the restaurant a couple of hours later. We'd often eat lunch in my home. Dennis wasn't a half-bad cook, though his range was limited to barbecue and a wide variety of stir fry. After lunch, Dennis worked at the restaurant, and I managed the vineyard and winery throughout the afternoon, and then I'd come home, get myself dinner, and make one last trip around eleven when the restaurant was closed and Dennis had finished his shift. We had different days off, and I often felt a little out of sorts on the weekends, when Dennis worked and I didn't. My house, which had never before seemed lonely, was bothering me if he wasn't home.

In the rare evenings we had together, we'd often just sit on the couch, both of us reading, or watching movies—once I figured out how to turn on the bloody closed captioning on my DVD player. Dennis had mimicked my tongue sticking out while I'd worked on the remote, my glasses perched on the end of my nose.

One evening in the early spring, Dennis admitted that reading lips was tiring, so I bought a copy of *ASL for Dummies* and started reading it on the sly. My first attempt to say something to him—I tried to compliment his ass—made him chuckle in his breathy way, and he'd corrected me. He scribbled on a notepad.

Who taught you that?

I showed him the book. He stared at me a long time, then nodded. I couldn't decide if I'd offended him or impressed him in some way, but we began lessons and I learned that signing was far easier than interpreting someone else signing. Still, we made slow progress.

I started training for the next half-marathon, and when I'd come home from running, sweaty and still feeling the high, Dennis would tumble me into the bed, despite my protests of needing a shower, and he'd wrap his legs around me. We'd rut like animals, all swallowed cries and sweat and spit, and I learned that as tender as he could be, Dennis enjoyed sex this way—rough and quick. To my surprise, I learned I liked it myself, and loved to watch his face while I gripped his shoulders and shoved my dick into him with the sole notion of getting us both off, fast.

His breathy cry would always delight me, and when he'd come across his own chest, the pool of his spunk on the tattoo on his chest would always tip me over the edge right after him.

❖

After the vision of myself leaves, this watery version of Dennis looks out the window. I realize with a start that he is waiting to see me get into my car, and shake my head, angry at myself all over again. Dennis is fading. I take another swallow of the wine, and he sharpens.

He shakes his hand, and droplets of water and soap vanish before they can hit the floor. Startled by the movement, I look at him.

He raises his hand to the window and lowers his middle two fingers. His thumb is out, his index finger and pinky upright.

"What?" I say. I know that sign.

Through the window, I see my car pull away.

❖

The summer months were busy for me, and apart from the half-marathon, what little time I could scrape together for relaxation I spent in my pool. The heat was oppressive, and rain was scarce. I'd been struggling with the growers to make sure the soil was getting enough water from the wells and fighting to maintain the sometimes precarious balances in the earth, and it felt like a daily struggle to make sure everything went smoothly. Watching Dennis swim—he never wore trunks in my fenced back yard—was a delight, and after one particularly athletic session at the water's edge, I'd been unable to control myself and had hoisted the young man onto the pool's edge and fucked him in the shallow end. He'd shot across his stomach, green eyes never leaving mine while I pounded into him. When I'd come inside him—the only time he closed his eyes was when he felt me come inside him—I leaned over him, chest to chest, our skin sticky with his climax.

He smiled at me as I pulled out of him. His hands moved. *I have to go to work soon.* Our sex had made it too late for him to make the longish walk, which he sometimes enjoyed.

I groaned. The last thing in the world I wanted to do was drive back to the vineyard.

"I need to buy you a car," I said, jokingly. He smiled. He couldn't drive. But then, a thought occurred to me.

"What about a really good bike?" I asked. "Can you ride a bike?" He watched my lips, and signed again.

You don't have to buy me anything. It made him uncomfortable.

"I just gave you one of the biggest loads I've ever shot," I said, wagging my eyebrows. "Consider it a reward."

Dennis shook his head and squirmed out from beneath me. I stepped back into the water, surprised. He kept shaking his head and dropped back into the water, making for the ladder despite my useless protests. He wasn't looking at me, but still I was talking, a habit I couldn't seem to break.

"Dennis? Wait!" I bit off the words, finally remembering.

He had his towel wrapped around his waist by the time I caught up to him. When I took his arm, he turned, his eyes aimed low at the deck, frowning.

I'm sorry. What's wrong? I signed.

He looked at me, and there was such hopelessness on his face, I took him by the shoulders, and leaned in close.

"I'm an idiot," I said. "I'm sorry if I insulted you." His eyes watched my lips.

He nodded, barely. He drew his fingertips from his lips into the palm of his open hand. It meant *thank you.*

He went inside to change, and I sat at the edge of the pool and wondered what exactly he was thanking me for. The drive to the vineyard—and the one back—was tense. That night his lovemaking was almost frantic. His goal seemed to be to get me off, with no thought to his own pleasure, and I had to slow him down. Eventually, I just wrapped my arms around him, and we held each other. Both of us pretended I couldn't feel the wetness of his eyes against my chest.

"I think I fucked up," I said to Terry the next day. He was sitting in the restaurant office, piles of paper all over his desk. It made me cringe how disorganized he could be, and I was forever glad that his assistant seemed capable of sorting through his disasters to make sure everything was done on time.

Terry looked up at me from his desk. "The vines?"

I shook my head. "No. I think we've got that covered. They're going to till in some new fertilizer and soil. With a little luck, they also won't destroy all the vines that are growing in the process." I shrugged and sat down in the other chair. "It's Dennis."

Terry's smile was wide. "Trouble in paradise, Daddy Warbucks?"

I sighed. "It's not like that. He's not like that. He doesn't ask for anything." I shook my head. "In fact, that was my mistake. I offered to buy him a bicycle…I think I insulted him. I made him feel like a hustler or something."

Terry laughed. "Trust you to find the only hot fuck without an agenda." He shook his head. "You're such a lucky asshole."

I stared at him. "Thanks, Terry. You always know just what to say to make me feel better."

He laughed again. "Sorry, buddy. You're the one dickin' the help. If the boy doesn't want anything more than your cock, I say go for it." He grinned. "I'm sure you'll find a way to make it up to him. He's not the sort to stay pissed. Just fuck him good, and he'll come around."

I bristled. "He's not like the boys you hook up with."

"Why? Because he's deaf?" Terry shook his head. "Look. I'm glad you're happy. It's nice to see you happy. Lord knows, you work your ass off and you never do anything fun for yourself. I'm glad you're getting laid. You're lucky. You don't want to know how much cash I dropped on that last piece of trash."

I sighed. "You're such a misanthrope."

"It's why we didn't last," he agreed. "I'm not saying you're not a catch, Jesse. But let's be honest. The kid is hot, he's got that whole 'wounded' thing going on for him with the deaf stuff, and you fall for that crap hook, line, and sinker." He shrugged. "Just have fun. Go places, do shit, get him some decent clothes and shit. He's a boy—he's gonna get tired and move on eventually. Don't sweat it when it happens, just find another. Trust me." He wagged his eyebrows. "There's always another."

I went to go find Dennis in the kitchens, where he was working hard at the sink. He'd gotten a ride in with one of the other workers, and I hadn't seen him since the morning. When I tapped him on the shoulder, he turned, with a dark look on his face that vanished when he saw me. He smiled, looking a little bashful.

Sorry, he signed. Drops of water hit his shirt.

"Forget it," I said, and just like that the knot in my chest was almost gone.

He nodded.

"Movie tonight?" I asked him.

He nodded, then paused. *I'm closing. I might be late*, he signed.

Two staff stayed behind after the restaurant closed to double-count the deposit and lock up the safes. It usually didn't take longer than half an hour. "Do you need me to come pick you up?" I asked.

He shook his head. *I can get a ride, or walk.* He liked to walk in the nice weather.

I leaned in and kissed him, a quick peck on the forehead. He smiled, his crooked smirk firmly in place.

When I saw that smile was for me, some reflex flickered and I lifted my hand and curled in my middle two fingers, spreading my thumb wide.

It was an ASL sign: *I love you.*

He flinched. I felt my face burn. I reached for his shoulder, and he was tense beneath me.

"You don't have to say it back," I said.

He leaned forward, and kissed me—a long, lingering kiss. The ache in my stomach faded.

"See you tonight," I said.

He nodded.

But I didn't see him again.

❖

The air ripples. The sunlight is gone. I take another swallow, but Dennis fades. He loved me. I close my eyes for a moment, just a moment, to remember that sign through the window—something I never saw. I open my eyes again and turn.

Dennis is in the restaurant. I can see him, watery and pale, through the small window in the swinging doors.

I push through them. Dennis is standing, arms crossed, waiting for something. He checks his watch and frowns.

He's wearing the same shirt. It's the same day, I think. That night. The night he stole the money and left.

My stomach clenches.

The door opens, and someone walks in.

"What?" I say, but of course, neither of them answers.

I take another swallow.

❖

"He cleaned out both the safes," Terry said. "The shop and the restaurant, including the night's dinner earnings."

I rubbed my forehead. "What did the cops say?"

Terry sighed. "It was cash, right? They're not thinking it's likely we'll get it back. They've got people on the lookout for him, but…" He shrugged. "I'm sorry, Jesse. I…I wish it was different."

He looked terrible. I smiled at him. "I'm the one who got taken by the hustler," I said, each word burning in my gut. "Why do you look like shit?"

Terry just shook his head. "If I'd been smarter, I wouldn't have let the kid help with the closing. He wouldn't have known the ins and outs…"

"The safes have to be double-counted every night," I said. "That's how it works. Don't feel bad about it. It was my judgment call, not yours." I smiled, though I wanted to scream. "You get to say I told you so now."

Terry just shook his head, and made for the door. "Will we be okay?" he asked.

I nodded. "There's enough in the bank in the business accounts. It'll suck, don't get me wrong, but it'll be okay. No bonuses this year. And if it really gets bad, I can float the difference from my personal account."

"I'll handle the soil stuff," Terry said. "If you want."

I'd forgotten we were having the soil treated again. Damned dry summer. I smiled at him, genuinely relieved. "Thanks. I'd really just like to go home."

Terry nodded, and left.

I put my head down on my desk and cried.

❖

Dennis hadn't taken any of his belongings with him. I'd been at home, so he'd probably felt it wasn't worth the risk. I'd waited for him until nearly midnight before calling the restaurant. When no one had answered, I'd tried the vineyard, but no one picked up there, either. I'd waited another half hour, aware that Dennis had said he might be late, and growing more and more nervous. I'd called Terry, who'd picked up right away and told me he'd call the worker who'd closed the restaurant down with Dennis. Terry called me back and told me that according to the other staff, they'd closed the restaurant and gone their separate ways. Dennis had declined a ride.

Finally, I'd gotten into my car and driven the road between the vineyard and my home. There was really only one way to walk home, and he wasn't on it. I'd driven slowly, feeling sick—what if he'd been hurt? When I got to the restaurant, I saw some of the lights were on, and parked. If he'd come back, Dennis wouldn't have heard the phone ring when I'd called. I went inside and started looking for him. When I'd gotten to the restaurant's office and the door to the safe was wide open, I'd stopped, frowning at it for a long while.

I'd called Terry again, and then the police.

It was a lean autumn, but by winter we were doing well, and if we hadn't recovered the loss, exactly, we were breaking even again. We scored a favorable review both for the year's vintage and for the restaurant, and the two went a long way. I worked long hours, not enjoying my quiet home at all.

When the first frost hit in early January, for the first time since I'd owned the vineyard I didn't help with the picking. The grapes might be ideal for an uncommon red ice wine, but I didn't want to see them. I passed the whole event by, letting my staff deal with the process, and barely following up to make sure they were doing things correctly.

Going into the restaurant made me feel sick, and I hadn't stepped into the kitchens in months. By the time the red ice wine was ready, and it was time to taste it, instead of gathering the staff like I'd done for years and opening a few bottles for us all to try, I uncorked the bottle and had a single small glass in my office, after everyone else had gone home.

It was wonderful. Sweet, almost a honey bouquet, and a first-class finish.

"Molten strawberries," I said, but it didn't make me smile. The soil had been worth it—the impact on the wine was obvious.

I picked up the bottle and glass and left my office. I walked through the main building and went into the restaurant, locking the door after myself. I stood among the tables for a while, then walked into the kitchen through the swinging doors.

As soon as I saw the sink, I started shaking with anger. I put the bottle down and threw the glass across the room, hearing it shatter in the huge steel basin where Dennis had worked. It didn't help, and I ended up having to clean up broken glass for five minutes. By the time I was done with that, I felt thoroughly humiliated all over again, and reached for the bottle and drank a swallow of the ice wine like a hobo in an alley. It was an exceptionally good wine.

I pulled out my cell, and called Terry.

"The red ice wine is great," I said.

"You okay?" he asked.

"I'm fine. You can go ahead and start shipping it tomorrow."

I went home, the open bottle balanced between my legs, not caring if I was pulled over. Inside my house, I tipped the bottle back again, starting to feel a small buzz. This wasn't the way you were meant to enjoy a red ice wine. It was a dessert wine, something to enjoy on its own merit in small glasses. Maybe with a strong cheese, but certainly not with anything sweet. I poured it into a pinot noir glass and swallowed more.

By the time I'd finished the large glass, I was buzzing. I refilled the glass and sank onto my couch.

Dennis walked in.

I yelped, and sat up—but Dennis wavered and disappeared. I blinked, shaking my head. Tears stung my eyes.

"Oh, fuck you," I growled, and swallowed.

He reappeared. I froze, glass at my lips, and watched. Dennis was watery, a blurry vision through which I could see my bookcases. His hair was longer than it should have been, and he was wearing the faded shirt he'd worn the night...

I walked in after him, watery and indistinct.

"Oh Jesus," I breathed. I watched the scene play out silently. I saw myself speak, but there were no words. I saw him pick up the picture of Terry and myself, and I watched him walk over and kneel in front of me.

I swallowed more wine, and the image sharpened.

By the time the bottle was empty, I'd followed myself and Dennis into the bedroom and watched myself make love to the young man for the first time. After, I watched Dennis snuggle into my arms, and the smile on my face when I looked at him cut me to the bone.

"You're an idiot," I slurred at myself. Then I fell over and passed out.

❖

I came to when my cell rang, late in the following morning. I grabbed it awkwardly.

"'Lo?" My voice was rough, and my head was aching. Not the worst hangover I'd ever had, but still a hangover.

"You sound terrible." It was Terry.

"Ugh," I said.

"You need to take a day?"

"Yeah."

"Okay," Terry said. He paused, like he wanted to say more, but didn't. "Okay."

"Thanks," I said, and rubbed my eyes. At some point I'd crawled into bed. When I rolled to my side, a bottle rolled against me. I looked at it. Remembered.

"Terry, did you send out the red ice wine yet?" My heart was hammering.

"Yeah."

"Get it back."

"What? You said it was fine. I've shipped out quite a few already, and…"

"Get it back," I said. "No one drinks it. Got it?"

"I'll try," Terry said. "Shit. Is there something wrong with it?"

I thought about Dennis and myself, replaying in front of me.

"Yes," I lied. "There's something wrong with it."

❖

Terry and Dennis are arguing in front of me, though I can't hear what Terry is yelling, and for his part Dennis is just shaking his head and pointing at his notepad. I move closer, look at the notepad as Dennis holds it up in Terry's face.

It just says *I won't do it.*

Terry is furious. I've seen him like this before, once or twice, and I wish I could read lips like Dennis to know what Terry is screaming at him. Terry grabs Dennis by the shoulders and physically shakes him. Dennis steps back and writes on his pad again. When he holds it up to Terry, I try to get around to see, but Terry smacks it out of his hand, and it flies off and vanishes.

"Stop it," I yell, but they don't react. The bottle shakes in my hand.

Dennis shoves Terry, hard. Terry punches him—his thick fist landing hard in the middle of Dennis's face. He stumbles back, and his foot catches on something. He goes down, and Terry is on top of him, his hands wrapping around Dennis's neck.

"No," I whine. "No, no, no…"

The images collapse. The bottle is dry. My lover is dead. The last of his memories are gone with the wine.

I don't know how.

I don't know why.

But one of those I can answer.

❖

The police are here when Terry comes in to work. When he sees them, he seems to deflate, and I wonder how long he's been waiting for something like this to happen. I had them dig under the rows of vines from which the red ice wine was born, and when they called out that they had found something, I had closed my eyes, willing the world to slow down and let me not know, just for a moment longer.

Terry had had no time for anything elegant. And through the wine my Dennis spoke to me. Where else could my lover be? It all comes together. The rain, the grapes, the frost. The soil. The soil tells.

The police take Terry's arms. They tell him his rights. He looks at me, and I ask.

"Why?"

"Money," he says. "He was supposed to get access to your bank accounts." He looks at me, a pleading look on his face. "They're going to take my house."

I close my eyes and try to ignore all the sounds as they put Terry into the car and the rest of the business unfolds.

I stand there, eyes closed, and think of Dennis, and Terry, and death. A hustler after all, I think darkly, but it doesn't hold. I remember his hand at the window and swear I can taste molten strawberries on my tongue.

CHRISTMAS COMES TO OTTERS' GAP
JEFF MANN

Charles is only half a mile from the diner when he hits the patch of black ice. He's driving slowly in the sudden snowstorm, so the 180-degree slide his cherry-red Miata slips into is gentle, almost graceful, albeit thoroughly unexpected and not at all welcome. For a split second he thinks of that stupid song, "Jesus, Take the Wheel," but he's not particularly religious, and besides, he's always been a proponent of the maxim "God helps those who help themselves," and thus his hands remain on the wheel, though his white-knuckled twisting of it does absolutely no good. By the time the half circle is completed—too gradually to call it careening—and the jazzy little car has come to a stop, Charles is facing precisely in the direction from whence he came.

Dusk's falling over the Blue Ridge Mountains of Virginia. There are no other cars on this altitudinous road; in fact, Charles hasn't seen another vehicle for a good while now. It's Christmas Eve. Charles rests his head on the wheel; adrenaline, that chemical postscript, shakes his lean frame. "Fuck, I wish I were back in Richmond. Fucking hillbilly hinterlands," he mutters. His radio's still blaring Top Forty. Around him the forest is perfectly silent, the grays and browns of December disappearing beneath abrupt white the heavens sift down, like goose down, like bleached flour, like the cocaine Charles used to indulge in during his younger days, before he gave up such entertainments and became a writer for the *Richmond Times-Dispatch*.

When Charles has managed to resume some semblance of calm, he backs up, turns around, and continues up the mountain toward Otters' Gap, his wheels tracking parallels in the snow. "Better be worth the trouble," he growls, turning off the radio so he can more easily focus.

Anxiety's building in his chest in exact proportion to the increasing whiteness of the road. The Miata creeps along between darkening walls of woodland. Then the road crests the ridge, and here's Otters' Gap, a break in the mountains—once popular with Tidewater settlers moving over the wild steeps of the Blue Ridge to inhabit the Valley of Virginia, according to Charles's research—and there, to his relief, is the glow of the restaurant, just to the side of the road.

Charles pulls into the parking lot, which is empty except for a Ford pickup truck. He cuts the engine, leans back in the bucket seat, and closes his blue eyes. He's been a city dweller all his life; tortuous mountain roads covered with snow and slicked with perilous patches of ice are not among his enthusiasms. But he's bucking for a promotion, and lately that ambition has prompted him to take on the oddest and most challenging stories in order to impress his editor. In the last several months, those stories have led him all over the Commonwealth, from Southside tobacco fields to Arlington's traffic jams, from Eastern Shore sands to this remote and unnerving mountaintop.

This particular assignment sounded simple, before the unexpected snow complicated it: interview Dave Forster about his wildly popular diner, Otters' Den, which specializes in "Appalachian cuisine," whatever that is. When Charles tries to imagine it, all he can think of is mac and cheese from a box, baloney sandwiches, and possum: white trash food, what people in trailers eat. Still, thanks to New York chefs who've popularized such mountain ingredients as ramps, the diner has become the new place to go for city dwellers bored with urban options. Despite the several-hour drive, Washington DC and Richmond foodies, desperate for culinary stimulation, are making the trek to Otters' Den.

Charles grabs his backpack, heavy with camera, iPad, and other journalistic paraphernalia, clambers from his car, and edges across the lot. His loafers are not the best footwear for such weather, their soles being without tread and so about as slippery as that black ice previously encountered. His khaki slacks, blue oxford shirt, and brown tweed blazer are similarly unhelpful against the highland cold. He left sunny Richmond this afternoon too quickly to bother checking the weather forecast, and now, shivering before the diner, he's cursing himself for that mistake.

Otters' Den is an oblong cabin made of rough-hewn logs, which fits Charles's preconception of Appalachian architecture. It's two-storied, with a roofed porch along its entire length, where empty rocking chairs are dusted with snow. It all reminds Charles of those Cracker Barrel restaurants where, he assumes, ravenous rustics eat. About the diner loom bushy evergreens, boughs already sagging with snow. "Shit! Shit!" Charles mutters, climbing the porch steps and giving the wooden door a hard rap. His head's throbbing with lingering tension. "How the hell am I going to get back—"

The door's flung open. The slender silhouette of a man appears, backlit. "Mr. Murphy, right? Come on in, bud. I'm Dave Forster. Been waiting for you."

The voice is deep, slow, and warm, heavy with Southern inflection. Charles steps inside, brushing snow from his shoulders, from his styled blond hair and close-trimmed beard. It's dim but warm, a welcome change from the bitter storm outside.

"Hello, Mr. Forster," says Charles. "I'm really sorry I'm so late. Should have called. I wasn't expecting the snow, and my car isn't very good in it."

"Call me Dave. You need you a four-wheel drive, like my Ranger out there. Good to meet you," says the man, extending a hand. "Lord, ain't you tall?"

The two men exchange a firm handshake. The contrast between their heights is indeed dramatic. "I'm six feet three," Charles says, studying his host's thin, handsome face, the brown beard that begins along the top of his cheekbones, bushes out on his cheeks and chin, and recedes into brown swirls along his neck. *Well*, he thinks, *at least this assignment will provide me with some scenery apart from the landscape. This mountain man's downright adorable.*

"Hell, I'm just five foot eight," Dave says, releasing Charles's hand only to brush long brown hair out of his eyes. Chuckling, he adds, "Guess they grow 'em big in the city. Leave your stuff here," he adds, patting a side table, "and I'll give you a quick tour. You hungry?"

"Yes," Charles responds without thinking. He's admiring his host's compact frame. Dave's dressed in blue-jean bib overalls and brown work boots. Beneath the overalls, he's wearing a white athletic undershirt inside a half-buttoned red-and-black-checked flannel shirt. *A bit of rough, that's the phrase. He's one hot little ridge-runner. The guy could be a Raging Stallion porn star.*

"Good. I'll set you up with some supper, if you'd like. We're closed tomorrow for the holiday—ever'body 'round here, other'n going to church, stays home on Christmas or visits with kinfolk—but I'll be cooking a bunch tonight anyways. Folks'll be coming in in droves day after Christmas, plus, since I knew you were coming—gotta admit I'm excited that your paper wants a story about my place—I thought I'd show you some of my specialties. Okay?"

"Uh, sure. So, *Appalachian* food?" Charles says, following Dave into a big room to the right. "So what is that exactly?"

Dave chuckles again. "You sound nervous, Mr. Murphy. Ever been up this way before?"

"Call me Charles. No, not really. I've spent my whole life in Virginia—Norfolk and Richmond—but I've never been in the mountains other than a conference in Charlottesville."

"Charlottesville's pretty, but it ain't really mountains. *These* are mountains. Now, this here's the main dining room," Dave says with a sweeping gesture. Charles takes in the long room with its log walls, an assortment of tables and chairs, a wagon-wheel pseudo-chandelier, and a big stone fireplace, unlit, at the far end. "It'll be bustling day after tomorrow. Got another dining room at the opposite end of the building. And here," he adds, pushing through a swinging door, "is my favorite place, the kitchen."

The room's spacious, with a big fridge and wide granite counters along the left side, upon which several foil-covered pies rest. On the right, a huge gas stove is set beside an old-fashioned woodstove. On both, pots are bubbling. In the back, a picture window gleams above a heavy wooden table. Beyond the steamed sheet glass, snow continues to fall, huge fluffy flakes drifting down among the pines. Somewhere, a radio is playing country music faintly. The space is very warm, and full of delicious odors. Charles shucks off his blazer; his stomach growls.

"Have a seat," Dave says, pointing to a chair at the table. "Want a drink?"

"That sounds great." Charles drapes his blazer over the back of the chair before sitting down. "But I'd better not. I have to drive back to Richmond tonight."

"Tonight? Ain't happenin'," Dave says, opening the woodstove long enough to push in a log. An overall strap slips off his shoulder; with a thumb, he hitches it back up. "You're lucky you got up the mountain before it really started coming down. Look out there. It ain't s'posed to stop till late tomorrow afternoon. It's a real White Christmas."

"Oh, hell, I should have checked the weather report," Charles grouses. "Is there a motel around here?"

"Nowhere close. You can stay here, bud. I got a guest room upstairs."

Charles rubs his forehead. "That's really nice of you. Are you sure?"

"Yep. Be good to have the company."

"All right, thanks. So yes to that drink. It might help my tension headache. Driving in snow scares the hell out of me."

Dave fetches a mason jar from inside a cabinet. He sloshes it around and grins. The liquid inside is as clear as water. "How about some local spirits?"

"You mean—?"

"Yep. You came here to experience Appalachian food." Dave flicks the oven on. "Let's us start with some Appalachian drink." He pours a liberal amount of the jar's contents into two tumblers.

"Moonshine? Really?"

Dave smiles, taking a seat. "You never had white lightning before?"

"Oh, no. Is it…safe?"

"Of course. A buddy of mine brewed this. I ain't giving a guest any popskull. You like hard stuff like rum or whiskey or vodka?"

"Sure."

"Then you'll like this." Dave lifts his glass. "Welcome to Otters' Den."

"Thanks," says Charles. Their glasses clink. Hesitantly, Charles takes a sip. It burns, yes, but not as fiercely as expected. He takes a second sip, this one larger, then a third. Between the heat of the woodstove, and now the liquor, Charles is feeling more relaxed than he ever imagined he could be in such a foreign environment.

"It's real strong. Take it slow," Dave warns.

"You bet," says Charles, looking into his host's prettily lashed green eyes. Studying the curve of Dave's full lips beneath his bushy brown mustache, the plastered chest hair curling over his A-shirt's ribbed white and pooling in the pit of his neck, Charles feels the first stirrings of a hard-on. If this were one of his favorite dance bars in Richmond instead of a remote cabin, he'd be moving in fast, laying on the aggressive flirtations that have netted him many a hot bottom, but, as it is, well, he's heard about how devout and backward hill folks are, so he keeps his lusty admiration carefully concealed behind a casual we're-all-just-straight-boys-here façade.

"Sorry you're stuck." Dave looks out the window at the snow, which is slanting sideways in a rough wind, and takes a swallow of moonshine. "I know you must hate missing Christmas Eve and Christmas Day with your family."

"I'm single." His last dismal attempts at dating—with well-off Bryan, classy Brad, sleek Jonas—flicker through Charles's mind. They bored him; they were too much like him; in mere weeks he stopped calling them back. "And I don't pay much attention to holidays. Too busy with work. This place is as good as any to spend Christmas. But how about you? Am I interrupting family time?"

"Naw." Dave grins, shaking his head. "I'm single too. My last boyfriend and I parted ways six months ago."

Charles gapes. His shock has many facets: that this butch, scruffy-bearded guy is queer; that he so casually admits it; and that, despite his homosexuality, he's living up on this mountain, out in the middle of nowhere.

"You're *gay*?"

Dave nods. "Yep. Ever'body in Bedford County knows that. I'm sorry. Did I shock you? I figured a cosmopolitan city boy like you would be broad-minded. You ain't one of those nasty pious types, are you?" His beautiful green eyes narrow.

"Me? Oh, God, no. I'm gay too!" Charles blurts.

"Yeah? Really?" Dave looks pleased. "Well, that's cool. Now you're doubly welcome." Again he extends his hand; again the two men shake. "It's always a treat to meet other gay guys."

"I'm just surprised to find a...someone like you way out here."

"In the boonies, you mean?" Dave laughs. "More of us out here than you'd expect. I'm from here, buddy. Lived in DC a few years and hated it. Got homesick as hell. Hated the crowds, the goddamn traffic jams on the beltway. So I moved back here, back to Bedford County, when I was twenty-five. I'm thirty now."

"Thirty? Me too. Don't the rednecks give you trouble, though? If you're so open?"

"Rednecks?" Dave snorts. "Hell, friend, *I'm* a redneck."

"You know what I mean," Charles says, shifting uncomfortably in his chair and taking another sip of his drink. The liquor's warmth, glowing in his head and spreading through his long limbs, is making his speech less guarded than it might normally be. "Homophobes. Religious types. Moral Majority and all that."

"Well, they would. Except my daddy's a prominent politician roundabouts. Plus, when I lived in DC, I was kinda intimidated, so I figured, since I'm small-built, it'd be a good idea to earn a black belt. I've whipped a few asses, some surly types who came in here juiced up on beer and wanting to kick the queer around. So, no, that kinda folks don't bother me no more." He nods to a gun rack near the back door. "And there's that shotgun there. She's only one of my prizes. I got a gun safe in the basement. Even got me an antique Confederate pistol. That's a treasure."

"Wow! A gun safe? You're one dangerous mountain man." Charles shakes his head. "I'd better watch out."

"You've seen *Deliverance* too many times," Dave says, unscrewing the mason jar. "You want to eat now? Or you want to drink for a while? The way the snow's coming down, you'll definitely be stuck here for a day'r so. We could save the interview for tomorrow. Tonight, you could just hang out. We could talk while I cook."

Charles's gaze ranges over his host, returning to that tempting thatch of chest hair. Their glances meet and hold for a long moment. *Christ, he has pretty eyes.*

"Let's drink," says Charles. "This stuff's tasty. I'll just consider another round research."

"That's the attitude. Sounds good to me." Dave smiles, a flash of white inside that wild bush of beard, and pours. The easy confidence of his expression impresses Charles. His own good looks—tall, sinewy, long-waisted body; oval model's face; fashionable clothes; brooding and intense turquoise eyes; thick, product-spiky golden hair; and neatly trimmed blond beard—tend to unhinge men, making them pushy and needy. This one, Dave, he seems relaxed, solid, free of that desperate clinging and panting horn-dog lust that has so rapidly turned Charles off in date after date.

"Okay, I got to get to cooking," Dave says, moving to the counter. "You mind?"

"That's fine, dude." Charles looks out at the falling snow. "Should I take notes?"

"Do that tomorrow. Just enjoy your drink. In a bit, I'll set you up with a plate of food you won't forget." Dave pulls out a battered bowl, into which he measures cups of flour. From a cabinet, he fetches a can of baking powder. "You warm enough?"

"Yes, thanks. It's toasty in here." Charles stretches, trying to banish the last tension from his limbs. He gives his host's butt—small and round beneath the overalls' denim—a long look while Dave's back is turned. *Wonder if he's a top or a bottom? Butch as he is, I'm guessing the latter.* Charles takes a long sip of moonshine and licks his lips.

"It *is* toasty. Woodstoves always pour out heat. In fact…'scuse me." Dave slips the overall straps off his shoulders, unbuttons and removes his flannel shirt, then replaces the straps. Now Charles can scrutinize his host more easily: defined pecs, hard-muscled, lithe arms, and brown fur feathering over the top and sides of the A-shirt.

"You're, uh, built," Charles says, knowing full well that the statement, despite its casual intonation, might be construed as an expression of erotic interest. "You lift?"

Dave graces Charles with a lazy smile, just this side of flirtatious. When Dave reaches up to pull Crisco from a shelf, Charles can make out the thick hair of Dave's armpits.

"I do. Got a weight set in the basement. You?"

"No. Aerobics and yoga, though, when my schedule allows."

"City boy stuff." Dave grins. "But it seems to do the trick. You look real fit. Twice as handsome as the picture I found online."

"Online?" Charles laughs. *Yes! He thinks I'm handsome!* "You looked me up online?"

"Yep. I figured I should check out the paper and the reporter, see if everythang was legit. Don't worry; I'm too busy running this place to be a stalker. Hell, I ain't got time for online porn, much less stalking." Moving to the fridge, Dave pulls out a carton of buttermilk.

"So you have a computer?"

"Don't sound so surprised. It's a MacBook Pro, actually. Most of us 'hillbillies' are computer literate."

"Oh, hey, I didn't mean—"

"Relax, bud," Dave says, adding a few clumps of Crisco to the bowl. "You're out of your element, I get it. I feel that way ever'time I'm in a city. So, a lesson in Appalachian food. You wanna see me bake a batch of biscuits? This zinc bowl was my Nanny's; the recipe's my daddy's."

"Sure. I can barely heat soup. I've never seen anybody bake anything."

"Git over here, then. And bring your drink."

Charles rises, takes a sip, and strolls over, positioning himself behind Dave. From this angle, if he bends forward, the much taller Charles can study the curves of the shorter man's chest and the shallow valley of brown hair between his pecs. He can even make out the nubby impression the cook's nipples make against the undershirt. Charles can smell him too: a peppery deodorant mixed with his natural musk, mingled with faint scents of grease, and, oddly, vanilla. "Okay. Show me, Chef Forster."

"Okay." Dave cranes his head back and grins up at Charles. "You're one long tall drink of water, that's the expression. So," he continues, returning to his task, "you cut in the Crisco...so. You add buttermilk...so. Now you work it up, yep, that's about right. Now..." Dave sprinkles flour on the counter and dumps the mess of dough out. "Now you knead...like so. Over and turn. Over and turn. Get it good and smooth, like a baby's bottom."

Wonder if your bottom's smooth or hairy? Hairy, I hope. Charles takes another swallow of the booze, feeling comfortably toasted already. Now that he knows that his host is gay and thinks he's handsome, his inveterate flirtation skills are edging to the fore, and so, after a second's hesitation, he rests a hand on Dave's shoulder and gives it a soft squeeze. "So I get some of these biscuits?"

"In a little while, I promise." Dave pauses in his kneading, turning long enough to give Charles a big wink. "I can tell you're a little dubious about mountain food, so it's my job to convince you and your readers that we Appalachians know how to cook."

"Convince me, dude. Want some?" Charles lifts his glass.

"Sure." Dave inclines his head and drinks from Charles's glass. "Thanks. So where you go when you go out in Richmond? I've had some beers and burgers at Babe's with a lesbian friend of mine, the few times I've been to town."

"I tend toward the dance clubs. Barcode or Nations. You dance?"

"Some. When I go to DC, which ain't too often, I dance with a couple Bedford County friends of mine at Town Danceboutique. James and Phil live up there now, in Adams Morgan—they're kinda fey, so living around here was pretty hard for them. I stay with them when I'm in town. Most often, though, I go to the Green Lantern or the Eagle… or wherever Bear Happy Hour is these days."

"The leather and bear crowd, huh?" Charles laughs. "No wonder you call this place Otters' Den." He lifts his glass to Dave's mouth; the smaller man takes another sideways sip. Charles resists the urge to slip his hand inside Dave's undershirt, to move forward another couple of inches and press his erection against Dave's back. "I guess we're both otters: lean and bearded."

"Yeah. I like the way your beard's trimmed, bud. Classy. You hairy too?"

"Yeah." Charles sighs. "I love body hair on other guys, but I don't like it on myself. I've been thinking about shaving my chest or having it waxed—body hair isn't very fashionable these days—but so far, I've just been too busy to do it."

"Fuck fashion. Give me hairy any day. I'd say you look damned fine the way you are. If you don't mind me saying so."

"I don't mind you saying so. I appreciate the compliment." Charles flushes with pleasure. He's self-aware enough to know his own vanity. Flattery's his favorite food.

"My guess is you get lots of compliments. You look like a fashion model." Dave pats out the dough with his flour-whitened hands, then pulls a cookie sheet from a rack. "Well, anyway, this diner was named after the gap—used to be plentiful otters round these parts, not many left—but, yeah, the wording's a fortuitous coincidence. Hey, would you reach in that fridge and fetch me a tin that says 'Grease' on it?"

Charles does so. "So what is this?"

Dave takes it from him, opens it, scoops out a gray-white waxy substance, and drops a few dollops onto the cookie sheet, which he then slides into the heated oven. "Bacon grease."

"You keep it in a tin?"

"Son, bacon grease is the secret ingredient of Southern cooking. You don't look like you need to watch calories, lean as you are. Relax. You can get back to salads and tofu when you return to Richmond." With that, Dave cuts the dough into circles, pulls the cookie sheet from the oven, moistens both sides of the rounds in melted grease, then lines them up and returns the sheet to the oven. "Twelve minutes," he says, brushing his hands on his overalls and setting a timer. Taking Charles's glass from him, Dave finishes it with a gulp. "More?"

"Sure. Though I'm a little buzzed already."

"You ain't used to this the way I am." Dave pats Charles's forearm before pouring them both half a glass. They take their seats. They gaze at each other and smile. They look out on the deepening storm. They gaze at each other again. *Oh, yes, I think I know in what direction this evening's headed*, Charles thinks. *Fuck, I'm hard.*

"Yep, you're right." Dave's face is pink with drink. "You *are* hairy." His eyes are fixed to the top of Charles's oxford shirt.

Charles blushes. He tugs at the fur sprouting over his top button. "Yeah."

"Lord, *don't* shave it. It's pretty. Color of honey. I'm glad you came by, city boy," Dave says, bumping Charles's knee with his own. "Like I said, it's good to have company. I could do with more gay friends. Last time I hung out with another queer was Master JW down in Roanoke, back in September. We might go to MAL together this coming January. That's Mid-Atlantic Leather, for you vanilla boys."

"I've heard of it. Yeah, I guess I'm vanilla. So far. Though leather... I've always been curious. My ex-boyfriend Tom, he bought me a pair of handcuffs, and once he and I took turns...it was hot. Master JW? You a bottom?"

"Why you want to know, bud?"

"Just curious." Charles smiles sheepishly. "Am I getting too personal?"

Dave laughs. "No such thang. Yeah, I'm mainly bottom, though I flip my tops every now and then. You?"

"So warm in here." Charles undoes the top button of his shirt, deliberately displaying another few inches of chest hair. "I'm mainly a top. I'm versatile, though. Whatever the other guy wants. I'm easy. Not easy as in getting around a lot—I'm too busy trying to snag a promotion, just easy, like…sorry, I'm…I'm not usually so…"

"You're squirming. A guy as hot as you shy? It's *real* cute. Why don't you take your shirt off?"

"What?" Charles is used to being the aggressor, yet this little guy is ordering him around? It's fucking arousing. "Well, I don't…"

"You been flirting with me ever since you got here, ain't you, city boy?" Dave stands. "Ain't you?"

"Yes. I think you're adorable."

"*Adorable?* How about hot, dangerous, rough, wild, all them other Appalachian stereotypes?"

"Well, yeah, all that. I didn't mean—"

"Now you're 'bout to apologize again. Hey, I'll take 'adorable.' Okay, I ain't as used to that 'shine as I claimed. Around men as hot as you I get nervous, so I drink too fast. So I'm a little toasted too. Nevertheless." Dave slams a fist down on the tabletop. "Git your shirt off. Now! Or no biscuits! How's that for a threat?"

"Yes, sir." Amused, excited, Charles unbuttons his shirt and shucks it off. He looks down over his body. Too soft, too hairy, not sufficiently defined. Yet Dave seems to feel differently.

"Oh. Oh. Goddamn." Dave steps toward Charles and wraps an arm around Charles's narrow waist. "Okay, you're just fucking beautiful," Dave sighs, running a tentative finger over Charles's thick chest hair. "Okay, not only am I kinda drunk, I'm being a bad host. I'm real sorry for coming on so strong. It's bad manners."

Charles strokes Dave's shaggy head. "Relax, dude. The attention's more than welcome. I'm disease-free, by the way. You?"

Dave nods. "Oh, yeah. Tested six months ago. Haven't been with a man since then."

"How about you feed me all that delicious-smelling food you've been cooking? We'll figure out the rest later."

"Sure, bud. You're just so handsome that…well, okay." With both hands, Dave pats Charles's bare chest, then gently pushes him away. "You…sit. Here it comes, the mysterious hillbilly food you've been wondering about. I hope you're hungry?"

"Yes, indeed," Charles exclaims, draining his glass.

The oven timer goes off. Dave slides biscuits from the oven, then spoons and forks food from pots atop the stoves. In a few minutes, he's set full wineglasses and heaped plates on the table. He's about to take a seat when Charles raises an eyebrow. "Your turn, Dave."

Dave gets the shorthand. He tugs his A-shirt off, tossing it into a corner.

Charles takes a deep breath. Now he can see the little man's plump pecs, the thick brown hair pelting his belly and torso, the pink nipples surrounded by that rich rug of fur. "Damn, Dave, you're…"

"Dive in, city boy. I've given you just a few spoonfuls of everythang, so you'll have room for dessert. I got several pies waiting for us."

"All right," says Charles. "I'm famished." Seizing his fork, he begins.

Dave provides a culinary gloss as they feast, as Charles groans and smacks his lips with delight. "Okay, the wine's elderberry. Kinda sweet, I know. Most homemade wine is. And that's brown beans and cornbread. Real hillbilly fare. Add some of this to it. Chowchow: it's a homemade relish. That taste for sweet-sour, the German immigrants brought it over. And these are stuffed peppers, and these are cabbage rolls. And here's greens: a little bit of collards, a little bit of kale, some creecy greens and some mustard greens. Splash on the Tabasco; that's a great addition. That there's pulled pork simmered in barbecue sauce; put that on a split biscuit with some of this cole slaw. Only way to eat barbecue. And here's some potato salad…and some deviled eggs. Some broccoli salad, some pea salad…"

Dave falls silent. The two men eat, and eat, and eat. Their flat bellies grow less flat. By the time they put down their silverware, those bellies are taut and bulging.

"Uhhf." Charles groans. "I'm pretty stuffed."

"Me too. Full as a tick. Maybe we should wait for dessert?"

"Yes. I really want to try those pies, but not for a while yet."

"In that case…" Dave stands. He stumbles, then straightens. "Shit, I'm drunk. Your fault. Too damn handsome…" Grabbing Charles's hand, he pulls him to his feet and flicks off the kitchen lights.

"Come on now," Dave directs. Charles follows him through a doorway into a tiny antechamber. Inside are a narrow cot heaped with comforters, a paper-cluttered desk, a bookcase, and an armchair.

Dave pushes Charles down onto the mattress. "Get naked, big man," he mutters. "After I put the food away, we'll cuddle, sober up some."

Awkward with too much drink, Charles does what he's told. Stripped, he falls back onto the cot. Dave shucks off his overalls and stands naked beside him. "God, you're glorious," Dave whispers, caressing Charles's hair and arranging comforters over him. "I'm so glad you're here."

"Damn," Charles sighs. "Me too." He reaches up, runs his fingers over Dave's hairy belly, grips the cook's erect prick, cranes forward, and runs his tongue over the cockhead—surprisingly large for such a small man, Charles's 'shine-soaked brain registers. Then Charles slumps back beneath the blankets and passes out.

❖

What wakes Charles is something heavy across his hips, something tightening around his wrists. His eyes blink open. Dave, still naked, is straddling Charles's waist and roping his hands together before him.

"Oh, here we go. You leather types." Charles musters just enough struggle to encourage Dave to force his hands above his head. Charles's erection bumps Dave's butt; Dave's erection bumps Charles's belly.

"Relax, city boy. You trust me, don't you?" Dave's beard brushes Charles's beard. Dave's lips brush Charles's lips.

"Yeah, I guess I do." Smiling, Charles submits, allowing Dave to continue his knot-work. "But we're not about to act out a *Deliverance* scene, are we?"

Dave chuckles. Done binding Charles, Dave bends, nuzzling his mouth. They kiss, deeply, lengthily. "City boy raped by hillbilly? Naw. I'm mainly a bottom, remember?" Dave wiggles his butt against Charles's prick. "I promise it'll be real fun. Want some dessert? I have several courses in mind."

"You bet."

"Up then." Dave, slipping off the cot, hauls Charles up by the several feet of rope hanging from his wrists. Again they kiss, the taller man leaning over, the shorter man craning upward. "One more thang," Dave says, picking up a bandana from the desk. It's red, white, and blue, the pattern of the Confederate flag. "Big Rebel buff here. I attend reenactments every chance I get." Pressing the folded length of cloth over Charles's eyes, he ties it behind the big man's head.

"All right?"

"Yeah. I guess. I'm a little scared now."

"Good. Don't you worry, city boy. I got you. I take good care of my captives." Pulling on the wrist-tether, Dave leads blindfolded Charles through the darkness. A door creaks; they pass into the scents and warmth of the kitchen.

"Easy, bud. Watch that chair." Dave's hand protectively cups Charles's naked hip. "Here we are. Sit."

Charles fumbles behind him, finding a solid shelf.

"It's the kitchen table. Now stretch out. It's solid. It'll hold you."

Charles obeys, lying down on the hard wood. Dave pulls Charles's hands above his head. The rope goes taut. When Charles tugs, he finds himself tied down. Dave spreads Charles's legs; now rope's knotted around Charles's right ankle and pulled tight, now Dave does the same to Charles's left ankle. Charles shifts and writhes, only to find his movements limited to mere inches in any direction.

"There you go," Dave sighs with audible satisfaction. "You all right? Into this? Looks like it." A fingertip slides down Charles's erection.

"Actually, yeah. This is hot." Charles smiles into the darkness.

"Ain't going nowhere for a while, are you? Ready for dessert?" A fingertip brushes Charles's mouth. When Charles parts his lips, the finger traces his tongue. When Charles tightens his lips, the finger fucks that tightness.

"*Damn*, you're big," Dave sighs, stroking Charles's hard-on. "You tall lanky boys always have huge dicks. I'm gonna love having that fat thang up in me."

"Ump." Charles grunts around Dave's finger and nods. The thought of fucking Dave's hole has him so cock-stiff he's in pain.

"First course," Dave says, pulling his finger from Charles's mouth. The bound-down journalist can hear crinkling, scraping, then Dave nudges his mouth. "Open up, big boy."

Charles grins. He extends his tongue. Intense gelatinous sweetness floods it.

"That's pecan pie."

Charles chews and swallows. "Fuck, that's great! And I have to say, this is the hottest scene ever. You hillbillies are marvelous perverts."

Dave guffaws. "Well, hell, that's the sweetest thang any man's said to me in years. Okay, next. Say 'Ah.'"

"Ahhhh."

This taste is jiggly, creamy, with a tinge of spice. "Wow, what's that?"

"That's custard pie. Real old-fashioned. Dusted with nutmeg."

Dave rings the changes—buttermilk pie, shoofly pie, sweet potato pie, apple crisp, blackberry cobbler—just a forkful each. Charles groans and chews, savoring every bite.

Padding of bare feet. Clink of plate and fork in the sink. "That it?" Charles lifts his head, grinning at his unseen captor.

"Naw."

The table creaks beneath Charles as Dave clambers onto it. He straddles Charles, then lies on top of him. The two men kiss, grinding their loins together.

"Got several courses left," Dave rumbles huskily. "You just lie back and count your blessings, city boy."

First, fondling and lapping, Dave makes lengthy love to Charles's sensitive nipples. *God, he's good*, Charles muses, when his pleasure-flooded brain isn't washed entirely free of words. Next Dave sits astride Charles's chest, cups the back of his neck, pushes his cock between Charles's lips, and fucks his face with short strokes. Dave's dick is slender but it's long, almost as long as Charles's own, bumping the back of his captive's throat. Charles groans and slobbers, relishing Dave's pubic musk and pounding vigor.

"A few more courses, and we're done," Dave mutters, pulling his cock from Charles's appreciative mouth. The smaller man slides down to Charles's groin, giving each nipple a quick nip as he descends, squeezes his balls, and engulfs Charles's cock with his wet mouth. The bound-down man moans and thrashes; Dave's skill is so well honed that, within moments, Charles is approaching climax.

"Oh, God, I'm close!"

"Ah, ah. Not yet." Dave's mouth frees Charles. There's the ripping of a condom packet, the squirting sound of lube. A gooey chill covers

Charles's rampant cock. "Here we go," Dave sighs, straddling Charles's hips. "Been a long time since I got fucked. Big as you are, we got to take this slow."

And so they do, Charles, despite his pulsing ardor, doing his level best not to thrust upward—wildly, hurtfully, and too fast—into that delicious, descending tightness, Dave's ass muscles opening gradually, Charles's cock gradually edging inside. "Whoa! Oh! Slow!" Dave blurts. "Hurts! Fuck, you're huge. Okay. Easy. Go ahead."

Now the last inch slides up inside Dave's tight hole. The smaller man rests on Charles's groin, wiggles his rear, tightens his sphincter around Charles's thick column of flesh, and gives a long, blissful sigh. "God*damn*, it feels *great* to be filled up like this."

With that, their matching rhythms begin. Lips nibble lips; Dave pinches and tugs Charles's nipples, clenching his ass muscles around Charles's cock. Soon, with matching moans, they're done, Charles's a latex-sheathed climax deep in Dave's ass, Dave's a copious spurting across Charles's belly hair.

Another few minutes, and Dave's cleaned them both up and put the desserts away. Dave pulls off the blindfold and frees Charles's feet. Leaving his hands bound, Dave leads his smiling and sleepy guest upstairs by his wrist-tether. Soon, the two men are snuggling together in Dave's big bed, Charles's bound arms around Dave's small frame, Dave's face nestling against the bigger man's chest. Outside, the blizzard continues, heaping the pines, the cabin roof, Charles's snazzy Miata, and Dave's rusty Ford.

❖

Charles wakes at dawn with a raging hard-on. Stealthily, he picks at the rope about his wrists with his teeth, freeing himself. By the time Dave, yawning and blinking, comes awake, Charles has his host's hands tied together and anchored to the headboard. Giggling, Dave struggles. Giggling, Charles wrestles him down and rolls him onto his belly.

"I'm going to plow you again, hillbilly," Charles announces, hauling Dave onto his elbows and knees. "I'm going to rape your pretty ass." He gives one plump cheek an open-palmed slap.

Dave yelps, only to lift his ass higher. "If you insist, city boy. There's, uh, rubbers and lube in the bedside table there."

"Yum, your ass is as hairy as I'd hoped. I guess that means I'll have to open you up with my tongue. I can't resist eating a hole this furry. Would you like that? Want your redneck ass eaten?" Charles runs a forefinger down Dave's crack, then lifts that finger to his mouth, wets it, and nudges Dave's hole.

Dave whimpers. "Hell, yes. Please." He buries his face in the blankets, bound hands clenched beneath his chin, and lifts his butt higher still.

"Good boy." Charles grips Dave's butt cheeks, spreads his pink ass entrance with his thumbs, licks his lips, buries his face in Dave's crack hair, and begins.

❖

Christmas is a triple idyll: romantic, gustatory, and erotic. Snow continues to fall, though the wind dies down and the storm slows as the day progresses. Dave and Charles sleep late, then, dressed in baggy sweats, gobble a big brunch Dave prepares, complete with Bloody Marys made from Dave's home-canned tomato juice. "So, that's sausage gravy on the biscuits," Dave murmurs as they contentedly stuff themselves. "Jimmy Dean sausage, it ain't got much fat, with a little onion added. Scrambled eggs, that green stuff is ramps I picked over the hill last April and froze, they're a kinda wild onion—got to use a cast iron skillet and lots of butter. Fried apples…brown sugar, cinnamon, a little bacon grease. You want more coffee, stud?"

Their afternoon's divided between kitchen and bedroom. At first they're efficient. Dave cooks some, talks some. Charles pulls out his interview questions, taping Dave's responses. Then they get to kissing, squeezing each other's crotches and rear ends. Now Dave's on his knees by the woodstove, sucking Charles's cock. Now both men are naked, Dave's bent over the kitchen table, and Charles is slapping and biting Dave's buttocks. Now Dave's on his back on the bed upstairs, legs hooked over Charles's shoulders, whimpering as Charles pushes his fat cock up Dave's ass and nips Dave's torso with his teeth. By the time five o'clock arrives and Dave's pouring them glasses of 'shine, Charles's cock is chafed and Dave's asshole is sore, his chest and butt cheeks covered with the blue bruises of love-bites.

Come suppertime, Dave and Charles, both gently buzzed, sit down to another down-home meal: country ham biscuits, corn pudding, fried chicken with cream gravy, pickled beets, and green beans cooked with fatback. Sated, Charles props his feet up. Dave fetches his banjo and lights a candle. They relax in the warmth of the woodstove, Charles drowsing, hands folded across his belly, Dave picking out old ballads while, outside, the storm fades and a snowplow scrapes by.

After dessert—Dave has half a slice of shoofly pie, half a slice of pecan, while Charles indulges in a heap of apple crisp topped with vanilla ice cream and a drizzle of maple syrup—they go to bed early, sleeping soundly, snuggling close. Come morning, Dave's hungry butt nudges Charles awake. Charles roughly fucks Dave on his side, jacking him with his hand. They both come, bucking and shouting. Charles pulls Dave into his arms, his cock growing soft inside the smaller man. Curling up together, they fall asleep.

❖

"Road's nice and clear," says Dave.

"Looks like it," says Charles, sliding his backpack into the Miata's passenger seat.

Snow's falling in clumps from sun-bright pines. Melt's dripping off the diner's eaves.

The two men stand by Charles's car. "Thanks for breakfast," Charles says, resting his hands on Dave's shoulders. "Buckwheat cakes, maple syrup, and sausage: That'll keep me going till I get home and well after."

"Just in case that ain't enough…" Dave hands Charles a paper bag. "In there's a couple of country ham biscuits. For the road."

They fall silent with that uncertainty that, after passionate and unplanned lovemaking, composes so many partings. *Is this over, a one-time thing? Or is this connection worth the risk of continuing?*

"Look, bud," Dave drawls. Taking Charles's right hand, he kisses a knuckle. "I know you must have loads of boyfriends waiting in the wings, and I know it's a good ways from here to Richmond, and I'm just a scruffy ole redneck, but…come back sometime. If you want. If your schedule ever—"

"I'll mail you a copy of the paper your story's published in. If you'll e-mail me." Charles pulls a business card from his front pocket.

Inside him, the customary battle rages. *Lives too far away. Backgrounds too different. Best lay I've ever had. So sweet, so gentle. Damned dangerous, this tender feeling.*

"Oh. Okay. Sure." With a brisk nod, Dave takes the card. He drops Charles's hand and takes a step back. "Well, better get in there. 'Spect lots of folks'll be coming by for dinner today."

Fuck it. I'm thirty, for Chrissake. I've spread enough wild oats. When am I going to meet a guy like this again? "Hey, Dave." Charles grips Dave's arm, squeezing his hard little biceps. "You ever get weekends off?"

A hopeful smile lights up Dave's face. "Ev'ry so often. Rarely."

"You free next weekend?"

"Naw, I gotta work. Closed Sunday, but open Saturday. Why?"

Charles brushes Dave's thick bangs to the side before kissing his brow. "Well, I'm free, I'm pretty sure. Guess that means I could be driving back up this way. That all right with you?"

"Really?" Dave nods. "Yeah. That'd be great."

"Only if you cook for me."

"Sure. How about, uh, beef stew, corn muffins, and collards? And I got a recipe for apple stack cake I'd like to try out."

"That sounds wonderful. I'll provide the wine, okay? To be honest, that elderberry stuff is far too sweet for me." With a wicked grin, Charles pats Dave's ass. "How about I bring those handcuffs of mine? I'm thinking you'd look pretty hot bent over the kitchen table with that Stars-and-Bars bandana tied between your teeth, your hands cuffed behind you, and my cock stuffed up your ass."

"God, such nasty talk," Dave exclaims, rubbing the front of his overalls. "Hell, yes. More kink would be much 'preciated, as would a long plowing."

"I think I can get up here late Friday night. I'll have work to do Saturday, but I can do that on my laptop while you're running the diner. I'd have to leave Sunday evening, okay?"

"Yep!" says Dave. "I'd sure like to see you again."

"Feeling's mutual." Bending, Charles takes Dave in his arms. For a soft, brief moment, their lips meet. "Good-bye, hillbilly."

"Bye, city boy. Be careful going down the mountain."

They exchange a hard hug. Charles starts up his engine, turns on the radio, and spins off. In his rearview mirror he watches Dave's figure rapidly diminishing. Just before Charles turns a corner and the diner disappears, he sees Dave wave.

Best Christmas I ever spent, thinks Charles, descending the Blue Ridge. *Is this what I've been needing, a country boy? Is it really time I started getting serious about someone and thought about settling down? Surely not. With a mountain man? Surely not! But...those beautiful green eyes, that sweet smile, that tight, eager, furry ass...damn. Never to see him again? Incomprehensible.*

By the time Charles has reached the interstate, he's left doubt behind. Fumbling out his iPhone, he punches in his new boyfriend's number, preparing to detail for Dave the several positions in which he plans to pound him when next they meet.

THE CAFÉ FRANÇOISE
JAY NEAL

*C*afé au lait, s'il vous plaît."
        Non, I have not been back to this spot for some years, ever since Hélène died, I suppose. I had no reason—no desire perhaps—nothing to bring me back to this side of the Seine.

At first you might think it looks the same here since the War, but how can it? War is a filthy, ugly thing and none of us can be the same afterward. You see these trees lining the boulevard? How majestic and placid they look, spreading their shade over the sidewalks, but they too are changed because of the things they have seen passing beneath them in the streets.

Yes, this café, it also has changed, *bien sûr.* The building looks timeless, the young lovers leaning together in the corner, the two old men playing chess at their table—they all look as unchanging as *la Bastille* that once stood on this spot, but even that is gone. It is all an illusion, my friend, all an illusion.

From everywhere out here you can see the Genius. You see? There, on top of the July Column in the middle of the *Place,* the statue of the "Genius of Freedom"? She was our guardian angel. "By the Genius we'll get through," Hélène always said.

This used to be called the Café Françoise. That's how I knew it then, during the war. It was owned by Hélène, *la belle* Hélène. She was a very smart businesswoman. She made her money in the first war with a house of prostitution or something equally disreputable. Then she bought this place and settled down to become respectable and take care of us all. Perhaps only somewhat more respectable.

Many people passing by thought she had named the café after herself, but how could that be? Her name was Hélène. So I tell you now: she named it for her husband! *Oui*, her husband. He was a famous *chanteuse*, a singer who performed in ladies' clothing in the nightclubs near here. His name on the stage was "Françoise." Before the war the streets shimmered with the lights of the nightclubs. After the Germans came—well, the singers continued to sing and the people continued to dance, but the lights seemed dimmer and the shimmer had gone missing. But, by the Genius, we got through.

Wartime makes for strange bedfellows, *non*? Two of the least likely met right here at the Café Françoise, their stars crossed with the inevitability that war can create.

Jean-Pierre lived in a room just there, a small room behind that window on the fourth floor above the café. He worked here in the café, managing for Hélène the staff of waiters, who seemed to be changing with some frequency. Of course, you guess that was a false story to hide the truth. Jean-Pierre and Hélène were part of *la Résistance*, a very active part. They helped people escape from Paris, where they were not safe, into the countryside of southern France, where they might be safer during the time of occupation.

Needless to say, escape took time and planning. One couldn't simply travel from Paris into the countryside and take a train to Switzerland or Spain. Remember, this was the time of *Nacht und Nebel* in the occupied zone. The Gestapo would have been happy to give us free passage to that detention camp in Alsace if they could catch us in activities of *la Résistance*. Naturally we were not keen to disappear into the "Night and Fog," never to be seen again. And so we worked at the café as waiters and cleaning staff while we waited for our false papers and travel itineraries to be put together in secret.

From this place it was mostly homosexuals who were fleeing from the occupation that was crushing their beloved home city. I know: I was one of them, working here, waiting on customers and waiting for my chance at freedom to arrive. It was a tense time, and very dangerous, but by the Genius we got through—at least, some of us did.

This was a good place for smuggling people away. You see, across the *Place*, where the Opéra Bastille was built, that used to be the *Gare de la Bastille*. Trains and people came and went all the time, creating confusion and making opportunities for clandestine departure from the city.

Of course, the *Militärverwaltung in Frankreich* knew this too, and their headquarters was only three kilometers away: the cat sleeping near the mouse's hole. Perhaps it meant an extra *frisson* for us, snatching the cheeses away so near to the cat's nose. But you could guess that sooner or later the Gestapo would start to smell the mouse and send a cat to investigate the situation. But who could have known that the cat would be so beautiful—so dangerously beautiful? His arrival was utterly prosaic and we mice had no sense of impending doom.

The long, black cars favored by the Gestapo were ubiquitous in Paris by then and we had lost all fear of them. We were undaunted when one stopped in front of the café. It was only when the car door opened and a tall, young Gestapo officer stepped out and strode to the café that we suspected—well, that something would happen. We really had no idea at first what it might mean for us that the Gestapo had come sniffing around.

What did they already know about us and what went on here that they sent such irresistible bait to catch their mice? Surely, we knew, such a thing could not happen merely by accident.

This man was one of the very few persuasively Aryan-looking men of the Gestapo. Tall and blond, he was broad at the shoulders, broad at the waist, and broad at the hips; not fat, but hefty and solidly built, like the honest farm boy that he probably was. Most disarming was his radiant smile. I'm sure he was a successful interrogator: Who wouldn't want to tell him anything he wanted to hear?

He arrived on a sunny April afternoon. I was cleaning tables set out on the sidewalk after our lunch rush. We weren't very busy, only two or three tables still occupied. He chose to sit out of the sun, at a table in the shade of the awning.

Jean-Pierre appeared and the officer ordered, in surprisingly unaccented French, "A coffee and a piece of torte."

Jean-Pierre asked, "Which flavor torte would the gentleman prefer?"

He shrugged. "Whichever is tastiest." He looked intently at Jean-Pierre for a moment. "You decide for me."

When Jean-Pierre walked away to get the order, the officer took from his coat a small notebook, from which he read a bit then wrote a note or two.

Jean-Pierre reappeared and set a coffee and slice of torte in front of the man, who looked at it and smiled his satisfaction. "Ah,

Schwarzwälder Kirschtorte! I see you have discerned my tastes already."

Jean-Pierre inclined his head in discreet acknowledgment.

The man consulted his notebook. "The proprietress is Madame Hélène DePuys. Is that correct?"

"That is correct."

"Is she here this afternoon?"

"No. She never arrives before the hour of nine in the evening. Nothing to speak of ever happens here any earlier."

"I see. And who is in charge until she arrives?"

"I am."

"And your name is?"

"Jean-Pierre Renard."

He made a note. "Perhaps, then, I can rely on you to satisfy my needs. I am *Kriminalinspektor* Klaus Nördlingen."

"That would be my pleasure, I'm sure, *Herr Kriminalinspektor.*"

"Thank you, that's all for the moment." Nördlingen returned his attention to his notebook but—was this just my imagination?—he did glance at Jean-Pierre as he walked back into the café.

Nördlingen enjoyed his refreshment at leisure, apparently relaxed in the afternoon sun, watching what little traffic passed in front of the café. At length he stood, left a few coins on the table, and walked back to his waiting car. As soon as he was inside the car drove off. Thus began what we were certain was to be continued surveillance of our operation by the Gestapo.

As the next few weeks passed, Nördlingen became a regular visitor to the café. His car would arrive and wait for him at the curb while he enjoyed his refreshment. Each day he arrived later and later. Before long he was there at a time to have his supper at an inside table. Soon enough he was there to watch the cabaret that started after nine o'clock.

All the time he was served by Jean-Pierre. It only made sense. Jean-Pierre was the constant in our operation, the one who was always there, who would always be there after the others of us had left, the one who could maintain a consistent cover story. Besides, the rest of us were too jittery to trust ourselves with a Gestapo officer regardless—or perhaps because of—how undeniably attractive he was.

So, of the two, who did his job too well? Who was the infiltrator and who was the infiltrated? Klaus Nördlingen was sent by his bosses to break through our cover and reveal our secret organization. Jean-Pierre Renard was to spin a web of deceit and make it convincing that we did nothing more illegal at the café than running a black-market operation in smuggled alcohol. As they penetrated each other's confidence, who suspected that they would find each other's soul?

They became lovers. By the end of his third week visiting the café, Nördlingen was sharing Jean-Pierre's bed. This fact they could not hide from me for the simple reason that I shared Jean-Pierre's room. There was a divider, *bien sûr*, but it was only a stained blanket hanging from a wire across the room. While it hid their activity from my eyes it could not conceal the sounds of their lovemaking from my ears.

Was their liaison ill-considered, dangerous, incendiary? *Bien sûr*, but what does young love know of fears like that, of ill-considered liaisons, of future difficulties? Only the present mattered, and it was a war. Do not forget that. I would have envied Jean-Pierre his luck at winning Nördlingen, but I was too buoyed by their love for each other and the hope it seemed to promise for the future.

I'm a little embarrassed to say so, but it was not without benefit, my lying on the other side of the hanging blanket. Yes, of course they knew I was there, but that was easily forgotten in the midst of their passion for each other. Besides, I could be trusted with their secret, not only because I was part of *la Résistance* group, but also because I was part of their passion. As they gave each other pleasure in the dark next to me, I gave myself pleasure with my own hand. Yes, they made love to each other and I made love to myself while I listened.

Would I ever forget their first night together? It was long after we'd closed the café, so the whole building was very quiet and very dark because of the blackout.

The sound of lips and tongues on skin is very distinctive, *non*? It was vivid in my ear, listening to Jean-Pierre kiss his lover on the neck as he unbuttoned Klaus's tunic. The rustle of clothing being removed confirmed my aural image.

With their clothes stripped off they could lie silently next to each other, feeling their warmth, feeling their bare skin touching over the entire length of their naked bodies: Jean-Pierre short and dark, hairy and rough; Klaus tall and blond, smooth and soft. The contrast in their bodies delighted my mind's eye.

I was young, I was hot-blooded—and I was horny. War was a time of deprivation, *bien sûr*, but clinging to each other provided some relief from the terror and sex offered some optimism for the future—that there would even be a future! Imagining the motions that accompanied the sounds of their lovemaking was not so difficult for me. Besides, when you get down to specifics, how many really different things can two people do with each other, particularly while trying to keep entirely silent in complete darkness?

Kissing arouses me greatly, and they certainly did a great deal of it. Lips smacked, joined and pulled apart, lubricated and guided by tongues exploring in moist mouths. Locked in embrace, the two moaned as their erections stiffened and pressed more rigidly against each other.

I could discern Klaus's sounds of pleasure as Jean-Pierre shifted his attention first to kissing Klaus's neck, then gliding down to kiss Klaus's chest and nipples, nipples no doubt rigid and sensitive with urgent desire. Klaus's shuddering intake of air told me that Jean-Pierre had grabbed Klaus's yearning erection with his hand, making exploratory strokes all the while he teased Klaus's nipples. When the torture became too great, Klaus clapped his hands to Jean-Pierre's head and shoulder, trying to make their two bodies into one, crushing themselves together in love and fear.

When it began I could easily identify the familiar sounds of joyous cocksucking, but it was more difficult to say who was doing exactly what to whom. There was enough sound—and ample moaning—for me to presume that Jean-Pierre and Klaus were both involved in giving and receiving in a noble display of *égalité* and *fraternité*. Hard dicks in welcoming mouths, lips and tongues on balls—these sounds are not so pretty to make it worth describing in detail but we all know the remarkably pleasurable sensations they accompany, and the satisfaction that goes with giving and receiving that pleasure. I felt almost a part of their lovemaking as I gave myself solitary—and silent!—pleasure in the dark next to them.

The pace of our mutual activities increased, only to be halted suddenly when I heard Nördlingen whisper, "*Bitte, ficke mich jetzt.*" I stopped stroking my own dick while I listened to them rearrange their position. My anticipation was keen; I felt that my orgasm could arrive at any moment.

I cannot say with certainty whether they assumed a face-to-face position but I easily imagined it so, for the romance and the intimacy. Jean-Pierre's moment of entry was made clear by the somewhat clenched *"Ja—Ja—Ja"* of Klaus's encouragement and enjoyment.

I matched my rhythm to theirs: slow, deliberate, savoring the sensations at first. How is it that something we do thousands of times can seem new and fresh each time? Before long their measured sensuality gave way to fevered urgency, the irrepressible urgency to reach the goal, to achieve the climax, as quickly as possible. Fortunately, as we increased our pace, my own increasingly heavy breathing was masked by the inchoate moans and grunts from Jean-Pierre and Klaus expressing that shared satisfaction that is impossible to express with mere words.

We all arrived at our release simultaneously. I came silently, still maintaining the fiction that I was not witness to their consummation. Jean-Pierre and Klaus, while evidently intending to demonstrate a certain discretion, nevertheless were rather noisier as they reached their climax, quickly collapsing in a heap of cooing and giggling, relaxing into an intimacy of touching and caressing and whispered endearments. My exhaustion and satisfaction were complete; I fell soundly asleep and never knew when Klaus left Jean-Pierre alone in his bed for the night.

I longed to share another secret evening with the two lovers, but it never happened again. Surely it would have attracted too much attention and raised too many questions if Klaus were seen to be absent too frequently in the night from his official accommodations. No, after that first night the two lovers stole their moments together during the young Gestapo officer's official afternoon visits or, more commonly, as a brief interlude in official surveillance during the evening cabaret that began at nine or ten in the evening, but never before Hélène arrived.

They believed they were discreet, as all secret lovers do, but anyone could see the passion burning in their eyes when they looked at each other, and they looked into each other's eyes at much greater length than any customer would with his waiter. When Jean-Pierre hovered to take Klaus's order, or when he brought that afternoon's refreshment or that evening's supper, they moved next to each other too closely, as though their mutual attraction pulled them inescapably together, as if an undeniable law of nature, a gravitational force, had developed between them and them alone.

As time passed their indiscretion grew more worrisome to me. By this I do not refer to any jealousy on my part. *Oui*, I've admitted that I envied Jean-Pierre his luck with conquering Herr Nördlingen in such an unlikely setting, but I did not feel at all jealous. No, my fear was that what I could so clearly see happening between them, others might see with equal clarity, and others might not be so romantically disposed toward the two lovers.

My fear proved to be no idle worry. Also observing—with very keen interest—was the man we knew as Monsieur Cochon, so called either for his piggy little eyes, or his piggy little snout, or his piggy little face, or perhaps for his piggy little body or his exceedingly piggy demeanor. Regardless, he was a regular patron of the café, and a perpetual irritant.

Whenever Nördlingen was in the café, Jean-Pierre was nearby and M. Cochon watched them closely. He saw the way they looked at each other, the way they spoke to each other, and he no doubt kept a careful record of the times when they disappeared upstairs together. His interest in the affairs of others would have been merely insensitive and intrusive until the afternoon when I saw Cochon approach Nördlingen's table and speak quietly to him for several minutes, only to scurry away quickly when Jean-Pierre emerged from the kitchen. Seeing this, Jean-Pierre remonstrated with Klaus, but Klaus looked insouciant. Whatever Cochon had in mind to say to Nördlingen, whatever proposal he had to offer, it would likely lead only to trouble. The incident left me gravely concerned for Jean-Pierre's safety and the integrity of our operation at the café.

That evening when Hélène arrived I pulled her aside to tell her of my concern.

"You know," I said, "that we are being closely watched by the Gestapo?"

"You refer to the beautiful young German who sits here and eats every day," she said. "Of course, what else could he be?"

"His name is Klaus Nördlingen. You know that he and Jean-Pierre are carrying on a secret liaison?"

"To see them together is to know. I think this is a secret that is not so very secret."

"Does this not worry you?"

"Love is always a happy thing, but falling in love is always a risk, especially when the seeds of love grow in the rocky soil of war."

"Their secret is evidently known to M. Cochon."

"He is a piggy little man of no real consequence."

"I saw him earlier talking secretively to Nördlingen. I worry that our operation may be compromised, that there may indeed be consequences."

"Perhaps he hopes for a little bit of success at blackmail, eh? It's a difficult time—he is trying to provide for his ailing sister. Perhaps you should show more charity, try to understand."

But I felt that I did understand fully and could see with clarity the danger that Hélène chose to deny. I get no satisfaction from knowing that I was soon proved to be correct: There are situations that are bigger than ourselves, sequences of events that we trigger and participate in but over which we have no real control.

It was only a few days later when the precipitated events finally occurred. It was still early in the evening—the cabaret had yet to begin, but it would soon since Hélène had already arrived. It was to be a festive evening, too: Françoise himself would be giving a special performance later on.

I had been in the kitchen gathering some plates of food to deliver to a table of rowdy young men restless for the show to begin. I heard noise in the café: yelling, angry yelling in a woman's voice. It was Hélène! How unlike her, I thought, to raise her voice during opening hours in the café. I stepped out of the kitchen into the hallway at the rear of the café to see what could be the cause of this unseemly behavior.

It surprised me little to see that it was M. Cochon as the root of the trouble. He was standing, abashed and helpless, some little distance from the zinc bar while Hélène, from her place behind the bar, hurled volley after volley of invective at him.

"You little rat! Why have you betrayed your friends like this! You filthy pig! Dying on a garbage dump is too good for a traitor like you!"

Everyone in the café was silent, riveted by the thrill of this melodramatic scene. Jean-Pierre stepped out of the kitchen and stood behind me.

"Whatever is going on out there?" he asked.

"It seems that Hélène is showing M. Cochon some charity."

M. Cochon, verbally trampled upon as he was, felt no need to yell back at Hélène. Was I imagining the hint of a smirk on his face? Reasons why this might be so started forming in my mind until the sound of breaking glass interrupted my thoughts.

At first the source of the sound was not evident, but as those of us who had been engaged in this drama watched M. Cochon slump to the floor it soon was obvious that the sound was that of the large window at the front of the café shattering as a bullet passed through it on its flight toward M. Cochon's head, its evident target.

All was silent for several seconds. M. Cochon—the now late but certainly unlamented piggy little informer—was suddenly just a bleeding lump on the floor. Shock and delayed comprehension enforced the silence. Then, at once, the noise and confusion of the reality broke through that barrier.

Mayhem erupted. The doors to the café flew open and a dozen or more young Nazis poured in, trying to spread quickly through the crowd, but there were so many people it was difficult for them. All the people in the café had stood up at once and begun trying to move, everyone looking for an escape from this uncertain situation. Everywhere was noise and jostling. A few people, some couples, managed to get free and passed us in the hallway, moving hurriedly toward the rear door of the café, apparently left unguarded.

Jean-Pierre was casting his eyes over the crowd of people, searching. Anxiously, he mumbled to himself, "Where is he?" I looked toward the front door just as Nördlingen himself strode in. He paused, also surveying the crowd of people. With his greater height he spotted us quickly and began swimming in our direction.

"He is here," I said to Jean-Pierre. "He has seen us."

Nördlingen reached us and pushed us back into the shadows of the hallway. His speech was urgent. "We have very little time left. Events now are out of my control."

Jean-Pierre was agitated. "But what has happened? I thought you would protect us!"

"We are betrayed and I am in no position to protect anyone now."

"But how can that be? We had it all worked out. It was all arranged."

"Listen to me: That little pig ratted on us to my superiors. They know about your entire operation and they insist on shutting it down. Tonight. Now."

Jean-Pierre was not comprehending—the shock of it all was clearly too great for him. Frustration broke through Nördlingen's thin veneer of composure. He forcibly threw Jean-Pierre against the wall, pinning his lover there with his left forearm. His right arm slowly rose up to reveal a semi-automatic pistol in his hand. He placed the pistol with its barrel pressed up beneath Jean-Pierre's chin.

Klaus's words were measured. "They are testing me. They know about us. They sent me here with orders to kill you." The gun did not waver a centimeter.

Jean-Pierre looked with resignation into Klaus's eyes. "Shoot me, then. Kill me now, this instant! Without you, without our love, I have nothing to live for."

In a voice meant only for Jean-Pierre to hear, Klaus said, "You will always have my love." He closed his eyes and leaned forward until his lips reached Jean-Pierre's lips. They kissed, with passion and abiding love, but also with calm acceptance of their fates. Klaus never moved the gun from Jean-Pierre's throat. I steeled myself for the shot, already picturing Jean-Pierre's lifeless form sliding to the floor.

But the explosion never came. Nördlingen never fired. They broke their kiss, their final farewell, and Klaus let his hand with the gun sink to his side.

Nördlingen's voice was quiet and strangely calm. "Run," he said. "Run now. Run for your lives. Run, and do not look back."

We left. Jean-Pierre hesitated but a moment before he grabbed my hand and turned to lead us through the flood of people clogging the hallway. His pace was unhurried but deliberate, focused on our immediate goal of reaching the back door of the café, our door to potential freedom, before we were trapped and captured by the dark forces then at loose. I did look back—but only once—when I thought I heard a gunshot. We were not being shot at. It was only much later that I realized the implication of not seeing Klaus Nördlingen still standing in the hallway where we'd left him barely seconds before.

Inside the hallway it was dark and crowded with people, people everywhere crushing against us. When we finally reached the door and passed outside it was still dark and crowded with people but there was a palpable difference. The very air itself seemed fresher and we felt already more free for breathing it in. Yet we did not dare stop to savor the sensation. Danger was all around us in the blackout of Paris. Right there, right then, it felt as though all of Paris pursued us.

Fortunately for me, Jean-Pierre knew which way to go, where to turn. As we passed through one side street to another dark alley, we saw fewer and fewer people until at last it was our footsteps alone that echoed against featureless walls.

We finally arrived at an anonymous door. A soft, coded knock followed by a few whispered phrases efficiently gained us entry and found us securely hidden in a safe, secret room somewhere in Paris. To this day I have no idea who our benefactors were on that occasion, who I have to thank for my life. Over the course of several days we were visited and given food by caring faces I'd never seen before and would never see again. Occasionally Jean-Pierre would have lengthy murmured conversations with our visitors, gauging the danger of the situation we would face outside. Eleven days after we'd arrived at this safe house, he judged it finally safe enough for us to leave on our flight for freedom.

Sometimes the memory of our escape seems blurred and indistinct; at other times I feel like I can remember every moment in too-vivid detail. We moved from city to countryside, village to farm, always under cover of darkness, desperately hoping to evade detection. Everywhere we saw devastation and hardship, but everywhere we were helped along by people who still believed that there might be a life after the war, a reason to survive. There were several times when we thought we were surely discovered and could not avoid capture, but somehow we managed, staying alive by our wits, our determination, and the good will of others.

Jean-Pierre and I traveled this way for twelve weeks, the entire summer of 1943, the longest summer I had ever known. When we finally reached Geneva, my feet and my soul were so weary I could travel no farther. Switzerland, however, was a good destination for me: Its wartime neutrality was holding and I had some distant relatives there I could call on to help see me through to the peacetime that I increasingly thought might actually arrive.

Jean-Pierre had another destination in mind. On our travels he had begun dreaming of starting a newer, simpler life somewhere along the south coast of France. He would not be staying with me in Geneva.

How to say good-bye to someone who, through trials and shared experience, had become closer than a twin brother? There is no way, so we shared one last coffee together at an outdoor café on the *Lac Léman*.

"Can I not convince you to stay here?" I asked.

"I'd be a burden to you, a constant reminder."

"You mean I'd be a constant reminder to you."

"This is not the place for me to find my new life."

"Do you know where you are going?"

"The southern coast."

"That's a big place."

"I'll know it when I arrive."

There seemed nothing else to say, but I tried. "Thank you for everything."

"We both owe our lives to each other."

Before the next silence could become too uncomfortable we finished our coffees and stood up.

"I wish you the best of luck in your new life," I said.

He clapped his hands to my shoulders and gave me a short kiss. "Farewell, my brother."

He turned away and left me. I watched him go. He never looked back.

Jean-Pierre Renard stayed on the south coast of France after the war; he never returned to Paris even for a visit. I saw him once in Marseille some fifteen or twenty years later. He told me he had settled in a nearby village, where he made his living doing something with the boats for the fishing fleet. He was not very forthcoming about his new life but he told me he had been living with the village butcher for a number of years in rooms over the butcher's shop. He seemed happy.

Unlike Jean-Pierre, I had felt directionless without Paris to guide it. I could not stay away. I returned in 1949 to try to pick up the threads of my life, but it was never really the same—and who could expect that it would be? As I grew older nostalgia came knocking, so I began asking around about the people who had once been such a part of my life.

For Klaus Nördlingen I had imagined many possible scenarios, but all of my imaginings were wrong. He had not survived the war. In fact, he had not survived our final evening together in the Café Françoise. As

I should have realized at the time, the gunshot I heard was the sound of Nördlingen taking his own life. He helped us escape and then took the only escape that seemed left to him. Somehow it seemed sadder that I only learned of his sacrifice long years after he had died.

Françoise DePuys continued on with very little change. He sang here at the café every weekend until 1959, when he died rather slowly from cancer of the throat. Hélène DePuys took care of him through his long suffering but it took its toll on her. When she lost Françoise she lost all of her effervescence.

Not long after her beloved husband died she sold the Café Françoise and moved into a small, overheated apartment on the top floor of the building across the street. Through her window she could watch the comings and goings at the café that used to be hers. On warm summer evenings she would open her window and listen to their cabaret. I was with her when she died in 1972. She surely would have said, "By the Genius, we got through." True enough as far as it goes, but who is to know how or when we will end our days? Not even the Genius can guess that.

MISTAKES WERE MADE
TRISTAN COLE

Spencer

Unbelievable. For the second time, I was a success, and for the second time, my family was taking it away from me. My new eatery had just opened two months ago, and we were the rage of the East Village within weeks. Then my mother called.

"Spencer, we're going to give your new little business to your cousin, Chaz."

"Mother, I don't see why my success has to be forked over to relatives because—"

"—mistakes were made. Yes. I'm sorry, darling. That side of the family has been needing...erm...help for some time now, and we really should do our part, don't you think?"

No, actually. Our extended family was a clan of former millionaires, thanks to my parents' bad investments and Ponzi scheming. So, yes, my family funded my ventures, which allowed them to take over at any time. But, really, it's not my fault that they're lazy inheritance leeches who should be in jail.

I'm not a genius, but I work hard, and I have a knack for ideas. First, I thought of Quarter to Dawn, a diner that opened at midnight and closed just before sunrise. The suburban kids thought, "Ooh, it's run by vampires," and they flocked to the Lower East Side for food they could have gotten anywhere.

For my second attempt, Herculaneum, my hot-assed boyfriend, Connor, may have had the inspiration that saved the restaurant from failing. Reclining like Romans isn't the easiest way to eat, but after Connor suggested installing individual tables that could be raised or lowered with a push of a button or shifted from left to right, people thought it was fun. I had another hit.

Connor pointed out that the novelty would wear off, so we needed quality Mediterranean cuisine to go with the theme—dishes with grape leaves or dates and fancy wines from Tuscany. Whatever. I figured Connor himself would keep business coming. He looks incredible as a toga-clad waiter. Seeing his thick bare legs was enough to arouse nearly every customer, but it made me nuts because I'd seen him in much less. He hardly ever let me fuck him, and it drove me mad.

And now he was face-down on my bed only wearing white briefs and white socks, watching porn on my tablet when he said he needed to study. He may be kind of smart, but he doesn't apply himself. There's a reason he goes to some fourth-rate "alternative" college.

For a moment I wondered if he'd be upset once he found out what my parents were pulling, but the more I stared at Connor, the more the urge to maul his twenty-year-old body overwhelmed me. I went back to my prattling mother and said, "Fine, fine. Chaz can have the restaurant. I have to go. Bye."

I tossed the phone on the mahogany credenza and leapt in the air, the bulge in my shorts landing squarely in the cleft of Connor's tight, round ass.

"Oomph. Geez, Spencer, what's your deal? I already told you—"

"Yeah, yeah, yeah. You don't want it. I'm too big." I tugged on his thick brown hair, pulling his head back. "Come on, boy. Try it again. It'll be better."

"Nooooo. I'm too tight."

Why did his whining make me hot? I imagined him whimpering under me as I pounded him, his mouth contorted in both agony and need. There was a small hole in his briefs. Not even really a hole, just a threadbare spot that could easily be—

"Hey!" Connor yelped as I ripped his underwear wide open. I grabbed his bare buns with both hands, massaging and groping him hard as I purred in his ear.

"C'mon, I want that ass. Now. Let me fuck it."

He let out a small moan, and I felt his hips grind against my sheets, so I knew he was turned on. But he protested. "Spence…you know I can't. You're too damn big and too damn rough."

"I'll be gentle this time."

"No, you won't."

True. No, I won't. I pushed off him in a huff and paced back and forth before plopping down in my computer chair. Connor had gone back to his porn movie. I guess I should be glad for his porn addiction. He waited tables because he needed cash to keep his dad from discovering his expensive habit.

"So, you're just going to lie there and tease me with your bare hole?"

He turned to look at me. "Well, what the heck am I supposed to do?"

Put your pants back on, goofball. "Nothing. I'll think of something." I opened an Internet window and started a guest account for TopCraver.com. I'm not stupid. I see all the "surprise butt sex" footage he watches. I know what he wants.

"You *should* think of something, Spencer. Think of something different this time. Something your parents won't take from you for some reason. I mean if you're tired of that bullshit."

"What are you talking about?"

"Didn't that phone call have to do with taking your restaurant again? Next time do something they won't want to know about because it's…I dunno…embarrassing to their high-society values or something. Why not a place like Nouvelle Justine? You know, the S&M restaurant where you eat out of dog bowls?"

What? How did a twenty-year-old know about that place? I was twenty-eight, and I'd never been there.

"So do something like that. Something almost…illegal, maybe, and your parents will leave you alone."

I ignored him. I was in the chat room typing "Will someone fuck my boyfriend's ass?" I turned on my webcam, aimed it at Connor, who wasn't looking my way, and within seconds, the screen lit up with messages.

You know the quote from that philosopher, Plato, who said, "He had a beautiful face, but if you saw his smooth, bare ass, you'd totally forget he had a face"? Yeah, that's not exactly the quote, but *that* is Connor. He's naturally sway-backed, so it seems like his ass is constantly being offered up for the fucking.

I need that, said the first guy who messaged me.

How big are you? I typed.

Seven.

Sorry. Too big. I didn't explain I needed a small-to-average cock because then I would get downward lies instead of up. I waited for someone to lie his way up to six.

It was only three minutes before I found Brandon, a guy who had the supposed right-sized dick and lived close enough to my high-rise that he could be in Connor in under half an hour. He told me six, which I figured meant five, especially since his picture showed only from the waist up. Five would open Connor up for my eight. Brandon looked older and chubby, probably couldn't pound Connor's ass too hard. Excellent.

I'd just typed *C'mon over* and given him my address when the phone rang. It was Chaz. I realized I'd seen his dick in the gym locker room at Hulldrake Academy and thought, *Ha, he's smaller than me* and *he's two years older.* Also, he was gay. And somehow a top, even with that small cock.

And he only lived three blocks west.

I typed *Wait, hold on* to Brandon.

"I understand I've been called in to take the helm at Herculaneum. So I'd best master the principles of being a restaurateur, eh what? I'll require your help." Honest to God, every time I heard Chaz speak he sounded more like Thurston Howell the Third. "Perhaps you could act as my assistant, if you've nothing better, until you start a new little something."

Bite me. I lowered my voice so Connor wouldn't hear. "Actually, I need *your* assistance fucking my boyfriend. In exchange, maybe you could be *my* underling for a few weeks, and then I'll turn it over to you." After all, taking the manager's salary for a bit longer would mean I'd need less from my folks.

I heard Chaz inhale. "Wait, you mean...the waiter boy from the restaurant? I'll be right there."

Most excellent. I looked back to the computer screen and saw I hadn't hit Send, so Brandon never saw the *Wait, hold on.* He'd sent *leaving now*, and the screen said he'd signed off. Whoops.

Connor

I was studying for my Peace Studies class by researching ways gay porn might lead to more peace when someone buzzed up. I yelled, "Did you order pizza or something?" to Spencer, but he'd disappeared somewhere, probably into his closet to find the pants where he'd left his wallet so he could tip the delivery guy. I went back to my movie, but then, holy shit, the next thing I knew there was a tall, bald guy with a beard and glasses taking off his jacket and staring right at my naked ass.

"Spencer, what the—" I scrambled to cover myself with my hands. "Why didn't you tell me someone was coming in so I could get dressed?"

Spencer emerged from the closet. "Because you're not getting dressed. You're getting your ass fucked, so I can get in there myself."

"Wait, *what*?" I looked at Spencer. He hadn't gone to get his wallet. He'd gone to get some lube and condoms. He was friggin' serious!

The stranger dude grabbed my ankles, flipping me and yanking me toward the edge of the bed, and then threw my legs in the air. I felt like I should protest, but Spencer must have been paying more attention to the movies I watch than I realized. This was exactly my fantasy, and the new guy could tell that from my erection. I may have been reflexively pushing back on the mattress to get free, but I moaned as the guy lubed my hole.

Spencer made impatient gestures with his hands. "Come on. Hurry up, dude. I want to get in there as soon as possible."

"Patience, Spencer. I assure you I will be ravishing this ass for as long as I can."

My God, they're treating me like I'm just a hole. I exhaled as adrenaline flowed up from my gut to my brain. This was perfect.

The guy had managed to roll a condom down his length with one hand, and he was already thrusting into my crack, trying to push in hands-free. He missed on the first thrust, the second, and then the third I felt the burn of him pushing in. My mind spun like I was drunk on a roller coaster.

The shock of Spencer letting a total stranger get my ass was turning me on as much as the guy's dick, but all I could think was *What the hell? What the hell? What the hell is he doing?* and then—*What the hell am* I *doing?* I'd stopped trying to get away. Now I was just obediently keeping my legs up so he *could* get my ass. Why? Because I'm a wannabe slut. I've wanted a scene like this for so—ohhh, geez, he's worked his way in deeper, stretching me like crazy.

Deep breaths, Connor. Deep—

"Oh! Yo, yo! Too fast! Too fast! Please! Just—"

"Relax. You'll adjust to my girth. Now let me enjoy you."

He sank in me to the balls and started thrusting again. I moaned, my brow furrowed with the pain. I didn't want to break the getting-fucked-without-permission fantasy, but I had to ask, "Why are you giving my ass to a total stranger?"

Spencer kneaded the bulge of his shorts while he watched me get plowed. "He's not a stranger. That's Chaz, my cousin."

Oh, right. I hadn't been paying attention, but maybe Spence had mumbled something on the phone about trading my ass to keep the restaurant. God, that's fantastic. I've never allowed myself to be so easy. I'd never been watched before. And now I knew I loved having my ass given away. I have the most insane boyfriend in the entire world and God, this dick hurts, but in a good—

Someone else buzzed up.

"Now, *that's* a total stranger."

"What!" *What the fuck is happening to me? I'm a good boy. I don't let total strangers have my ass.*

"Sorry, Connor. Mistakes were made," he said, leaving the room.

"Unnnh, ohhh! If it's a mistake, why are you letting him in?" Spencer didn't answer. Chaz continued fucking me like nothing else was happening, and my hole throbbed with the invasion.

"Mmph! Unnh! What is Spencer doing?" I wondered aloud.

"You're too tight for him to fuck, so he's having other tops stretch your ass incrementally." Chaz pumped my hole harder, and I clenched my teeth.

Spencer returned with a bald, fat guy who had to be well over forty. That may sound unattractive, but his expression was a combination of steely confidence and bottomless lust that made me bite my lip in heat.

I looked up at Spencer. "Unnnh! Jeezus! All this so you can fuck me? Couldn't you have just bought a couple dildos?"

"Oh, yeah. Didn't think of that. Oh, well. Too late now."

Chaz kept going harder and harder as if he were showing off to the new guy how good he was at owning my hole. All this greedy fucking was making me feel faint. Why was I so turned on getting pounded by a guy whose glasses and shaggy beard made him look like a librarian bear from 1975? He was so pale, he'd probably been locked in the library that long, and considering how viciously he attacked my ass, he hadn't nutted since then either. He'd winded himself from plowing so hard that he stopped, caught his breath, and pulled out, still stiff as iron. Chaz held my legs up and made a "please, help yourself" gesture to the new guy. I closed my eyes and took deep breaths to calm down. If I didn't, I was either going to come or scream.

Pot-bellied, bald Brandon came at me with his fully hard dick. He pushed my legs back farther with strong, calloused hands.

"Damn, you've got the ass of a porn star," Brandon said in a breathy baritone as he lined his prick up with my hole. "I'm never going to stop fucking it."

"Holy-gah-unnh!" God, his dick might not have been huge, but it was too big for me. It was at least six thick, veiny inches. I pressed my hand against his stomach to keep his cock at bay, but he pushed my arm away and thrust all the way in. "Jeezus, oh my God!" *I can't believe this. I am the kind of guy who gets his ass fucked by total strangers. Gang fucked, in fact.* "Oh! Nnnh! Oh!" The dude had my legs back and my ass up high enough that I could see his dick go in and out of me. I watched in utter disbelief. Each stroke stuffed my hole to near the breaking point, so I grabbed a pillow from behind me and bit down on it. After many minutes of moaning and whimpering in agony, the pain decreased, and it felt more like a massage.

"Yeah, this ass is meant to be mounted all day every day." The guy looked at me liked he dared me to disagree. The feeling that this stranger basically wanted to enslave me sent a hot, shameful wave of delirium to my brain, and I had to pinch off my dick not to come.

Then Brandon switched with Chaz, who now wore a ribbed condom. He slammed in, pounding even harder than before.

"Oh! Nnnnh! God, oh!"

I saw Spencer lubing up his cock. I shook my head in dazed amazement. I'd never been watched. I'd never been with a stranger. And I'd never been gangbanged.

And now I had no control over stopping it. That thought sent another surge of heat through me, and this time there was no way I could hold back from coming.

"I can't fucking believe this, Spencer! Oh! Oh, God!" I wailed as I pulsed out wave after wave of come.

Spencer

I booked our flight to Puerto Vallarta on a private jet service instead of a commercial liner. That meant I got to fuck Connor's ass twice at 25,000 feet. If I craved his ass before his "breaking in," I was obsessed with it now. Furthermore, after exploring his exhibitionist desires, I knew what kind of restaurant I needed. After all, it was Connor's suggestion to create something my parents wouldn't touch, right?

I'd told Connor, "New York won't allow a restaurant where you'd wait tables in chaps, would it?"

Connor had been hesitant. "You're being serious? Then someplace where I don't know anyone. *At all.* New Orleans? San Francisco?"

"If its reputation is accurate, New Orleans might have enough bribable cops to make it work, but that could get insanely expensive so...*Aha.*"

"And isn't dining room nudity probably a health code issue— Aha? Aha what?"

"We'll leave the country and open something where bribes aren't expensive. South of the border, perhaps."

I investigated several resort areas that seemed attractive to gay clientele. However, Chaz, who'd left Herculaneum in the care of his siblings because he wanted to keep working together, insisted Puerto Vallarta was the "San Francisco of Mexico." It was obvious Chaz wanted more shots at Connor's hole. He wouldn't get them, but if it meant he'd fly out to scout properties for me, I'd let him believe he would.

Outside Puerto Vallarta, Chaz found a secluded enclave where gay men with money liked to party: Playa Peligrosa, which Chaz told me means Fat Pelican Beach.

Convincing Connor to take a leave of absence from school was difficult, but I helped him write his advisor a bullshit proposal so he'd receive course credit, leaving out the fact that his "intercultural experience" would be working as a nearly nude waiter. I did promise Connor I'd make him more of a business partner later if I thought we'd be profitable without his rump on display. That was highly doubtful, but Connor would get over it. He was fun, sweet, and a great piece of ass, if a bit whiny. I knew I shocked him with the freaky things I wanted him to do, but I hoped he'd stick around.

The new restaurant would be called Wild Oats, and we planned to use "avena sativa" in our food. It's a syrup from oats I've read is an honest-to-God aphrodisiac. I'd gone to some lengths to envision an atmosphere that would feel natural to see a waiter in chaps and a harness while surrounded by the tropics. Black leather chairs and dark wood sounded appropriate, and they'd be lit by tiki torches in the shape of Aztec skulls. But Connor pointed out that those materials, if only protected by palm-thatched palapas, wouldn't do well in the elements, so I said, "Fine. I just want black. Dark. Mysterious. Figure it out."

Connor thought we should focus more on the food—hire a chef from a fancy culinary school, advertise "innovative molecular cuisine" made with locally caught fish and a wide selection of California wines. I said "sure, sure." The restaurant would really be about exposing Connor's ass, which meant I had to identify the people to pay off. It turned out Chaz already knew someone.

"Eight hundred American each week," said Franco, the police chief for Playa Peligrosa and some neighboring villages. I shrugged and nodded, more put off by the way Franco undressed Connor with his eyes than by the size of the bribe. Franco had thick salt-and-pepper eyebrows, but other than that, he seemed young to be a police chief. There was definitely a look in his eye that said "don't fuck with me," and he had an unsettling habit of stroking his nightstick.

"I will monitor everything," Franco added with a slow blink of his long eyelashes. "Make sure no one gives you trouble, of course." He winked at Connor, which made him fidget, but I saw Connor's gaze go down to the officer's crotch. Hmph.

"Sure we shouldn't look somewhere else?" I asked Chaz later, but he waved his hand dismissively.

"The chief's obviously queer. This area is crawling with older gay tourists who are horny and want a place where they can eat food that won't make them sorry they came to Mexico. We couldn't ask for a better situation, Spencer."

"I've found some oat bread recipes that could be prepared with avena sativa syrup," Connor said, for once using a computer for something besides porn. "And here's something about a fish called a corvina that's super trendy."

"Sure," I said to the back of Connor's head. *But maybe instead of researching, you should be doing some nude tanning, because the success of this venture depends on your baby-smooth bubble ass. Yep, yep. It's all about your ass.*

Connor

The day that Spencer lost Herculaneum changed us both. Everything seemed to center around sex now, rather than the new restaurant. I was sure he was letting details slip. For example, why was I the only waiter? Spencer assured me weeks ago he'd hired, like, three other guys, but it dawned on me I'd never seen any kind of paperwork or heard any names mentioned. "They're hot," he said. "They're experienced with restaurant work."

We opened before we were ready. We needed more tables, more chairs, and, well, more food. The first night started slowly, which was fortunate because I couldn't concentrate, knowing my ass was completely bare and available for groping. The slightest breeze against my skin made me lose my place when I attempted to rattle off beverage options or ask for orders in my mediocre Spanish. Only three of the eight tables were occupied: two older American men in flowered shirts, two Mexican businessmen who were probably in their forties, and that police chief, Franco, sitting by himself and doing shots of Spencer's most expensive tequila…on the house.

The customers devoured the fresh oat bread like they hadn't eaten in weeks. All four ordered ceviche, which was lucky since it was the only dish the chef didn't have to "improvise" thanks to our limited supplies. The Americans took photos of my backside with their phones, and before they were half done with their meal, all the tables were filled and there were several parties waiting.

I practically ran from table to table, refilling wine and delivering orders, when one of the two Mexican businessmen grabbed my waist and didn't let go. His hand was hot on my bare skin. I gave him a "can't you see I'm busy" look and attempted to gently move his arm. It didn't work. The man called Spencer over.

"I'd like to order the special dessert now," he said.

Spencer grinned. "Absolutely." He beckoned Chaz to come over.

"I wasn't aware of any special dessert," I said, and since the lady delivering tres leches cakes hadn't shown up, it would have been nice to know we had anything at all.

"That will be five hundred dollars. American. Cash only," Chaz said, with his hands behind his back. Without hesitation, the businessman produced his wallet and started counting out hundreds.

"What dessert could possibly cost five hundred dollars?" I wondered aloud. The guy finished counting and began groping my ass. *Oh, no.*

"You cannot be serious," I said to Spencer.

"Thank you so much, Mr. Valdez," Spencer said as he took the money, and Chaz handed the man a condom. "Get up on the table, Connor, and spread your legs."

"*What?* In front of everyone? No way!" I realized, too late, that it sounded like I'd be fine with this as long as there was some privacy.

Spencer pressed me back toward the table. "Yep. You're gonna to lose that whore ass to him in front of everybody."

That whore ass, he said. The words made my head spin and my stomach clench with heat. Damn, now I *needed* to lose my whore ass to this Valdez dude more than anything. The next time Spencer pushed me toward the table I fell back on it, Chaz clearing away plates to make room for my upper body.

Valdez was on his feet now. My head swam with bewilderment. Why did I want this? Why was I fine with this happening? But lust overwhelmed confusion as I lifted my legs and watched Valdez yank off my chaps. All conversation stopped as Valdez unzipped to reveal his thick, hard dick. It pointed right at my hole. Spencer lubed me, Valdez slipped on the condom, and less than a minute after I found out what "special dessert" meant, my ass was getting fucked in public. As I moaned helplessly, looking from customer to customer, I tried not to worry what everyone there thought of me. I saw not looks of disgust, but of fascination. My continued shock at being publically plowed sent an icy thrill flooding through me.

"Look me in the eyes while he fucks you," Spencer growled. The look on his face was a crazed one. Obsessed. His breathing was almost as hard as mine.

Valdez stabbed my hole harder to get my attention. "No. Look at me," he said. "Only me."

"No, you're my boyfriend," Spencer barked, "and you're giving your ass to someone else in front of the entire restaurant. The least you can do is look at me while—"

"What do you mean 'giving'? You sold my ass to him. *You* said I had to lose it to him!"

Valdez grabbed my face and turned my head toward him. "If you look at him again, I'll make it so you can't walk for a month."

Valdez rammed twice as hard as before, again and again and again. I wailed and moaned. The table rocked so violently under my back I was certain it was about to collapse.

Valdez still looked furious. "Look only at me. Describe to everyone what's happening to you, young man."

"I'm...I'm getting screwed."

"More. Louder!"

"I'm losing my ass to you—"

"Louder! Shout it! Don't stop!"

Oh, God, this was going to make me come. "I'm losing my ass! You're fucking my ass in front of everyone. Your huge cock is slamming my hole so hard, I think I'm gonna die." I felt the euphoric rise in my gut. I was getting closer and closer with each thrust. "Oh! Nnnnnnh! Aaaaaah!"

Valdez began to shout and bellow. "Yes! Yes! *Dios!*" He started screaming in Spanish, and he came inside me at the same I let loose. White jets coated my chest as I wailed in ecstasy and pain. With the final few thrusts, he pumped so hard that the table almost did turn over, but Chaz caught me and Valdez's dining companion grabbed the table.

Valdez pulled out amidst a smattering of applause. Again, I practically fell off the table, panting as Chaz kept me from stumbling to the floor, but Spencer swatted my rump twice and said, "Get cleaned up and get back to work."

"Are you crazy? After that, there's no way—"

"Don't kid yourself, Connor. That ass-fucking was the hottest thing ever in the history of everything. You know you want to go back out there with your naked and freshly fucked ass vulnerable to another attack, and second, we're going to make a mint if the word spreads about what happens here."

"No. Just no, Spencer."

"You wanted a restaurant too wild for my parents to touch, right?"

"I can't do this night after night."

"You won't have to. We'll get other boys. You're management, remember?"

Spencer's pupils were dilated, and I had him figured out. I didn't understand the "cuckold fantasy," but he was lying to me because nothing got him harder than seeing me, his boyfriend, fucked and then fucked again before he took his turn ravaging my "whore ass" himself.

"This is not a good idea," I said, although I knew I'd jump at the chance if I were sure my parents, friends, and classmates would never find out.

Spencer grabbed my crotch and whispered in my ear. "You already know it's the best idea imaginable, don't you? I promise nothing bad will happen."

A shiver of heat went through me, and I inhaled deeply. "Let me think about it." I picked my chaps off the floor and went indoors to the washroom. It was dark and cool, and I spent a couple minutes washing off and calming down. I put my chaps back on and twisted so I could look at my ass in the mirror. I was sore, my rectum throbbing a bit, but things looked…good. In my head I heard Chaz's voice saying "now that's an ass that's meant to be fucked nonstop," and my dick stiffened again. I took a deep breath and headed in the direction of the dining room, but I was stopped in the doorway by Franco.

"You are actually going back out there?" he said with a puzzled shake of his head.

"Yes," I said, biting my lip as I saw him appraise me from head to toe.

"Then you enjoyed what happened?" He puffed on a cigarette. Through the tendrils of smoke I saw the look on his face, and I knew he wasn't asking out of sheer curiosity.

"Y-yes," I said. I inhaled deeply to stop trembling. "I guess I must have." I returned to the dining room without looking back.

I remained shaken—stammering, and breathing hard as I served customers. "Yes, the heart of palm is fresh, not canned. A vegetarian entrée? It's not on the menu, but they can make a jicama stew for you. What beers do we have? Negra Modelo and Tecate, but nothing on tap." The customers behaved as if nothing wildly insane had just happened. Valdez sat, drinking coffee and chatting with his friend.

"I'd like that special dessert, too, please," said a loud voice behind me. It was one of the Americans who had arrived first. Oh, God. There was more murmuring and gasps of shock, but also some notable licking of lips and adjusting of chairs to get a good view.

Spencer practically vaulted to the guy's table. "Certainly. Five hundred dollars, please. Chaz? Can you get, er, supplies for Mr. Walsh?" How did Spencer know all these customers' names? This felt suspiciously like the night he got on TopCraver.net when I thought he was ordering pizza.

"Four hundred," Walsh said. "I'm not paying full price for seconds."

"Perfectly understandable," Spencer said, snapping his fingers at me and pointing to the customer's table, indicating I was to bend over it. I didn't understand myself. I chose to come back out here bare-assed when I could have found my pants, called a taxi, and left. *I'm crazy for doing this.*

Walsh pressed down hard on my upper back and my chin hit his table. In seconds, he'd put on a condom, mounted my ass, and starting fucking me. My face burned with shame. Once could have been for novelty, for the sake of pushing the envelope and crossing off the wildest item on a bucket list. But a second time? Now everyone in the room is thinking, "Ah, that's why this place is terrible. It's not a real restaurant and he's not a real waiter, just a hole for everyone's pleasure." Why did that thought make my cock even harder?

The older guy stretched me, but he got it in without too much of a tussle. Yep, saying that everyone was getting to see my "whore ass" get fucked was accurate. I moaned in humiliation as I saw customer after customer watching my rump get viciously pumped, the sound of the guy's balls slapping my ass with every thrust. Walsh's companion leaned over and dribbled his white wine over the back of my head. Between the guy licking my ears and my own moans and cries, I could barely hear what sounded like an argument.

"—charge a Mexican five hundred, but this man only four?"

"Franco, come on, you know why—"

"You also made my friend pay first, but this man hasn't produced the money and he's getting the boy's ass already."

"There's no problem. I'll charge him five hundred."

Walsh pumped me harder. "Like hell, you will. Now both of you shut the hell up and let me fuck this ass."

Walsh grabbed me by the back of my head and rode me faster and deeper. I heard him start growling and then screaming "Oh! Oh! Oh!" The pain in my hole was making me whimper and moan as well, but my eyes were on Spencer and the police chief. They were locked in a staredown. The chief stepped forward and Spencer backed up.

"We have a problem," Franco said to Spencer. "Perhaps you want to go to jail?"

Walsh still had his dick in me, but upon hearing that he pulled out and backed away. Tables cleared.

Franco had his handcuffs out and started toward Spencer, but to my amazement, he handcuffed me.

"I'm sorry, young man. You've violated decency laws, you see. I must take you now."

"No, please, don't take Connor!" Spencer offered the officer the five hundred he'd just been paid. Franco grabbed the money but led me away anyhow.

Shit. "Spencer, you promised nothing bad would happen!"

"I'm sorry, Connor!" Spencer called after me. "Mistakes were made. I'll think of something, I…I promise."

I asked if I could put on pants first, but Franco acted like he didn't hear me, and my stomach tightened at the thought of being locked up bare-assed in a Mexican jail. I made a mental note to see a shrink about the fact that dangerous men made me batshit horny.

Twenty minutes later, Franco literally had me over a barrel. I was completely nude except for my harness. We were outdoors behind a dilapidated shack, my butt balanced on the edge of a wooden keg filled with a liquid that smelled of alcohol. The derelict shack must have had electricity as a bare bulb lit my body from above. A knotted chain with one side ending in a metal ring held my balls captive. The other end was fastened to a rusty iron door knocker two feet away. There wasn't enough slack for me to turn over, so I lay there in silence as the officer smoked a cigarette and stared between my legs. He ran a finger up the length of my crack. "So nice," he whispered. I said nothing, just squinting under the glare of the bulb and sucking in dusty air.

"There are few men in this part of the world who enjoy getting their asses fucked," he said. "Or will admit to it, anyway, and allow it to happen." He rubbed my hole in slow, round and round motions. "And none that anyone actually wants to fuck. Until now."

He turned on his car radio and out poured Spanish rap. As he lit a second cigarette, I heard a car approach, slow down, and then roll to a stop just out of my view. Before the car door slammed shut, I made out the engine of a second approaching vehicle.

The man who came around the corner was tall and thick, muscles bulging from under his white tank top and jeans. Once I saw him closely, I had a feeling he might have been a Beta or Zeta or whatever the gang was called. His face was craggy and scarred, and he had tattoos on his forehead and neck. Not a trace of a smile, and as he approached, I could see the hungry look in his eyes. Not only cruel, but starved.

He whipped out a hundred peso note from his jeans pocket and tossed it at Franco. Before Franco had even pocketed the money, the new guy was manhandling my ass cheeks hard, and I groaned as he began squeezing, spanking, and pinching me rough enough to bruise.

Then I heard him unzip and line up his dick.

Wait a minute. What was a hundred pesos worth? An hour ago, a guy had paid five hundred dollars for my hole, and now my ass was sold for about...

Seven bucks.

Franco pointed at me to put my legs in the air. I did, and the dude bent his knees and shoved his dick in. I tried not to cry out, but I couldn't control it.

"*Pinche niño bien,*" the guy muttered as he started stroking in and out. "*Pinche gringo. Tu culo es nuestro, putito. No vamos a parar de cogerte nunca.*" I didn't totally know what he was saying, but I caught something about them owning my ass and fucking it forever. Ohhh, *God, please don't let this be too bad. Just...bad enough.*

The guy was at least as big as Spencer, and his pace went from fast to ferocious. I heard two car doors slam and more voices, but I had no idea what they were saying because the sound of the guy reaming me and my own grunts and yelps drowned out the words. After maybe five minutes of being piston-fucked, the pain in my hole was so bad I screamed. The guy stopped, and rubbed my stomach, perhaps to calm me down. The unexpected kindness filled me with relief even as I was aware it shouldn't. I looked through my sopping hair at the new men surrounding me. They stroked their dicks, patiently waiting. The first guy was another beefy man, and again, he had a hardened, intense face that looked like it belonged to a biker or prisoner, but his rumpled business clothes and wedding ring combined with his famished stare made me suspect he'd reined in his needs, perhaps for his family's sake, for years. Now he needed to ream my ass like a damn maniac.

The second man looked familiar, even in the shadows. Chaz!

"Hey! Help me. Pay them off, Chaz!"

"He's here to take a turn, *putito*," the officer said. "Part of our agreement was that if he brought you to me, he fucks your ass as much as he wants but Spencer, never." The shreds of relief I'd felt vanished, but my dick was so hard and my ass so in need, blunting my panic.

Still, my predicament was settling in. I looked at the chain that had me by the balls. God, fuck. I wasn't going to get away. My erection was so rigid, it felt like my whole groin was hard. I whimpered and lifted my legs, volunteering for more. Franco, the officer, loosened the chain and threw my legs in the air. As he slammed his cock in me, I could only gurgle and gasp in protest. My ass was pumped harder and harder as I was flipped from position to position by man after man. I only felt the amazing ache in my hole and my pounding heartbeat. The chain was adjusted again. I was put on the ground on all fours, watching more men give Franco a hundred pesos each. Someone yanked on my harness as he stuffed his cock in me and started pumping hard.

Jesus Christ. I was the son of a CEO and an honors student in college, but here I was in the dirt, barking and getting my ass ridden like a ten-dollar whore.

Or a seven-dollar whore.

The animal needs around me ignited my own, but I resisted the urge to grind and push back. After all, it probably turned them on more if they thought I didn't want it. I felt the jab of each stroke, the slap of balls against my ass, and the sweat dripping from my hair. My eyes were unfocused to the point that the faces were blurs, and all I heard were my moans, the sounds of my ass getting fucked, and the snickers and taunts of the men enjoying my humiliation.

All I'd said was "hey, how about creating a restaurant your parents won't want to touch," and now I suspected my ass was going to be enslaved for a damn long time. Franco was fucking me again, and he yanked the chain to give my balls a vicious tug. "Ohh!" I bellowed. That hurt so good, but I couldn't take much more. But I might have to. Shit, what if my life was going to be about my ass getting gangbanged from now on? God, that's so perfect that I'm gonna come. Oh, Jeez. Oh, God, how mistakes were made…

ACQUIRED TASTE
WILLIAM HOLDEN

O
h my God." I groaned as I slipped it into my mouth. I closed my eyes, savoring every drop of the warm, salty cream. I didn't swallow. I wanted to hold out a little longer. The earthy flavors lingered on my taste buds. I licked my lips to catch the cream that dribbled from the corner of my mouth. A wave of heat swept over my body. Beads of sweat broke out across my brow. My balls contracted. My cock stretched. I gave into the urge. I swallowed.

"Christ, Dean, keep your voice down, people are staring at us." Cameron whispered from across the table.

"This spaghetti carbonara is unbelievable." I opened my eyes. Cameron did not look amused. "You have to try this." I twirled my fork in the mass of carbohydrate goodness.

"No thanks." He pushed the fork out of my hand. It fell on the table splattering the bits of bacon and cream over everything. "Jesus, fucking, Christ, Dean."

"What's your problem?" I took another mouthful, letting the flavors take me to a more pleasurable place so that I could ignore Cameron's pissy attitude. My cock pushed against the shrinking space in my underwear. I felt a drizzle of precome trickle down my thigh. The urge to fuck rushed through me. I moved my right hand up my leg. My cock was a solid shaft of flesh. "Did you say something, Cameron?"

"Never mind, I've lost my appetite. I'm going out for a smoke." Cameron threw his napkin over the plate and left the dining room. I took another bite, leaned back against the seat, and let my finger draw little circles up and down the shaft of my throbbing cock.

The pits of my arms became wet and sticky. I could smell my own perfumed sweat seeping through my T-shirt. I took a sip of water and noticed a man peering out from the kitchen. He looked to be in his early forties. A dark five o'clock shadow covered his otherwise hairless rectangular head. Bright orange flames etched into his skin snaked their way out of the collar of his shirt. The flames licked the ridge of his jawline. Our eyes met. A half smile crossed his thick lips. He ducked back behind the swinging doors. I took another bite of the pasta as I continued to rub myself off under the table. The sensory overload intensified.

I heard the front door open and looked behind me expecting to see Cameron. Through the window I could see him outside on the sidewalk. He lit up a new cigarette. His red hair appeared darker under the streetlights. I tried to think of him naked. His pale skin covered in those soft, silky red hairs always sent me over the edge. Even as horny as I was, the idea of running my tongue through the orange-red hair of his ass did nothing to quench my desire.

A fit of laughter erupted. I turned my attention away from my boyfriend and focused on two couples sitting in a booth across the room. They raised their wineglasses. The clink of the crystal shattered through the air, impossibly loud. I twirled my fork, took a bite, and continued to stroke myself while watching the odd behavior of the two couples.

The men kept glancing up from their steaks to look at one another. Their glances grew to long stares. A few moments later I noticed one of the men slipping the dress shoe off his foot. He took a bite of his T-bone steak. He licked the bloody juice from his lips as he stretched his leg out to caress the other guy's ankle with his socked foot. He slipped his toes under the hem of the guy's pants. They looked at each other as if nothing was out of the ordinary. The younger man moved closer to the edge of the seat, spreading his legs further apart. He reached down and grasped the curious foot. He brought the man's toes to rest upon his crotch. They smiled at one another as if their wives were not sitting next to them.

"Dean," a distant voice called. I ignored the voice as I watched the man's foot squeeze and massage the other man's crotch with his toes. The women continued to talk as if nothing was happening.

"Goddammit, Dean, let's go." Cameron dropped into his seat. "I've been out there for over twenty minutes."

"So?" I spoke to him as I continued to watch the events unfold across from me. I forced my eyes back to Cameron. "Sorry…"

"Don't bother apologizing. I've paid the bill, let's go."

"But I haven't finished my meal." I looked up as our waiter walked by. "Excuse me, could I get this to go?"

"Of course, honey." I watched his firm ass sway back and forth in his black slacks. I wanted to fold him over one of the tables and bury my face in his stale, damp ass. He looked back at me and winked as if reading my mind. I looked down at my lap. A wet spot of precome had formed on my jeans.

"I need to go to the bathroom."

"Can't you fucking wait?"

"What is your problem tonight? I'm just going to take a piss. I'll be right back." I stood up at an angle so that Cameron wouldn't see my raging hard-on or the wet spot in my crotch. I turned my back on him as my body cleared the edge of the table.

I stopped halfway to the bathroom and leaned against a chair as a wave of pleasure rippled through my body. *Holy shit. I'm going to come.* I gripped the edge of the chair with both hands, as my cock spasmed. My body shook as I unloaded several thick spurts of come into my underwear. I ran to the bathroom as the waves of pleasure increased. I stumbled into the first stall as another surge swept through my cock. I leaned my head against the cool metal surface. My pulse drummed in my head. "Oh, shit!" I leaned against the door, bracing myself with the metal walls. My knees buckled. "Oh, Jesus." I grabbed the top edge of the walls. "Fuck!" My body quivered. My cock pulsed as I shot another thick, gooey stream of come.

The bathroom door swung open. I covered my mouth to help stifle my groans as another orgasm, stronger than before, exploded from my cock. I peered through the half-inch opening between the door and the stall. The two men from the booth stumbled into the bathroom as they clawed at each other's bodies.

"Rick, what are we doing? Fuck, our wives are out there." The younger man panted as he unzipped his pants and pulled out his thick, uncut cock.

"Shut the fuck up, Steve. I don't want to think about them." Rick pushed Steve against the row of sinks and dropped to his knees. "I just have to have your cock in my mouth." He grabbed the thick base of Steve's cock, pulling the foreskin back as he went. He hesitated and then slipped the large, swollen head into his mouth.

"Shit, that feels fucking good." Steve moaned. "Yeah, suck my big throbbing cock."

I released the buttons of my pants and tugged them, along with my underwear, down to my knees. My pubic hair was sticky with come. I ran my hands through the tangle of hair, capturing my cooling jizz. I watched the two men getting wild with lust as I beat myself off.

Rick unzipped his blue pin-striped slacks and fished inside the fly. He pulled his cock out. It hit the tile floor in a wet smack. Rick moaned with Steve's cock lodged deep in his throat. I felt another rush. I jerked myself fast and hard as I watched these two men getting off together. My release was stronger than anything I could have expected. I let out a scream as the intensity of the pleasure released. My body rattled the door as my cock unleashed three, then four heavy jets of come. It slid down the chilled metal surface, leaving a thin, creamy white sheen in its path.

"Jesus, someone's in here." Steve threw Rick off his cock. They both scurried to hide their exposed cocks.

"Fuck." I opened the door and leaned against the stall. "I'm sorry, guys." My body covered in sweat was near exhaustion. I was thankful that the unusual cravings had subsided. "Don't worry," I panted. My eyes darted between their wet, dripping cocks. "I won't...I...oh, shit, I gotta go." I pulled my pants up, grabbed a paper towel to clean the come from my fingers, and then left the bathroom. I stood in the small hallway with my eyes closed, hoping to slow my breathing before going back to Cameron. I could hear Steve's grunts as their unexplained desires resurfaced.

"You ready?" I didn't stop at the table. I paused briefly to grab my to-go bag. I couldn't look him in the eyes.

"I've been ready for... Turn around." His hand settled on my shoulder. "Is that what I think it is?" He turned me around. "Jesus, did you fuck someone in the bathroom?"

"Don't be ridiculous."

"Your neck." He reached up and stretched the collar of my T-shirt. "And your chest, you have sex blush. You fucked someone in there, didn't you?"

"No, I didn't." I looked around the restaurant. The two women sat with solemn expressions on their faces, talking. They appeared oblivious that their husbands had gone missing. I turned my attention back to Cameron. "We are not having this conversation here." I turned and left the restaurant.

"Don't walk away from me," Cameron yelled as he stepped out onto the sidewalk. "I know how you get after sex. You can't tell me those red splotches came from something else."

"I jerked off in there. Are you satisfied?" I glared at him. "And put that cigarette out. I can't stand to kiss you after you smoke. It's disgusting."

"You couldn't have waited till we got back to my place?" He lit the cigarette.

"No."

"No?" That's all you're going to say? Then why not invite me into the bathroom with you? That would have been hot. We're always talking about new places to fuck."

"Maybe it's because you weren't the one I wanted to fuck tonight." The words fell from my mouth before I knew what I was going to say. I could see the hurt in his eyes. "Look, I'm sorry, I didn't mean it. It just happened."

"You don't have to worry about kissing this mouth tonight." He took a drag of his cigarette and blew the smoke in my direction.

"Cameron."

"Don't." He pulled away from me. "Thanks for a great evening, Dean. I'll walk home from here. I need to clear my head."

"Aren't you overreacting to my beating off? Jesus, I masturbate all the time. What's the big deal?"

"It's not. Never mind. I'll call you in the morning." I watched his body disappear into the shadows. His footsteps echoed in the crisp night air.

I walked to my car and sat in the dark. The smell of the carbonara filled the car with its tantalizing aroma. I slipped the Styrofoam container out of the bag and opened it. Nestled in the center of the leftovers was a smaller container with a note attached to it. I pulled the note from the box and read it. "You left without ordering dessert." The stares of someone unknown to me pricked my skin as I read the note a second time. I looked across the parking lot. There was no one around, yet the feeling of someone watching me persisted. I opened the small container. Inside was a five-layered dessert, cut into a perfect circle. A tiny plastic fork rested against the side of the box.

A nerve twitched in the pit of my stomach as the anticipation or craving of pleasure rose through my body. My hand trembled like an addict needing his next fix. I tore into the alternating layers of cake and mousse. The chocolate, butterscotch, rum, and hazelnut flavors opened a flood of emotions. A chill ran over my body. Gooseflesh broke out over my skin, causing the hair on my arms to stand up. I took another bite. My body shivered as if it were mid-January instead of September. Despite the icy chill that covered my body, sweat broke out on my forehead and in my armpits. My nipples quivered as if something or someone was biting them.

I felt light-headed. My body ached as if I had just been fucked senseless. I set the container in the passenger seat and stared at the food. Its aroma beckoned me to take another bite. I closed my eyes, trying to clear my head, holding on to the key in the ignition, praying I could get home. I looked across the parking lot as the headlights illuminated the night. The man I had seen earlier in the kitchen watched me from the restaurant door in the alley. I felt his eyes upon me. His presence filled the air as if he were sitting next to me. I looked down in my lap as I felt my cock stir. I saw the pulse of my cock thumping against the denim. A low, steady drumming echoed in my ears. The man disappeared behind the door. I pulled the keys from the ignition, opened the door, and walked down the alley.

The chilled night air seemed impossibly warm against the coldness of my skin. I shivered from the icy sweat running down my back. My footsteps crunched against the rough surface of the ground. I approached the door. I looked around the empty alley, opened the door, and stepped inside. I slid my hand along the door to soften the noise when the lock engaged. The kitchen was immense, impeccably clean, and empty. I looked at my watch. It was only ten fifteen. I walked toward the two-way doors. They rocked back and forth in opposite directions. I held them open and looked into the dining room. Customers filled nearly every table, yet their laughter, their spoken words were silent to me, as if someone had pushed the mute button on a television.

The sound of metal clanging startled me. I turned around. Several large pots rocked back and forth from their ceiling racks, yet I was alone—or so I thought. I walked through the kitchen, as if playing a game of hide-and-seek. In the back corner, an enormous refrigeration unit stood with its door ajar. I entered. My breath crystalized in thick white puffs through the chilled air. Metal shelves covered in a light frost lined the left side of the room. To my right, various cuts of meat hung from fifteen or twenty hooks suspended from the ceiling. I was about to leave when a voice came from behind me.

"Did you like your dinner?" The man's voice was sensual, deep, and hypnotic.

"Jesus." I turned around. Even in the dim light, I could see the flames coming out of his collar. My cock stirred in my pants as the strange cravings rushed through my body. "I…it was…"

"I make the bacon myself. In fact, I make all the meat myself. I have a secret way of smoking it." He pulled a knife from his breast pocket.

"I should go." I eyed the knife in his hand. The dull light of the room reflected off the sharp metal blade. "I'm sure you have customers to attend to."

"You don't want to leave, do you?" He placed his hand on my arm. His gentle, firm touch ignited my cravings to be fucked. "I'm Benjamin, the owner and chef. Here, have another piece of my meat." He slipped the knife through a slab of meat, pulling it away with his thumb. I opened my mouth, taking in the salty meat. "Tell me, Dean, What is it you desire?"

"How do you know my name?" I swallowed, letting the heat swell within me. The uncontrollable urge to come returned. My balls cringed as my cock pulsed and spasmed.

"I know that you want me, Dean, almost as much as I want and need you."

"Why me?" I grabbed hold of the edge of a shelf to support my weakening legs as an orgasm raced through my body. "Shit."

"Because I love you, Dean. Why else would I give you so much pleasure?" Benjamin leaned into me and licked my neck. I came in my pants.

"But I don't…"

"Shhh…" He held a finger to my lips. "Don't say it, Dean. The words would wound me, and I've suffered intolerable pain over the years. I cannot take that from you, not ever. I need you to want me, Dean. You do want me, don't you?"

He took the knife and raised it to his neck. He smiled as he brought the blade down, cutting the thread that held each of the buttons on his uniform. His chest was a solid mass of muscles covered in short, clipped hair. He let the chef's coat fall to the floor. The orange flames of his neck ran in a single fiery line between his pecs, and then branched out into burning reds and yellows as the flames spread out across his stomach. A thin black line rose from the tip of the top two flames, and encircled each of his large dark nipples. His tits grew from the icy air as he pulled me to him. I pushed against him, trying to resist the urge, yet knowing it was no use. I ran my tongue over his right tit, flicking it and then biting it. The sharp blades of his chest hair poked at my skin. "Tell me that you want me, Dean."

"I want you." I moaned as my tongue ran through the wet, silky hair of his armpit. I sucked the chilled sweat from his pits, savoring his bitter oils. I moved my tongue up his neck, following the licks of the flames. He pushed me away from him. Our eyes met. I become lost in his gaze. I felt the temperature in the room drop. It chilled the sweat that lay on my skin. He gripped the hem of my T-shirt and pulled it up over my head, bending down and licking my navel. His hot, meaty tongue caressed my body, running along the thin trail of hair that led from my stomach to the denser patch covering my chest. His tongue came to rest on the cleft of my chin. "God, please kiss me."

"I am not God." He pushed me away from his body. "Take your pants off."

I pulled the shoe from my foot. He curled his finger and smiled. I tossed the shoe in his direction. He caught it and held it to his face. I could hear him inhaling. He moaned and took another long, deep breath of the odors of my sneakers. I pulled the other shoe off and it landed by his feet. I unbuckled the belt and then released the buttons of my jeans, stepping out of them. The arctic air covered me like a clammy blanket. Despite the cold, my cock was rock hard. The front of my underwear had iced over where my precome had saturated the fabric. I shivered as the temperature continued to drop.

"All of it." He dropped my shoe as he watched me slip the underwear down my legs. "Yes, that's more like it."

"Please fuck me. Make me come, do whatever you have to, but make these cravings stop." I looked down my naked body. Crystals of ice from my sweat-dampened body clung to the hairs of my chest. My cock, hot and swollen, leaked intermittent streams of precome. It clung to the tip of my cock before releasing and pooling at my feet. I approached him.

"You don't want the cravings to stop, do you?" He threw me off him. I landed on the floor. "Do you want to go back to the passionless existence you had with Cameron?"

"It was great with…how did you…?"

"Then why are you here, Dean, if I am not the one you want? Do you want Cameron?"

"No," I gasped through icy breaths.

"Then tell me, Dean, who do you want?"

"I want you." My voice cracked as the frosty air caught in my throat. I sat on the chilled tiles as my cock ached for release. Benjamin stood over me and kicked his shoes off. I could see the heat of his feet radiating from inside his shoes. He unbuttoned his pants and pulled the zipper down, exposing a dense patch of golden blond pubic hair. The orange flames that ran down his stomach ended in a single black point at the base of his cock.

"Beg for it, Dean. I need to know that you want me." He began to laugh as he slipped his hand into his pants. He stroked and pulled on his cock, tormenting me by not giving me what I wanted. What I needed.

"Please give me your cock, Ben. I need that fucking dick shoved up my ass."

"That's more like it." He let his pants slide down his thick, muscular legs. His massive cock swung freely in front of him, in front of me. The point inked into his skin spread out and covered his entire shaft in black. The head of his cock was tinted a deep red.

I crawled over to him. My body trembled from the cold and the cravings. I needed to satisfy one of them. His large foot stopped my advance. He pressed it into my face. I inhaled the aromas of his foot, still warm from the confines of the boot. It did nothing to quiet the cravings. I slipped my tongue through my pressed lips. The stale sweat of his foot made my cock squirt. A thick, gooey rope of come splattered across his shin and foot. He reversed his footing. I licked my own come from his large toe, running my tongue over the coarse blond hair that covered the top of his foot.

"Tell me that you love me, Dean."

"I…" The words caught in my throat. I shook my head. I watched as he took the knife to the slab of meat. He licked the thin slice and then bent down in front of me. The urge was too much to resist. I wanted the tiny sliver of flesh, but knew what I had to do to get it. "I love you, Ben." Tears welled in my eyes from the release of emotions as I bit into the meat. I jerked myself hard, desperate to come again and relieve the pressure.

"That's it. Go ahead and get yourself off. It's not going to do you any good. The cravings won't stop until I make them stop." He picked me up and threw me against the metal shelves. I felt the cold metal attaching itself to my exposed skin. "I'm gonna fuck you good, my love, and then when I'm done with your ass, we'll get down to business." He bit down on my shoulder as he impaled me with his enormous cock.

"Son-of-a-bitch!" The pain of his initial thrust ripped through my body like a jagged knife. I felt his cock squirm inside me as he moved his hips back and forth. My body shook without control. "Fuck!" I bent my head between my outstretched arms and watched as I shot thick, white ropes of come. Steam rose up through the air as it sprayed across the frosted shelves. The cravings continued to build, racking my body with the most painful desires. "Oh, God fuck me harder, please."

"You want more?" He pulled out of me and turned me around. His spicy breath battered my face. He cupped his hands under my sweaty armpits. He lifted me into the air and then plunged me downward, impaling me on his rigid cock. He pumped me up and down as if he was fucking a rag doll. His cock drove deeper into me, swelling and filling me with pain and pleasure. I looked at him. His face was a twisted grimace of emotions. He laughed between grunts. My cock slapped back and forth between our stomachs, spraying our bodies with precome with each pleasurable smack.

"Fucking Christ!" I began to gasp as he fucked the breath from my body. My head swam with the pressure that continued to build inside me. Then a burning heat rushed through my battered cock. The first explosion showered our faces. He licked my come from his lips, groaned, and continued to skewer me with his dick, forcing me to come again in rapid succession, covering our bodies in my white release. My body went limp. I faded in and out of consciousness as he impaled me one last time upon his still-rigid cock. The motion stopped. He pulled me off and threw me to the cold tiled floor. I lay there panting, shivering, and scared. The cravings continued to swell within me.

The sound of metal against metal filled the room. I raised my head off the floor. Ben stood a few feet back from me with his butcher knife and a honing stone. There was a gleam in his eyes as he focused on the blade running along the edge of the stone.

"Please, don't hurt me." I crawled away from him, fearing the cold edge of the knife as he sank it into my body.

"Hurt you?" He stopped and looked at me. "I would never hurt you. I love you, Dean. Don't you know that by now?" In two short steps, he was upon me. He knelt down and stroked my hair. "The only one who can hurt you now is you. Are you feeling okay? You look needy." He fondled my cock. "Do you need more of my gifts?"

I nodded in response, not wanting to admit verbally that I was still horny as hell and unable to control my impulses. "Please, what do you want with me?"

"As I said, we have business to attend to." He pulled me off the floor and propped me up against the shelves. "Your pleasure or pain depends on you." He walked in the direction of the back wall, toward a heavy tarp that I had not noticed before. "You, my love, are my apprentice. You will learn my trade tonight." He pulled the heavy plastic down.

"No, God, please no," I cried in disbelief and horror as I looked at Cameron hanging from the wall. His feet rested on a wooden plank. His arms stretched out perpendicular to his body, with a single nail in the center of each palm.

"Don't worry, my love, he's not dead. The angry mood I placed him in this evening during dinner had a little something extra to relax him. It will also ease his pain. Trust me, he's very much alive. It has to be that way. That's part of my secret. The meat has to be fresh from the bones." His laughter filled the room. "Most people think that warm skin makes for a closer shave, but I have to disagree. The hair comes off much cleaner when the skin is chilled." He took the blade of his knife and ran it through the thick bush of fire-red hair that surrounded

Cameron's cock. The thin fibers gathered on the floor. Stroke by stroke, I sat paralyzed with fear as Benjamin scraped the hair from Cameron's body.

"I'll do whatever you ask." I crawled over to him and grabbed his leg. "Please, don't do this." I begged for my boyfriend's life.

"Oh, my love." He shook his head at me. "I'm sorry. You misunderstand. I'm not going to do this. You are."

"You're fucking crazy. I'm not butchering my boyfriend." I let go of his leg. I crawled away from him. "No, no, no." I shook my head in a slow back-and-forth motions, continuing to chant my response until it was a whisper of my former voice.

"You said that you love me, Dean." He took a small paring knife from his pocket, sharpened it on the stone, and pressed the tip below Cameron's right nipple. It slipped into the skin with precision. "It's as simple as this." He cut a small one-inch piece of meat from Cameron's body. Cameron mumbled something in his fogged state. His body quivered. "Would you like a taste of him?" He placed the piece of Cameron's skin on the tip of the blade and slipped it into his mouth. He ran the blade across his own tongue, painting his mouth with Cameron's blood. "There's nothing better than a fresh piece of meat. I realize it's an acquired taste, but one you'll get accustomed to." He came to me. "It's your turn, Dean." He handed me the knife. "Do it quick before he wakes up, or the last thing he'll see is his boyfriend cutting away his flesh."

"No." I took the knife and threw it across the floor.

"I know what you want." He grabbed my swollen cock and stroked it. I couldn't help but groan from the pleasure. He removed his hand and let my cock drop to the cold floor. "You need to understand where I'm coming from, don't you?"

"Please just beat me off. God, I need to come so bad."

"We'll take care of that." He walked over to the hanging slabs of meat. He looked a couple of them over and then shaved a sample from one. He brought it to me. I opened my mouth, no longer caring who or what he fed to me. I chewed the tougher piece of meat, waiting for the pleasure to rush through my body, and with it relief. Instead, sadness consumed me. I began to cry with heavy sobs. "Yes, that's it. Feel the pain of my sadness. It has been my sole companion. The knowledge that it shall never leave burns a hole inside you. It nests and festers in that empty, hollow place you call a heart. Cry all you want. The tears may end, but the sadness will live forever." He walked across the room and cut a piece of meat from another slab.

"No." I said through the tears. "I can't do this anymore. How can you live with so much sadness?" I reached out and grabbed the knife on the floor. I turned my wrist over and raised the knife, wanting nothing more than to end the pain and suffering he felt.

"No, you fucking coward!" He ran toward me. He pulled the knife from my hand. "You don't get to take the easy way out. This is your destiny, my love. I selected you out of all the others. I will not let you disappoint me."

"Please, make it stop."

"You want the sadness to end?" His tone was soft, sensual. He touched my shoulder as if he cared. "My love, you must eat this. If you don't, I'm afraid I might have to wake up your boyfriend and rip him to shreds. You will hear his agonizing screams for the rest of your life." He grabbed my hair and dragged me across the floor. "You wouldn't want that, now, would you?" He embraced me. We rocked. He hummed an unknown song while I cried in his arms. "Will you please eat this for me? I do not want to lose my temper with you. I so hate violence." He ran his thick tongue up my cheek. His hot saliva clung to my skin.

I opened my mouth and let him slip the meat onto my tongue. It was bitter and spicy. The sadness faded. We continued to rock. I looked up at him. He smiled at me.

"There, that's better than crying, isn't it?" He kissed my head. "It's more productive anyway." He laughed.

"Fuck." I groaned as my body became flushed with a searing heat. My heart pounded in my chest as I felt an incredible anger rise inside me. "What…you…son of a bitch. How can you…?" Despite the cold, sweat dripped down the side of my face.

"You'll want this." He handed me the knife. "Don't fight, my love. It will only make things worse."

"You son of a bitch!" I raised the knife and pointed it in his direction. The rage, *his* rage ripped through me. He laughed as I slammed the knife into his chest. I felt the blade tear through his skin. I shoved it deeper into him. He continued to laugh as he gripped my hand and pulled the knife out of his chest.

"You can't hurt me, though I know that is where the anger lies."

He raised the knife to his mouth and licked the edge of the blade. "You know what you must do."

"I want to hurt something. I need to release the anger." I looked up at Cameron crucified on the wall. He moaned in his sleep-induced state. "Why are you doing this to me?"

"Isn't it obvious? I am the teacher, and you are my pupil. You should be honored that I have selected you to run my restaurant."

"I don't want this." I looked past the blade and stared at Cameron. The rage grew inside me, taunting me, calling me to act.

"It will come. It always does. I've never had to fail a student." He stood and lifted me with him. "Embrace the anger, Dean. Feel the control. Feel the power that it gives you."

"No." Even as I spoke my response, I could feel my heart hardening. The pulse felt hollow as I adjusted my grip on the handle of the knife. The anger screamed through my body. Yet behind the burning fires of hell, I felt the control and power that Benjamin was offering. I tasted it behind the anger, the sadness, and the seduction. Yes, this was what I had longed for. It's what I had waited for my entire life, and it was finally at hand.

"Do it, my love. Give over your life to me. Free yourself from this world, and from those you are about to leave behind."

"I don't know how."

"Yes, you do. Follow the instincts that I have given you, my love. With me by your side, you cannot fail."

"No." Benjamin led me to the back wall. I looked at Cameron, the man I once loved, the man who would smoke and then want to kiss me with his soiled breath; the man who used to tell me how to do things his way, because his way was the only way; the man who wanted everything and gave nothing in return.

"I can feel the anger rising. Yes, that's it. Embrace the gifts I have bestowed on you."

I felt a smile curl the side of my mouth as I let the emotions take control. I plunged the knife into my boyfriend's chest, feeling the tip of the blade scraping the metal wall behind him—fingernails on a chalkboard came to my mind. My mind flashed images of dying memories. I could taste Cameron's ass on my tongue, feel his cock pulsing inside me as his hot come filled me with delight. I dragged the knife downward, letting it come to rest on the pelvic bone. There was no time for him to scream. His death was quick, easy, and satisfying. His warm blood saturated my hands and body. I became aroused at the thought of his body covering mine—a full-body orgasm that spewed his life out onto the floor. I took my bloody hand and jerked myself off. Come sprayed from my cock and mixed with Cameron's blood to pool on the floor between us. I gutted him, being careful not to damage the precious meat. I carved a small sliver of his stomach and placed the bloody piece of meat in my mouth. He was sweet and tender.

"You are doing well, my love." Benjamin's voice echoed in my head. "Give into the pleasures, my emotions, and my tastes that you have acquired."

I walked out of the refrigeration unit while Cameron's body drained. I looked at the clock while I sharpened my knife. My cock pulsed with excitement and desire as I contemplated the dinner menu, with Cameron as the featured guest of honor.

THE MUNCHIES
ROB ROSEN

I wasn't stoned. Per se. I mean, there was pot at the party, and I was, well, sitting nearby when it got passed around. But I didn't take a toke. More than once. Um, well, twice. Three times at most, but I barely inhaled. The third time.

Okay, so, fine, I was stoned.

But to be fair, in California it's only a ticketable offence. Not even a misdemeanor, just an infraction. Barely even illegal. Barely. Though, well, maybe driving while stoned is a no-no, I suppose. Which is why I stopped just after I'd gotten off the freeway. At the all-night donut shop. See how civic-minded I was? I wasn't even thinking about how starved I was. Mostly.

Plus, all that blinking neon was so, uh, *pretty*. Drawing me in like a moth to a flame.

Fresh, then *Donuts*, from pink to green, over and over and over again. Very hypnotic it was. Meaning, I suddenly found myself parked just outside, at one in the morning, all by my lonesome.

I hopped out, grinning as I made my way inside the exceedingly bright shop, the shelves lined with row after row of sweet, doughy delights. My mouth practically watered at the sight of them. Practically, I say, because I had a severe case of cotton-mouth by that point. Go figure.

"Hello?" I rasped, my throat still a tad burned. I mean, who doesn't have a bong these days? Primitive, right?

A guy came out a split second later, a vision in all white. A veritable angel, he was, eyes so sparkling blue that they made the sky jealous. "Howdy," he said. Then, "Whoa, dude, you're seriously stoned."

"Nuh-uh," I managed to say, a flush of red working its way up my neck.

He chuckled, the sound running down my spine like a runaway train. "Dude, a *case* of Visine couldn't get all that red out. Plus, a one in the morning donut run can only mean one thing."

"I'm, uh, diabetic and my sugar level got dangerously low?" I tried.

"The munchies, dude," he corrected me. "For sure."

I sighed and leaned my arms on the counter, my eyes now fixed on the Boston cream-filled ones. Like they were shouting at me. *Eat me!* Meaning I relented. "It would've been the height of rudeness to, uh, just say no."

Again he laughed, my nerve endings now sizzling at the very sound of him. "And wasteful. You were just being…*green*…so to speak."

I touched fingertip to nose and dreamily glanced back up at him. "Exactly." Then I pointed down at the case. "I'll take one of those." Another point. "And those." And another. "And those. And that one, with the blueberries." Each point got more urgent as my stomach loudly grumbled. *Hurry!* it shouted. And then, lastly, of course, I pointed to the Boston cream-filled one. *Bless you!*

Quick as a wink, he had it all boxed up. "That'll be five and a quarter, buddy," he told me.

I withdrew my wallet and shoved my fingers inside the, *gulp*, empty slot. Still, the silver credit card quickly came to my rescue. Sort of.

The baker dude pointed to the now-obvious sign that hung beneath the cash register. NO CREDIT CARDS. CASH ONLY. "Not like we have big-ticket items here, dude. Sorry," he said. "Anything in the car?"

"Nope." I just about cried, the tears welling in my eyes. Almost. Because, yes, they too were dry as a bone now. "Can I just, um, you know, owe it to you? Please? Pretty please"—I pointed to the powdered donut on the top shelf—"with sugar on top."

He shook his head. "This ain't Goodwill, dude." Then he leaned in, handsome face barely a foot from my own. "But maybe we could *come* to an arrangement."

And, oh, yes, he did emphasize that word, stuffed it so full as to make the jelly donuts seem empty in comparison. "An arrangement? Like I mop your floors or wash your pans?"

He winked. "Nope. You ever bob for apples?" He leaned in even closer, eyes shimmering before mine, like a pool on a hot summer's day. Like you'd want to dive right on into them.

"Been a while," I replied, crotch throbbing as I leaned against the cool, hard glass. "Why, you got apples back there, too?"

Again he shook his head. "Just donuts, buddy."

I scratched my head in confusion. "How do you, uh, how do you bob for donuts, then?"

Again he chuckled, only this time it was tinged with something else. Something that made my heart go *kathump, kathump*. Or that might've been my cock. Hard to tell, what with my head still so pot-cloudy. "See, I hang them off my rod and you bob for them," he explained.

I squinted my eyes. And, all things considered, they didn't have far to go. "You hang them off a rod and I bob for them?"

Once more he shook his head. "*My* rod, not *a* rod."

I would've gulped again, but the last one fully depleted my spit supply. "Here?" I managed.

Now it was his turn to point. "Kitchen, dude. If you're game, I mean. Otherwise, hope your cupboards at home aren't as bare as your wallet."

I looked from him to all those glorious donuts, rack after rack of them, all seemingly glowing behind the glass, calling for me, yanking at my very doobage-encrusted soul. "Deal," I squeaked out.

His shake switched to a nod before he took the box and motioned for me to follow him, locking the shop as he headed to the back. "On the floor," he quickly commanded, tossing a white chef's jacket for me to use as a pillow, nice guy that he was. And hard guy, too, if the straining coming from his white work pants meant anything.

I paused, but did as he said, my tummy now obviously in complete control. Fucking munchies. Then again, guy was way cute. And getting cuter by the second as he kicked off his clogs and unbuttoned his chef's jacket, a fine matting of curly brown down coming into view, then tight pecs, thick pink nipples, a flat belly also covered in hair. "Guess you abstain from your goodies," I couldn't help but chime in with.

He smiled and winked, fingers brushing the button to his cottony slacks. "A lot of jogging does the trick. Then I can eat all I like."

"Lucky you," said I, arm behind my head as I gazed up at him.

He opened the box of donuts and then cupped his tenting crotch. "Lucky *you*."

The slacks fell to the ground. Baker dude was going full-on commando, his mammoth cock jutting up and out, curved a bit to the side, balls so low they were practically in another area code. "Lucky me," I echoed. Which, of course, was a gross understatement. Especially once he started hanging those yummy-looking donuts off his equally yummy-looking cock, one after the next, until all four were crammed on and his wide helmeted head was jutting through and poking out, dripping copious amounts of translucent precome. Made your mouth water. If you weren't stoned. And had water to, um, burn.

He walked over and stood behind me, his cock swaying above my head, donuts so tantalizingly close that I could practically taste them. "Shame only one of us is naked, though," he said, swinging the goods back and forth.

Stoned as I was, horny very much won out over modesty. Meaning there were two naked dudes in that small kitchen of his in no time flat. "Better?" I asked, once again prone, again staring up at all that stunning donut-covered man-meat.

He moved in an inch, feet on either side of my head, then crouched down, hairy asshole winking out at me, balls resting on my forehead, so that the donut nestled against the base of his shaft was now pressed to my hungry lips, the heady aroma of dick and donut wafting up my nostrils. "Better," he replied, dipping down a few more centimeters, until I was chowing down, the impossibly soft dough popping inside my mouth before gliding down my throat.

When it fell off his prick, he fed me the rest. To return the favor, I reached behind my head and stroked his hole and balls, yanking them back, which had the added bonus effect of his dick dunking further down, allowing me even easier access to the next donut, the stellar blueberry one. *Mmm. Yu-fucking-um.*

"Think you can make it all the way down the line?" he asked, moaning as I swirled my index finger around and around his crinkled hole.

Chewing and swallowing, I managed a, "There a prize if I do?"

He tapped the box behind him, the lone donut still waiting its turn inside. "For sure, Munchies Dude. Creamiest prize this side of the Mississippi."

"And the other side, too, I'd imagine." Which meant that I eagerly started in on donut number three, half of his rod now in plain view, the other half still, well, *doughified*. Which is kind of like glorified only yummier. Then with my mouth now covered in crumbs and flakes of glaze, I started in on the last one, a cake donut, yeasty and perfect. When it was done, it was just my finger now up his ass and his exposed cock above my mouth. "I'm ready for that prize, Mister Baker Man."

That chuckle of his returned as a swarm of butterflies took wing inside my belly, all of them happily sugar-coated now. Then he reached behind and removed that delectable cream-filled number. He held it out and above my chest before gently stuffing his prick inside, the gooey center dripping out and down as he slowly fucked it, his hefty balls rubbing this way and that atop my head, my index finger pummeling his hole.

Slicked up and creamy, he removed his delicious-looking dick and slapped it on my lips. "Your prize, dude."

Ravenous all over again, I slid out from under him, finger included, and flipped over, his prick in my grip in no time flat, then down my throat even faster. Never has a cock tasted so sweet, I figured, or gone down so fattening. Then I glanced up as I sucked him off, his head thrown back, jaw slack, moans and groans ricocheting around that small kitchen of his. I mean, he might've known a thing or two about baking, but I won the blue ribbon in sucking dick. A regular Betty Cocker I am. And, of course, I was now eager to spread my gooey glaze on him, too. Icing, as it were, on the cake. Or his chest. Or mine. Or both. And soon, I hoped.

I popped his prick out of my mouth, the excess cream gliding down my chin. I licked it off with my tongue. "What do I get if I make you come?"

He pried his pretty blue peepers open and stared down at me. *"If?"*

I nodded and gave his cock a tug. "Well, this ain't Goodwill, dude. Or so I've been told."

He smiled and reached down to tousle my hair. "Dozen donuts, then."

I spanked his prick, sending it careening this way and that, bits of glaze flinging outward. "That all?"

"Baker's dozen," he amended with, eyes aflame now, cock steely stiff as it came to a midair halt. I paused. As did he. "*Two* baker's dozens, I mean."

I hopped up and closed the gap between us, my lips on his in a white hot instant. "Deal," I whispered, sucking on his lips and again working his pole with my palm.

"Deal," he whispered back, mashing his mouth into mine, his chest into my chest, hairy belly to smooth belly, until it was impossible to tell where he ended and I began. "Fucking deal." And with that, he pulled me to the tiled floor, both of us crouching, my hand on his pole, his on mine, him pulling my nuts, me pulling his, all while we swapped some heavy spit. Thank goodness. Because by then I had absolutely none left of my own. It was like a whole bale of cotton had been shoved inside my mouth, along with his slicked-up tongue, which he was slithering and snaking around my own as he worked my tool.

Soon enough, we were completely in sync, our hands stroking in unison, balls pulled to the max. And *his* max was nearly floor-level. "Close," I soon groaned, pushing the word down his throat as I exhaled heavily, legs starting to buckle as his pace quickened on my rod.

"Closer, dude," he replied, sweat cascading down his forehead and into my mouth, the salt hitting the back of my throat like a bullet.

And then we shot, together, two geysers of spunk shooting this way and that, thick wads of it hitting my belly and thighs and calves before dripping down to the floor below, more of it splashing his chest and stomach, which was rapidly rising and falling as he shot and shot and shot, band after aromatic band of sticky man-sap.

"Fuuuuck," he moaned up to the ceiling, his cock so thick in my grip that it was almost impossible to hold on to.

"Fuuuuck," I echoed back as he shook every last drop of pungent come out from my pulsing prick, until the floor was slick with jizz.

Again his mouth found mine as he pressed his hirsute sweaty body into me, softening dicks pressed up snug, his hands roaming my back, mine his stellar ass. He chuckled into my mouth as we fell to our knees. "Still got those munchies?" he asked, slapping my ass.

I shrugged and gently bit his lip. "I'm good. But a tall glass of milk wouldn't hurt."

He hopped up and disappeared somewhere. When he returned, he had two frothy glasses and two clean towels held up for me. "Take your pick."

Naturally, I dove for the milk. Anything to wash the cotton down with. That and the four donuts and dick-infused Boston-cream. Then we wiped off, the floor included, and I got dressed, as did he. After that, he sent me on my merry way, two baker's dozens of delicious donuts in hand.

When I again was sitting in my car, I glanced up at the flashing neon sign. *Fresh*, then *Donuts*, from pink to green, over and over and over again. Not as hypnotic this go around, the pot-cloud at last lifting from my addled head, but still awfully pretty. Though I was sure to never look at a donut the same way again. Fresh or not.

I smiled as I started my engine, only to shut it off again when he came running out. "Wait!" he shouted.

I rolled down the window. "Did I forget something?" I asked.

"Nope, I did." He held out his hand. "Pete," he said, his smile so big and bright as to make all that glowing neon seem pale in comparison.

"Glenn," I told him, hand in hand, those butterflies of mine swarming all over again.

"Nice to meet you, Glenn," he said, leaning in and down, a peck on the lips before he stood back up. "And if you should ever get the munchies again…"

"…I'll come right over."

He chuckled, naturally. "Emphasis on the *come*."

I nodded and shot him a wink before starting the engine up again. "Emphasis on the come, Pete," I said, slowly backing away. "Emphasis on the come."

A DIGESTIF

Wasn't that a sumptuous feast?

I'll just leave the bill here and check on a few other diners before I pick it up. In the meantime, you might want to leave a little note to the chefs for their brilliant entrées. If it weren't for these folks, this dive would never be able to stay in business. And speaking of business, thanks are also due to Radclyffe and the wonderful folks at Bold Strokes Books for setting the tables, lighting the candles, and running down to the wine cellar for more libations.

Personal thanks also go out to my fellow blogger, critic, and co-conspirator William Holden as well as the telephonic support of Dale "Old West" Chase and to my usual confidantes, Ryk Bowers, Keith Lucero, and John Couture, who, after suffering through three books with me, now know more about the writing and editing business than any of them ever wanted to.

But where would any restaurant be without butts in the chairs? Thanks and appreciation go out to everyone who wandered in off the street, attracted by the wonderful smells from our banquet. Good cuisine means nothing without someone to partake in it. We hope we've sated your appetite for the moment, but remember that whenever you get hungry again, we're open twenty-four seven.

And we appreciate your patronage.

Our Chefs

DAVID PRATT won a 2011 Lambda Literary Award for his novel *Bob the Book*. His story collection, *My Movie*, was released by Chelsea Station Editions in March 2012. David has directed and performed his work for the theater in New York at the Cornelia Street Café, Dixon Place, HERE Arts Center, the Flea (in a workshop led by Karen Finley), on WBAI-FM, and in the New York International Fringe Festival. He was the first director of plays by the Canadian playwright John Mighton. David is currently at work on two more novels and the book of a musical.

KARL TAGGART is a supertaster, so he knows whereof he speaks. Since food is often a challenge, he concentrates on other appetites, which leads to occasional erotica writing. His stories have been published in various anthologies as well as *Men* and *Freshmen* magazines. This latest story is an attempt to entertain as well as enlighten readers about the plight of those afflicted with extra taste buds.

DALE CHASE (dalechasestrokes.com) has written male erotica for fifteen years with over 150 stories in magazines and anthologies, including translation into German and Italian. She has two story collections in print: *The Company He Keeps: Victorian Gentlemen's Erotica* from Bold Strokes Books and *If The Spirit Moves You: Ghostly Gay Erotica* from Lethe Press. Her first erotic novel, *Wyatt: Doc Holliday's Account of an Intimate Friendship*, is due from Bold Strokes Books in fall 2012. Chase lives near San Francisco.

JEFFREY RICKER (jeffreyricker.wordpress.com) is a writer, editor, and graphic designer. His first novel, *Detours*, is available from Bold Strokes Books. His writing has appeared in the literary magazine *Collective Fallout* and the anthologies *Paws and Reflect, Fool for Love: New Gay Fiction, Blood Sacraments, Men of the Mean Streets, Speaking Out, Wings, Riding the Rails*, and others. A magna cum laude graduate of the University of Missouri School of Journalism, he lives with his partner, Michael, and two dogs, and is working on his second novel.

The oddest thing STEVE BERMAN has ever put in his mouth is fermented mare's milk—a beverage he drank on the steppes of Mongolia. The oddest guy he has ever had in his mouth would be a purportedly heterosexual artist who only drew gay furries. Is there a correlation between the two? Yes. Both were salty. He would like to point out that he does write other things than erotic metafiction. Case in point: his novel, *Vintage: A Ghost Story*. He lives in southern New Jersey.

A transplanted Westerner, J.D. BARTON has worked as a freelance writer, social worker, and health care professional. Drawn to open spaces, he strives to include as much of the outdoors as he can in his writing, which includes novels and radio plays. When not writing, he spends time with his boyfriend and listens to Motown and all the great 70s singer-songwriters who inspired him to write in the first place.

TODD GREGORY is the author of the bestselling erotic novel *Every Frat Boy Wants It* and its sequel, *Games Frat Boys Play.* He has edited numerous erotic anthologies, including *His Underwear, Wings, Rough Trade* (Lambda Literary Award finalist), *Blood Sacraments* (ForeWord Award finalist), and the forthcoming *Raising Hell.* He has published numerous short stories, and his next novel, *need*, will be released by Kensington in December 2012.

LEWIS DESIMONE (www.lewisdesimone.com) is the author of *Chemistry* and *The Heart's History*. His work has appeared in *Christopher Street, James White Review, Harrington Gay Men's Fiction Quarterly*, and *Second Person Queer: Who You Are (So Far), The Mammoth Book of Threesomes and Moresomes, Charmed Lives: Gay Spirit in Storytelling,*

Best Gay Love Stories: Summer Flings, I Like It Like That: True Tales of Gay Male Desire, and *My Diva: 65 Gay Men on the Women Who Inspire Them*. His contribution to the latter was reprinted in *Ganymede* and *Best Gay Stories 2010*. He lives in San Francisco, where he is working on his next novel.

DANIEL M. JAFFE (danieljaffe.tripod.com.) is author of *"Jewish Gentle" and Other Stories of Gay-Jewish Living* (White Crane Books, 2011) and the novel *The Limits of Pleasure* (Bear Bones Books, 2010). *The Limits of Pleasure* was a finalist for a ForeWord Magazine Book of the Year Award when first published in 2001 and was later excerpted in *Best Gay Erotica 2003*. His short stories and personal essays have appeared in dozens of anthologies and literary journals.

HANK EDWARDS (www.hankedwardsbooks.com) is the author of the hot and funny Charlie Heggensford series: *Fluffers, Inc.*, *A Carnal Cruise*, and the Lambda Award Finalist *Vancouver Nights*, all from Lethe Press. Three other books are available from Loose Id: *Holed Up*, *Destiny's Bastard*, and *Plus Ones*. His self-published paranormal novel, *Bounty*, and sizzling short story collection *A Very Dirty Dozen* are available for download. Every Monday Hank posts free m/m reads to his blog as part of the Story Orgy writer's group.

'NATHAN BURGOINE (redroom.com/member/nathan-burgoine) lives in Ottawa, Canada, with his husband, Daniel. His previous erotic fiction appears in *Tented*, *Blood Sacraments*, *Wings*, *Afternoon Pleasures*, *Erotica Exotica*, and *Riding the Rails*. His non-erotic short fiction appears in *Fool for Love*, *I Do Two*, *Saints & Sinners 2011*, *Men of the Mean Streets*, and *Tales from the Den*. He loves ice wine, but not the winters that make it.

JEFF MANN has published three poetry chapbooks: *Bliss*, *Mountain Fireflies*, and *Flint Shards from Sussex*; three full-length books of poetry: *Bones Washed with Wine*, *On the Tongue*, and *Ash: Poems from Norse Mythology*; two essay collections: *Edge: Travels of an Appalachian Leather Bear* and *Binding the God: Ursine Essays from the Mountain South*; two novellas: *Devoured*, in *Masters of Midnight:*

Erotic Tales of the Vampire, and *Camp Allegheny*, in *History's Passion: Stories of Sex Before Stonewall*; two novels: *Fog: A Novel of Desire and Reprisal* and *Purgatory: A Novel of the Civil War*; a book of poetry and memoir: *Loving Mountains, Loving Men*; and a volume of short fiction: *A History of Barbed Wire*, which won a Lambda Literary Award. He teaches creative writing at Virginia Tech.

"The Café Françoise" shows what can happen when an author of German heritage studies too much French in school. JAY NEAL adores most any type of diner, whether it has a long, shiny stainless-steel counter and serves blue plate specials, or a zinc-covered drinks bar in Nazi-occupied Paris serving outlawed absinthe—provided the music is appropriate to the setting. And what of love in a diner? Love is always grand, especially when it's inappropriate and dangerous—in fiction, at least. In reality, Neal and his partner lead a grand life of domestic tranquility in the suburbs of Washington, DC, where they fulfilled a long-held dream by being married in 2010.

TRISTAN COLE is the author of *Porn Star Slave* and *Harvey's Bargain*. He occasionally updates his blog, *The Dark Mind of Tristan Cole*. He is originally from North Carolina.

WILLIAM HOLDEN's (www.williamholdenwrites.com) writing career spans more than a decade, with over forty published short stories in erotica, romance, fantasy, and horror. He is co-founder and co-editor of Out in Print: Queer Book Reviews at www.outinprint.net. His first collection, *A Twist of Grimm*, is a Lambda Literary Finalist. His latest book, *Words to Die By*, is available through Bold Strokes Books.

ROB ROSEN (www.therobrosen.com), author of the novels *Sparkle: The Queerest Book You'll Ever Love*, the Lambda Literary Award–nominated *Divas Las Vegas*, *Hot Lava*, and his latest, *Southern Fried*, has had short stories featured in more than 150 anthologies.

ABOUT YOUR WAITER

Editor of *Tented: Gay Erotic Tales from Under the Big Top* (a Lambda Literary Award finalist) as well as *Riding the Rails: Locomotive Lust and Carnal Cabooses* and the forthcoming *Tricks of the Trade: Magical Gay Erotica* (both Bold Strokes Books), JERRY L. WHEELER lives, works, and writes in Denver, Colorado. He and William Holden co-founded Out in Print: Queer Book Reviews (www.outinprint.net), and reading for this blog takes up much of his time. What's left is misspent in fleeting encounters with men best described as trashy. Some on work release programs. Despite this predilection, he still manages time for writing, including book reviews, short stories, essays and a novel-in-progress called *The Dead Book*. Please feel free to contact him at either Out in Print or his website, www.jerrywheeleronline.com. Furry men with tats and shady backgrounds please step to the front of the line.

Books Available From Bold Strokes Books

Oath of Honor by Radclyffe. A First Responders novel. First do no harm…First Physician of the United States Wes Masters discovers that being the president's doctor demands more than brains and personal sacrifice—especially when politics is the order of the day. (978-1-60282-671-7)

A Question of Ghosts by Cate Culpepper. Becca Healy hopes Dr. Joanne Call can help her learn if her mother really committed suicide—but she's not sure she can handle her mother's ghost, a decades-old mystery, and lusting after the difficult Dr. Call without some serious chocolate consumption. (978-1-60282-672-4)

The Night Off by Meghan O'Brien. When Emily Parker pays for a taboo role-playing fantasy encounter from the Xtreme Scenarios escort agency, she expects to surrender control—but never imagines losing her heart to dangerous butch Nat Swayne. (978-1-60282-673-1)

Sara by Greg Herren. A mysterious and beautiful new student at Southern Heights High School stirs things up when students start dying.(978-1-60282-674-8)

Fontana by Joshua Martino. Fame, obsession, and vengeance collide in a novel that asks: What if America's greatest hero was gay? (978-1-60282-675-5)

Lemon Reef by Robin Silverman. What would you risk for the memory of your first love? When Jenna Ross learns her high school love Del Soto died on Lemon Reef, she refuses to accept the medical examiner's report of a death from natural causes and risks everything to find the truth. (978-1-60282-676-2)

The Dirty Diner: Gay Erotica on the Menu, edited by Jerry L. Wheeler. Gay erotica set in restaurants, featuring food, sex, and men—could you really ask for anything more? (978-1-60282-677-9)

The Marrying Kind by Ken O'Neill. Just when successful wedding planner Adam More decides to protest inequality by quitting the business and boycotting marriage entirely, his only sibling announces her engagement. (978-1-60282-670-0)

Sweat: Gay Jock Erotica by Todd Gregory. Sizzling tales of smoking-hot sex with the athletic studs everyone fantasizes about. (978-1-60282-669-4)

Dark Wings Descending by Lesley Davis. What if the demons you face in life are real? Chicago detective Rafe Douglas is about to find out. (978-1-60282-660-1)

sunfall by Nell Stark and Trinity Tam. The final installment of the everafter series. Valentine Darrow and Alexa Newland work to rebuild their relationship even as they find themselves at the heart of the struggle that will determine a new world order for vampires and wereshifters. (978-1-60282-661-8)

Mission of Desire by Terri Richards. Nicole Kennedy finds herself in Africa at the center of an international conspiracy and is rescued by the beautiful but arrogant government agent Kira Anthony—but can Nicole trust Kira, or is she blinded by desire? (978-1-60282-662-5)

Boys of Summer, edited by Steve Berman. Stories of young love and adventure, when the sky's ceiling is a bright blue marvel, when another boy's laughter at the beach can distract from dull summer jobs. (978-1-60282-663-2)

Calendar Boys by Logan Zachary. A man a month will keep you excited year-round. (978-1-60282-665-6)

Buccaneer Island by J.P. Beausejour. In the rough world of Caribbean piracy, a man is what he makes of himself—or what a stronger man makes of him. (978-1-60282-658-8)

Twelve O'Clock Tales by Felice Picano. The fourth collection of short fiction by legendary novelist and memoirist Felice Picano. Thirteen dark tales that will thrill and disturb, discomfort and titillate, enthrall and leave you wondering. (978-1-60282-659-5)

Words to Die By by William Holden. Sixteen answers to the question: What causes a mind to curdle? (978-1-60282-653-3)